Advance Acclaim for *When Mockingbirds Sing*

"Billy Coffey is a minstrel who writes with intense depth of feeling and vibrant rich description. The characters who live in this book face challenges that stretch the deepest fabric of their beings. You will remember *When Mockingbirds Sing* long after you finish it."

—ROBERT WHITLOW, BEST-SELLING AUTHOR OF *THE CHOICE*

"Some stories invite you in, but Billy Coffey's *When Mockingbirds Sing* grabs you by the collar and embraces you flat out. Beautifully written with characters made of flesh and bone, Coffey haunts you with truth, compelling you to turn the page. His best book yet."

—MARY DEMUTH, AUTHOR OF *THE MUIR HOUSE* AND *DAISY CHAIN*

"An engrossing novel on so many levels. A story of mystery, hope, opening our ears in a way we can truly hear, and the choice of belief. Coffey has penned a captivating tale that will linger with you long after the final page is turned."

—JAMES L. RUBART, BEST-SELLING AUTHOR OF *ROOMS* AND *SOUL'S GATE*

"*When Mockingbirds Sing* is a lovely, dark, fervent tale that grips and won't let go. At some point, I entered its pages so fully, the sky opened up and gale winds blew outside. It's that good."

—NICOLE SEITZ, AUTHOR OF *SAVING CICADAS*
AND *THE INHERITANCE OF BEAUTY*

"*When Mockingbirds Sing* by Billy Coffey made me realize how often we think we know how God works, when in reality we don't have a clue. God's ways are so much more mysterious than we can imagine. Billy Coffey is an author we're going to be hearing more about. I'll be looking for his next book!"

—COLLEEN COBLE, BEST-SELLING AUTHOR OF
TIDEWATER INN AND THE ROCK HARBOR SERIES

when mockingbirds sing

BILLY COFFEY

THOMAS NELSON

Since 1798

NASHVILLE   DALLAS   MEXICO CITY   RIO DE JANEIRO

Published in Nashville, Tennessee, by Thomas Nelson. Thomas Nelson is a registered trademark of Thomas Nelson, Inc.

Thomas Nelson, Inc., books may be purchased in bulk for educational, business, fund-raising, or sales promotional use. For information, please e-mail SpecialMarkets@ThomasNelson.com.

Scripture quotations are taken from the Holy Bible, New International Version®, NIV®. Copyright © 1973, 1978, 1984, 2011 by Biblica, Inc.™ Used by permission of Zondervan. All rights reserved worldwide. www.zondervan.com; the King James Version of the Bible.

Published in association with the literary agency of WordServe Literary Group, Ltd., 10152 S. Knoll Circle, Highlands Ranch, Colorado 80130.

Publisher's Note: This novel is a work of fiction. Names, characters, places, and incidents are either products of the author's imagination or used fictitiously. All characters are fictional, and any similarity to people living or dead is purely coincidental.

Library of Congress Cataloging-in-Publication Data

Coffey, Billy.
  When mockingbirds sing / Billy Coffey.
    pages cm
  ISBN 978-1-4016-8821-9 (trade paper)
  1. Christian fiction. I. Title.
  PS3603.O3165W48 2013
  813'.6—dc23

                                                2013000165

Printed in the United States of America

13 14 15 16 17 RRD 6 5 4 3 2 1

My daughter says the Rainbow Man is real. I believe her. Not in the sense that every parent believes his or her child, but in the sense that I have the luxury of firsthand experience.

She was four when he appeared at the edge of her bed—bright and friendly and sparkling. I would hear the whispers coming from her room late at night. I would walk in and see her sitting up against her pillow, staring at that spot, waiting to continue their conversation about the Higher Things. They got along famously.

My daughter loved the Rainbow Man. And honestly? I think he loved her right back.

He went away after a few months in somewhat strange circumstances that I will not delve into here. However, I will say this—the descriptions of the Rainbow Man you'll read in these pages are the descriptions my daughter gave me those years ago.

So this story is for you, baby girl. I hope he (or is it He?) approves.

God did this so that they would seek him
and perhaps reach out for him and find him,
though he is not far from any one of us.

—ACTS 17:27

There's a bit of magic in everything
And then some loss to even things out.

—LOU REED

saturday

Seven Days Before the Carnival

1

In those long days between the town's death and its rebirth, everyone had a story of how the magic came to Leah Norcross. Whether that magic was divine or devilry, real or imagined, hinged upon the teller. And though many declared they had trusted all along, the fact was that in the beginning no one believed but Leah and Allie, and not even they could have known what that carnival week would hold. And as for who was there when the magic first appeared, that would be Leah's father. Unfortunately, he was too busy worrying about Leah's birthday party to notice.

Tom Norcross shielded his eyes from the morning sun and checked his watch. On the driveway to his left, three men unloaded wooden chairs and a gleaming but dented popcorn machine from two panel trucks with *Celebration Time* stenciled in swollen red letters on the sides. Tom looked up as one of the men passed him with an armload of chairs.

"Gonna be a hot one, Dr. Norcross. Shoulda ordered you some shade along with all this stuff."

Rick? Nick? Tom couldn't remember the man's name.

There were more pressing things to consider. He checked his watch again—9:17 now, each tick of the second hand like a tiny exclamation point—and did his best to smile.

"Should have. And it's just Tom. You can leave off the doctor part."

"Will do."

The man—Tom decided it was Rick—joined the two wheeling the popcorn machine and disappeared around the corner. Tom fidgeted with his hat and reversed his course along the sidewalk in front of his family's new home. His eyes went first to the twisting lane that led to the empty road below, then through the open windows of the old Victorian. Ellen was somewhere inside, probably pulling the tubs of ice cream from the freezer or helping to set up the cake. She had been awake for three hours, Leah long before that. Tom suspected it was anticipation that had pushed his wife from bed so early for a Saturday. He suspected it was that same expectation that had awakened their daughter, though one tempered by a measure of don't-get-your-hopes-up.

But Tom's hopes? Up. Because Barney Moore had a plan.

Of course, that plan depended upon Barney's timely arrival, and if there was one thing Tom had learned in his two short months of country living, it was that time carried little weight in Mattingly.

He checked his watch again—9:30.

"He'll be here."

Ellen stood on the white wooden porch behind him. She'd exchanged pajamas for faded jeans and a pink T-shirt that accentuated her blond hair and blue eyes. Both reduced Tom to a lovesick teenager despite the wariness she displayed. Or perhaps because of it.

"Barney was supposed to be here an hour ago," he told her.

"Yes." She took a step closer, which Tom matched. "But this was all Barney's idea. He'll be here. He probably just had to be careful with Mabel."

Under normal circumstances—normal being five years ago more or less; Tom couldn't remember when it all started, though Ellen enjoyed reminding him how—a wife would take that moment to offer some sort of physical bolstering. A hand on the arm, a kiss on the cheek, a pat on the rear. Anything besides the nothing Ellen gave. Tom didn't think his wife realized this and didn't feel like broaching the subject. There was Barney to worry about. Besides, pointing out what Ellen wasn't doing might prod her into mentioning that the touchy-feely street ran both ways.

"Where's Leah?" he asked.

"Out back overseeing the temporary amusement park you had trucked in."

The jibe was slight but still pricked. "Like you said, Barney's idea."

Ellen said, "It was Barney's idea to invite everyone. The Deluxe Princess Birthday Package from Celebration Time was yours." She took another stride forward to the top step but still didn't descend. Her hands rested on her hips. "You can't fix everything, Tom."

He doffed his hat and rubbed the sweat from his brow. Rick/Nick was right, it was going to be a hot one. Maybe hot enough to keep everyone away.

Tom checked his watch again. "I just want today to be perfect."

"I know." Ellen's hands went from her hips to behind her back in a posture Tom saw as one of trust. "I want today to be perfect too. Maybe too much. I'm sorry, Tom. Sometimes it's just hard. Truce?"

A rumble came from the east side of the street below. They both looked, but the source of the sound was hidden by the magnolias bordering both sides of the lane. An engine popped and sputtered, sending a cloud of blue smoke above the trees that was caught and then swirled in the hot breeze. Finally, Barney Moore's old green pickup appeared. It weaved from one side of the lane and eased back into the middle.

Ellen smiled. "Told you. Take the world off your shoulders, Dr. Norcross. Everything will be fine."

"I'll let you know in a couple hours."

They shared a smile. Tom could not speak for his wife—reading her gestures was one thing, reading her heart was sadly another—but to him it felt warmer than even the summer sun on his back.

"I'll go get Leah," he said.

Tom waved to Barney and followed the men with the tables and chairs around the house, where the backyard's three acres affirmed that Ellen's remark about the amusement park wasn't far off the mark. The Moon Bounce was finished. Per Tom's directions, it had been placed far enough from the tables and chairs that the children's play wouldn't disrupt adult conversation. The yellow-and-blue castle jiggled in the June breeze, its puffy bottom inviting a multitude of tiny bare feet. The air smelled of popcorn and flowers. Banjos and fiddles resonated through two towering speakers between the Moon Bounce and the tables. The deejay had been part of the Deluxe Princess Birthday Package as well, but it was Barney who had chosen the music. Not exactly Tom's style, even if he couldn't help but drum his fingers against his jeans. Tied everywhere possible were hundreds of balloons—red ones and orange ones and green and blue. And yellow, yellow especially, Leah's favorite color. A banner hung between the two large maples by the house. The pink and purple letters spelled out HAPPY 9TH BIRTHDAY LEAH! The Celebration Time men placed their tables next to ones already decorated with mounds of silverware and glasses. Tom caught himself thinking there weren't enough people in the whole town to fill all those places.

He took the four steps from the stone path onto the back porch, where the birthday girl sat atop a faded and chipped picnic table that had come with the house. Leah peered out toward the far edge of the yard where the white fence abutted a small hill. Her yellow dress was tucked around her scrawny legs like a cocoon. Small patches of sunburn on her face and neck mingled with chalk-white skin. Not-quite-folded hands rested in her lap. Her left thumbnail rubbed her right in short, panicked strokes that matched her breathing.

"H-hey, Puh-Pops," she said.

"Hey, Leah-boo."

Tom sat beside her on the picnic table and smoothed out a wrinkle in the hem of her dress. He knew the stutter would be there (that birthday wish had sadly gone unfulfilled for the last four years), but he had hoped it would at least remain at the usual degree. Instead, what was usually manageable had grown worse. It was the stress, of course. Too many things, too many people.

"Whatcha doing?" he asked.

"Just wuh-watching," she whispered.

Her eyes remained on the hill, where two shaggy pines grew at awkward angles in a skewed, fairy-tale simplicity. The hill had been Leah's favorite place since the move. Tom had considered trying his hand at building a playhouse up there for her, though he thought Barney might be better suited for it.

"There's luh-lots of s-stuff here, Puh-Pops."

Tom placed a hand on Leah's knee. Her thumbnails stopped

rubbing as one hand went over his. Her gaze never wavered. Tom turned her thumb over and winced. The sight gave him shivers despite the heat and broke his heart despite the happy surroundings.

"I know you asked me not to do all this," he said. "Couldn't help it, I guess. This is your day, and I love you."

"You luh-love me t-too much to duh-do what I ask," Leah said, then she pursed her lips and shook her head. "I m-mean that guh-good, not b-bad. It's all so p-pretty. It'd make for a guh-good p-picture."

A yellow balloon by the tables slipped free of its moorings. It floated upward and stuck into one of the maples. Leah didn't seem to notice.

"Maybe later."

She looked from the hill to Tom. "I'm scuh-scared no one will c-come, Puh-Pops. No one wuh-will come and no one wuh-will notice me."

"I know." Tom leaned over and kissed the top of his daughter's head. Her long black hair smelled of Ellen's shampoo. "But it's your birthday, and your mom and I have something special for you. Mr. Barney's bringing it right now."

Leah's eyes went from woeful to bright. "Is Muh-Miss Mabel w-with him?"

"She is. Want to come see?"

Her mouth tried to say yes but instead hung open in the thick air. Leah didn't have to say what she thought. Tom knew "coming to see" wasn't nearly as easy for her as it sounded, and it sounded nearly impossible.

"Suh-sit with m-me for a minute, Puh-Pops?"

"Sure."

The Celebration Time men put the finishing touches on the backyard. Leah filled Tom in on the goings-on of the strangers around them. The big man—Leah said his name was Rich, not Rick—set the last chair by the last spot at the last table and slapped its back. He was eager to leave for his son's baseball game. The man still by the Moon Bounce making sure the engine was working was Derek. The engine was just fine—Tom could hear the whirring all the way from the picnic table—but Derek was stalling because he didn't want to go home until his wife left for the store. The rainbow man was on the hill. Marty, Gill, and Eddie were already on their way to the big trucks out front. They were in a hurry because of the wedding they had to set up for back in Camden that afternoon. And the deejay didn't care much for the music he was playing, but that was okay because he was getting paid for it anyway.

Tom asked, "How do you know all of that?"

Leah shrugged her bony shoulders. A small bead of sweat broke out on her upper lip. "If you're smuh-small, p-people around you will suh-say most anything b-b-because you aren't there."

"Well, I see you. And I can't believe what a big girl you're becoming."

Tom kissed the top of her head again and let his lips linger there as he tried to find something prudent to say, some sort of sage advice or practiced wisdom. None came. Dr. Tom Norcross had tried several times over the past two months to regard his daughter as a patient, thinking that would help him smooth out the deep wrinkles in her life. But in the end that notion never worked. Love always got in the way.

They sat there watching the balloons dance and hearing the birds sing. Tom decided everything was perfect. As perfect as it could be.

"What'd you say about the rainbow on the hill?" he asked.

"Nuh-not a r-rainbow, Puh-Pops. The R-rainbow M-man."
Leah pointed to the two pines and grinned. "Suh-see him?"

"No."

"I d-do." Her grin turned into a smile. "He sees m-me too.
He's s-s-singing."

Tom followed Leah's eyes. The two pines slouched in the
heat, forming patches of shade over a thick bed of brown needles. A mockingbird flitted from the fence onto a limb. Its
song called out.

"When did he show up?" he asked.

"Juh-just now."

Tom nodded. He didn't think Leah was talking about the
mockingbird. Which meant this was a new something to add
to the long list of his daughter's ailments. The little he could
recall of imaginary friends was not enough to form a professional opinion, but the father in him didn't think the sudden
appearance of one coupled with the worsening of her stutter
was a good sign. Especially not that day.

"Ready to go see Mr. Barney and Miss Mabel?"

"Ok-kay, Puh-Pops," she said. "S-stay close?"

"I won't let you go."

They rose from the picnic table and walked around the
house hand in hand. Leah stopped at the corner for a last look
at the hill. Tom hoped the wave she offered the pines was
good-bye rather than hello.

2

Barney Moore lifted the soiled John Deere cap from his head
to get a better view of the surroundings. "Never thought I'd
see this day, sure enough," he said. "Tarnation, ain't it a sight?"

The old Dodge passed through the opening in the white wooden fence that guarded an expanse of emerald grass. The lane was smooth despite its age, the line of magnolias so old they were casting shadows back when Barney was still sitting on his daddy's knee.

"Ain't this a sight, Mabel? Lookit that house, up on the hill like some kinda citadel."

Mabel offered no response. She sat hunched over in the passenger seat. Her chin lay against her chest. A pink sliver of tongue poked out from between her teeth.

"Mabel? Hey there, honey."

Barney let go of the wheel and shook his wife hard enough to wake her but easy enough that his panic didn't show through. The Dodge drifted to the right as her eyes opened into two pale holes. There was a tinny *ahh*, followed by a sharp cough.

"There ya go. Gonna have to get Doc March to take a look at that hack you're gettin'." Barney took the wheel and steered the Dodge back into the center of the lane. His free hand dabbed the thin string of drool that escaped the corner of her mouth. Her bottom lip trembled as he did. Mabel had always been ticklish. "Look up there, Mabel. Ol' Henrietta Fox woulda lost her supper if she caught a body up in her lane, and here we are drivin' right on up to the *house*. Ain't that somethin'?"

Mabel tapped four fingers against her leg in a steady rhythm and said, "I *love* you."

"Now don't get all jittery just yet," Barney said. "Still don't know if this'll work, but I got a good feelin'. I know Reggie's gonna show. Reggie shows, so will everybody else."

Barney patted Mabel's hand. He checked the rearview mirror and smiled at the blanket fluttering in the truck's bed.

The pickup sputtered past the last of the magnolias and circled around to a yellow Victorian that stood like a monument to better times. Flower gardens bloomed in yellows and oranges and reds along the front and sides. An American flag hung from a tall metal pole. Two panel trucks from Celebration Time sat in front of the detached double garage. Dr. Norcross waved as he made his way around the side of the house. His Ellen stood on the porch. Barney pulled into the small opening left by the trucks and smiled through the open window.

"Hiya, Miss Ellen."

"Hello, Barney."

Barney pulled on the handle and pushed, pushed again, and then heaved his hefty frame against the rusty door until it yielded. He retrieved the wheelchair from the bed and lifted Mabel into it as Ellen approached.

"It's so nice to see you." Ellen bent toward Mabel and touched her on the arm. "I'm happy you're here, Mabel."

"I love you," Mabel said. Her smile was frail and confused, but a smile just the same.

Ellen grinned and glanced at the blanket-covered object in the back of the truck. "Is that what I think it is?"

"It be," Barney said. He adjusted the thick glasses on his face and lifted his cap. "Gave her one last coat of lacquer yesterd'y evenin'. Go on an' have a peek."

Ellen eased over to the bed and pulled back on the blanket. There was an *oomph* as the air left her lungs. Her eyes widened. She ran a finger along the wood grain and shook her head. That was always Barney's favorite part.

"Purty, ain't she?"

"Leah's going to love this, Barney. It's just what she needs."

"You gonna wait until the party to give it to her?"

"No," Ellen said. "We're going to give it to Leah now. Partly because we don't think we can keep it a secret any longer, but mostly because it'll soften the blow. You know, if the day doesn't go well."

"Now, Miss Ellen, I know y'all only been here two months, but you just gotta have some faith. Why don't you give Mabel a little push into the carriage house while I get this outta the truck. Need to shine her up right quick."

Ellen wheeled Mabel into the garage and got another "I love you" for her effort. Barney carried Leah's present from the truck to the middle of the concrete floor and removed the blanket. He pulled a shop rag from the chest pocket of his overalls, turned his cap backward, and went to work on the thin layer of grime that had accumulated more from the blanket than from the two-block trip from the Treasure Chest.

"She an artist, your Leah?"

Ellen set the brake on Mabel's chair and said, "A budding one, at least. Leah loves to draw. I think it helps her, especially now. We're still getting used to things."

"Figure it's a shock, movin' from the city," Barney said. "Us country folk do things different. Not better, I reckon, at least not in some ways. Just different. Never been up here to the Fox home, as we call it. Seems an awful big place for just three people."

"We just fell in love with the house," Ellen said. "The upstairs needs some remodeling, so we're just living in the downstairs for now. The previous owner made a fantastic master bedroom in the back of the house."

"Henrietta Fox never cared much for steps once age took hold of her," Barney said. "Heard she had some work done."

"We turned the parlor into Leah's bedroom. She wanted to stay close."

"Can't blame neither of you for that," Barney said. "New

town, new house. I imagine all that strangeness would be hard on a little'un."

"We like it here just fine. People have been very nice. Very . . . welcoming."

"Ayuh." Barney finished, slapped the rag against the wood one last time, and stepped back for a last look. Mabel approved with a small, catlike *eck*. The rag went back into his front pocket, the blanket back over Leah's present. He turned back and smiled. "You're nice to say that, Miss Ellen, though I know it ain't true. That's one of them kindly lies that won't get you sent to hell for the tellin'. I know y'all are stuck by yourselves."

Ellen had no answer. Truth don't need an answer, Mabel liked to say. Or used to.

"Ain't no excuse for it," Barney said, "but there's reason. Most folk here got kin buried either in their fields or over in Oak Lawn goin' back generations. We all grown up together, you see? Like a family. Takes us awhile to get used to people from Away. But you said your Tom's one of them headshrinkers, so I expect he can explain all that."

"He can," Ellen said, but she said it in a funny way that told Barney she was going to ask Tom no such thing. "And I can understand it too. It's just that Leah can't. The move's been hard on her. Tom says that deep down, people just want to be loved. Leah gets plenty of that from us, but not so much from anyone else. Because she's . . . how'd you put it? 'From Away.' But the truth is that she didn't fare much better back in Stanley. She's just so shy. Shy and scared of her own shadow. We've taken her to speech therapy and counseling, but her progress has just been so slow. I guess the truth is it doesn't matter where Leah is, Barney, she'll always be from Away. Mabel's the only one she's really taken a shine to. Isn't that right, Mabel?"

"I love you," Mabel said. She coughed again.

Ellen smiled and turned back to Barney. "We're just trying to pull Leah up out of that dark hole before it's too late. I don't know what's keeping her and Tom."

The Celebration Time men interrupted to say everything was ready and they would be back in the evening to pack up. They hoped the birthday girl had a great time and that everyone showed, given that it was gonna be a hot one. Ellen and Barney thanked them.

"Hard rain falls on us all from time to time," Barney said when the men left. Mabel looked at him. Her fingers danced on the vinyl armrests of her wheelchair. More spittle leaked from her mouth. Barney retrieved his shop rag and tended to her dignity. "Ten years ago when Mabel had her stroke, Doc March said 'twas a miracle she survived. Said the same when she started talkin' again, even if all she says is the same thing over an' over. We's in a dark hole too for a while. But we'll get there, Mabel an' me. Your Leah too." He struggled with the pride that threatened to cut off his next words and managed to set it aside. "Want to thank you again for the chance to make your young'un's present. We need the money, don't mind sayin' that. But I needed the satisfaction more."

"And we want to thank you for doing such a magnificent job." Ellen took three steps toward the blanket and reached out. She drew her hand back as two shadows crossed the garage's entrance. "Here they come."

Tom was smiling when they entered. He said hello to Mabel—"I love you," she answered—and shook Barney's hand. Leah's eyes went up long enough to see the covered something in the middle of the floor.

"Where have you two been?" Ellen asked.

"Th-there's a man in the buh-backyard at my special puh-place," Leah whispered to her. "He was suh-singing."

Ellen exchanged a look with Tom, who shrugged.

"Hello, little Leah," Barney said. "Happy birthday to you."

"Hello, Mr. Buh-Barney." Leah's eyes went from Ellen's to her own feet. She smiled at her shoelaces. She stepped around her parents and brushed the hair out of Mabel's eyes. "Hello, Muh-Miss Mabel."

"I *love* you," Mabel slurred.

When Leah said she loved Mabel back, Barney thought he saw tears in Ellen's eyes.

Tom said, "Leah, your mom and I want to give you your present now, before everyone comes."

There was another downward smile and another upward glance.

"Go ahead, honey," Barney said. "From what your momma says, it's just what you need."

Leah inched toward the middle of the garage and regarded her gift as if it had teeth that could bite. She took a step back and pulled down on the blanket. It slipped free without a sound and dropped to the floor.

The easel was nearly as tall as Leah, stretched upward on four wooden legs with a perpendicular workspace half as wide as the frame was tall. The wood had been sanded and primed to a glow so bright it seemed to pulse with life. A roll of drawing paper was fastened to the top, the first page pulled through a small opening at the top and held in place by three wooden dowels at the bottom. Just below the dowels, a pullout drawer adorned with a brass knob beckoned. Leah reached out a shaky hand and opened it. A wooden divider ran crossways through the inside of the drawer, separating an assortment of wide and thin brushes in the back and seven small jars of watercolor paints—red, orange, yellow, green, blue, indigo, and violet, all arranged in rainbow order. Her eyes bulged at the sight and cut toward Barney. There was a small click as she pushed the drawer closed.

"Well?" Ellen asked. "What do you think?"

Leah turned away, head down and smile there, and ran toward the sound of her mother's voice. She hugged Ellen and then Tom. Then she walked over to Barney and hugged him as well.

"It's the muh-most b-b-beautiful thing I've ever suh-s-seen," she said. "Thank you so muh-much, Mr. Buh-Barney. It's so w-wonderful."

Barney's arms went slack and then tightened around Leah's yellow dress. His smile was as big as his eyes were wet. That was always his favorite part too.

"No, child," he said. "Thank you."

Leah let Barney go and turned to her father. "C-can I puh-paint now, Puh-Pops?"

"Not quite yet, Leah-boo. The party's ready to start."

Those last words were a noxious cloud that hung in the air longer than the exhaust from the Celebration Time trucks. Tom was the first to mimic Leah's downward gaze. Ellen followed. Mabel was last, though Barney thought that was more due to weariness than worry.

"Now let me tell y'all somethin'," Barney said. "Mattingly folk like to keep to their own, ain't no doubt about that. But we're also plenty nosy, and that's what I'm countin' on. Ol' Henrietta Fox lived up in this house for years and didn't let no one near the door. That white fence y'all got on these five acres? Might as well've been Fort Knox, and I ain't kiddin'. Now she up and passes on into the next life, God rest her soul . . ."

Barney held his hat to his chest. He wouldn't continue until Tom did the same. The doctor did, though reluctantly and without knowing why.

"She passes on, and a family of city folk move in. And now there's this birthday party for their young'un, and ol' Barney's done spread the word that everybody's invited. Trust me, they's gonna come."

Barney's impassioned plea fell on deaf ears. That was just as well—secretly, even he didn't believe his words.

Yet just then from beyond the raised garage door came the sound of slowing vehicles. A caravan of trucks and cars wound its way up the lane toward the house. Dozens of them in slow procession, there and not and there again as they moved among the magnolias. Rusty tailpipes and chattering voices sent the robins and jays into neighboring yards.

"They's comin'," Barney said. He let out a "Ha!" that made Tom and Ellen smile and Mabel profess her love. That joy was balanced by the fear in Leah's eyes. Barney placed a hand upon her shoulder and told her it would all be okay. The hard part was over. Everything would be bright now.

3

Allie Granderson had been in the middle of the convoy that approached the people-from-Away's big fancy house. In the backseat of her daddy Marshall's truck, to be exact, and with Mary Granderson's reminder to behave like a lady fresh in her mind. That exhortation had dwindled the moment she spotted the puffy blue-and-yellow bouncy-bounce in the backyard. It had gone away completely when she saw Zach Barnett crawl inside.

It had taken awhile to jump her way over to him. It wasn't a woman's place to call on a man—so her momma said—which meant a bit of craftiness was in order. Allie had jumped with the smaller kids near the front first, her friends in the middle second. The June breeze barely seeped through the tiny holes of the nylon mesh that enclosed the space. By the time Allie had gotten close to Zach, the air whiffed of sweat and feet.

He and his friends had welcomed her—the boys in town respected Allie as nearly an equal. She could jump as high, run as fast, and throw rocks as far as anyone. When it came to recess games, she was often picked before all the boys except Zach.

Dear, sweet Zach, who had just moments before performed an awkward but successful somersault in the Moon Bounce solely for Allie's benefit. They'd jumped until their feet were slick and their knees ached. Then Zach had whispered in Allie's ear that she was pretty. That had been enough for them to sneak away to the side of the house.

"I love you, Zach Barnett," Allie had told him, but only after she'd looked to make sure the side of the house was theirs. "I'm gonna be your missus one day. So let's just peck right here, and we'll be promised."

Zach had balked at the idea at first, saying that kissing girls was gross and he was too young to be entertaining thoughts of holy matrimony. And then he'd added that just because a girl could kick a ball and chuck a rock didn't mean she'd grow up to be pretty and make a good supper. But there was magic in the air that day, and that shine had crept through the tiny holes of the Moon Bounce and clung to them even if the breeze had not. Zach had turned his head to make sure they were alone and then aimed his lips at Allie's jaw. She bucked at first— Allie expected a peck on the cheek but never *that*—but then felt her knees weaken. She opened her eyes to see a yellow balloon untangle itself from a tree and float into the blue sky.

"Don't you go blabbing, Allie Granderson," Zach said. "You do, and I won't love you no more."

Then he ran off, leaving her to swoon.

Now she mingled amongst the crowd and tried to get the feeling back in her legs. Allie found her parents beside the biggest popcorn machine she'd ever seen, talking with a man she did not know. Barney and Mabel Moore were with them. To Allie's dismay, so was the sheriff. She took a deep breath and tried to act natural.

"Where you been, young'un?" Marshall Granderson asked.

"Playin' in the bouncy-bounce," Allie told him. "Hey there, Sheriff Jake. I ain't seen your son nowheres."

"Okay," the sheriff said. "I expect Zach's with Kate somewhere."

Allie nodded, proud of her subterfuge. "Can I have some popcorn, Momma? And hey there, Mr. Barney." She bent down to find Mabel's eyes and yelled, *"I love you, Miss Mabel."*

"I love *you*," Mabel told her.

Barney smiled at Allie and tugged on one of her pigtails. He turned to the strange man beside him. "Tom, this here's Allie Granderson, Marshall and Mary's daughter. Allie, this is Dr. Norcross, Leah's daddy."

"Very nice to meet you, Mr. Doctor Norcross," Allie said. She curtsied despite her cutoff jeans and T-shirt and winked at her momma. "This is the best party ever. It's even better than the carnival. Are y'all comin' to the carnival? Best time in town all year long."

The man smiled and dug a silver scoop into the mound of popcorn. He was about her daddy's age, maybe younger, but thin with just a speckle of gray at his temples. His cap was new and bore neither a fishing hook nor camouflage. Still, Allie liked him.

"I expect we might," he said. "Nice to meet you, little Miss Allie Granderson. And thank you for coming." He handed Allie the bag and said to the rest, "Really, thank you for coming. Ellen and I were afraid the heat might keep everyone away."

"We wouldn't miss it for the world," Marshall said. He slapped Tom on the back hard enough to buckle the doctor's knees, which made the sheriff steady him and Allie laugh. "Everybody in town wants to know all about the city folk what bought crazy old Henrietta Fox's house. God rest her soul."

Marshall doffed his hat with those last words. Mr. Barney and Sheriff Barnett as well. Allie was impressed that Mr. Doctor did the same. Maybe he wasn't so city after all. People wound their way through the crowd and stopped to say hello, though few introduced themselves to Mr. Doctor and no one bothered to speak to Barney or Mabel, not even the mayor and his wife. Allie munched her popcorn and wondered how people could be so mean.

"Tom," Mary asked, "where would your Ellen be? I'd love to tell her how grand this all looks."

"She's over with the cake," Tom said. "I'm sure she'd be happy to meet you."

"Where's your daughter, Mr. Doctor?" Allie asked. "I ain't saw her yet."

"You know Leah?" Tom asked.

"Nosir, I just know her face. I was in fourth grade last term and Leah in third, but we rode the long bus together. Most kids said Leah shoulda rode the short bus since she lurches her words, but they's just mean."

"*Allie,*" Mary said.

Allie shrugged a *What?* "I didn't say that, Momma. Promise."

"It's okay, Allie," Tom said. "Leah's just shy. That's why Barney came up with the idea to invite everyone." He settled his hands on his hips and looked out over the summer day. Not to where people were, Allie noticed, but where they weren't.

He pointed to the end of the yard. "There she is, up on the hill there. Why don't you go tell her the cake's ready?"

"Okay," Allie said. "Great party, Mr. Doctor. Sheriff, I'll tell Zach hi if I see him, but I probably won't. Bye, Momma and Daddy and Barney." She raced off with popcorn in hand, stopped, and turned to yell, "I love you," to Miss Mabel. The old woman's eyes were closed, her head slumped down toward her chest. Allie blew her a kiss instead.

Chatter and squeals gave way to breeze and birdsong as Allie approached the hill. Leah sat curled up under the pines writing in a notebook. Her pretty yellow dress was spread out around her. She would mark on a page and look into the air beside her, speak and then listen, then write again.

"Hey there," Allie shouted. She waved as she ran, jostling popcorn from the bag. Her pigtails smacked the sides of her head. "Hey, Leah. Happy birthday."

Leah looked up and dropped her pencil and notebook. Her heels dug into a pillow of brown pine needles, pushing the rest of her deeper into the trees until her back met the white fence. She looked as though she were about to be attacked by a wild animal.

"Hey there," Allie said again. "Don't do that, you'll get your dress all sullied." She reached the hill and peered into the trees. Leah's knees were drawn into her chest. The look on her face was absolute horror. "Hey, I'm Allie. We rode the long bus together."

Leah's mouth trembled. The muscles in her throat went tight/loose/tight. Allie thought something was about to come out of Leah's mouth, and it was something not nearly as nice as a *Hey there* back.

"Hey," she said, softer this time, "it's your birthday. Your folks are pretty great to go all out and invite everybody, huh?

Not even the carnival's this nice. Are you going to the carnival next week? Maybe I'll see you there. Happy birthday, by the way. Why are you up here all by yourself? Are you okay? You look like you're gonna yark. Who ya talkin' to up here?"

Leah's cheeks puffed out like a squirrel with a mouthful of nuts. Her lips trembled and then parted. What came out wasn't as good as *Hey there* and not as bad as her breakfast, but instead something in the middle—a wet, cavernous belch that sounded very much like *BAAAAWP*.

Silence followed. Allie looked at Leah and Leah at Allie, her eyes too frozen to look away. The color in her face matched the white on the fence.

"D'you hear that?" Allie's eyes darted from one side of Leah to the other. She drew a finger to her lips in a motion so slow it could have been made in molasses. "Shh. I think there's a rhino in here. Must be the same one that follers my daddy round. That sorry thing's always makin' noises and tryin' to get my poor daddy embarrassed. Sorry about that."

Leah blinked. And then—almost—a smile.

"Happy birthday, Leah."

Leah swallowed hard and managed, "Th-thuhuh-thanks."

Allie wiggled herself between the branches and found a small spot in the bed of needles beside Leah. The mass of people below looked like ants that had happened upon lunch. Children ran and played (Zach was now introducing himself to Mr. Doctor, and the sight of him made Allie's stomach flutter as if hungry), the adults laughed. Birds darted from tree to tree looking for scraps of food. Allie offered the little popcorn that was left in her own bag. Leah shook her head no.

"Whatcha doin' up here all by your lonesome? You're the birthday girl. This is your party."

Leah wouldn't say.

"Hey," Allie said, "I know all about your stammer. It's okay. Way I figure it, you don't mix your words nearly as bad as most folks round here do."

"It's buh-better up h-here," Leah whispered. "Everybody luh-looks s-smaller."

"That's kinda weird. Hey, what's this?"

She picked up the notebook from the ground. Leah's hand moved to snatch it away but returned to her lap. Her thumbs rubbed together.

"Hey wow, these are *great*." Allie flipped through the book one page at a time and realized Leah hadn't been writing, she'd been drawing. There were pictures of her father and mother, of herself, of their big house on the hill. "I mean, these are, like . . . awesome."

"Thuh-thanks," Leah managed.

Allie reached the last page, a half-finished sketch of a smiling man with big eyes and music notes coming from his mouth. She held the picture up to Leah.

"Hey, who's this?"

At first she didn't think Leah would answer (or could—the horror in her eyes had dulled but was still there). Finally she said, "Thuh-that's the R-rainbow M-man."

"See," Allie said, "you can talk. I talk a lot. Daddy says it's my spiritual gift. I take that as sweet talk even though I know he's just makin' fun."

"H-he was suh-singing to m-me," Leah said. "Puh-Pops couldn't hear h-him earlier. He couldn't even see h-him." She paused. Allie thought it was either to take a breath or rest her sputtering lips. "C-c-can you s-see him?"

"Nope." Allie closed the book and looked at Leah until the shy girl's eyes looked back. "You mean he's here right now?"

"He's b-beside me."

Allie leaned herself around Leah's shoulder and winced when a branch poked her in the ear. Nothing was there but the blanket of pine needles and one lonely caterpillar that didn't look like a rainbow man at all.

"Leah, you know that thing about my daddy's rhino weren't real, right? I was just tryin' to settle you is all."

Leah sighed and rubbed her thumbnail again. "You don't buh-lieve me, d-do you?"

"Didn't say that, I was just makin' sure. You really see something there?"

Leah nodded.

"You mean he's, like, a spirit?"

Leah looked near to where the caterpillar rested. "He luh-looks m-more like m-magic. Do you buh-lieve in m-magic?"

Allie nodded. "I imagine so. What's he revealin' to you?"

Leah looked to the caterpillar. "He's suh-saying I have to buh-lieve in the M-Maybe."

"What's the Maybe?"

"I d-don't know."

Allie shrugged and said, "Well, lotsa folk round here believe in the magic. See those mountains yonder?" Leah's eyes looked up to the rounded spires beyond town that rose like giant blue waves against a clear sky. "Folks say they're fulla magic and that sometimes it spills out over town and flies over people. They say Mr. Andy Sommerville found the magic awhile back. Mr. Sheriff Jake Barnett found it too. That was after, out in Happy Holler. His son Zach told me that, Zach bein' the boy I'm gonna marry. But I can't say no more about that, you bein' from Away."

"I duh-don't think my puh-pops buh-lieves in m-magic," Leah said.

"Well, maybe you should ask him." Allie took Leah's hand.

"Speakin' of which, come on. Your daddy said it's time for cake."

Leah jerked her hand away. "I'm juh-just going to stuh-stay here. The R-rainbow M-man's walking duh-down for me. He suh-said he'd b-be back in a m-minute."

Allie saw no caterpillars between them and everyone else, though she reckoned she could've missed plenty, given all that fluffy grass. Still, the only rainbows she saw were the clusters of balloons below.

"You can't just stay here."

"Why n-not?"

"Because I'm your friend now. That means you gotta go where I go." She grabbed Leah's hands again and pulled her out from under the pines. "Come on. Let's go down there. I wanna see if I can catch a sight of the rainbow man too."

Allie ran, giving Leah the choice to either follow or dis-locate her shoulder. She chose the former. The two skipped down the hill toward the mass of people below.

4

Reginald Arthur Goggins—Reggie to the good people of Mattingly every Monday through Saturday, Preacher Goggins or Reverend Goggins on the Sabbath—made his way through the gathering and considered his a job well done. Barney had been hawking the city folks' coming-out party to everyone he saw for over a week, with little result. That was to be expected. As much as Reggie thought of his fellow towns-people, he knew Barney's entreaties would fall upon deaf ears. It was hard to get people to listen when they were too busy pretending the person doing the talking wasn't there. Which was why in the end it had been Reggie himself who had spread the word that people should come. It would be the Christian thing to do.

He greeted Hettie Mayfield by the back porch of Henrietta Fox's old house, where people gathered for pieces of a cake that was big to the point of brazenness. The old woman took his hands as he prayed aloud for the cancer in her body. Jake Barnett, Kate, and Zach helloed. Reggie whispered a warning to Kate that she'd better lock her boy up in a few years, Zach would be driving the girls crazy by then. Kate replied that a forty-year-old man of God who still retained all of his hair and most of his physique would do well to heed that very advice, especially considering the honey-eyes certain unattached ladies of the choir offered while his back was to them every Sunday morning. Mayor Jim Wallis and his wife, Gloria, politicked with voters by a set of fancy banquet tables. Trevor Morgan—Gloria's nephew and editor of the *Mattingly Gazette*—stood by them scribbling in his notebook. Reggie greeted them all, asked how they were and how he could pray for them, told them if they needed anything, anything at all, the church was always open.

And it was. Day, night, and every time in between. Because Mattingly was God's town and Reggie Goggins was God's servant.

"Hello, Mrs. Carver," he called to a woman near the Moon Bounce. "Lovely singing last Sunday. You have the voice of an angel if I've ever heard one."

Lisa Carver waved back, the smile on her face brighter than the sun shining down on her. Reggie moved on and took in the balloons, the music, the fancy Moon Bounce, satisfied that he'd accomplished another of the tasks before him. The truth was that Lisa Carver couldn't hit a note to save her immortal soul, but the truth was also that Reggie had overheard Lisa's husband, Rodney, tell her such after last Sunday's service. The hurt on Lisa's face was a pain Reggie felt was his duty to set right, even if it did require a lie. Reggie comforted himself by saying it was all music to the Lord, and praise be to Him.

He found the Moores and Grandersons by the popcorn machine with two people whom Reggie took as the hosts. Barney waved him over and shook his hand.

"Tom, Ellen, this here's Reggie Goggins. He preaches down at the First Church of the Risen Christ, biggest church in town."

Ellen extended her hand. Tom, however, did not. Reggie thought this odd but took no offense.

"Nice to meet you, Reverend Goggins," Ellen said. "We appreciate you stopping by today."

"A pleasure." Reggie said hello to Marshall and Mary and bent down to see if Mabel was awake. He kissed the top of her head and nodded toward Barney, who offered a not-so-hidden sigh of relief. The poor old man always feared Mabel would one day fall asleep and never wake again. "And it's Reggie, ma'am, least on Saturdays. Beautiful house you have, simply wonderful. Called on y'all once or twice since you moved in, but no one was here. Nice to finally meet you both. Where's the birthday girl?"

"Allie was on the hill with her a bit ago," Mary said.

The hill was clear but for grass and pines. Tom and Ellen scanned the crowd, their lips pursed. Ellen reached for Tom's hand.

Reggie didn't see reason for their worry and supposed it was still the city in them. He tried to break the tension by offering, "Never can tell with kids, I suppose. But 'children are an heritage of the Lord: and the fruit of the womb is his reward.'"

"Amen," said Barney and Marshall.

Reggie turned to Tom—a psychologist back in the city, rumor had it—and said, "Tom, plenty of fine churches in Mattingly. Your lovely family would be welcome to visit mine, of course. The Moores and Grandersons can attest to its standing."

"I appreciate that, Reverend," Tom said. He still hadn't offered his hand. "We don't go to church."

Ellen said, "We're spiritual but not religious."

The only sounds were the crowd's prattle and fiddle-play from the speakers. Reggie supposed it was his place to say something, he being the beloved town pastor and the Norcrosses being spiritual but not religious, but it was Barney who asked what most everyone in the group wondered.

"What the heck's that mean, Miss Ellen?"

"I suppose it means we ask the same questions religious people ask; it's just that you believe there are answers to those questions and we don't."

Tom's eyes were on Reggie, jaw muscles flexing, ready to . . . what? Pounce? Reggie thought no, it couldn't be that. But it was as if the wind had changed and dark clouds had gathered around them. Something had struck the mean place inside Tom Norcross's heart, and Reggie had no idea what or why.

Barney raised his hat and scratched his head. Mary waved to someone. Anyone.

"What good's a question if there ain't no answer to it?" Marshall offered.

Before Ellen or Tom could respond—and Reggie was very much looking forward to *that* answer—Allie appeared alongside a little girl so pale and fragile she looked sickly. Their cheeks were flushed, their mouths panting. Tom and Ellen looked genuinely surprised. To Reggie, their reaction only added to the ambiguity of the moment.

"Hey there, Preacher Goggins," Allie said.

She hugged Mary and then Marshall. Leah followed suit with her own parents and then wedged herself between them. She apologized to Ellen for the condition of her dress. Reggie took a step forward and put his hands on his knees.

"You must be Leah. Happy birthday to you."

The little girl grinned at the grass and said nothing.

"Get some good presents?"

Still the silence. Tom nudged Leah's shoulder and whispered for her to say something.

"M-Mr. Buh-Barney m-made m-me an easel," she mumbled. She tried to look at Reggie but somehow couldn't. "I'm s-supposed to muh-make him a p-p-picture to s-say thanks. It's what he nuh-needs."

Barney smiled and said, "Why, thank you, little Leah. That's awful kindly."

"Leah saw a spirit," Allie announced. "He was a-singin' to her up on the hill there and then he came down here. Y'all seen a spirit, Momma?"

"Can't say we have," Mary said.

Chuckles spread through the group. Reggie thought that perhaps had more to do with the relief of moving past what had just been said than anything else. Still, he noticed the only one other than himself not laughing was Tom, who looked more concerned than amused.

Ellen looked at Leah, who had now found something on the front of her dress to take her mind off her shoes. "Did you see something up on the hill, Leah? Maybe it was someone at the party."

"There wasn't anyone on the hill," Tom said.

"It was luh-like m-magic," Leah told them.

Reggie took that opportunity to say, "Would you like to see some magic, Leah? Real, true magic?"

Leah's chin moved upward to Reggie in slow motion.

"I already h-h-have," she said.

For reasons Reggie could not understand, those words gave him chills despite the hot day.

"Well, if you want to see more, you just come down to First Church this Sunday. Plenty of magic there. Allie here can tell you that, can't you?"

"Yeppers," Allie said, though at the moment she seemed more concerned with looking for Leah's spirit than being a good fisher of men.

"Life on earth is a wonderful thing, but life with God is better."

"What'd you say?" Tom asked. He stepped forward to Reggie. The two men stood like boxers before a fight—Tom snarling, Reggie wondering why. They were not much different in size or age, though the good doctor had puffed out his chest and lifted his chin to appear both taller and bigger. Marshall took a step forward and looked to Reggie, unsure what was happening. "Tell me that again."

"I said life with God is better."

"That so?"

Tom was closer now. Reggie could feel puffs of air on his face from the doctor's nose.

"*Tom,*" Ellen said. She left Leah's side and grabbed her husband by the elbow. His body turned toward his wife, but his eyes remained on Reggie. "What are you doing? Not in front of our *guests.* I'm so sorry, Reverend."

Reggie looked past Tom and said, "No apology necessary," though one surely was. Not to the Grandersons, who stared slack-jawed at Tom, nor to Barney, still rubbing his head, nor Mabel, who had, to Barney's relief, now awakened to offer a barely there *ahhh*. Not even to Reggie himself. No, Reggie thought, the apology should have gone to Leah, who huddled against her mother and began polishing her thumb. Her head bobbed up and down as if listening to a faraway song.

"I think it's best if you just go, Reverend," Tom said.

"You can't be kickin' the preacher out," Barney said. "Reggie came down here special, Tom. Saturday is his gettin'-ready-for-preachin' time. You can't blame a preacher for spreadin' the Lord around."

Tom said nothing.

"It's okay, Barney," Reggie said. "I'll be going. Marshall, Mary, Allie, I'll see y'all tomorrow. Barney, I'll see you this evening?"

Barney nodded. "Sure thing, Reg."

Reggie bent his head around Tom and said, "I love you, Mabel." Then, to Leah, "Happy birthday again, little Miss Norcross."

"Thuh-hank you, Ruh-Reverend," Leah mumbled. She still worked on her thumb. A nervous habit, Reggie thought, just as that stutter must be. If she was doing all that on the outside, how must her insides be? No wonder the poor child was conjuring up people to talk to.

"Ellen, nice to meet you. Tom, if you should change your mind—"

"Won't happen," the doctor said.

"God can reach anyone, Tom. Seen it myself."

"I'll have nothing to do with your God, Reggie, and I won't have such talk spoken in my house."

The silence that followed was broken only by Allie, who offered a low, "Oh Emm *Gee*."

Reggie turned to leave, thankful that the others attending the party had been too busy talking and playing to bear witness to the rudeness of what had just happened. He made his way back through the crowd, pausing to say hello and goodbye, then climbed into his truck. He sat there for a long while, replaying the scene over and over in his mind to understand where things had gone wrong. By the time Reggie reached the end of the winding lane, he was sure of two things. One was that he would have to pray for the family from Away. The other was that they were trouble.

5

The heat finally got the better of everyone's curiosity around noon. By one thirty, the Celebration Time men had returned to pick up what they'd dropped off. They'd even disposed of the trash—evidently a hidden perk of the Deluxe Princess Birthday Package. By three, the yellow Victorian's backyard had returned to its formerly serene and empty state. And by four, Leah had still not come out of her room and Ellen had still not spoken to Tom.

He told himself both were understandable. The day had simply been too much for Leah. Ellen had to all but hold her in place while the crowd sang "Happy Birthday," after which Leah and her new friend had escaped back to the hill. If there was one bright spot to the party, Tom thought it was Allie. And if there was one dark spot, it had been meeting the good Reverend Goggins. That little kerfuffle had not only almost ruined the party, it had also frightened Leah and shattered the fragile truce between him and Ellen.

The worst part was that they couldn't know why he'd

reacted with such anger. Ellen couldn't read the thick folder marked GLADWELL, MEAGAN that now lay open in his hands. Leah wouldn't understand what it meant if she did. Tom had refashioned the small opening between his life at home and his life at work such that only he could fit through. That was the only way he could keep his daughter blissfully ignorant of the hardness of the world for as long as possible, and the only way to ensure that his wife would not nearly ruin his career again.

He closed the file and set it on his desk. The small office just off the living room wasn't much—aside from the roll top, there was a leather love seat, a cherry bookcase stocked with psychology books, one silk plant, and a file cabinet—but it was enough for Ellen to refer to it as Tom's Home Away from Home. That most times she said those words in a slightly higher octave than usual was proof of one of life's great ironies—the old wounds were the ones that seldom healed, while the fresh ones tended to scab over quickly. He rose from the chair, closed his desk, and decided it was time to apologize. He'd start with Leah. Not just because it had been her day and her party, but also because her forgiveness would come easier.

Ellen was in the kitchen. What remained of Leah's party had been scrubbed, cleaned, and put away. A bottle of wine rested on the center island beside a half-empty glass—Ellen's way of dealing with most things, the strange and the stressful among them. Though it had gone unspoken, Tom knew the party had meant just as much to his wife as it had to his daughter. Ellen was the kind of person who needed to be liked, would go to any lengths necessary to ensure acceptance. He thought of that as she took another sip, and he thought of how much things had changed around them and how little had changed between them. Journey's "Don't Stop Believin'" echoed through the radio on the counter. Ellen took a sip and looked at Tom, took another sip. Strands of blond hair spilled over her left ear. Her hand moved to the crystal that hung from her neck. The sapphire in her eyes had dulled to a powder blue and was sadder but no less appealing. Tom held up one finger—hold on to that feelin', the expression said—and continued down the hallway to the parlor that was now Leah's bedroom. The door was cracked open. He knocked once and entered.

Leah stood in the far corner of the room, the easel between her and Tom. She wore what was once the white apron Ellen used for cooking. Now it was artist's attire, coated with splatters of paint. Bits of green and gray and white peppered her face and hair. Oversized dollops of yellow puddled on a plastic drop cloth from the garage. Leah whipped the fat tip of a slender brush in short, purposeful strokes so powerful that they wobbled the easel. Her eyes were trance-like, her breaths shallow.

"Whatcha doing, Leah-boo?"

"Hey, Puh-Pops." Her eyes never left the page. "I'm m-making a thank-you for Mr. Buh-Barney. Be done in a s-second."

Tom sat on the edge of the canopy bed and smiled. "It's awfully nice of you to do that for Barney. It was a good idea."

"It is g-good," she said. She dipped her brush, stared at the page, and resumed. "But it w-wasn't m-my idea."

"Can I see?"

"Not yet," she said. "There's wuh-one over on m-my desk that's r-ready, though." She dipped the brush into a small bowl of water beside her, wiped it on the front of her apron, and chose another color. "It's the fuh-first one I d-did. You can h-hang it up f-for me if you w-want. I did that one all buh-by myself."

He walked to the desk on the opposite side of the room where the painting lay, its brushstrokes dry but still glistening.

Along with his own likeness, Leah had painted Ellen, Barney, Mabel (complete with wheelchair and an "I love you" speech bubble jutting out from her mouth), the Grandersons, and herself. Bodies were little more than stick figures with right angles for arms and legs. The sky was a flat afterthought. Clouds were oblong boxes, trees squiggly and full. There was no doubt the painting was a Leah Norcross. Generalities were compromised in favor of particulars. Bodies and scenery were unimportant. It was Ellen's eyes and Tom's own smile, Barney's strong hands and Mabel's doughty spirit, the Grandersons' familial love. The painting wasn't about *what* these people were, but *who* they were—the heart of the matter.

"This is really wonderful, Leah."

"Th-thanks, Puh-Pops. I can draw b-better on my easel, don't you thuh-think?"

Tom didn't, not really, but said yes, absolutely.

She dipped her brush again and said, "I thuh-hink it's because it has luh-love in it."

"The easel?"

"Yes. It has Mr. Buh-Barney's love. Tacks are on the desk, Puh-Pops."

Tom shook out four thumbtacks from a purple bowl on the desk. There was precious little space left on the walls. All the apropos preteen posters of singers and movie stars hung here and there, but the rest of the space was quickly filling with the noble attempts of a fearful little girl to not only define her world but shrink it into something more manageable. Tom placed Leah's newest attempt in a small space near the window beside other recent works. Some were of the house, others of Ellen or himself, but most were self-portraits. Lined up side by side in chronological order, Leah had rendered herself in each sketch with the same long black hair and round face, but the smiles had regressed to grins and then to frowns. The heart of the matter. Which made the still-shiny smile she'd given herself on her newest masterpiece all the more pleasing. Whatever regrets Tom still harbored from the party faded that moment into a deep sea of warmth.

"Leah, I want to apologize for the way I talked to Reverend Goggins today. I can't tell you why I did it, but if I could, you would understand."

"That's okay, Puh-Pops. I just fuh-figured—" Leah stopped, spellbound again, eyes wide. Tom was about to ask her what was wrong when she finished. "—it w-was about your wuh-work. M-Mommy says you get muh-mad sometimes because you luh-love too m-much."

Tom supposed that was as good a way of putting it as there could be.

"But I shouldn't have done that to the reverend. It wasn't a nice thing. Are we square?"

Leah said, "Yuh-yeppers," but Tom thought she didn't realize what she was agreeing to. Her focus was still on the paper. He looked back to the painting by the window. Her smile was still there—that was the important thing—but there was no denying that Leah had taken a step forward in her abilities. Maybe she was on to something with the easel. The colors were brighter, the strokes bolder. And there was something he hadn't seen the first time.

"Hey, Leah-boo, what's that behind us in your picture?" Tom moved closer to the paper. It seemed nothing more than a dollop of colors.

Leah stopped painting and studied him. "Puh-Pops, do you buh-lieve in m-magic?"

"I believe in grand things," he said. The something was nothing more than a smudge, he decided. A slip of the brush.

Brushes were harder to manipulate than colored pencils or Crayola markers. "Things that make us wonder. But I think magic is a kind of mystery, and mysteries are just questions we can find answers to if we look hard enough. So, no, I guess I don't believe much in magic, just good tricks."

"Then it's juh-just nothing," Leah said. She set the brush down. "I'm d-done, Puh-Pops. Wanna see?"

"Sure."

He looked away from the smudge and returned to the edge of the bed. Leah took a deep breath, tore the page from the easel, and turned it around.

"What do you thuh-hink?" she asked.

Tom's shoulders slumped as all feeling left his body. His brain, formerly sharp enough to understand the whys and hows of his wife's anger, stuttered to a stop.

He called out the door, "Ellen."

"What's wruh-wrong, Puh-Pops?"

A part of Tom knew that his jaw had loosened itself and was now hanging where his chin once was. What's wrong? He didn't know. Or he did, but explaining it to Leah would be like explaining the color red to a blind person.

"Ellen, can you come in here, please? Can you come here right *now*?"

The hard tinkle of Ellen's wineglass hitting the kitchen countertop sounded as if it were a million miles away.

"Leah," he asked, "how . . . ?"

Heavy footsteps down the hall. Ellen appeared at the door. She may have meant to ask what was so important to interrupt her vino therapy, but when she saw Leah's painting, all she managed was, "Whaa . . ."

"Hi, M-Mommy," Leah said. "I puh-painted a thank-you p-picture for Mr. Buh-Barney. It's what he n-needs."

Ellen walked into the room and slumped down beside Tom. Leah stood by the easel with the painting in front of her—one arm wrapped around the top of the page and the other hand holding its bottom, as if shrouding her own nakedness. Ellen reached for Tom's hand. He had the vague understanding that the truce was back on after all. Strangely, that didn't seem to matter. All that mattered was the picture in front of them.

The field was dense and emerald, washed in a rain just past. Droplets of water covered the blades of grass, each of which had been painted in singular precision—hundreds of them, thousands, covering the bottom third of the painting. Above the field, gray clouds gave way to their white cousins, both of which were sprinkled with patches of cobalt sky that united them in a seamless, almost illusory effect. A rainbow spilled from the largest patch of blue in a perfect arc into the middle of the field. Halfway between sky and meadow, the colors transformed into pieces of gold that showered down into an overflowing clay pot. Piles of gilded coins were scattered around the pot in a pattern that was at once haphazard yet perfectly symmetrical. Written at the bottom was a smiley face and *Thank you Mr. Barney Love Leah.*

"What's the muh-matter?" Leah asked. "D-don't you luh-like it?"

Tom tried to work his lips, happy that at least "It's . . ." came out.

Ellen finished with ". . . wonderful," but that was all she could manage without the benefit of another breath. "Leah, how did you paint that?"

"I juh-just listened," Leah said. "The easel has Mr. Buh-Barney's l-love in it, Muh-Mommy. All it t-takes is l-love and l-listening, I guess."

Ellen started, "But . . . ," then fizzled. It was more than Tom could say for himself. "There's . . . *gray*, Leah. You don't have gray paint. You painted in colors you don't have."

"I muh-mixed them. It's easy." Leah placed the painting on the top of her desk to dry, then turned back to her parents. "I nuh-need to guh-het this to Mr. Buh-Barney this afternoon. It's i-important. Allie can go w-with me. She says we're fuh-friends now. I'll c-call her. Is that okay?"

Ellen said nothing. Tom, at least, nodded. He wondered how much of his wife's wine was left.

6

Though only a few blocks separated the Treasure Chest from the Norcross house, Barney was just getting Mabel home. The old Dodge had sputtered and spat and finally died just after they'd turned out of the winding lane. He couldn't leave Mabel there alone, and he didn't think he could push her all the way back up the hill to Tom's house. He didn't have a cell phone to call Reggie or Marshall or Jake. Those who passed did not see him. Barney couldn't understand how that could be, what with him standing there waving them down. But they'd passed on anyway, their eyes to the opposite side of the road or down at their radios. He was left with no other course than to try and figure out himself what had gone wrong with the truck. Thankfully, the problem was little more than a mucky battery cable in need of a good spit and polish with his shop rag. He filled Mabel in on the solution when he climbed back into the truck, but she had slumped over against the window.

"Mabel? Hey there, old girl."

She didn't move. Barney fought the urge to panic and gently shook her arm.

"Hey there, honey. You okay?"

Mabel's eyes fluttered and her lips parted. "I love you."

Barney smiled and loved her back. The old hoopty fired up on the second try and carried them onward. Barney took a left at the light (a blinker; Mattingly had only one stoplight and that one was mostly ignored) and drove into downtown. The smell inside the truck was enough to force his head out the window.

"It's okay, Mabel." Barney supposed Mabel was fine with the odor, even if a bit of it had gotten down his throat. "We'll be right home."

Pebbled sidewalks and ancient trees lined the four square blocks of shops and restaurants, anchored by the town hall and the sheriff's office. The Old Firehouse Diner stood to Barney's left. He waved as a few customers straggled out, their bellies full and cholesterol high. No one waved back. The next right was Second Street, which flowed into an alleyway that dead-ended in front of a two-story edifice of peeled and fading brick. A cobbled sign hanging from the door said simply The Treasure Chest.

The Dodge settled in the second of seven parking spaces in front of the building, these empty but for tall weeds poking through asphalt that had last been sealed back when Mabel still knew the world around her. The Treasure Chest had turned a profit that year, enough to pave the lot and buy a new lathe for the shop. Barney lurched out of the truck and retrieved Mabel's wheelchair from the bed, then eased her down into it.

"Home now, Mabel," he whispered, to which he received a shallow *mmmm* that gave him relief.

The wooden front door creaked and opened into the

middle of the store. Barney retrieved a rock to prop open the entrance while he wheeled Mabel inside. The last of the day's sun struggled through the grime on the windows, highlighting a shower of dust motes and rows of neatly placed marble rollers, wagons, and dollhouses. An assortment of wooden trucks and cars lined the far wall. Barrels of building blocks and Lincoln Logs stood in the middle of the room under signs that read Ahoy! 20 Cents Each! A hand-cranked cash register sat on the warped counter. The shelves behind it were stocked with jars of candy and lollipops, all of which had been purchased around the same time as the parking lot had been sealed. The air was thick with pine and cedar and must. Barney kicked the rock out of the way to let the door swing back. He turned the sign in the window from BLIMEY, CLOSED to AHOY, OPEN out of habit rather than necessity.

The building had seemed a castle when Barney and Mabel first signed the loan not more than two months after their marriage. The Treasure Chest was to be their business, yes, but more than that, it would be their home. The Realtor (that would be Margie Black, a cousin to Mayor Wallis, though Barney didn't hold that against her) had been quick to point out the prime business location and the fact that there was even a basement, something no other building in downtown Mattingly possessed, given the steep costs of boring into the rock upon which the town proper had been built. All was bright until the business faded and Mabel took ill. Now only ghosts roamed the aisles of toys and stood at the counter. There were times when Barney would stand in the middle of the store and hear the echoes of children now grown with children of their own.

The pungent odor, mixed with the smell of wood and forgottenness, did not allow him to pause for those sounds that day. Barney gathered his wife of fifty-four years from her wheelchair and cradled her up the stairs to their one-bedroom apartment above. The door clanked against the rubber door-stop and swung back toward them, almost bumping Mabel's head, but Barney moved out of the entranceway and stopped the door with his foot.

"Sorry 'bout that, Mabel," he said. "Reckon I gotta mind my own strength."

Barney kicked off his shoes upon entering—Mabel had always been a stickler for tidiness. He figured if there was one blessing in the dementia that had followed his wife's stroke, it was that she did not care about the peeling wallpaper and cobwebbed corners that had come to define their home. She could not comprehend what their life had become.

He took her to the sofa, careful not to lay her on the cush-ion with the broken spring, and then collected what he needed from the bathroom. He placed a towel under the small of Mabel's back and removed her pants without disturbing her. His forearm went under her knees and pushed them toward her chest, while his free hand undid the tape. Barney was mind-ful not to pull the diaper away—he'd done that before, and the result had been two messes to clean up, one hers and one his—but instead left it beneath her. He collected a handful of wipes and cleaned her from front to back, dropping the used ones into the stained diaper. He continued until the final wipe returned unsoiled. The diaper and wipes went into the garbage can. Baby powder went into the fresh diaper and onto Mabel. Barney checked her for rashes and then pulled the dia-per on until it rested at Mabel's waistline.

"There now," he whispered. "Good as new."

Mabel peeked through her eyelids and made a gurgling sound. Barney patted her arm and wiped a tear from his eye.

He had always been a man of faith. He knew God was a kind and merciful God, a God of love. And yet in secret thoughts he would never share with anyone but Reggie, Barney knew that God was also cruel. The Moores had prayed for years to be blessed with a child. Barney redressed Mabel's frail body and realized the good Lord had finally gotten around to granting that petition, only the child turned out to be his own wife.

He dropped his wallet and keys onto the kitchen table beside the unopened mail from the day before. From the hospital mostly, though there was also an envelope from the power company and one from the insurance place. Each stamped with *Past Due* or *Final Notice*, just in case Barney had failed to notice the sense of urgency in the letters and phone calls that had preceded them. He left them there and checked on Mabel's breathing, then settled into the broken cushion on the sofa.

"Well, I'd call that a success," he told her. "Sure, there was that little hiccup with Tom and Reggie, but it passed by. Who in the world is 'spiritual but not religious'? I don't even know what that means. Do you, Mabel?"

Mabel didn't say. Her fingers danced on the pillow beside her. Barney wondered what tune she played and didn't ask. He figured that answer would be the same as her answer to the Norcrosses' fuzzy faith.

"And that little Leah, such a fine girl. Kinda trapped in herself, I reckon. She's sure taken a shine to you, Mabel. I wonder why that is?"

Mabel didn't say.

"She loved that easel. Did you see her face, the way it lit up? Like a million tiny lights. She even hugged me, an' the way her momma and daddy looked, Leah don't hug nobody. It was like it used to be when a little girl or boy got somethin' I made. You remember those times?"

"I *love* you."

"I love you too." He reached for the blanket draped over the sofa and covered her. "I'm gonna go downstairs for a bit. Reggie'll be here in a little while to watch you while I run your errands. You just rest now. You rest and dream of the ocean. I know how you loved—love—the ocean, Mabel. I'm gonna take you back there one day. You wait and see."

Barney kissed Mabel on the cheek and watched as she drifted away to that foggy place where she lived. He sat with her for a long while in front of the open window. Beyond the alleyway, cars passed and people strolled and the world went on without him. It was that sense of lonely disconnect that bridged his thoughts from what was happening around him then to what he would do that night under the guise of his errands. It was a shameful act. Shameful and desperate. He sniffed and rubbed his eyes.

"But I reckon if you're hungry enough," he whispered to Mabel, "even poison tastes good."

7

Allie padded down the sidewalk that led into town and felt as if a giant weight had lodged itself in her brain. She supposed Leah felt the same, since her head was down and she was rubbing at her thumb again. Probably the only thing that kept her upright was the Hello Kitty book bag she was wearing with Mr. Barney's picture inside.

Everything Leah had told her was still crashing around in Allie's mind when she spied Jane Markham sitting on the sidewalk ahead. In Jane's hand was a half-eaten orange Popsicle melting in the sun. Jane had not gone to Leah's party and would not, declaring the day before to a gathering of classmates at a church softball game that "anyone who'd be friends with somebody like *that* needs srain burgery." Everyone had laughed. Everyone always did what Jane wanted, as she was the most popular girl in the whole entire fourth grade. Allie had laughed too, not just because Jane was popular and they were friends enough, but because switching the *b* and *s* in "brain surgery" was nothing short of comedic gold. But that had all been before Preacher Goggins called and asked the Grandersons to attend the party because it was the Christian thing to do, and it had been *way* before everything Leah had just told her.

Jane looked up as they approached, and there was nowhere for Allie to hide. The Popsicle went from pointing skyward to across the street. A thin runner of orange goo dripped from the stick to the sidewalk. Jane had seen them, Allie knew that just as she knew soon it'd be all over town that she was now best friends with the stuttering girl who lived in Henrietta Fox's old house.

"Well, what're you gawkin' at, Jane Markham?" Allie asked.

Jane said nothing, just sat there with a how-dare-you glare, and the more she did so, the angrier Allie became. Leah's head found her shoes and she drifted into the grass of Jane's daddy's yard. Allie pulled her back. In for a penny, in for a pound, that's what her momma always said. Allie hadn't known what it meant until that moment. They passed Jane, and Allie said, "You better pick your jaw up before a fly lays eggs on your tongue."

They walked on in silence, Leah now next to her. A faint smile was on her lips.

"Don't you worry about her none," Allie said. "She says somethin', I'll set her straight. Now, you wanna tell me all that again?"

Leah's smile disappeared. Her voice was soft and distant. "I'd really luh-like it if I duh-didn't have to."

Allie shook her head. "Friends, I sure can pick 'em. They told me, you know. My other friends, I mean. 'Don't be friends with her, she's as odd as a football bat,' they said. But no, I didn't listen. I had to be a good *Christian*. Jesus wept."

Leah looked from her thumbnail to Allie and asked, "You duh-don't want to be my fuh-friend anym-m-ore? I thought you buh-lieved."

"I didn't say that," Allie answered, though she had to admit the not-being-friends part had crossed her mind. As for the other, well, "It's just that . . . *geez Louise*, you know?"

Leah nodded and resumed her scratching.

Allie stopped midstride, grabbed Leah's hand, and asked, "What are you doing to your finger?" A brief tug-of-war ensued. Allie countered by putting all her weight on Leah's elbow— "Don't make me hogtie you"—and pinning her. Leah surrendered her thumb. "Holy wow, Leah, there's a *hole* in your *thumb*."

Leah braced against Allie and pushed, freeing herself. "It's nuh-not a *h-h-hole*," she said, "it's a *puh-p-place*." She lowered her eyes and resumed walking. "I get n-nervous sometimes."

"Okay," Allie said. She ran to keep up. "One thing at a time. We'll work on your thumb later. And since you don't want to repeat it all, I'll do it. Because that ain't the sort of stuff you say once and never again, Leah Norcross. So I'll talk, and you just nod or shake your head. Okay?"

Leah nodded.

"Okay, so before the party you see this man that no one else can see, and he's a-singin' to you."

Nod.

"And he was with us earlier up on the hill."

Nod.

"And he's walkin' right beside us right now."

Nod.

"Stop nodding, Leah."

"He's ruh-right here," Leah said. "I had to tuh-tell somebody. I'm too small to d-do this all b-by myself. I asked Puh-Pops if he buh-lieved in magic, b-but he s-said there's just good truh-tricks. You said we were f-friends, and you're the only f-friend I have. The R-rainbow M-man said you'd help me. But you don't buh-lieve me, d-do you?"

Leah scratched at her nail again. Allie let her. One thing at a time.

"I didn't say I *didn't* believe. I just need proof is all. Everybody needs proof about stuff they don't believe, Leah. That's how they start believin'."

They walked on. The quiet side street lined with plain homes and baseball fields gave way to fancy homes and churches. They were close. Snyder Avenue would lead to Jackson, Jackson to downtown, and downtown to the Treasure Chest.

Leah said, "I'll guh-give you pruh-proof. What do you w-want?"

"I want to see him."

"You c-can't. And n-no, I don't nuh-know why. Isn't the p-painting enough?"

The rolled-up piece of paper stuck out from the top of Leah's book bag. For a moment, Allie thought yes. That was enough. That painting looked so real she could almost smell the rain and hear the gold coins clinking out of the sky. Leah went to work on her thumbnail again. Allie realized as well as a child could that the gully in Leah's thumbnail wasn't the only one she had.

There was another gully somewhere deep inside herself, and Leah was ready to fall into it.

"Well, what's he look like, then?"

"I cuh-can't describe him," Leah said.

"Proof, Leah. You have to try."

Leah looked to the side where Allie wasn't. The waning sun cast two shadows on the gray sidewalk.

"He's three tuh-times bigger than my smuh-small," she said. "And he g-glows, but it's not like g-glowing." She paused, eyebrows scrunched, looking for words her mouth couldn't form. "I duh-don't think the him I suh-see is the real him. I think it's juh-just all the him he wuh-wants me to see."

Allie kept her stride beside Leah, which wasn't easy given that her friend—and she now considered Leah a friend, there was no going back on that one—was a good four inches taller. How could Leah think she was too small to go downtown by herself?

"Tell me more," she said. "What's he sound like when he sings?"

Leah looked to the shadows again. "Suh-sometimes it's like a b-baby laughing. Or like the r-rain. Right now it suh-sounds like an ocean w-wave. Not like it's c-c-crashing, but kind of luh-like it's c-crashed and g-going back over a million tuh-tiny shells. It's m-music l-like I've n-never heard. It's so buh-beautiful it hurts my ears. My m-mind can't hold it."

Allie looked to Leah's opposite side and strained to see. Aside from the shadows and the grass, there was nothing. A part of her heart felt heavy, almost guilty. It didn't sound right to be jealous of someone who was so afraid of the world that she'd worn a hole in her thumb, but it was envy just the same.

The T in the road ahead meant Main Street. First Church

sat on the left. Preacher Goggins's truck was in the lot. Across from that was the park, which was already undergoing its transformation into fairgrounds for the carnival next weekend. Four firemen were busy stretching a banner across the street between two telephone poles. MATTINGLY SUMMER CARNIVAL, it said, and underneath, THIS SATURDAY FUN FOR ALL!!

"T-tell me about the cuh-carnival," Leah said.

"It's only the biggest thing ever. Everybody comes. There's rides and games and stuff. It's awesomesauce. Are you going? We can go together."

Leah said, "We'll b-be there," but the words came out flat, as if being there was more a matter of having to than wanting to. "Do you buh-lieve now?"

"More than I did," Allie told her.

"W-well, what else do you wah-want me to do, Allie? I've tuh-told you everything I c-can. You have to buh-lieve. He wants you to guh-go into the Maybe with muh-me."

Allie didn't know what that meant and didn't ask, there already being too much in her head. She considered her options. Only one remained. It would be a risk, but only if Leah was telling the truth.

"I got a secret no one knows. If he can tell you what that secret is, then I'll believe."

Leah bent toward the shadows and listened. Allie looked away. She couldn't decide if it was because watching made her uncomfortable or if it made her scared.

"*Oh Emm Juh-jee*," Leah whispered. "You kuh-kissed a *b-boy*."

Allie felt all the muscles in her face slacken. She froze and pulled on Leah's arm.

"How'd you know that?"

"He tuh-told me."

"What else does he know?"

Leah shrugged. "I d-don't know, but I think he nuh-knows everything. Do you buh-lieve me now?"

"Yes. Will you ever tell anyone?"

Leah crossed her fingers, spit on them, and crossed her heart. "Nuh-never."

That was good enough for Allie Granderson.

They reached Main Street and turned right at the diner onto Second. The steady churn of cars and voices was swallowed by the empty brick buildings and old signs of the alleyway. It was as if this one street had balked at the chance to carry on with time, choosing instead to remain behind.

"Why are we really taking this to Mr. Barney?" Allie asked. "Not that I mind, a'course. I like him fine. Miss Mabel too. It's just that a lot of folk don't pay him no mind no more. That picture ain't just a thank-you, is it?"

"The R-rainbow M-man didn't tuh-tell me. All he suh-sang was that it's what Mr. Buh-Barney needs."

"Why's he need it?"

"He duh-didn't say."

Allie looked at the empty space beside Leah. "You know, for a guy who knows everything, he ain't much on sharing."

The sign on the door read AHOY, OPEN. The two entered. Their eyes slowly adjusted to their surroundings—candy behind the counter, dollhouses everywhere, toys made with love for no one to love them back. A faint bow in the wooden floor marked the path most traveled, leading from the door to the back. A wobbly set of stairs was in front of them. Two swinging doors stood to the right. Another door was to their left. It was to this door that Leah walked. Allie stopped her.

"That's just the basement. Ain't nothin' down there but empty."

"Yuh-yell if anyone's here," Leah said.

"Why me?"

"B-because it'd tuh-take muh-me too luh-long."

Allie raised on her tiptoes and hollered over the shelves and barrels. "Hey there, anybody home?"

A rustle from the back of the store, then silence. Allie followed as Leah made her way toward the two swinging doors that led into Mr. Barney's shop. They took one door each and pushed. The room on the other side was just as old and sad as the one they'd left. Cobwebbed machines sat scattered amidst worktables of varying size and states of disrepair. Tools hung backward or upside down on pegs along the wall. On the far end a broom handle propped open the large garage door.

Allie felt a tug on her sleeve. Leah said, "He's over thuh-there."

Mr. Barney was at the far end of the shop, perched on a wobbly stool beside an even wobblier desk. Stacks of paper surrounded him, some in piles even taller than Allie. Along the top of the desk were frames that held yellowing pictures of boys and girls holding toy cars or sitting in wagons. Tacked to the wall above these were thank-you cards scrawled in large, curvy letters.

Allie thought being surrounded by such adoration would bring a beam to anyone's face, but she didn't think Mr. Barney was smiling. His head was bent over the desk and hidden by his right hand. The shudders in his back and shoulders were different from the sort laughing would cause—jerky and shallow rather than steady and long.

"I think he's crying," she whispered to Leah. "We should go. Nobody worth their bones wants anybody seein' them blubber, that's what I say."

"Nuh-no," Leah said. "It's im . . . *port*ant. We huh-have to."

Allie's fingers slid down Leah's arm until they found her hand. The two girls crossed the width of the shop to where Mr. Barney sat. As they neared, the old man's sobs became plain.

Leah reached out and touched him on the shoulder. Mr. Barney spun around and nearly fell off the stool, then raised his hands to his face. He reached for the rag in the pocket of his overalls and dabbed his eyes.

"Hey there, Mr. Barney," Allie said. She smiled to make up for the sadness in her words.

"Allie?" Barney reached for the glasses lying cockeyed on the desk and wrapped them around his bulging ears. "Leah? I'm sorry, girls, I didn't hear y'all come in."

"That's okay," Allie said. "We just figured you was busy is all. We didn't see you bawlin'."

The old man blushed and shoved his fingers under his glasses. The big circles they made produced sucking sounds against his skin.

"Oh no, I weren't cryin'," he said. "Just got a bit of sawdust in my eyes is all. Been busy today, whole lotta busy. Just me an' Mabel, you know. What brings you two ladies down here today?"

Leah's voice was small. "I huh-have something f-for you, Mr. Buh-Barney." She unzipped her book bag and pulled out the rolled-up sheet of paper. "It's w-what you nuh-need."

8

Of all the duties involved in being a small-town preacher, this was Reggie's favorite. Not studying the Word, not preaching it (though he had to admit preaching it was right up there), but applying it.

Living it.

For years there had been whispers that he could retire from preaching and become mayor, a fact that even the current mayor, Big Jim Wallis, willingly conceded. Not because Reggie possessed any sort of political acumen, but because he was so well liked. So *sought out*. Which was why the short walk from church took longer than it should have. Children stopped him to say hello, men to ask for prayer or advice, women to flirt. Reggie understood that a man in his standing—relatively young, relatively handsome, and unattached—would be appealing to some of the town's bachelorettes. He only hoped what few women who pined for him understood there was no room in his life for another love. His heart belonged to his God and his town, nothing more.

Reggie's thoughts were still on the Norcross family, and that bothered him. He had already prayed for them, had given Tom and Ellen and sweet Miss Leah to the Lord, which was all he could do. Yet the family from Away lingered still, and Reggie could not understand why. Those thoughts finally began to shift as he turned at Second Street and walked down the small alleyway to the Treasure Chest. Unfortunately, his heart now pondered Barney and Mabel Moore.

A life devoted to supplication and Scripture could provide the answer to most any question (Reggie shook his head at the whole "spiritual but not religious" nonsense), and the answer to the suffering lives of Barney and Mabel should be no different. All Reggie had to consider was Job, that good man ruined by the devil for the glory of God. Or Joseph, who was bound by chains only to rise up and rule all of Egypt. The problem was the Moores had yet to rise up. They were still being sacked and shackled.

Why? That was the question that had preyed on Reggie's

mind for years, and one that remained unanswered. The Moores had been faithful to both their church and their God, but that had not prevented Barney's financial troubles or Mabel's worsening condition. As a result, their social status had been reduced from pillars of the community to pitiable laughingstocks. Aside from himself, the Grandersons, and the Barnetts, the town all but shunned Barney and Mabel. Even at church, that place where Christian love should be most evident, they were relegated to the purgatory of the back pew and given only the slightest passing greeting. It was as though the town likened them to a debilitating virus spread by mere acknowledgment. Deep down (and despite his best efforts to prove to the town otherwise), Reggie simply believed folks were afraid Barney's failure would rub off on them.

It was all part of the Mystery, the unseen hand of God. Only He knew why some were blessed and others cursed. All Reggie was privy to was the knowledge that while he could not change the world, he could change tiny pieces of it. Which is why he kept watch over Mabel every Saturday and Wednesday evening so Barney could run errands. It was a small act, but an appreciated one. A necessary one.

Reggie walked into the Treasure Chest and heard voices from the shop. He pushed through the swinging doors. Barney stood near his desk looking at a large sheet of paper. Allie Granderson and Leah were with him.

"Hey, Barney," Reggie said.

Barney and the girls looked up. Allie waved. And was that a smile on Leah's face?

"Reggie," Barney said, "come on over here and take a look at this."

He weaved among the worktables and discarded tools to where they waited. Barney's eyes were red and his cheeks puffed.

"Hey there, Preacher Goggins," Allie said. She gave him a sideways hug that Reggie returned.

"Hello there, Miss Leah," Reggie said.

"H-hello."

The girl's smile was still there. Reggie noticed it wasn't a joyful smile but a shy one, a grin of secrets.

"Look at this, Reggie," Barney said. "Leah painted me a picture on the easel I made her. You just look at this."

He handed the painting over. Reggie's eyes bulged at the landscape—the beauty of it, the exactness, the sheer *perfection*. It was as if he held not a likeness of the world, but a world itself. His hands began to shake.

"Ain't that somethin'?" Barney asked. "You ever seen its like, Reggie? 'Cause I sure ain't, not in all my seventy-three years."

Reggie looked down at Leah and asked, "You painted this, child?"

"Nuh-not exactly," she said. "The R-rainbow M-man helped a luh-lot."

"The who?"

"Leah's spirit," Allie said. "You know, the guy we were lookin' for at the party?"

Reggie tried to smile, but his mind was split between the numbness in his lips, the picture in his hands, and the fact that he was actually asking, "You say a spirit helped you paint this picture?"

"He s-showed me how to m-mix the wuh . . . w-watercolors," Leah said. "He's m-magic. Do you buh-lieve in m-magic, Ruh-Reverend?"

"I believe in the Lord, Miss Leah."

"I think it's just wonderful," Barney said.

Reggie brought Leah's painting so close it felt as if he would tumble into it. He offered the picture back to Barney.

"Wuh-we'll be going n-now," Leah said. "I know you have stuh-stuff to do, Mr. Buh-Barney."

Barney shook his head at the painting and placed it on his desk. He wrapped the two girls in his arms. Leah hugged Barney back. Her left hand patted his head as if comforting him.

"Good-bye, girls," he said. "And thank you so much. Y'all have no idea."

"You're welcome, Mr. Barney," Allie said. "And don't worry, we won't tell nobody about your bawlin'. Bye, Preacher Goggins."

"Good-bye, Allie," Reggie said.

The girls headed for the swinging doors hand in hand. Leah paused just before leaving and cocked her head to the side, as if listening. She turned back to Reggie and said, "Chuh-cheery-bye, Ruh-Reverend. Please be cuh-careful of the n-newspaper b-b-box."

She left then, taking her mysteries with her.

9

Barney climbed into his truck with the Dodge's keys in one hand and Leah's rolled-up watercolor in the other. He'd meant to mount the painting in a place of honor above the shop desk but couldn't. It didn't seem right, leaving such a beautiful thing to gather dust. The engine gasped to life (*There's one miracle*, he thought), but the truck didn't move. He had to take one last look before leaving.

He unrolled the paper and let out a low whistle. "Tarnation, child. How'd you do somethin' like that?"

The setting sun behind him cast its warm glow over the page, giving the illusion that the images were swirling.

Something was different. The colors were brighter (*Of course they are, dummy*, he thought, *the sun's a-shinin' on it*) and the image clearer, yes. But also something else. Something like—

The page inched closer until it almost touched his nose.

"Now, what's this about, little Leah? What you got goin' on here with ol' Barney?"

He lowered the paper and scratched his head, wondering if what he saw had been Leah's intent or the light playing tricks. Barney would have to decide later. He had to go so he could get back before Reggie started suspecting.

His first stop on those Wednesdays and Saturdays was always the pharmacy—Barney's way of both reminding himself what was most important and alleviating whatever nagging jabs his conscience offered. On this night he picked up Mabel's blood pressure pills and something for her cough. According to the story he told Reggie, afterward entailed a quick trip down to the Dairy Queen for a sundae and then a leisurely loop around Route 620 back home. That was a lie—Barney considered it unlike the lie Miss Ellen Norcross told him; this one possibly *could* send a person to hell—but a necessary one. Instead of turning left out of the parking lot of Spencer's Pharmacy to the Dairy Queen, he turned right toward the town of Camden.

Perhaps this was the gutter of last resort. Barney had considered that possibility often over the past months. That he, once an Important Man, had been so trampled by life that the hole in which fate had placed him could only be escaped by the granting of some twisted miracle. As the dim lights and dirty streets of Mattingly's wayward sister town loomed, a thought nudged its way forward in his mind that the only thing worse than being spiritual but not religious was being religious but not hopeful.

He pulled into the lot of the 7-11 and made sure he knew

no one inside. Unlikely, but not outside the realm of possibility. Leah's rolled-up painting went into his back pocket.

Barney said hello to the cashier and walked to the left front corner of the store. The display offered everything a fraught soul would need in order to turn desperation into further failure. Tickets were stacked in two separate bins beside a collection of tiny green pencils with VA LOTTERY stamped in gold on the sides. A large electronic sign flashed above him on the wall announcing the current jackpot. That night it was 250 million. Barney pulled a ticket from the bin and reached for one of the pencils.

In the months since he'd first offered his soul to the Gods of Good Fortune, Barney had played every combination of numbers he could summon—his birthday and Mabel's, their anniversary, the date the Treasure Chest opened. Anything that could bend luck his way. Aside from that one glorious night when he managed to pick a single correct number out of six, all Barney had gotten out of the deal were a few hundred more miles on the Dodge and what very well could have been a small ulcer. Now, as he stared at the box on the ticket—there were actually five boxes, making five chances to win, but Barney only played one and thanked God at least for *that*—he pulled Leah's painting from his pocket and unrolled it across the plastic surface of the booth.

The numbers were still there.

In the clouds above the field was the number 23. Barely visible, but there just the same. A 42 sat in the blades of grass along the left edge of the paper. A 5 was molded into the side of the clay pot in the middle of the field, along with a 4 in the rainbow. The grass along the bottom of the page hid the number 2. And written into one of the coins that spilled from the pot was a final digit—7.

Can't be, he told himself. *You're losin' it, Barney. You're brain's just as broken as Mabel's.*

Maybe. But when you are crawling through the sewage in the gutter of last resort, you will take whatever glimmer of hope is offered, because even poison tastes good.

Barney filled out his ticket and took his place in line. What came next was the sort of inner conversation between the fairer side of the human soul and its uglier counterpart that often sprang up in places where beer, condoms, and lottery tickets were offered with no questions up front and have-a-great-day on the end.

The man in front of Barney turned around and spotted the ticket in his hand. "That's a sucka bet, ol'-timer," he said. He wore a tattered ball cap and the grime of a long day spent either in a factory or under the hood of someone's minivan. Two of his front teeth were gone, replaced by a chasm of black. In his hand was a worn ten-dollar bill. "You play the scratchers. Scratchers where it be."

Barney thought yes, maybe, but the scratchers wouldn't be enough to dig him and Mabel out of their hole. Scratchers would be a spade and a bucket. But the Powerball? The Powerball was a backhoe.

Ball Cap paid for his scratchers and placed the stack atop a trash can by the front doors. He went through them one by one, shaking his head and cursing each time.

"What you want?" the young cashier said. The girl was tattooed and had earrings in her nose.

What do I want? Barney thought. He thought of Mabel and the *Past Dues* and *Final Notices.* He thought of Reggie, who at that moment was looking over Mabel, and he thought of Jesus, who at that moment was looking over Barney's black heart. He shifted his weight and heard Leah's thank-you crinkle in his pocket. He thought of how no little girl could create such a thing, and he thought of the rainbow man whom she said helped her. *A spirit*, Allie had said. *It's what you need*, Leah had said.

He handed the cashier his ticket.

"Two dollars," she said.

And with that, Barney Moore dug through his overalls and handed over six quarters, three dimes, two nickels, and ten pennies that would come to define the short life he had left.

Sunday

Six Days Before the Carnival

1

Tom woke to an otherwise empty bed and smelled breakfast. He understood the notion that each new day was the Universe's way of offering a do-over, but that was a philosophy he had never personally embraced. Starting life anew took time and persistence. Yet the world was full of people who believed their problems could be overcome easily. People who wept themselves to sleep each night only to wake believing everything was different—that everything had changed—only to repeat the cycle. And even though Tom pitied such people, he was also thankful for them. Those were the ones who gave him purpose. The ones who sought him out when their worlds crumbled. The ones he was born to help. And not only did Tom feel a kinship to them, he'd married one.

He crawled from under the covers and eased into the hallway, careful of the weak spots in the hardwood floor. Leah's bedroom door was still closed. She'd been up late—the thick wall of silence between Tom and Ellen had been somewhat balanced by the surprising jingle of Leah's laughter through the thin walls between bedrooms—and he didn't want the creaky boards to wake her. Not until he'd made sure the truce was back in effect. Tom had assumed it was when Leah unveiled her painting and Ellen had taken his hand, but no. After Leah had left with Allie, the warm front had lifted and the cold front had settled back in. Ellen hadn't so much as sneezed in his direction the rest of the night.

Her back was to him and bent over two sizzling pans, sausage in one, eggs in the other. Ellen stabbed at the eggs with a spatula and released a cloud of steam that worked its way into the fans above the stove. Sunshine flooded through the open windows, casting her yellow bathrobe in a warm glow.

"Morning," Tom said.

"Good morning back." The words were clipped, business-like, though when she turned Tom was happy to see a slight smile. "Hungry?"

"Very."

"It's almost ready. Our little Monet's still asleep."

Tom thought of Sundays past, when he would wake hungry for more than breakfast. Back when he would find Ellen in a different kitchen bent over different pans and he would offer his good morning with a kiss on the back of her neck. Back then he was the one who would have said Leah was still asleep. He would turn the stove off and lead Ellen to the bedroom, where they would offer themselves in an act that was not only symbolic of their love, but also the means by which Tom could render himself numb to his life and Ellen could find a temporary awakening to hers. But now there was only that statement of fact—Leah's still asleep—and nothing more. And in those three words was all the proof Tom needed that we could gaze upon as many rising suns as there were stars in the sky, but in the end their light could only shine upon our yesterdays and never erase them.

"I figured we'd just let her sleep a bit," Tom said. "She had a big day yesterday."

"She certainly did. That painting, Tom. Could you believe that painting? And she went down there to give it to *Barney*. With *Allie*. Leah's never gone anywhere without us." She shook her head and turned back to flick at the pan of sausage. "And then last night? How many times since the move have we lain in bed listening to her crying? And there she was giggling and talking to herself." Ellen turned around again. Tears welled in her eyes. "It was all so . . . *strange*."

"Oh, I don't think I'd call it strange. She said the easel had Barney's love in it, and that's why she could paint so much better. I don't know what that means, but maybe the easel really does have something to do with it. The angle or something. Or maybe she just has some latent talent. She draws all the time. She's bound to get good at it."

"That's kind of a stretch, don't you think? What she painted wasn't just *good*, Tom."

A part of him thought, yes, it was a stretch. But even a savant had to be bad at some point, right?

"I think we shouldn't let that picture overshadow the fact that Leah made a friend yesterday. That's why we did all of that, right? And she had a great time. As great a time as she'd allow herself, anyway."

But Tom knew rationality had never been the comfort to Ellen that it was to him. Far from offering his wife the value of another vantage point, his words had only brought to the forefront what the morning was supposed to have taken away.

"I had a nice time. Mostly." Ellen flipped the burners to low and pulled three dishes out of the cabinet to her left. "I try to let bygones be bygones, Tom. I figure that's the only reason we're still together, and I know I've caused as much hurt as I've been hurt myself. But this? No."

She walked past him and set the plates on the dining room table. Ellen's cheeks were flushed. Tom didn't think it was from the hot pans.

"I'm sorry," he said.

"I know." She passed him again, this time to fetch three glasses. "That's the thing. I know you're sorry, you know I'm sorry. Sorry is all we say, and usually that's good enough. But we all had a stake in that party yesterday, not just Leah. I need to be accepted by this town, Tom, and you go all half-cocked on the *preacher*. What in the world got into you? You said things would be better here. You said it would be *different*."

That was the moment Tom Norcross decided his wife had suffered enough. For too long Ellen and Leah had been shoved aside and relegated to ghosts on the periphery of his life, though Tom believed that to be just as much Ellen's fault as his own. She likely believed that as well, realizing that no matter how much she tried and no matter how much she wished otherwise, Ellen could not counsel the counselor.

But he would tell her now. He would tell her despite the fact that he'd told her something else once that ended up nearly costing them everything. He would tell her that his outburst in front of their new friends was not because of the Reverend Goggins but because of GLADWELL, MEAGAN and the false faith by which she had already been ruined. He would tell Ellen, tell her everything, and then she would hold him and his tears would dry against her yellow robe and they would walk down the creaky hallway to their bedroom and offer themselves as they had those Sundays past. Because each new day may not erase the days before it, but it could still be a first day. It could still be a beginning.

But just then the floorboards creaked. Leah walked into the dining room too asleep to know where she was. One hand rubbed an eye, the other her hair.

"Good morning, sweetheart," Ellen said. She offered a look to Tom that said their discussion was over, at least for now. They did not agree on much, but they did when it came to arguing in front of Leah.

"Hi, M-Mommy."

Tom walked over and picked Leah up—she was nine now, but she would always be his little girl—and gave her the kiss on the cheek he'd been saving for Ellen. "How'd you sleep, little girl?"

"Good, Puh-Pops," she said, though the deep yawn that followed said otherwise. "M-Mommy, I'm hungry."

"Coming right up. Have a seat. Tom, help me?"

Tom followed Ellen into the kitchen and asked, "Milk or juice, Leah?" He turned for her answer. There was only an empty space where Leah had stood. "Where'd she go?"

Ellen shrugged and grabbed the pan of eggs. The floorboards in the hallway creaked again, this time followed by a *thump, thump, thump* that made Tom peek around the corner and furrow his brow.

Leah returned dragging a small blue-and-yellow plastic chair. Tom recognized it as one belonging to the play set they'd bought years ago for Leah's Barbie-doll-and-teddy-bear tea parties. Leah had deemed such activities childish as her ninth birthday neared, so the table and chairs—along with the Barbies and teddies—had been banished to the back of her closet. Yet now there the chair was again, recalled for duty.

The chair went in the empty spot at the table. Leah stepped back, bowed, and swept her hand in a wide arc that began behind her head and ended at the blue-and-yellow seat.

She straightened and took her accustomed place across from Ellen's chair.

"What are you doing, Leah-boo?" Tom asked.

Leah yawned and rubbed her eyes. "Huh, Puh-Pops?"

"What's the chair for?"

"Oh, th-that. It's f-for my fruh-friend."

"Your what?" The silverware was still in his hands. For a moment Tom forgot where the forks and knives belonged.

"My fruh-friend." Leah yawned again, then added, "He w-wants to sit w-with us."

He heard a chuckle from the kitchen. Tom placed the utensils and gave the plastic chair a wide berth.

Ellen brought breakfast to the table one pan at a time. She swept four links of sausage onto Tom's plate, two onto hers. She paused at the empty place, spatula in one hand and pan in the other, and said, "Should I fix a plate for your friend?"

Tom said, "I don't think that's necessary, Ellen," and gave her a look that said she should know better. But she didn't, Tom knew that. Part of it was revenge for his actions the day before. A bigger part was that while his life was governed by facts, the former Ellen Bosserman had chosen to dwell under possibilities. It was always *Who?* and *What?* with him. With her, it was always *What if?*

Ellen looked at Leah and raised her eyebrows.

The plastic chair didn't answer Leah's look. For a few odd seconds, no one spoke. Then she said, "He's nuh-not hungry right n-now, M-Mommy, but he wants me to suh-say thank you."

"My pleasure."

Ellen fetched the eggs and ignored her husband's stares. The three sat down to eat.

Tom said, "So tell me about your friend, Leah. What's his name?"

Leah paused with a forkful of eggs halfway between the plate and her mouth and looked toward the empty chair. "I tuh-told you yesterday, remember? He's the R-rainbow M-man."

"The rainbow man," Ellen repeated. She cut her eyes to Tom and smirked. "That's a great name. Is that because he's made of rainbows?"

"Nuh-no," she said, trying the bite again.

"When did he show up?" Tom asked her. He heard his voice go flat and felt his left palm resting against his chin—Counselor Mode. Ellen kicked him beneath the table.

"A little buh-bit before you c-came to get muh-me," she said. Bits of egg fell from her mouth. She took three more bites in quick succession. "You know, right b-before Mr. Buh-Barney gave me the easel."

"Does he talk to you?"

Leah said no, and Tom thought that a small victory. But then she added, "He m-mostly suh-sings. Remember me telling you thuh-that yesterday, Puh-Pops? Before you got m-mad at the puh-preacher because you luh-love too much?"

"Yes," he said. "Yes, that's right." He smiled at Ellen and then Leah, thankful his daughter had just explained his craziness the day before in a way he could not.

"He sings, huh?" Ellen asked. "That must be pretty. What's he sing about?"

Another bite, another look at the empty seat.

"Lots of stu-huff. Secret stu-huff, mostly. Like puh-painting Mr. Buh-Barney that p-picture. I'm going to p-paint more too."

"He's singing to you now?" Tom asked. He got another kick and removed the palm from his chin.

"Yuh-yes," Leah said.

Ellen asked, "What's he saying?"

"What's going to huh-h-happen."

"What's going to happen?" Tom asked.

"I only nuh-know s-some." Leah finished the last bite, pushed her plate aside, and let out a gratified sigh. "That sure was g-g-good, M-Mommy. I think I'm gonna g-go get dressed."

Leah pushed back her chair and rose. The floorboards creaked as she made her way back to her bedroom. The yellow-and-blue plastic chair remained at the table. Tom considered the possibility that Leah had left it behind intentionally.

"I don't like this, Ellen," Tom said.

Ellen sipped her milk and sighed. "There's nothing wrong with having an imaginary friend, Tom. Everyone's had one. I had one. It was a little rabbit dressed up like a fairy princess."

Tom's palm went to his chin. "Really?"

"Analyze me all you want, big guy. You're stuck with me."

He rolled his eyes, feigning exasperation, happy that they were talking about something other than Reverend Goggins. "Fine. But I never had an imaginary friend."

"Oh, come on."

Tom shook his head. "Never."

"Not even a little rabbit dressed up like Sigmund Freud?"

"Cute *and* funny, that's you," he said, and for the first time that morning, Tom Norcross smiled.

Leah called from her bedroom, "He c-can hear you, you nuh-know. Don't be duh-dillydallying. You both should g-get dressed too."

Ellen laughed, Tom shook his head. And then Leah added two words that would have been prophetic had they not been such an understatement.

"It's guh-gonna be a b-big day."

2

Standing on the large carpeted podium with Bible in hand, watching the sunshine bestowing fresh life to old accounts through stained glass—the suited men tall and steeled, the hatted women fanning themselves with folded bulletins—hearing the claps and the amens and seeing heads nod and hands raised, comforting the wounded, preaching the Word, feeling the Spirit a-loose. This was Reggie's favorite time. The town may have had their eyes on the coming annual carnival, but to Reggie the carnival came every Sunday.

"Faith," he called out in his preaching voice, and the congregation amened again. "Faith is what we need. Faith is what God calls us to wield. The Book says it is 'the substance of things hoped for, the evidence of things not seen.'"

Yes, called the crowd.

"Faith is our defense against the darkness of this world, from the suffering, the sickness, the hurt, and the torment. Faith is the means by which we are able to withstand the evil day. 'For we wrestle not against flesh and blood, but against principalities, against powers, against the rulers of the darkness of this world, against spiritual wickedness in high places. Wherefore take unto you the whole armour of God, that ye may be able to withstand in the evil day, and having done all . . .'" Reggie lifted his hands in the air and walked from one end of the stage to the other, looking first to the choir behind him, then to Lila McKinney at the organ beside him, and finally to the congregation before him. "'. . . having done all . . .'" Their hands skyward, their lips praising. "'. . . to *stand*.'"

And then a thunder of claps that tingled Reggie's cheeks. Lila fingered four quick notes of hallelujah. Praise the Lord, the people said, and Reggie knew he had reached the tender places inside them, because applause and nods and amens meant agreement, but *praise the Lord* meant just that.

In the back row, Barney Moore raised his hands as if to embrace heaven itself. He'd exchanged his usual overalls for a blue suit and tie. Mabel was parked beside him in the aisle. Her eyes were bright this day, her grin brighter. Praise God. Reggie prayed the ailing woman could still understand his Sunday words—any words—but the only comprehension she showed was when Lila played the organ that was once Mabel's own in brighter times.

Even from the stage, Reggie could see her fingers mimic the notes. Mabel had always loved her hymns and sang them still, as much as she was able. The offertory that morning had been "Worthy of Worship," one of her favorites. Mabel had fingered the keys in her mind along with Lila and moved her mouth to the words. *Worthy of rev'rence, worthy of fear,* sang the congregation. *I love you, I love you, I love you,* mouthed Mabel. Reggie prayed as he walked—*Bless the Moores, Jesus, bless them and let them see Your face.* He knew Barney and Mabel had wrestled against the powers and principalities, knew they were trying to remain upright, trying to—

"Stand."

He let that word hang in the air and took another lap around the stage. His steps were confident, big. The Grandersons sat in the middle on the right side of the congregation. Reggie winked at Allie, who winked back. Brent Spicer, head of the deacons, sat beside them with his own family and his usual scowl. Mayor Wallis and his wife, Gloria, sat in the front pew, Trevor Morgan beside them. The newspaper editor had exchanged his notebook and pen for the King James. Reggie thought it would serve Trev well if he did that more often.

"This is a hard world."

The crowd nodded.

"This is a hard world and these are tough times. And what do we need, friends? Do we need some more government stimulus?"

No, the people said.

"No sir, we do not. It is by faith that the great deeds of God can flow, it is by faith that the devil can be vanquished, it is by faith that the hardness of this life can be overcome. We do not need government stimulus, friends, we need *faith* stimulus."

Amen, called the crowd, amen and praise the Lord, the Spirit alighting itself upon the gathering in a wave that stood many up and left others slumped in their pews. Reggie walked up and back, hands raised, chin high, big, like a general rallying his troops, Reggie's town, God's town.

"Who will give a witness today?" he asked. Reggie pointed his worn Bible outward to the crowd like a sword unsheathed. A Bible that is falling apart usually belongs to someone who isn't, he often said. "Who will stand today and tell of the power of God?"

"I'll stand, Reggie," Barney called from the back. "I'll speak on the Power."

The electricity in the air still moved, though now it came in swirls rather than waves. The congregation turned to the back of the church. What came next was an awkward silence as people decided for themselves whether to look upon Barney with pity or look away from him in embarrassment. What could he say of the power of God? He might as well have asked to speak on how to split the atom.

Reggie waved him forward. "You come on up here, Brother Moore. You come right here and give your testimony."

Barney gripped the pew in front of him and eased himself into the aisle. People settled back into their seats as he bent over and whispered something in Mabel's ear. Dozens of church bulletins waved in the hot air like tiny white windshield wipers. A hum settled over the multitude as Barney reached the stage. He smiled at Reggie, then turned toward the townspeople and gathered his words.

"God is real," he said.

The congregation politely applauded. Reggie said, "Amen."

"No," Barney said. He held up his hands to quiet the people. "I mean He's *real*. I been sittin' in that back row there since I was a young'un. Been taught all my life the Lord's a-walkin' with me. Knew it in my head, but not in my heart. I reckoned He's real enough to talk to, but not real enough that I expect Him to heed. But He inclined His ear last night, that's what I come up here to say. And then He declared."

Someone said, Hallelujah. Reggie thought it was Lila at the organ.

"That's right," Barney said, "He declared. Y'all know the troubles me an' Mabel been through. Been tough on us. We tried to keep at it, but we kept gettin' knocked down."

Many in the congregation—Reggie thought it was more than half—looked away.

"Well, God just stood us back up." He turned to Reggie again. Reggie saw the man's face was red. Barney's voice halted. His words came in spurts. "Preacher, me an' you's friends. I gotta confess what's been full on my heart. Those nights you been watchin' over Mabel whilst I'm out? I did more than run over to the pharmacy and drive around town. I'd drive on over to Camden too."

Reggie nodded as if to say, *That's okay, Barney, don't you worry about that one bit.* Barney turned back to the front.

"You see, I been callin' on the Lord for a long while, but there weren't no answer. So I figured I'd strike out on my own."

Barney paused and lowered his head. Reggie took a step closer. He meant to say that we all stumble in life, we all limp and need to lean on the Lord.

But then Barney said, "So I started playin' the lotto."

Reggie's knees weakened. The congregation murmured amongst themselves. Deacon Spicer rose halfway up out of his place in the pew and then settled, unsure whether he'd heard right.

"I know," Barney said. "I weren't proud of it. Y'all gotta see I didn't have no possibilities. Me an' Mabel, we was done. I lost my faith, but the Lord took pity on my sin. I thought He was cruel, but He's pardonin' instead."

Barney reached into his suit pocket and produced a square slip of paper. He held it up like a shining light in a dark place.

"I got this'un here last night," he said. "Brought it home in shame like I always did, an' then I watched the TV right at eleven. And, well . . ." His voice cracked. Tears spilled out onto his cheeks like tiny rivers of fire lit by the sunlight through the stained glass windows.

Reggie thought of how Barney had looked the day before in his shop and how Allie swore she'd tell no one of his sorrows.

"It's a dad-gummed holy miracle," Barney stammered. "I got the windfall. All two hundred fifty million of it."

Reggie wasn't sure if the room hummed or if the sound was just in his head. Barney held up his ticket to craning necks. Hands could not get to mouths fast enough to silence shrieks and gasps. Many stood, driven to their feet not by the Spirit but by sheer marvel. Allie Granderson stood atop her pew, holding on to Marshall with one hand and Mary with the other.

"I love you," Mabel called out.

Barney's other arm mimicked the one in the air as he tried to calm the swell.

"I know a lotta y'all were over at the old Fox place yesterd'y for little Leah Norcross's birthday. Her folks were kindly enough to ask me to build her an easel, since Leah likes to draw." Barney put the lottery ticket back in his pocket and pulled out a folded sheet of paper.

Reggie didn't have to watch him open it to know what it was.

"This here's what she gave me. Her an' Allie brought it down to me last evenin'."

Now more people stood. Voices grew louder. For the first time in Reggie's ministry, he felt the moment was bigger than himself.

"Leah said 'twas what I needed, an' I needed it just then. I was in an awful spell, cryin' over Mabel. I do that a lot. I'm just scared I'm gonna lose her. But then I left to go to the pharmacy and to Camden, and I knowed what Leah meant. I'm a-standin' in front of y'all not to brag about what the Lord done with me—I'm here to say what the Lord did through that young'un. He done touched her with the magic, just like he did to Andy Sommerville and Sheriff Barnett. I know that because these here numbers that I won by are in little Leah's picture. She drawed them all beforehand."

Now it was a frenzy. Allie Granderson shouted, "Oh Emm GEE!" Congregants left their pews and hastened to the front as if Reggie had made an altar call. Allie followed them and then, realizing that Mabel had been left alone, walked to the back to keep her company. She put one hand on Mabel's shoulder and rose to her tiptoes, trying to see.

Reggie grabbed Barney's arm and gently pulled the old man to himself. "What have you done, Barney? This isn't the Lord's doing. You have to know that."

Barney looked at Reggie as if the preacher spoke in another

language. The crowd pushed in, asking to see the ticket, wanting to see the painting. Barney pulled the piece of paper from his pocket again and lined it up with Leah's picture. He pointed to the 23 on the ticket and then to the clouds Leah had painted. The people moved closer, straining to see. Trevor Morgan had left his Bible on his pew and taken his notebook and pen with him. Later, after the bad had happened and before the worst had come, Reggie would remember that sight. He would remember that more than anything else. Mayor Wallis stood beside Barney. His arm was around the old man as if he were the prodigal son.

"Please, everyone," Reggie said. He used his preaching voice, hoping that would shepherd his flock back to their places. "Return to your seats."

Reggie Goggins's mind was full of many thoughts in that moment—that the Spirit had been quenched by sin and curiosity, that Deacon Spicer was well on his way to throwing Barney out of church, that Mabel was once more in front of the organ in her broken mind—but the one thought that outweighed them all was that he was being ignored in his own church.

"What's this?" Barney asked. "It ain't there no more. Why ain't the number there?" He went through the other numbers and let his finger dangle over the painting. "Ain't none of them there no more."

Reggie tried to step forward and say of course the number wasn't there, none of them were, that not only was everything Barney had said impossible, it also wasn't the issue at all. The issue was what he'd *done*.

But just then someone in the jumble said, "It's another miracle," and Reggie froze.

To his astonishment, he counted six *Praise the Lords*.

3

The caravan that made its way up the Norcrosses' lane was not as long as the one from the day before—two vehicles rather than fifty. The first was Barney's rusty Dodge. Trailing behind were the Grandersons. Allie unlocked the door on Marshall's truck before he could park. Her white dress with yellow flowers—her Sunday usual and the only girly thing Mary could ever convince her to wear—fluttered in the breeze as she ran up the steps and onto the porch. Mrs. Norcross waited at the open front door. The smile she wore was a mix of greeting and confusion.

"Why, hello, Allie," she said. "What brings you—"

"HeythereMissEllenma'am." Allie ran past her and into the house. Tom and Leah were on the leather sofa gandering at the fancy flat TV on the wall. "Hey there, Mr. Doctor."

"Hello, Allie," Tom said. "What's going—"

She walked right past him and took her strange new friend by the hand. "Hey, Leah, me and you gotta parlay."

"Whuh-what's wr-wrong?" Leah asked.

Allie guided Leah out the back door of the yellow Victorian as Ellen welcomed the Grandersons and the Moores through the front.

"Why's Mr. Buh-Barney s-smiling like that?" Leah asked.

"Just come on," Allie said.

Allie pulled Leah off the porch and into soft grass still flattened by the day before's footsteps, past where the popcorn machine and Moon Bounce had stood, to the underside of the two pines on the small hill where they'd first met. They sat side by side as green boughs enfolded them in silence. Somewhere in the limbs above, a robin squeaked its protest and lit for the maple nearer the house.

Leah's thumbnails found each other. The dead space beneath the trees filled with rubbing sounds. Her voice was shaky and small: "Wh-what's happening?"

Allie said, "Leah, I'm gonna ask you somethin', and you gotta be for reals, okay? No pretendin', because we're pals."

"I duh-didn't tell anyone about y-you and Zach Buh-Barnett," she said. "I p-promise, Allie."

"I ain't talkin' about that," Allie said, "but thanks anyways." She slid her hand between Leah's thumbs. "And stop rubbin' at your thumbnail before you spark a fire. Now, you keep honest, hear?"

Leah nodded, though her lips quivered and her throat did that tight/loose/tight motion again. She looked around the brambles that surrounded them and settled on a spot in the needles. The hand with the unblemished thumbnail settled there.

"Did you put those numbers in that picture we gave to Mr. Barney?"

Allie studied her, careful to watch for the things she herself did whenever she fibbed, which she told herself was not often. Leah did not look away, did not ask Allie to repeat the question, did not take offense. She simply said, "Wh-what numbers?" and Allie believed her.

"Mr. Barney gave a witness in church today."

"What's a wuh-witness?"

"It's when you stand up in front of everybody and speak on the good God's done you," Allie said. "But never mind that right now. What matters is that Mr. Barney says he won on the lotto last night. I mean, like, all the pennies in *heaven*, Leah. And he says he knowed what numbers to play on account they was all in your picture. So I'm gonna ask you again—did you put those numbers in there?"

"N-no," Leah said. Her eyes bulged. Allie thought for sure another *BAWP* was near. "All I duh-did was listen."

Allie shook her head. "I don't even know what that means."

Leah looked to where her free hand lay. Her voice was low and hushed. It was a tone of wonder: "I just luh-listened to what he s-s-sang, and then I puh-painted it. He said it was what Mr. Buh-Barney needed."

It wasn't that Allie had forgotten about the Rainbow Man, it was more that she had misplaced him. Too much had happened since, and a child's mind rarely dwells upon the past. But now, yesterday and today merged in the forefront of her mind like jagged pieces of a puzzle, snapping together to form one incontrovertible whole.

"Zonkers, Leah. He's really real, isn't he? The Rainbow Man."

Leah offered Allie a look that was part shock and part hurt that had nothing to do with her cursing.

"I thuh-thought you already buh-lieved that. You t-told me you duh-did yesterday."

"But that's different," Allie said. "And it don't matter, because I believe all the way now. Holy cow, Leah. You and the Rainbow Man just made the Moores bajillionaires. Outta everybody in town . . ." She snapped her fingers as another piece of the puzzle fell into place. "*That's* what makes it a marvel. Most folks say the Moores are accursed, even though my momma and daddy think they just fell on hard times like Job. You don't know about him 'cause you ain't covered in the blood, but he was this good man who did all the right things and loved the Lord a whole bunch, but God let th' devil at him just to make a point. Poor Job lost near everything, just like Mr. Barney and Miss Mabel did. They ain't got no fam'ly, though. All Job's fam'ly died except his wife, who was pretty much a biddy."

Leah shuddered. "Thuh-that sounds awful."

"I know. But God touched Job with the magic at the end. That's the only way He could fix him proper again." Allie looked over her shoulder. She saw nothing but some dry limbs and a gray spider spinning its web. "I think the Lord's movin' you with the magic now too, Leah."

Allie thought that should have been enough to make Leah smile, but none came. There was a war being fought between Leah's eyes and chin, a clash of dread and hope that erupted in a series of flinches that had nothing at all to do with being so close to a spider. Aside from those spasms, Leah was motionless until she looked back over her shoulder. The hand that cupped the brown pine needles twitched but did not move. Allie thought if it did, Leah would go at her thumbnail again.

"I duh-don't know who God is," Leah finally said, "but I nuh-know the R-rainbow M-man wouldn't luh-let anybody get hurt just to pruh-prove some p-point. He didn't tuh-tell me Mr. Buh-Barney would w-win the lottery, and I duh-don't know anything about any nuh-numbers." Now she turned all the way around so that Allie was looking at the house and Leah toward the fence behind them. "The R-rainbow M-man duh-doesn't tell me everything. Juh-just the things I n-need to know."

"And me," Allie said. She turned to face the small space between them and the fence. The spider had retreated. Only the limbs remained. Cracks of sunlight drifted down upon them. Allie didn't know if the Rainbow Man was there or not, but she guessed something was. She could feel it. She figured it was the same way Mr. Barney had felt those numbers. "We're friends now, remember. That means I'm with you. So whatever he bares to you, you need to bare to me."

The war was fresh on Leah's face. It was a tossing and turning, a reaching out and a pulling back.

"I know your daddy can't imagine such things," Allie said. "I think my folks are strugglin' to imagine too, least when it comes to what Mr. Barney said about your numbers. I can imagine fine, though. Truth is, I had a friend no one could see once. An' I ain't talkin' about that rhino my daddy says follows him around, 'cause I know that's just his body makin' noises. I mean a real pretend friend. Her name was Daphne. She weren't magic or nothin', but we still played together. Then one time a whole day went by and I didn't say nothin' to her at all, and then it went on for another day too, and then after that she just went away. I don't even remember what she looks like now." Allie was surprised that she had to pause and shore up the emotion that threatened to leak through her eyes. "Sometimes I wonder if I killed her. Not with my hands, but just with my heart. I don't want that to happen to your Rainbow Man, Leah. He's special. Killin' him would be an awful burden to bear."

Leah considered those words. Allie hoped they would be enough to provoke a little more reaching out than pulling back. She had never told anyone of what she feared had happened to Daphne, not even her mother, and telling it now revealed a small hole in her heart where Daphne had once lived.

"He wuh-wants me t-to do something," Leah said. "The R-rainbow M-man, I muh-mean. And I d-don't know what it is yet, so you d-don't have to ask. Whuh-whatever it is, he's g-going to help me. He suh-says he w-wants you to help me too. He suh-says he's g-going to s-sing us whuh-what to do n-next if we want to nuh-know."

"Okay then." Allie bowed her head and folded her hands. She nudged Leah with her elbow to do the same. "You just go on and direct us what to do, Mr. The Rainbow Man, and we'll set about to doin' it. Amen." She looked over to Leah. "Is he singin'?"

Leah nodded. "He suh-says it's already st-started."

"What's started?"

"I duh-don't nuh-know. All I nuh-know is that it's gonna be ruh-really guh-good, and then it's gonna be ruh-really buh-bad." She looked away from the spiderweb of limbs around them. "You stuh-stay right wuh-with me, Allie."

"I ain't goin' nowhere," Allie said.

This time, Leah smiled.

4

Barney had spent the short drive to the Norcross house rehearsing three different ways of expressing what had happened. None had seemed to satisfy Mabel. Now, as they sat in Tom and Ellen's living room along with the Grandersons, he decided the best course would be to dole out a little at a time. As Barney had witnessed at church, spewing it all out in one breath would only overwhelm them. Barney only hoped Marshall and Mary could keep quiet and not jump ahead, and that he could finish the account before Tom's phone started ringing. He thought Marshall could. But the way Mary fingered the gold cross around her neck (which was what she always did when nervous) made Barney want to hurry things up.

"I got this here last night," Barney said. He reached into his pocket and handed the ticket to Tom. "Never told nobody, but I been doin' it awhile. I guess when you hurt enough, a body's apt to try most anything to feel better. Reckon you can understand that, Tom, you bein' one of them head doctors."

Tom looked at the slip of paper and handed it to Ellen. Her head cocked to the side the way Mabel's sometimes did when she tried to remember something. She took the newspaper from the coffee table and flipped to the second page. Mary's hand went out to stop her and then withdrew, as if something had whispered that small act would bring the story to a close before its time.

"Anyways, Mabel's always in bed when the numbers are called on the TV. I reckon that's more good than not." Barney took his wife's limp hand and patted it. "She don't know much of what's goin' on anymore, but I'd still feel shamefaced if she was sittin' there with me while those Ping-Pong balls tumbled out. Mabel's a good Christian woman. She don't like the lotto. Ain't that right, Mabel?"

Mabel smiled as they all looked at her.

"So I stay up myself with the TV down low," Barney said, "and last night—"

"Oh my," Ellen said. Her face was hidden by the splayed newspaper, which now crinkled as her hands dropped to her knees. She handed the second page to Tom along with the ticket. "What did you do, Barney?"

Tom's eyes went from the ticket to the page where, much to the chagrin of a good many of Mattingly's clergy, Trevor Morgan always included the winning numbers in the Sunday edition of the *Gazette*. Tom moved closer to the sofa's edge with each number he read. He dropped both the newspaper and the ticket on the coffee table when he was done. His hands were shaking. Ellen was laughing.

"It's a miracle, Tom," Barney said. He smiled—Barney couldn't help it, Ellen's laugh was infectious and had spread to both Mary and Marshall—and tried not to let that affect the seriousness of his words. "An' I have your Leah to thank for it."

"Leah?" Tom asked.

"Yessir." Barney reached into his other pocket and unfolded Leah's painting. He spread it out over the coffee table on top of the newspaper. "Those numbers on that ticket? They were *in* her paintin'. Hidden-like. I saw them just as I was leavin' to go to Camden."

"What?" Ellen asked. She bent over the painting. Tom followed her.

"I don't see any numbers," Tom said.

"Well, that's the thing," Barney told them. "They ain't there no more."

The phone rang. Tom and Ellen both looked at it as if it hadn't rung much in the past two months. Ellen rose to answer it and bumped her knee against the coffee table. Barney didn't know if it was because she'd gone light-headed or because she just couldn't stop looking at her daughter's painting. Mary stood up with her and blocked Ellen's path.

"Better not," she said. "Not yet, anyway."

"Why?"

"Because that's probably Trevor wanting an interview," Marshall said. "That man was all in a tuff when Barney gave the church his news. He's smellin' a story. Best not to give him one until y'all have a handle on this."

The machine picked up after the fourth ring.

"Hello, Mr. and Mrs. Norcross. This is Trevor Morgan of the *Mattingly Gazette*. We met yesterday at your lovely daughter's party? Just wanted to touch base with you about Barney Moore's good fortune and ask if I could stop by later on this afternoon. Maybe talk a spell. Give me a call at your earliest convenience. My number here is 764-4591."

The line went dead and was replaced by a dial tone that for some reason perked Mabel up enough to mutter, "I love you."

"Holy cow," Ellen said. She thumped back down on the sofa. Tom studied Leah's painting.

"Barney," he said. "You just won the lottery. You're

a *millionaire*. I mean, the odds alone are . . . but you know Leah had nothing to do with this, right? I mean, that's just ridiculous."

"It ain't ridiculous, it's a miracle, just like I said. I know you an' Ellen don't believe in such things, y'all bein' spiritual but not religious, and I don't know what that means. But ain't no other word *for* it, Tom. Those numbers were there. I'll swear it. I might be a lotta things, Tom an' Ellen Norcross, but I ain't no liar."

"We didn't say you were, Barney," Ellen said. "But you have to understand that it's just kind of, you know . . ."

"Impossible," Tom said. He turned to Marshall and Mary. "You guys don't really think Leah could do something like this, do you?"

"I've never seen a painting like that, Tom," Mary said. "And Allie told me about this imaginary friend Leah has."

Marshall, who had been mostly quiet thus far (and Barney figured he knew why), now said, "Stranger things have happened in Mattingly, Tom."

"That's true, Tom," Barney said. "Sheriff Barnett found this hole up in Happy Holler awhile ba—"

"Barney," Mary interrupted. She shook her head.

Barney cursed his slip of the tongue, though he couldn't help but think of what Jake had found in those dark woods and added, "It's all connected."

The phone rang again. This time the caller hung up before the machine asked for a message. The back door opened. Allie and Leah ran into the living room. Leah headed straight to Barney and Mabel and wedged herself between them. She gave Barney a hug and Mabel a kiss on her cheek.

"Cuh-cun-gratulations, Mr. Buh-Barney," she said. "Allie tuh-told me."

Barney placed his hand at the back of her head and said, "Thank you, little Leah. From the bottom of my heart."

"Leah," Tom said, "Barney thinks you put some numbers in your painting that helped him win all that money."

She looked at Allie, who moved from Mary's lap to as close to Leah as she could get. Allie nodded slow.

"I puh-put the n-numbers there, Puh-Pops," Leah said.

"See there?" Barney said. And even though he had upon several occasions questioned the validity of what exactly he *did* see in that painting, he told Tom and Ellen that he never doubted one bit. "I knowed it."

"Leah," Tom said, "don't lie."

"I'm not luh-lying, Puh-Pops. I don't nuh-know why they're nuh-not there n-now, but they wuh-were."

Tom sighed. Ellen offered Leah a look of wonder that was much like the one she'd given the phone earlier.

"So Trevor's holding this big press conference tomorrow morning at the park," Barney said. "He said this is the biggest story since"—*since Jake Barnett found that hole*, he almost said, but then he remembered the Norcrosses were from Away—"since forever, practically. I'd like y'all to be there, Tom an' Ellen. An' you too, Allie. And a'course Leah, since she's largely responsible."

"We'd be glad to," Ellen said. "Leah?"

"Shuh-sure, M-Mommy."

"Barney," Tom said. He tugged at the collar of his shirt and slid a bit away from Ellen on the sofa. "I have to work tomorrow."

Ellen closed her eyes and mumbled, "I can't believe you, Tom."

"Buh-but you c-can take the muh-morning off, c-can't you, Puh-Pops?" Leah asked. "I nuh-need you there w-with m-m-me."

Barney couldn't believe he'd heard such a thing from a father. He'd never be one (except maybe to Mabel, of course), but he suspected his heart had been right enough even in the bad times of Mabel's stroke to know that your own comes before your job. There was a cleaving on Tom's face, a push one way and a pull the other that said Tom at least knew that. It also said Tom knew that the scales upon which we placed our treasures never balanced. They always tilted more toward the things we wanted than the things we had.

"I'm sorry, Leah-boo. It's important."

Allie spoke up and said, "So is Leah, Mr. Doctor. She's more important than the crazy people you gotta listen to."

"Allie," Marshall said, "that's enough."

"We should probably go," Mary told them. "Barney, would you like some help getting Mabel to the truck?"

Barney said, "That would be fine, Mary." He rose from his chair and collected the ticket and Leah's painting from the coffee table. Tom and Ellen looked at Leah, who was rubbing at her thumb. "I'm sorry if I caused y'all some pain. It's okay if you gotta work, Tom. Really. But I'd like to see Ellen and Leah there tomorrow anyways, just to share in me an' Mabel's joy."

"We'll be there, Barney," Ellen said. "Won't we, Leah?"

"Yuh-yes," Leah whispered. She let go of her thumb and turned to Barney. Her tears made her eyes glisten. "I'm suh-so happy f-for you, Mr. Buh-Barney. It's what you nuh-needed. And d-don't you wuh-worry. You and Muh-Miss M-Mabel are guh-gonna be just fine nuh-now. Your d-day's come."

There was a magic to the little girl's smile. Barney knew then without a doubt that she had been touched by God. He believed her. He believed her every word.

Monday

Five Days Before the Carnival

1

Tom hated Monday mornings. Hated having to exchange jeans for khakis, hated the drive into the city. Hated having to crawl through that small space between work and home and come out on the other side alone. His client list had been halved, his office hours cut back to Monday, Wednesday, and Friday. He and Ellen had finagled the bills and their investments to such that even with his lower salary, the inheritance from Ellen's father (that would be Robert Bosserman, who had before his death presided over an empire that included not only Big Bob's Classic Cars but also Big Bob's Housewares and Big Bob's Kountry Kitchen) would allow them to live in relative ease in a town where the cost of living was next to nothing. It was perfect, the American dream, and yet misery still followed.

He stood in his office and watched the rush-hour traffic below stagger and stall along the littered streets of Stanley, Virginia. He'd often wondered how he had managed for so long to think such a panorama warm, even comforting. Now he regarded it as alien. Strange what changes a mere two months among mountains and dirt roads could bring.

Then again, it was not nearly as strange as what changes a mere two days could bring to a little girl.

He reached into his pocket for his cell phone and dialed home. There was no answer, though Tom knew Ellen and Leah hadn't yet left for the park. The truce had been off again the moment the Moores and Grandersons left the previous afternoon. Even Leah wouldn't speak to him. Tom had cut back on his patient load and uprooted his family to the boondocks, but in the end even that hadn't been enough. He left a message saying he hoped everything went well and that he'd check on them later.

The outer door opened and closed. Tom checked his watch for no reason. That sound could only mean Rita, and Rita meant it was precisely 7:45. The openly callous curmudgeon and closeted saccharine grandmother had been many things in Tom's twelve years of professional practice—receptionist, bookkeeper, and (twice) bouncer—but she had never been late.

"Morning, Tom," she called through his closed office door.

"Morning."

Tom walked from the window to his desk. The polished cherry surface was empty but for a computer, a telephone, and a stack of the day's patient files. What mementos Tom brought through that small opening between home and work were kept locked in the top left drawer. He removed the brass key from his pocket and pulled out the stack of Leah's drawings—of himself and Ellen, of Leah and her not-quite-there smile, of their old house in Stanley and their new one in Mattingly. All drawn with the shaky, unskilled hand of a little girl searching for the heart of the matter. None like the one she had produced Saturday afternoon, and none with veiled magical numbers.

"It just doesn't make sense," he said aloud.

A knock at the door. Rita entered wearing a powder-blue dress that nearly matched the color of her hair. Her tiny heeled shoes left dimples in the carpet. The deep lines that framed her mouth into an ever-present look of sourness bowed out in their middles—her idea of a smile. The morning newspaper was tucked under her arm, and in one hand she carried a plate bearing two lemon muffins and a cup of coffee. With the other she pushed the door shut behind her.

"How was the party?" she asked. She set the plate and the paper down on his desk.

Tom folded Leah's drawings and placed them back into the drawer. "You wouldn't believe it."

"I told you everything would be fine, even if you're stuck down there in hillbilly hell. Heard about the guy who won the Powerball. You know him?"

"Barney Moore. He made an easel for Leah as a birthday present. The town's having some sort of news thing today. He wanted us there. Ellen and Leah are going."

"Why aren't you?"

He tapped the stack of files in front of him, but mainly the one on top. Tom could never say it, could barely allow himself to think it, but the one on top was the only one that mattered.

Rita turned around the chair that rested between the desk and the leather sofa in the middle of the office and sat.

"I see," she said. "I want you to know I respect that, Tom, even if it's something Ellen and Leah struggle with. I guess you probably even looked over that file this weekend, didn't you? You had the choice of which patients to keep and which to refer elsewhere, but you hung on to her. You can't let her go."

Tom took a sip of his coffee. "Some patients stick with you."

Rita shook her head. "They all stick with *you*. That's why you think you have to be the one to fix everything, or nothing will get fixed. So, you ready?" She stood up as if to say he didn't have a choice.

"How is she?"

"Nuts and hopeless. Doesn't take a fancy doctor to see that."

He did not scold Rita. Tom had realized long ago that along with receptionist, bookkeeper, and twice bouncer, Rita also served as a voice for those things he would not allow himself to accept. She turned to leave.

"Rita, can I ask you something?"

"Sure, but make it quick. There's an open window and a Gideon Bible out there. Might as well be weapons of mass destruction as far as she's concerned."

"Did either of your kids ever have imaginary friends growing up?"

"Of course not," she said. "You think I raised idiots? Why?"

"No reason."

Rita walked to the door and stopped. Tom thought she was about to say something, then realized she was merely gathering her strength. She looked like someone pausing at the threshold of home to feel the last bit of warmth before braving the cold. Tom placed a fresh box of tissues on the coffee table and followed her. He breathed, smiled, and walked out.

The woman corresponding to the top file on Tom's desk sat in the corner of the waiting room leafing through a two-month-old copy of *Glamour*. The irony had not escaped Rita, who now sat behind her glass cubicle shaking her head and smiling. The gaunt face and sunken eyes of the woman in the waiting room spoke of her weariness in bearing that unnamable weight Tom knew was common to all his patients. Her eyes glanced from the page to the area around her, though never high enough to warrant raising her chin. A car horn blew from the street below, making her flinch. Her jeans and denim shirt were twice the necessary size, as if to give the false hope that she could disappear into them and therefore go unnoticed. And yet despite all this, Tom understood that she had been pretty once and could be again. She looked up as he approached and offered a weak grin.

"Good morning, Meagan," Tom said. "Come on in."

She followed Tom into his office and settled herself in her accustomed place at the end of the sofa. Had she waited one moment later to reach for the box of tissues, the eruption of tears and spittle would have spewed everywhere—onto her, him, the leather sofa, maybe all the way to the windows—which would have only upset her more. It would have been a mess, and Meagan Gladwell was of the opinion that she was not allowed to make a mess.

"I'm so sorry," she said.

Tom's voice was flat and soothing. His chin was already in his hand. "You don't have to apologize for anything here, Meagan. It's important to let yourself grieve, okay? You're going through a very difficult time."

Meagan shuddered and poured her pain into the thick tissue she held over her mouth and nose. She wiped and took her position—legs crossed, head down, toes curled into the carpet as if grasping for something solid—and nodded okay despite the fact Tom knew she did not believe him. Meagan's life was based upon the necessity of being sorry. Her safety depended upon it, though the mottled green and gray bruises that peeked out from beneath her shirtsleeves confessed that her apologies no longer carried the persuasiveness they once did.

Tom pushed on. "Have you given any thought to what we discussed last week?"

"I'm still at home," she managed, which was enough for her to lunge for another tissue. "I'm afraid to leave, and I'm afraid to stay."

"I know."

"Do you know what's worse, Dr. Norcross?"

"Tom," he offered, as he had all the times before.

"Tom. Do you know what's worse? I honestly think we can work things out. It's not all Harold's fault. Takes two to tango, right?"

Tom wrote on the pad in his lap. As mistaken as her words were, they were still good for him to hear. One never knew what could spring forth from the silences of the heart, and what had just sprung from Meagan's meant she was holding steady. Once among Tom's thirty regular patients, she was now one of the fifteen he'd kept. She was also his most difficult. It had taken three months to crack the hard shell Meagan had by necessity constructed around herself. Her climb from Denial to Guilt had been slow but steady, but she had stumbled these past months. Months and possibly years from now would come Enlightenment and finally Responsibility, the last and most difficult stage of Battered Woman Syndrome. Assuming, of course, that Harold Gladwell hadn't killed her by then.

"You'd stand a better chance of working things out if Harold agreed to come here with you."

Meagan looked around the office—the desk behind Tom, the diplomas on the wall. Cherry bookcases filled with the collected wisdom of his profession's giants. Water cascaded down the Zen fountain in the corner. The fountain had been Rita's idea, a good one but not her best, that being reserved for her suggestion to never skimp on the tissues. The thicker the better, she'd said. Rita was a wise woman.

"You know there's probably more money in here than Harold makes in a year?" Meagan asked. "Not to mention this place is probably bigger than our apartment. I think that's why he gets so mad sometimes. Life didn't hand him much. He says that's my fault."

"That's not true," Tom said. "You can't believe that, Meagan."

She sighed and tossed her tissue into the rapidly filling wastebasket next to the sofa. "Maybe I can't. Do you think God is punishing me for the things I can't believe, Dr. Norcross? Do you think that's what He's doing?"

Tom's hand tightened around his pen. This, again—this was the reason for Meagan's stumble.

"I think that's an issue you should take up with someone of faith. I'm only concerned with your mind, Meagan, not your soul."

"There's more going on than my mind."

"I know this is difficult for you, Meagan, but we're making real progress. It's admirable to want to salvage your marriage, but I'm still going to recommend you reconsider staying in the house."

"God doesn't want me to leave."

Tom scribbled on his pad, mostly to rein in his anger. He wished Rita were there to say what he thought, wished she would grab Meagan by the shoulders and shake her, yell into her face, tell her that her notion of God was mauling her spirit just as much as Harold Gladwell was mauling her body. He thought of Reggie Goggins and his simple life of few cares, the sort of existence that lent itself to the very misguided fundamentalism that rendered Meagan a prisoner. It was easy to live one's life with faith and hope when your needs and wants were few. But when your world became a matter of living and dying, that faith and hope often resulted in more harm than good.

"If there's a God, Meagan, I'm fairly certain he would not want you to continue in your situation. But I don't want to talk about theology, I want to help you."

"You can't help me if you don't believe, Dr.— Tom. That's just it. You can't *understand*. God doesn't want me to leave." Meagan almost reached for another tissue but didn't. She merely stared at the box.

"We'll get through this," Tom said. He leaned toward her. "Meagan, I know some wonderful shelters in the area—"

"No, I can't."

"You have to understand that your faith—"

"It's not just that," she said. "It's something else too."

"What?"

Her eyes watered. Her lips trembled. She reached for another tissue.

"I'm pregnant."

Meagan gushed again.

2

Reggie had promised himself he would stay in his office that morning, far away from the hoopla outside. He'd even gone so far as to eat breakfast at the church rather than the diner. The candy bar from the vending machine in the hallway didn't settle as well as the eggs and bacon down on Main Street, but at least his conscience was calm.

His curiosity, however, wasn't.

He was at his desk working on next week's sermon when the first group of people passed the window. Reggie rose from his desk and grabbed the aluminum softball bat by the chair without realizing he'd done so. The thirty-four-inch Easton was pocked and chipped from years of use in the church soft-ball league (Reggie was the starting shortstop for First Church and had no qualms thinking himself to be the best ballplayer in town except for maybe Sheriff Barnett). It was also Reggie's secret weapon when it came to sermon preparation. Amazing, the thoughts that sprang from the fertile loam of his mind while holding that bat.

Lisa Carver, she of the sour voice, walked by with Rodney and their two children in tow. Reggie went to the open win-dow. The summer air was hot and clung to his face. A lone robin sang from one of the ancient elms in the church's court-yard. The Carvers continued on past, taking a right at the next corner and heading into the park.

More people followed, other families and groups of friends, many of whom attended First Church and none of whom cast a look in Reggie's direction. The young ones skipped and hur-ried, first running past their parents and then doubling back to urge them onward. Some carried balloons or signs that said CONGRATULATIONS BARNEY and WE LOVE YOU. Chatter and laughter filled the air. It was an excitement and expectation normally reserved for the upcoming carnival. Two news vans, one from Stanley and the other from Richmond, drove past. The scene was Reggie's worst nightmare.

He returned to his desk, where an open Bible lay beside a pad of paper. Reggie tried to concentrate on the task at hand but found his thoughts drifting to his town and his people, to poor Mabel—Barney hadn't called to ask if Reggie would come sit with her, which meant the crazy old man planned to bring her along—and of the way Barney had left her alone while he wallowed in the congregation's sudden adulation. He thought of studying the Word and preaching the Word, and then he thought of how it was more important to live the Word.

And that was when Reggie Goggins decided he had to go to the park. In the park was where God wanted him.

He walked outside and fell in step with the gathering stream of people. More—dozens more, maybe even hundreds—hugged the iron fence that bordered the park. A child ran past and clipped Reggie's leg, bumping his knee into the sharp corner of a *Gazette* newspaper box beside the pay telephone. Reggie winced, his hand shooting to his leg in reflex, then winced again when he found a small hole in his jeans that matched the deep scrape on his knee. The boy turned to apologize and then ran through the gate into the park.

Mayor Wallis stood on a makeshift stage that had been erected atop the pitcher's mound and thumped a microphone. Surrounding the stage were wooden frames of the booths and exhibits that would be used for the carnival. As the week progressed, those frames would be covered with tarps and decorated with American flags and banners. For now they served as leaning posts for expectant townspeople. Barney, Mabel, Allie, and Leah sat at a covered banquet table in the middle of the stage. Another microphone sat in front of them, along with a folded sheet of paper that had to be Leah's painting. Big Jim Wallis made his way over to pat Barney on the back and no doubt offer last-minute instructions. A woman from Away stood smiling nearby and straightened her black pantsuit.

The reporters at the front of the stage busied themselves with microphones and cameras. Townspeople waited under the pavilions on the hill above and in the tree shade below, watching and murmuring to one another about what had happened and how. It looked to Reggie as if a giant hand had scooped up everyone within ten miles and dropped them into that one small place.

He found a quiet spot next to an oak that offered a view

of both the crowd and the stage and rubbed his sore knee. Leah scanned the crowd from right to left. Her eyes settled on Reggie. She offered him a quiet wave that was no more than a simple raising of a finger. Reggie tried to smile back but couldn't.

Big Jim tapped the microphone with a thick finger and thanked everyone for taking time out of their busy day. He introduced Trevor to the reporters, reminded them that his nephew was the one who first broke the story and they shouldn't forget it. The crowd whooped, not because they were particularly fond of the mayor's nephew, but because he was one of their own. Big Jim then introduced the woman from Away as Mary Hill Rexrode of the Virginia Lottery, who had at his request taken the unusual step of driving all the way down from Harrisonburg to verify Barney's ticket. He then uttered seven words that set the wolves to howling.

"Mr. Moore will now take some questions."

Trevor was first, of course—"Trevor Morgan, of the *Mattingly Gazette*," he made sure to say—and cleared his throat.

"Barn, how's all this feel?"

Barney coughed and moved his mouth close to the microphone in front of him. The screech made Leah jump and Allie laugh. Mabel's eyes went from closed to open and then closed again. The microphone picked up her thick cough. Barney eased his way forward again as if the thing in front of him would bite if he weren't careful.

"It feels good, Trev," he said. "Real good."

Another reporter, she from the *Richmond Times-Dispatch*: "Has your ticket been verified, Mr. Moore? And what will you do with the money?"

"It's been proved, all right," Barney said. "But I expect I'll hang on to my ticket for a while. Can't really speak to why. Private stuff, I reckon."

Reggie heard the sadness in those words and wondered what it meant. He thought perhaps the Spirit was working on his old friend, stirring him, cracking his heart. As difficult as it was for him to hear Barney give voice to the war within him, a part of Reggie was comforted. Maybe it wasn't too late.

"As for what I'll do," Barney continued, "we got some bills to pay. My wife, Mabel, that's her dozin' beside me, she's been sickly. I'm gonna make sure she's taken care of proper. Maybe I'll get us a nurse to help out. I think I'll buy her a piano. Mabel, I mean. Not the nurse. Mabel's always loved her music, and she plays in her mind still. I don't reckon she'll be able to play it, though. Maybe the nurse will. An' I gotta fix the shop up some. I own the Treasure Chest just a couple blocks over. Make toys and whatnot. I s'pose that's how this all started. And I'll give my tithe to the church a'course, since this is all the Lord's doin'. That's First Church of the Risen Christ, you can see the cross on the roof out yonder over those trees." Barney paused so the reporters could follow the finger he pointed. None of them did. "Reverend Reggie Goggins presiding. Best church in town, at least to me. Sorry I got a little windy there, ma'am. I'm a mite nervous."

Reggie closed his eyes and prayed that the length of Barney's answer would drown the six words he'd said that would damn them all. He prayed, and as he did he felt his top teeth bite down on his lower lip. It was a childhood habit, one that Reggie's mother had gone to great lengths to break. He thought of Leah and her thumbnail.

That prayer went unanswered, because the next question came from a reporter from the Charlottesville *Daily Progress*—"Do you think God really had a hand in your winning, Mr. Moore?"

"Ayuh," Barney said, and then he nodded his head in case

interpretation was required. "Ain't a doubt in my mind. It's an answered prayer for me an' my Mabel. We was in the straits and sinkin' for sure, but the Lord took pity on us." He paused here again. Just in case the newspeople from Away did not take his cue for a second time (and just in case Reggie harbored any thoughts that a part of Barney's soul was not yet lost), he added, "God don't want nobody sufferin' an' poor. Y'all make sure to write that down. That's important."

The wolves obliged.

"How long have you been playing the lottery?"

"Not long," Barney said. He was getting comfortable now, enjoying the attention. "Just a few months, ever since Mabel's stroke and we ran outta money. Tried all sorts of numbers, but none worked. Then my little angel Leah came along. The Lord spoke through her."

Leah had sat motionless since the interview began. Now she flinched at the mention of her name. Reggie didn't see Tom in the audience and felt a tinge of respect for the city doctor. One moment, especially one as strange as their first encounter, did not offer a full picture of a man. There were muted places within every person that were hidden from all but God. Barney had taught Reggie that. He had taught Reggie that one never knew what could spring forth from the silences of the heart.

Ellen, however, sat beside Marshall and Mary Granderson in the front row. She pushed her fingers upward against the corners of her mouth, showing Leah how to smile.

"I made Leah an easel for her birthday," Barney said. He unfolded the sheet of paper and held it up. "She drew me this as a thank-you. Purty, ain't it?"

Cameras hissed. Leah flinched. Allie leaned over to whisper something in her ear.

"She an' Allie here gave it to me down at my store. That's the Treasure Chest, quality toys for a low price, open Monday through Saturday. Anyways, I was goin' out to buy my ticket t'other night. That's when I seen the numbers the Lord wanted me to pick. They was right there in the picture."

Barney moved his hand over the painting. The wolves howled Leah's name in unison, shouting their questions, smelling blood. Reggie understood then that what was before him was no longer a story, it was an event. The wolves would circle his flock in search of the weak and devour them. They would rip the seams of Mattingly and then leave as it all came apart. His town—God's town—would never be the same.

One howl rose above the rest and asked, "Leah, how did you know the numbers?"

Reggie saw Leah's throat move, but no words came. Her eyes reached out for her mother, begging her to do something. Ellen inched up the corners of her mouth. Reggie's heart broke for them both. Leah looked as helpless as Mabel, who woke from her daze long enough to cough and close her eyes again.

Allie rose from her chair and stepped between Leah and Barney. She put one arm around him and the other around her friend and leaned into the microphone as if they'd just won the big game and were about to announce a trip to Disney World.

"Hey there," she told the wolves. "My name's Allie Granderson. That's G-r-a-n-d-e-r-s-o-n. That's my momma, Mary, and my daddy, Marshall, sittin' there in the front row. Their names have the same first letter 'cause they were meant to be." She waved. The crowd chuckled. "That's Leah's momma, Ellen, there too. Her daddy had to work today. He takes care of the hurtin' folk. I'm Leah's friend. You can write that I'm her best friend, 'cause that's what I am.

"Anyway, Leah's shy 'cause of the hitch in her tongue, so I'm gonna be speakin' for her today since she just told me y'all are joltin' her. Truth is, Leah didn't know she was paintin' those numbers. All she wanted to do was say thanks for the great easel Mr. Barney made her. It's the Rainbow Man who gave Mr. Barney those numbers, and it's the love Mr. Barney put in the easel that let him, I think. Ain't too sure about that, though, so I reckon you better not write that down."

A wolf shouted, "Who's the rainbow man?"

"Leah's friend God," Allie said. "Y'all can't see him, no one can but Leah. He's prolly up here with us right now."

Reggie bit down on his lip more. He tasted blood. Ellen froze in her seat. Her fingers moved from the corners of her mouth to her cheeks in a motion that said, *Oh please no* rather than *Smile, baby, smile.* Cameras snapped like thunder. Voices yelled Leah's name, asking her if what Allie said was true, if she saw God and if God had picked Barney's numbers.

Leah turned her head and smiled.

Not to the crowd or her mother or her friend, but to Reggie. Leah smiled at him and him alone—a soft grin hidden in the folds of her fear.

Reggie knew then what had happened to this little girl. She was being loved and noticed. Whatever holes had been made in her life were finally being filled, and she was letting Reggie know she would make sure it would stay that way, no matter what.

Reggie gripped the side of the oak as Leah inched toward the microphone. The crowd hushed as she spoke her only words of the morning.

"It's truh-true."

It was the townspeople—Reggie's people—who reacted. Slow at first, as if they were trying to talk and understand her words at the same time, then faster. Louder. They pushed the reporters aside as they rushed the stage. Barney went for Mabel, who let out a small yelp as her eyes suddenly widened in full comprehension. Ellen became lost in the crowd and unable to reach Leah, which left Allie to take the place as protector. She stood up on the banquet table with fists raised, daring anyone to come near. Sheriff Barnett, Marshall, and Big Jim Wallis tried to hold back the crowd. Reggie ran from his place by the oak to help, to beg them all to see what they had become, but it was no use. The heaven of Mattingly was gone. Now only the hell remained.

3

Technology had never been Barney Moore's friend. He did not consider it an evil to be avoided, as did the Amish community in and around Mattingly who once frequented the Treasure Chest. Though they considered Barney an Outsider—their version, he supposed, of being from Away—they valued his old ways of doing things. It made him a kind of kin, if only in spirit.

No, technology would not steal one's soul, as Eli Yoder once said after collecting a marble roller for his son Jonas and climbing back into his horse and buggy. Barney had refused to suckle at the teat of modernity for a different reason. The truth was that the present sought to erase the past, and Barney preferred his yesterdays.

No, that wasn't it. The better truth was that innovation had stolen his livelihood.

The only example of modern-day-hocus pocus in his house was the cordless telephone and answering machine Mabel had won at a VFW raffle ten years ago. The Moores hadn't needed it—their old rotary worked just fine—so the phone had remained in its box on the top shelf of the hallway closet ever since. Barney now stood on a wobbly wooden stool and prayed it was still there and would still work.

"Ha." He turned to Mabel, who stared at him from her wheelchair in the living room. He withdrew his hand slowly from the shadows and brought the phone into sight. "Ta-da!"

Mabel clapped her hands and gurgled. In the past years Barney had become educated in that language spoken not by words but by the eyes. Mabel's eyes spoke to him then like some inner Morse code sent from the darkness within her, telling him she was still in there somewhere. Barney wished he could arrest that moment so that time could never rob him of it.

He stepped off the stool and brought the sealed box to where Mabel sat, ducking past the window so he wouldn't be seen. Outside, all seven parking spaces in front of the store were occupied by news vans. The crowd that had gathered after the news conference paced and talked amongst one another. Mabel coughed and placed her head on his shoulder.

"I know," he said. "That thing at the park wore me out too. An' I don't mind sayin' it scared me somethin' fierce. Didn't expect that many people really, though I reckon news travels fast. Ever'body acted like they ain't seen me in years. It's like the carnival came early."

Mabel's fingers moved over his forearms in a melody only she could hear. Barney pried the tape from the box in his lap. The rotary on the kitchen counter rang again. He patted Mabel on the arm and rose (mindful of the window), leaving the box with the new cordless beside her.

"Don't know why I keep doin' this," he told her.

Mabel didn't seem to know either.

Barney reached the phone on the fourth ring. He didn't know who it would be, though he had a fair idea of what he or she would want. And though answering the phone would pain him, Barney realized that not answering it would pain him worse. Tom Norcross had been right—in the end, people just wanted to be loved.

He said hello and stretched the cord over the sofa and back to Mabel. It was Boone Davis, who ran the tire shop out on Route 420. Boone Davis, who'd refused to give Barney credit a month ago when the old Dodge needed new tires.

"Good, Boone, good."

The customary *And how you doin'?* went unmentioned. It had taken a dozen calls for Barney to realize that not asking that question was best.

"Oh well, you know, Mabel's hangin' in there." Barney winked. Mabel gurgled again. "She's right here with me. Thanks for askin'."

The Styrofoam blocks around the cordless were crisp and intact, as if Barney had just brought the box home from the Super Mart in Camden. Modern technology. Mabel was still gurgling, the people outside were still gathering, and Boone was still talking about how the dad-gummed economy was putting a hurt on his business, but all Barney could think of was how Jonas Yoder's marble roller would one day be dust but those Styrofoam blocks would still be crisp and whole somewhere in the county landfill.

"Yep, ol' truck still needs some new rubber. But I ain't cashed in my ticket yet, so I still ain't got the money."

Barney found the cord to the cordless—a contradiction that made him chuckle. He unraveled it and plugged one end into the phone's base and the other into the wall as Boone laughed and said that was no problem, Barney could pay him later and hey, maybe after they could go down to the diner for lunch like the good old days.

The red light on the base read 0. Barney didn't know if that was good or bad. He decided to take a look at the instruction manual, which was currently upside down in Mabel's hands.

"Sure, Boone, I'll be down in a couple days . . . No, I'm gonna keep the store closed up today. Sort of a celebration with Mabel . . . Yeah." He chuckled. "I'm pretty busy . . . Okay, I'll see ya."

Barney hung up the phone and switched the line from the rotary to the cordless. He sat on the sofa, mindful of the noisy spring, and showed Mabel two crossed fingers.

"I love you," she said.

"I love you too."

The next call came not three minutes later. The cordless chirped three times before the line picked up. A too-loud robot voice announced that no one was available at this time and to please leave a message after the beep.

"Well now," he said. "What do you think of that, Mabel?"

Mabel coughed.

The message was from Allison Summers, who just wanted to congratulate her favorite customer and say that things had been slow down at the diner lately, real slow, and maybe Barney could pray for her "or . . . something."

Mabel's head lowered down and to the right. A line of spittle formed a delicate drop at the corner of her mouth. Barney wanted nothing more than to wake her—to talk, even if that conversation would be nothing more than banter with a child, because at least that child would want nothing more than his company. It was not the first time Barney envied Mabel and the gray curtain that was suspended between her and all else. The world could do nothing more to her.

He wiped the side of her mouth with his hand, kissed her cheek, and wheeled her into the bedroom. Her frail arms swung free as he lowered her into bed. Barney checked her diaper and her breathing and then lay down beside her. Sleep was close when a knock came at the front door.

Wonderful. Now they weren't just calling, they were popping in. Even with the BLIMEY, CLOSED sign on the window. He eased out of bed and closed the bedroom door, then made his way down the hall. Knocking again. Barney rubbed the tired eyes beneath his glasses and opened the door.

Neither he nor his visitor spoke until Barney chanced a smile and said, "Hey, Reggie."

"Hey, Barney." The preacher looked at him and then into the spartan living room. The phone rang. "Hope you don't mind that I snuck in through the back door of your shop. I figure you're busy, but you got a minute?"

"Sure." The answering machine did its *No one is available now* chatter and recorded a dial tone. *Good*, Barney thought, until he realized the caller would simply try again later. "Come on in."

Reggie limped into the room in front of the open window. Before Barney could warn him, shouts came from the parking lot below. Reggie ducked away and sat down on the sofa's good cushion. The knee of his jeans was torn, showing thin tendrils of drying blood. He rubbed it and offered an awkward smile.

"What happened to your leg?" Barney asked.

"Bumped it a little bit ago against the newspaper box at the park. It's fine."

Barney nodded. "Mabel's sleepin'."

Reggie waved him off. "That's okay. I'm here to see you, anyway." There was a mix of anger and disappointment in his eyes, like a father who'd just caught his son with a girlie magazine. "I didn't get a chance to talk to you at church, what with all the commotion. Or after. After, I just didn't feel like I could. But I guess that commotion wasn't near today's. This all took me by surprise, you know?"

"Kinda took me by surprise too, Reggie." Barney moved to the couch, mindful of the window and the spring, and sat next to the preacher. "But I had to share a witness. It was an answered prayer. I knowed it'd upset you, though, an' I'm sorry. I know how you rail on the lotto."

"There was a time when you did too, Barney."

Yes, Barney thought, but that was before the gutter of last resort. That was before the prayers had turned sour and the God of Blessing became the God of Cruelty.

"Coulda used you down at the park earlier. That was a sight."

"I was there," Reggie told him. "In the back, away from everybody. I wasn't going to go, I'll tell you that, though it wasn't for lack of love for you and Mabel and even those girls. Thank God the sheriff was there, or you'd all been crushed or worse."

The phone rang. *No one is available* . . .

Reggie pointed at the phone and said, "That's new."

Barney sighed and nodded. "People been callin'. Everybody, mostly. It was nice when it started 'cause most of them people ain't talked to me in years. Things're just so busy nowadays. People don't say hi no more."

Reggie looked at him again. This time Barney saw another look in Reggie's eyes, one he couldn't decipher.

"But then I figured it best if I just let the machine talk for a bit. They say *Good job, Barney*, and I expect that's what they really mean right off, but then it all turns to *Gimme this, Barney*. It ain't that I don't have a heart for the hurtin', Reggie. You know I do. Lord knows me an' Mabel seen our share of distress. I plan on helpin' plenty once I cash my ticket an' figure out who wants outta need and who wants outta want. But I gotta give my tithe first. You can be sure of that."

"I can't take your money, Barney."

Had Reggie grabbed the wooden stool that sat by the hallway closet and used it to beat Barney over the head, it wouldn't have hurt worse than those words. Barney's only consolation was that the preacher seemed hurt by it just as much.

"What you mean, Reggie? You know how much that'll be? Millions. Millions for the church, Reggie. For the kids an' the poor folk. Think of how much good that'll do."

Reggie smiled as if that were funny, and Barney saw his friend's face cleave just as Tom Norcross's had before, the push and the pull.

"Don't get me wrong, Barney. It's tempting. And it's appreciated too. But taking it wouldn't be right. I know you have good in your heart and I know you think this is all God's way of blessing you, but it's wrong, Barney. What you did was *wrong*. The lotto preys on people. It gives them a false hope. And now you're spreading that false hope too."

"But it ain't false, Reggie. I *won*."

"You did, but I don't see the Lord in it."

Barney shook his head. "How can you say that, Reggie?"

Reggie leaned over and looked Barney straight in the eye. "Because I know God, Barney. You know that. I spent my whole life knowing the Lord. I know who He is. I know *what* He is. And I know what He ain't too. God put me in this town to shepherd it. You think I take that lightly? I can't say I speak for Him if I don't know Him."

Barney tried to find reason to refute that but couldn't. It was the truth. Everyone in town knew that Reggie had God's ear just as much as God had Reggie's, knew that while people like Barney wanted to get rich, all Reggie wanted was to see the face of the Lord. Even the Methodists knew it.

"And you know what?" Reggie asked. "I think you're questioning things too. You're still hanging on to that ticket, Barney. You haven't cashed it in."

Barney said nothing. He leaned back into the sofa and heard the ticket crinkle in the front pocket of his overalls.

"I guess that's all I got to say," Reggie said.

"You ain't mad at me, are you, Reggie? I don't want you mad at me."

"I wish you would've gone to me or the church instead of the 7-11, but no, I'm not mad. Not at you, anyway."

"Well, you look mad. If it ain't at me, who is it?"

"Leah."

"Leah?" Barney asked. "Why in the world you mad at a little girl, Reggie?"

"She said she spoke for God, Barney. What you did was wrong. What she did?" Reggie shook his head. "That's dangerous. I fear she's brought a darkness to this town that's wrapped up in light, and that's the worst kind of darkness there is."

Reggie looked down at his hands and shook his head, then stretched out his bad knee. He rose from the sofa. Barney walked him to the door.

"I appreciate you stopping by, Preacher," he said. "I appreciate your honesty. An' I'm gonna give you some back now. Truth is, it hurt me somethin' fierce to resort to playin' the lotto. Maybe God weren't in it, but He's in Leah. I know He is. She said me an' Mabel gonna be just fine now. She said my day's come."

"She doesn't know what she's doing, Barney. She's just a lonely little girl who's conjured an imaginary friend with a bag full of lies. She's got you fooled, and Allie too. Allie I can see, she being just a child. But you?"

"You think Leah's little," Barney said, "maybe she is. But as far as her lyin', I reckon she weren't when she told you yesterd'y to mind the newspaper box, was she? An' now look at you, rubbin' your knee."

He didn't give Reggie the opportunity to respond.

"My day's come. You know how long I been waitin' to hear that, Reggie? Longer'n you ever waited for anything. You don't know hurt like I do, an' maybe that's why it's so easy for me to believe. Faith comes easy when you ain't got nothin' left. I know you don't understand that. I hope you never got to."

Reggie left without another word.

4

Allie hadn't minded the reporter people at first, at least not nearly as much as her momma and daddy had. Nor had she been scared when all those people went crazy after Leah answered yes to their questions. *Let 'em come,* she'd thought, then she'd stood up in front of Leah to protect her and vowed to fight them all if she had to, every single one. And she wouldn't even need her daddy's help to do it, because she was a Granderson and Grandersons were afraid of nothing.

"Want some more, sweetie?" her mother said.

"Sure, Momma, thanks."

Mary shook out another pile of French fries onto her daughter's napkin. Allie dipped one into the small container of warm ketchup and chewed. Along the riverbank, Marshall held a fishing pole in the water and looked from one side of the water to the other. Allie figured he was trying to spy anyone who might have followed them. She also figured no one had. Besides, if all those city newspeople could find their way out into the mountains just to take her picture, she'd just smile and say cheese.

"Having fun?" Mary asked.

"I reckon." Allie took a bite of her cheeseburger and shielded her face from the sun. This spot of woods was her daddy's favorite, though Allie found it too close to Happy Hollow for comfort. But on that day she thought of neither ghosts nor holes in the world; there was only sunshine and peace and the deer that fed in the meadow beyond. "I feel bad that Leah's all alone, though. I should be there with her, or maybe I shoulda brung her along with us. She needs me."

"She has her momma with her," Mary said. "I'm sure she's fine. They're not church folks. Tom said they were spiritual but not religious, and don't ask me what that means because I couldn't tell you. But they're still good people."

Allie shook her head. "Her momma ain't like you. I think she's sad. Sad and scared, but I don't know why. Leah don't tell her a lot of stuff, she just tells me."

"What about Leah's daddy?"

"Mr. Doctor loves too much." She took another bite of fries. "You know what that means?"

Mary didn't.

"Me neither. But he don't believe in the Rainbow Man."

Mary took one of Allie's fries and chewed. The thumb and forefinger of her free hand went to the plain gold cross around her neck. The way Mary rubbed it, so slow and with a smile, was beautiful in a way Allie couldn't explain. The sunshine glinted off her auburn hair like a halo, and her tanned skin looked almost golden. Preacher Goggins said everyone was special in God's eyes, even the folk who didn't believe in God at all, and Allie believed that because Reggie Goggins knew God better than anyone. But she also believed that some people had a special shine, and Mary Granderson was one of them. That was why Allie longed to grow up to be just like her momma. Maybe she would have a little girl of her own by then, one who didn't mind playing kickball or kissing handsome boys, and maybe if that little girl would find someone touched by the magic and a clamor would commence, Allie and Zach would take her to the woods for an afternoon of cheeseburgers and fishing to get away from it all just like Allie's own folks had.

"Do you believe in the Rainbow Man?" Mary asked.

"Sure I do."

"Why?"

Allie couldn't say. Wouldn't. Her momma might be her best friend in the whole wide world (besides Leah, of course, but that sort of best friend was different), might be the prettiest woman ever and have a crown of jewels waiting for her at the pearly gates, but Allie wasn't ready to tell her what she'd done with Zach Barnett on the side of Leah's house. Not yet.

"I just do. She explained him to me, and it sounded fairy-like enough to be real. Don't you think she's got the magic, Momma?"

"Maybe. That picture really was fine. But what about those numbers? Did she really paint them?"

"She said she didn't at first," Allie said, "but then she said she did."

Mary furrowed her brow. "Does that sound right to you? I mean, that's a pretty big thing. I know if I drew some numbers that did something that great for someone, I'd remember right off."

Allie took another bite and thought. It actually didn't sound right.

"You think maybe you should keep away from Leah for a while?" Mary asked. "All this with Barney . . . it'll get some people riled, Allie. You saw that yourself at the park. Me and your daddy don't want you getting caught up in it."

"No'm," Allie said. She couldn't believe her momma would ever say such a thing. "I can't forsake Leah *now*. She don't have like I have." Her words were coming quicker now. It was as if Mary had poked a hole in a hose and let loose a flood of water. Allie thought it was time to tell her momma everything, mostly. "She's got this place on her thumbnail that's got a *hole* in it, Momma. She starts rubbin' on it whenever she gets all worked up. Ain't that awful? That's just the worse thing I've ever seen. But she don't do it much when I'm around, and do you know why? Because I keep her safe and she can talk to me. She don't even lurch her words much when I'm with her now. And besides, she says the Rainbow Man needs her to do a task and he wants me to help."

"Got one!" Marshall yelled. He pulled his line out of the water to find a healthy trout on the end. He held it up as if it were Moby Dick. "Gonna eat good tonight, m'ladies."

"Nice one, Daddy," Allie hollered.

Mary took Allie's hand in her own. "You're a good girl, Allie. You're my girl. I'll say I'm not too sure what's been going on around here lately and I'm not too comfortable with you being mixed up in it, but I like Leah. I like her parents. And you know I love the Moores. But maybe God chose to shine on Mr. Barney just that one time, and maybe He just used Leah's painting to do it and not Leah. Do you think that might be possible?"

"I gotta help, Momma," Allie said. "'Cause even if you're shaky on what to think is true and ain't, I think Leah's been touched by the magic. I think the Rainbow Man ain't a man at all. I gotta be the one to show her that, 'cause Leah don't got nobody to tell her about the Higher Things. She told me I had to believe in the magic—she just called it the Maybe. Maybe you and Daddy need to believe in the Maybe too."

Allie thought that settled things as much as they could be settled and went back to her fries. She didn't think her momma believed in Leah's Maybe much. Then again, Allie also understood her momma knew that just down the road was the Hollow and Sheriff Barnett's hole. Some things just were. Just because you didn't understand them didn't make them less real.

"You're right," Mary said. "Leah needs you. She's such a timid little girl. And I think that she's too shy to say all this isn't true, especially now. You're a big girl, Allie. I trust you to do as you've been raised. You just be careful now, okay?"

"Yes'm," Allie said.

"And, Allie, please come to me with anything. Anything at all."

"I always do, Momma. We're besties."

They toasted with the last of the French fries as Marshall caught the rest of their supper in the sparkling river ahead of them. All memory of news reporters and lottery tickets and holy magic drifted from Allie's mind. What settled in was the slow awareness that on the back side of so much furor, she had found that rare and precious gift of a perfect day.

She vowed to enjoy it, and it was fortunate that she did. It would be Allie's last perfect day for a long while.

5

Tom finished with his fifth and final patient (DELACROIX, CHARLES the file said, age thirty-five, bipolar disorder) at four thirty, leaving him to reflect upon a day that seemed little more than a long rendition of the same sad story told from five different points of view. He'd tried twice to call home and ask how the press conference had gone, but both times the line had been busy and Ellen's cell had been turned off. Rita had popped her head into the office between Tom's third and fourth appointments to say she'd seen a clip on the Stanley newspaper's website. She'd only offered, "Quite the display down there in hillbilly hell." Nothing more. Her only other bit of commentary was written on the Post-it note she'd stuck to his office door before leaving. *Go home, Tom*, it read.

He emptied the mountain of spent tissues from the garbage can by the sofa into a larger one behind his desk and thought of gold coins gushing into an overflowing pot as they spilled into and over the receptacle. He gathered the tissues that had fallen onto the carpet and pushed them down into the bag, pushed them harder, then realized he could stand there the rest of the night and it would do no good—the can was simply too full.

It would be a two-bag day. Better than the three bags he'd taken out last Wednesday, but worse than Friday's single bag. Such was the life of a professional psychologist, where the difference between good days and bad was measured not so much by an increase of joy but a decrease of sorrow. Tom pulled another trash bag from the drawer and filled it. He then took the two bags in one hand, his briefcase in the other, and turned the lights out on another day of fighting the good fight.

He made an abrupt left toward the dumpster. It was technically the cleaning lady's job to dump the office trash each night. So Rita had reminded him, and upon countless occasions. And upon equally countless occasions Tom had reiterated that he had no qualms with Maria emptying the trash from the waiting and reception areas, but what was to be disposed of from his office was his job alone. It was Tom's private ritual, his way of ensuring that the burdens of his profession were no longer shouldered by Ellen and Leah.

He set the briefcase aside and hefted the dumpster's rusty lid. Rats scurried from deep within its bowels, scavenging for a morsel to satisfy their hunger or a bit of refuse to line their nests. The smell was rotten and bitter. Tom hoisted the bags— so light in some ways and so heavy in others—and watched as they disappeared into the darkness.

Yet unlike most days, Tom's ritual did not lessen the sadness he felt. He knew he could stand there all evening tossing tissues into the dumpster and still not forget Meagan Gladwell's mottled arms. He could not un-hear her tears or her sorrowed, twisted reasoning that faith trumped well-being. He could not let go of the notion that all the psychological prowess he could muster would be of little use to Meagan Gladwell. She was wandering, and she didn't even see that she was lost.

The cell phone chirped in Tom's pocket, jerking him from self-pity. He checked the number, smiled, and then didn't, then answered.

"Hey, Puh-Pops, it's yuh-your daughter Leah."

"Hello, my daughter Leah. I've been trying to call you all day. How'd everything go?"

"Nuh-not too guh-good, I'm afraid. You're luh-late, Puh-Pops."

"I know, I'm sorry. I'll be home soon. What happened at the news conference?"

"I ruh-really don't w-want to tuh-talk about thuh-that. You'll have to suh-see."

Tom climbed into his truck. The traffic beyond the parking lot snarled. Four thirty was an awful time to be leaving work. "Is everything okay? Talk to me, Leah."

"Muh-Mommy's pretty m-mad at yuh-you. Just w-wanted you to be ruh-ready for that. I guess muh-maybe I suh-sorta am tuh-too. I'm suh-sorry." Leah's voice cracked. She sniffed and tried to continue. "I nuh-needed you thuh-there, Puh-Pops. Allie and the R-rainbow M-man were thuh-there and Muh-Mommy too, but you wuh-weren't."

"I know," Tom said. And he did know. He knew that all the work he had to do meant leaving other work undone, work that was just as important and very likely more so, and it pained him in that moment that he considered the raising of his daughter just another something he had to do. He knew that every good man was torn between that which he'd been given and that which he was meant to do, and that those two things often shattered against each other like rock upon rock. Saying no to Leah meant saying yes to GLADWELL, MEAGAN and DELACROIX, CHARLES and all those after them, people who had nothing real left to tether themselves to except Dr. Thomas Norcross. Yet saying yes to them meant saying no to his only daughter and the one shining light in his own life. And though he had said it before and too often, he said he was sorry yet again.

"I nuh-know you are, Puh-Pops," Leah said. "You luh-love too m-much."

"I'll be home in a little bit, okay? I'll make it up to you."

"Ok-kay. Buh-be careful of the wuh-wolves. Chuh-cheery-bye."

"What wolves?" Tom asked, but Leah was gone.

Unlike the half-hour ride from Mattingly to his office, the ride back was usually a pleasant one. Like the trash bag ritual, it was another means of separating his two worlds of the brokenness in his patients and the love (shaky though it was) of his family. But even as four lanes gave way to two and city buildings melted against blue mountains, Tom could not find a sigh and a smile. Because by then, Dr. Tom Norcross was beginning to believe those two worlds were colliding, and that the darkness that defined the one was creeping into the other yet again.

He drove down Main Street to find the sidewalks littered with people. News vans fitted with communications dishes and long metal poles prowled the streets. Their drivers lurched and braked in the maze of narrow roads and one-way intersections. Sheriff Barnett was directing traffic away from a fender-bender between a jacked-up Chevy truck and a van from a television station in Richmond. He waved to Tom and offered a sad shake of the head. The air filled with blowing horns and curses. Reporters stood sentry on street corners with microphones and digital recorders in hand, goading passing townspeople into sound bites for the evening news. If the reporters were fortunate, they received cold silence. If they were not, they were told in no uncertain terms to leave.

More news vans and reporters were parked along the fence line in front of the yellow Victorian. Voices shouted as Tom approached. He tried to avoid them by cutting into the driveway, but Ellen's Lexus was parked sideways in front of the fence's opening.

There came a chorus of "Dr. Norcross" as Tom jumped out of his truck and hurried around Ellen's car. The reporters closed in. They called out questions about Leah and Barney, about what Tom thought and what he believed, demanding just a moment of his time. Tom's head thundered. Shards of white light shot out from the corners of his eyes. He raised his briefcase over his head and did not break his stride. If the presence of so many people—so many questions—affected him that way, how much more must it have affected Leah?

Ellen was alone on the porch swing. Tom waved as he cleared the magnolias and then extended his arms to the side in a what-in-the-world? motion. His wife neither answered nor acknowledged his presence. That's when Tom knew it was bad. It was bad, and it was his fault.

He climbed the front steps and sat on one of the rockers near the swing—close enough to talk, far enough to give Ellen space. Beyond the fence, the sun turned bright orange as it neared the mountaintops. The reporters snapped their pictures and spoke into their cameras, live from the small town of Hillbilly Hell, Virginia. Leah had been right. They were wolves, growling and sniffing and caring not what they devoured. Ellen sat with one leg under her and the other pushing against the wooden porch. The swing squeaked as it moved forward and back. Her gaze was outward toward the road. She fondled the crystal hanging from her neck. An open bottle of wine and an empty glass sat on the table beside her.

"What in the world is going on?" Tom asked.

Far below, across the street, the Norcrosses' neighbor—Ed Broomfield, Tom thought, though he wasn't sure the name was right—opened his door long enough to shout at the reporters. He retreated when the reporters turned their cameras and microphones on him, but not before offering them a gesture Tom was glad Leah wasn't there to see.

"Does that mean all this matters to you, now that your day at work is over?" Ellen asked.

"Ellen."

She shook her head. "No, Tom. I'm not going to say I'm sorry this time. You're not going to say you're sorry this time either. We *needed* you there, but you couldn't. No," she said, holding a finger in the air as if she'd just touched upon some greater truth, "you *wouldn't*. Because that stupid news conference was during business hours, and that's when Dr. Tom Norcross puts on his Superman costume to save the world, one paranoia at a time." She shook her head. Tom readied himself. "You and your hero complex. You have to heal the hurt. You have to change people. You ever think Leah and I need a hero too?"

Tom searched for words that would be enough to explain that the gash in his heart was just as wide as the one in Ellen's own, but he could not. The weight upon them was too heavy, the gulf between them too wide.

All he could manage was, "I had a two-bag day."

Ellen's eyes blinked. She nodded and said, "My day wasn't sunshine and cotton candy."

"Where's Leah? She called me before I left."

She pointed to the window behind her. "In her room trying to forget what happened."

"I just thought it wouldn't be a big deal. You and Leah could go, Barney would get his picture taken, end of story. What happened?"

She chuckled and pointed toward the road. "That look like the end of the story to you, Tom? And Leah wasn't just sitting in the crowd while Barney got his picture taken either. He wanted her up there *with* him, getting *her* picture taken. Allie too, and poor dear Mabel. What was he thinking?"

Ellen trailed off and shook her head. Mr. Broomfield appeared outside his front door again, this time armed with more than his finger. Tom didn't know if the shotgun the old man waved was loaded or not. There were volleys of shouts and curses from him to the wolves. Tom heard one of the reporters mention Sheriff Barnett and thought he heard Mr. Broomfield say that was a fine idea.

"And then what?"

"And then Barney starts talking about Leah's painting

and how the numbers he picked were in there, and then they started asking *Leah* all sorts of questions. She was so scared, Tom."

"Why didn't you get her out of there?" he asked, and then regretted asking it, knowing the reply would be, *That was supposed to be* your *job*.

"I started to, but then Allie told them that Leah didn't paint the numbers, the rainbow man did."

Tom's head dropped into his hands. "Oh no."

"Oh no's right. Now half this town thinks our little girl's got a direct line to God. The phone's been ringing nonstop, the reporters followed us here. That's why I parked the car at the end of the lane. Just to keep—"

She jumped at a rustle from the bushes on the side of the house and reached out for Tom's hand. In one thought he was thankful to take it, and in another he was sure that a parked car at the end of the lane would never be enough to beat back a pack of hungry wolves, especially so close to the six o'clock news. The shrubs parted. What peered out wasn't a camera-clad reporter, but a nervous old man.

"Hiya, Tom," Barney said. "Ellen. Sorry to slink up on y'all like this, but as you can prolly imagine, I'm tryin' to fly under the radar at the moment." He looked down to the road and shook his head. "Tried to call. Reckon your phone's been about as occupied as ours."

"Barney," Ellen said, "come on out of those shrubs."

"No'm," he said, "I ain't gonna. Those reporter people down there'll pitch a fit if they see me with y'all. I'm just gonna stay right here, if that's okay."

"Where's Mabel?" Tom asked.

As if on cue, a squeaky "I love you" came from the bushes.

"She's here behind me," Barney said. "Weren't much

trouble gettin' here, though I'm a bit winded from all the skulkin'. How's little Leah?"

"She's fine," Tom said. He ignored the look Ellen gave him. "She's resting in her room."

Barney nodded and looked at Ellen. "Sorry that ended so bad up at the park, Ellen. I was just tryin' to give credit where credit's due, which I reckon's why I'm here. Half that money's comin' your way when I cash in me an' Mabel's ticket." He patted the chest pocket of his overalls. "It's safe, don't want y'all to worry."

Ellen said, "Barney, we don't want any money. That's yours to keep."

Tom agreed. "We didn't have anything to do with that, Barney."

"Well, maybe not so much y'all as Leah," Barney said. "An' maybe not so much her as that Rainbow Man Allie talked about. I didn't know all that, by the way. I know they were sayin' Leah saw a spirit at the party. I thought they was just playin'. They weren't. Your little girl's got the magic, Tom."

Tom thought of Meagan and the tears her God caused her to shed—one bag's worth at least. He wondered if Barney would call that magic as well.

"Barney," he said.

The old man held up his hand through the bushes as if he were about to wave good-bye and disappear into another world.

"I know, Tom. But I'm speakin' the truth here. She shown me God ain't harsh, an' that might be a bigger miracle than even them numbers. Me an' Mabel's gonna be okay now. The Rainbow Man says so. My day's come."

"Please keep it, Barney," Ellen said. "Yours and Mabel's good fortune is enough payment for us. Tom's worked hard and sacrificed a lot"—she gave her husband a look that said *too* hard and *too* much—"to give us a good life. We don't need more than we have."

Barney shook his head and sighed in a way Tom found familiar. He'd heard at least five of those same sighs and seen five same shakes of the head that day at work.

"Everybody wants my money except for the folk I really wanna give it to," he said. "Me an' Mabel'll leave y'all alone now. And please tell Leah I's sorry. Say bye now, Mabel."

"I love you," Mabel called.

Barney shrank back into the bushes. Tom had no idea how he would cart a stricken woman back to the Treasure Chest without anyone seeing him, but he figured if anyone knew the back corners of Mattingly it would be Barney Moore, the richest man in town.

"I fuh-forgive you, Mr. Buh-Barney."

Tom and Ellen looked toward the door but saw no one.

"Hey there, Puh-Pops."

"Where are you, Leah?"

"Oh-over here in m-my room."

Tom and Ellen looked. Sometime between Barney and Mabel's arrival and departure, Leah had raised her bedroom window. A mass of black hair and the top of a colorless forehead peeked over the sill.

"I duh-don't want the wuh-wolves to s-see me," she said. "It was bad, Puh-Pops, like I tuh-told you."

"I'm sorry, Leah-boo. I truly am."

"I'm m-mad."

"I know. I should have been there."

"Nuh-not about that," Leah's forehead said. "You suh-said you d-didn't want that muh-money."

"We don't need that money, Leah," Ellen said.

Leah's voice lurched and spasmed as her words came. Tom could hear her frustration, not at her lack of clarity but at his and Ellen's lack of belief. She said they had told Mr. Barney no not because they didn't want the money but because they didn't believe him. But what Mr. Barney said was right, and Allie had been right too. The Rainbow Man was real. And not only that, he was in there with her singing at that very moment, singing that Ellen kind of believed but not really and Tom not at all, but that they both had to trust the Maybe. She said soon a lot of people would trust, because the Rainbow Man wanted her to paint another picture.

By the time Leah's breath had run out, the window screen was pocked with bits of saliva that her stutters had sprayed. She finished with, "And thuh-that's all I have t-to suh-say about that r-right nuh-now."

Her forehead disappeared beneath the screen, replaced by two bony arms that slowly closed the window.

Tuesday

Four Days Before the Carnival

1

Allie was old enough to understand that introducing someone to the Higher Things wouldn't be all sunshine. There was bound to be some clouds thrown in too. But she never thought she would have to sacrifice her morning cartoons.

She planned to check on Leah later in the day after spending the morning down at the Treasure Chest with her momma. Mr. Barney had called earlier to say there was a crowd at the door already, and these were paying customers rather than prying newspeople. He was going to need some help, and Mary had seized the chance. Allie's momma was like that, always eager to lend an ear to listen or a hand to help. But then Miss Ellen called just as the milk was going over Allie's Cheerios, and what Allie was hearing made her realize breakfast with the Roadrunner and Wile E. would have to wait.

"Sure, she can come over," Mary said. She held the phone in one hand and one of her favorite pink Nikes in the other. "I was going to Barney's anyway, so I guess we'll just meet you there? . . . Oh, okay, then . . . No, it's no problem. Are you all right, Ellen?"

On the television, Wile E.'s most recent scheme to nab the Roadrunner backfired. He sprouted wings and floated heavenward into a cartoon sky. Allie didn't think that seemed right. If anyone deserved the torment of eternal hell, it would have to be that mean old coyote. She set her bowl on the coffee table beside the folded morning newspaper. Allie had read all of Trevor Morgan's article earlier—"Local Man Wins Lottery with Miracle Painting." Allie was pleased that Leah and the Rainbow Man had been given just as much space as Barney himself.

"I can't imagine how hard it's been for y'all," Mary said. "Try not to worry, though. This will all blow over. It always does." She looked at Allie and walked from the living room into the kitchen—an old trick that never worked. Allie lowered the volume on the television and heard, "If you don't mind, can I ask if it's . . . like the other?" There was a pause, followed by an "Oh my gosh" that made Allie smile. The Rainbow Man must have sung again. She turned the volume back up and picked up her bowl as Mary said good-bye.

"Leah made another picture, didn't she?" Allie asked.

"Yes. Did you know about that?"

"No'm. But I reckon the Rainbow Man said it was time, and Leah's obliged to honor the magic."

"Mrs. Norcross wants you to come over. Leah says she has to take her picture over to Barney's, but she won't go unless you're with her. Wants you to maybe spend the night too."

"You don't mind?" Allie asked.

"No. I'll see you at the Treasure Chest, and I'm mostly fine with you staying there."

Allie let her spoon tinkle against the bowl in her lap. "What do you mean, 'mostly'?"

"Let's just say I think they'll all be better if there's someone else around. I'll call your daddy at work, but I'm sure he won't mind. Go pack some clothes and your toothbrush. And Ellen said Dr. Norcross is going to blow up the swimming pool, so pack your bathing suit too."

The swimming part more than made up for a morning sans *Looney Tunes*. Allie turned off the television and announced, "All right, then."

Allie understood her momma thought that Leah's Maybe was more like Leah's Probably Not. She also knew that what mattered to her momma was that Allie was helping Leah just as Mary was helping Mr. Barney. They spoke of many things on their drive to the Norcross home, of summer and dreams and fears, and at one point Allie almost confessed the kiss she'd shared with Zach. Then she thought against it. That was the sort of thing you took out once and could never put back in.

Two-thirds of the Norcross family was on the porch when Mary drove up the lane. Ellen's purse was already slung over her shoulder. Leah waved to Allie with the hand attached to her bad thumb. The other held another rolled-up piece of paper. She did not smile. Allie wondered how anyone could look so sad with God standing near. Mary rolled down her window and said good morning as Ellen and Leah made their way down the steps toward Ellen's car.

"Hi, Muh-Missus Granderson," Leah said.

She walked past and cast a look in Allie's direction that said *Help me* with no stutter at all. Allie kissed her momma good-bye, grabbed her bag of clothes, and got out of the car.

"Sure you're okay?" Mary asked Ellen.

"I'm fine," she said, but Allie thought Miss Ellen looked just as tired as Leah. Tired but braced. "Tom will be fine too.

Between the craziness here and all the craziness at work, he has a lot on him."

"I think you all do," Mary said. "Let me know if you need anything, okay?"

"Thank you."

More was said, but Allie was no longer interested. She opened the door of Miss Ellen's Lexus and climbed inside. The air was sticky and thick with the smell of coconut from the freshener dangling off the radio knob.

"Hey there," she said. "Brought my bathin' suit so we can swim later. Thanks for askin' me over. You okay?"

Leah said yes, but Allie knew it was a fib and thought she knew why. She jumped up from the seat and excused herself.

"I ain't squishin' him, are I?"

"Nuh-no," Leah said. "He can fuh-fit anywhere. It's Puh-Pops. He's not coming wuh-with us. He duh-doesn't believe me. Buh-but I bet if I wuh-was a crazy puh-person in his buh-big fancy office in the suh-city, he'd buh-lieve me thuh-then. If you luh-love some things t-too much, you duh-don't have luh-love left fuh-for anything else."

Allie wondered what kind of daddy would do such a thing and thought love didn't have much to do with it. "Did you tell him that?"

Leah shook her head. "Suh-some things p-people are suh-posed to nuh-know without being t-told."

Ellen finished talking with Mary and walked toward the Lexus with a surety Allie could never recall seeing in Leah's momma.

"I believe you," she told Leah. "And I'll help you too. What'd he tell you to draw this time?"

Leah unrolled the sheet of paper and spread it over her chest. Allie tried to take in the scene all at once but couldn't.

"Awesomesauce," she whispered. She looked from the page to Leah's face. "Are they—"

"Yuh-yes," Leah said. "I guh-guess this t-time it's not juh-just Mr. Buh-Barney that can s-see them, everyone can."

Allie tried looking at the page again. She tried to see and understand.

"Do you know what this means, Leah?"

"Nuh-no."

"It means this whole town's gonna go batty."

Ellen shut the door and asked, "Ready?" She didn't wait for an answer. The Lexus backed out of its spot by the garage and wound its way down the lane. Allie turned and looked through the back window. Mr. Doctor stood at the front door and watched them go.

"Puh-Pops sure seemed muh-mad," Leah said. "You duh-didn't even say good-buh-bye, Muh-Mommy."

"He's fine," Ellen told her. "Let's not worry about that. We have important things to do."

Allie mouthed a *We?* in Leah's direction. Leah shrugged.

"You okay back there, Allie?"

"Yes'm, right as rain."

The streets were empty. That wasn't much different from any other summer weekday, Allie thought. Most people were either already at work or hiding from the heat. Some, she reckoned, were hiding from the reporters as well. There didn't seem to be any of them out and about either, though. It was as if the town itself had inhaled and was waiting to blow.

"Look over there," Ellen said. She pointed to the marquee in front of the Mattingly Rescue Squad building. TOWN CARNIVAL JUNE 25 was placed on top, and below that CONGRADULATIONS BARNEY AND LEAH!!! "Isn't that wonderful, Leah? I mean, they spelled part of it wrong, but they got your name right."

"Awesomesauce," Allie said. She craned her neck to see if the sign had been replicated on the other side. It had. "Wow, Leah. You're famous now. Havin' your name on the sign is even better than havin' TV people ask you stuff."

Leah remained still. Her hands were folded around the painting in her lap. Ellen looked through the mirror. Allie shrugged at her.

"Leah, what's wrong, honey?" Ellen asked. "Are you still upset about Pops?"

"Nuh-no," came the answer.

"Good. We're almost there."

They continued on, past the church and under the carnival sign stretched across the road. Through the park's iron fence posts, the rough outline of booths and rides being set up popped into view. Strangely, no one was working yet.

"Where is everyone today?" Ellen asked.

Her question was answered when the Lexus turned right at the diner. Lining Second Street all the way to the Treasure Chest were dozens of cars and trucks. A horde of people bottlenecked at the front door, which was propped open by a large rock to ease the flow of customers.

"What in the world is going on here?" Ellen asked. "Mary said Barney was busy, but I didn't think he'd be this busy."

Allie leaned forward in her seat to get a view through the windshield. "Holy wow, Leah. You done made Mr. Barney famous."

Leah pulled her back and whispered, "He's huh-here."

"Who's here?" Allie asked.

"The muh-man I'm supposed to tuh-talk to."

"Well, of course he is, silly. It's Mr. Barney's shop."

"Nuh-not Mr. Buh-Barney," Leah said.

Allie looked down at the sound of crinkling paper. Leah scrubbed at the hole in her thumbnail.

2

For Reggie, Tuesdays were set aside for visiting the sick and shut-ins of his congregation. His first stop was always to see Mabel, and he'd decided that morning not to deviate from that routine. Regardless of Barney's moral lapse—not to mention his questioning of Reggie's knowledge of God's will—he was still a friend. And Reggie had always cherished Mabel's company, however faint that company might be. He'd expected to find her in her accustomed place and form—in bed and nearly catatonic. What he found instead could only be described as miraculous.

The Treasure Chest was hopping. Many were town residents—Reggie counted over a dozen members of First Church—but more than a few were from Away. Shopping. *Buying.* All in a frenzy of arms and legs and hands, a growing chorus of "This is wonderful" and "Wouldn't he/she/they love this" and, upon more than one occasion, "Give me that" and "I was here first."

Barney stood near the far wall by the basement door helping Allison Summers, who waitressed at the diner and filled in as church organist whenever Lila McKinney's arthritis flared up. Allison spoke to him in a low voice that wasn't necessary, given the commotion. Barney nodded and offered her an odd smile that was half joy and half disappointment. He scribbled something on a white pad of paper and tore off the top sheet. Allison gave him a peck on the cheek and carried the slip of paper to the front, where Mary Granderson cranked the lever on the old register. The bell on the cash drawer rang for the first time in a long while.

Mayor Wallis shook hands and wagged his tongue. Trevor Morgan took notes. Deacon Spicer prowled the aisles with the same scowl that had been present at church when Barney had given his witness. And there was Mabel herself, not running on all eight cylinders but on at least four of them, hunched in her wheelchair and within Mary's reach. She discharged a thick, phlegmy cough and drummed her fingers on the hand rest.

"Morning, Reggie," Mary said from the register. "Come to join the fun?"

"Came to visit Mabel." He stepped around a group of shoppers. "Guess I'll be visiting with more than her."

Mary laughed and helloed her next customer, an elderly man in a stained white shirt and tan pants with holes where pockets once were. He handed Mary another of Barney's white slips of paper and smiled.

Reggie moved to Mabel and crouched to see her face. The frail woman's eyes barely recognized him.

"How are you feeling today, Mabel?" Sweat gathered above her upper lip. Her cheek was leathery and warm. And though the crowd was boisterous, Reggie could hear the faint whistles that accompanied her exhales. "Mabel doesn't seem well, Mary."

Mary thanked the man with the holey pockets and waited for the next in line. "I think she's fighting a bug," she told Reggie. "Doc March is gonna stop by this evening. Barney gave her some medicine earlier. He's worried."

"I am too."

He patted Mabel's arm and straightened to take in the moment. It could be said that Reverend Reginald Goggins had recycled his share of sermons over the years, but the few times he had done so had been out of necessity rather than laziness. Certain things deserved a repeated going-over. None was as important as hearing God's voice. No other aspect of the Christian life was so misunderstood (Reggie mourned those poor souls who believed God spoke through such human foolishness as epiphanies and coincidence), and as shepherd of a town whose people connected nearly every happening to the voice of God, it fell upon his shoulders to set things right. It was a voice that had comforted Reggie through the years and had drawn him ever closer to the face of God. And it was a voice he listened for now as he beheld a once-dying business springing back to life and a once-cursed friend enjoying what he believed was his blessing. But that voice would not come. In the end, that was how Reggie knew before anyone that a dark trouble was approaching and that its first stiff breezes had already arrived. All he felt was a tiny sore spot on his head, the kind that meant someone was staring. His eyes settled upon the open door, where Leah Norcross stood with her mother and Allie Granderson.

The clamor inside the Treasure Chest ceased in that moment. Hands that reached for Lincoln Logs or toy guns or across the counter hung suspended as if fixed in time. Their focus settled upon the tiny girl with knobby knees and long black hair. Leah's focus seemed upon Reggie alone.

Barney left his spot by the marble rollers and made his way around the ogling customers.

"Little Leah. Come in, come in. Hello, Ellen, and there's little Allie too. How are you?"

"H-hello, Mr. Buh-Barney," Leah whispered. Her eyes were still on Reggie. She held up a rolled section of paper in her hand as Allie went behind the counter to give Mary a hug. "I huh-have a new puh-painting for you."

"A new painting?"

Barney's question unstuck the crowd and set the tempo in the room back into its former forward motion. They moved in unison toward the door and formed a loose circle around Leah and her mother.

"Yuh-yes," she said, and now the sore spot on Reggie's head really did feel sore. It felt like a burrowing, as if Leah's eyes were not so much looking at him but *feeling* him, his thoughts as plain to her as his face. "Wuh-would you luh-like to luh-look at it?"

"I sure would," Barney said.

"Wuh-would you luh-like us to show you, Ruh-Reverend?" she asked. "The R-rainbow M-man and me, I muh-mean."

"The rainbow man?" Reggie asked. "Is he here now?"

Leah said, "He's always huh-here, Ruh-Reverend."

Reggie listened for the Still Small Voice to direct him, and received more silence instead. The crowd waited. He felt he had no choice in what he said next.

"Sure, Leah. Come on over here."

She held the painting in her hand and parted the crowd like Moses waltzing through the Red Sea. Ellen followed her. As did everyone else, who now circled Reggie. Leah handed the paper to him and took her place beside Mabel, who opened her eyes long enough to mumble, "I love you."

"I luh-love you tuh-too, Muh-Miss Mabel," she whispered. And then, as if a little girl whose momma and daddy were spiritual-but-not-religious could know such things, Leah added, "Everything's guh-gonna be okay n-now."

There was an audible gasp from the crowd as Reggie unrolled the page. Even he was not able to keep his eyes from swelling. The emerald field and rainbow of her previous work had been replaced by a nighttime scene. A pale, full moon hung in a sky of stars, each swirling clockwise in an almost musical effect. In the distance, dark clouds gathered and spread. Shadowy trees scattered at the outer edges of the paper, their limbs gnarled and reaching—some downward toward the firmament, and others outward toward a representation of their town painted in the middle. On the tip of a giant twisted branch at the bottom of the page sat a mockingbird so lifelike its feathers seemed to ruffle in the unseen wind of an approaching storm. Its eye stared through the page with a clarity Reggie could not fathom. Musical notations emanated from its open beak, whole and half notes that morphed into the numbers 34720625 as they fell over the town.

"I think it's wonderful, Leah," Barney said. His voice was soft and church-like. "Truly so. These different numbers, are they?"

Leah nodded and put an arm around Mabel. She looked at Reggie and asked, "Duh-do you luh-like it, Ruh-Reverend?"

Reggie said, "I think it's beautiful, Leah," and his heart could not betray that truth. There were those in town now convinced this little unbelieving girl was a vessel through which God spoke, that her art was nothing short of some holy paint-by-number. Reggie was as sure that wasn't true as he was that God did not speak through wind and fire, but there was no denying Leah had a gift. A gift that would no doubt throw fuel on an already mounting blaze.

"Let's go hang this in the window," Barney said. He looked at Reggie. "Looks like I was right about the Lord's will, Preacher. He's gonna spread the wealth around."

Barney took Leah by the hand and walked to the front of the store, where Mary and Allie waited with four strips of tape. The crowd followed them only as far as the door and then headed outside to fan out in front of the window. Pens and scrap paper appeared as the numbers on Leah's painting were scribbled down. Only Reggie and Ellen remained behind.

"That's quite a talented young lady," he said.

"Talented?" Ellen chuckled. "Not really. Leah's always liked to draw, but it was never anything like . . . that."

Outside, several shoppers who hadn't managed to find a pen took photos of Leah's painting with their cell phones. Leah and Barney stood guard on the other side of the window. The pad of paper in Barney's hand went into the front pocket of his overalls. There was a soft crinkle as it rubbed against his lottery ticket. Mary and Allie went to check on Mabel, whose cough had worsened. Leah looked from the crowd outside to Reggie and smiled.

"Maybe some sort of latent talent," he told Ellen. "Such things have been known to lie dormant and suddenly spring to life."

"I thought that too at first," she said. "Guess I was just scared to think otherwise. I'm not anymore."

Reggie looked at her. "What do you mean?"

"Allie says Leah has the magic, and I think she's right. I've always believed in magic, Reverend. Tom makes fun sometimes when I go on about it." She touched the crystal that hung from her neck. "The Universe has touched my daughter. Leah's somehow tapped into something. If anyone should see that, I'd think it'd be you."

Reggie leaned on a barrel of Lincoln Logs and smiled—so "the Universe" had touched Ellen Norcross's daughter. In that one simple statement he understood the woman in front of him as one of those wayward souls who found more joy in pondering life's questions than in discovering its answers, who found comfort in keeping God broad and undefinable—the sort who would find no impropriety in praying to Jehovah while facing Mecca and sitting in the lotus position.

"The magic," he said. "That's what folks say when referring

to some occurrences that have happened here in the past. Others call it 'the Higher Things.' I don't care for either term myself. God isn't magic, Ellen. He doesn't fly over people—that's what they say happens from time to time—and He certainly isn't 'the Universe.' He's God. And though I believe He can and does touch people, I don't believe He's touched your Leah."

"You sound like Tom. He didn't want me to bring Leah down here this morning. He's a good man, Reverend, despite the opinion you may have formed of him. I think he was just trying to protect Leah from too much attention."

"I think that's probably a good idea, given the circumstances."

"I did too. But do you know what I've been thinking about all morning? How I met Tom. We were in college. I was in the dining hall one night. He literally bumped into me in line and said, 'I'm so sorry.' Just that, nothing more. But I had an epiphany in that very second. It was like I was hit by a beam of light. There was a crack of thunder in my head that said, *You're going to marry this man.*"

"Thunder?" Reggie asked, then had to force his head not to shake from side to side. "Was there fire and wind too?"

"No," Ellen said. "It was surreal, though. And it happened again a few months ago. Things weren't so good. Tom was working such long hours, and . . . well, something had happened between us, something hurtful that I did and I'm still trying to apologize for. Leah was withdrawing even from us. Tom wanted to move here, but I didn't think it was a very good idea. That's when I felt it again—*You need to move and start over.* I didn't think it was the voice of God, whoever he was. But I know it was now, because I heard it again this morning when Leah showed us her new painting. *Your daughter has been touched by God.* That's what the thunder said."

"That's not how it works, Ellen."

"I think you're wrong, Reverend. It's happened. It's happening to *us*. And you know what else I think? That maybe if God's touched Leah and I help her, He'll touch me too."

Ellen excused herself and went to her daughter. Barney asked her and Mary if maybe the girls could drop by later that evening. He had something special for them. The crowd trickled back inside the Treasure Chest. Leah stood in their midst, answering their questions with Allie's help, telling them about the Rainbow Man and how the painting was more his than her own. But it was the numbers they most wanted to know about. They hung on Leah's every word in the middle of the store just as they'd hung on Reggie's every Sunday morning. He tried to watch her and listen despite himself, but found he could not. Leah was too still, her voice too small.

3

Tom watched through the bedroom window as Leah and Allie chased three butterflies that skimmed above the backyard's green grass. Thus far, they'd come up empty. Allie had been close once, but the orange-and-black Monarch she was after looped just above her reaching hands. Leah had spent much of her time watching and only joined in when Allie forced her. Leah had never been much of a chaser, Tom thought. She preferred hiding.

But his daughter seemed to be getting the hang of things. Allie was a good teacher. She knew just when to prod Leah onward and when to give her space. She demonstrated the proper way to hold one's hands and how it was best to creep up rather than run toward. Tom thought Leah's new friend had the makings to be a good therapist one day. Leah made another attempt at a butterfly resting upon the edge of the small swimming pool Tom had inflated earlier. Allie guided her in. Leah almost made it, but at the last moment the insect flitted into the sky. Tom thought she would be disappointed at her failure, but the girls laughed instead and walked away from the pool to the hill at the end of the yard.

The hallway floorboard creaked. A shadow appeared out of the corner of Tom's eye. He didn't think it was Leah's imaginary friend but thought it would perhaps be better—much better—if it were.

"Hey."

"Hey yourself," he said.

Leah and Allie reached the hill. They snuggled under the hanging pine limbs and disappeared.

"Are you still mad at me?" Ellen asked.

Tom didn't know. A part of him, the part that ran contrary to much of what he once told his marriage therapy couples, still smarted from Ellen's decision to drive Leah to the Treasure Chest. He'd been adamant that she not. Okay, too adamant. And he hadn't meant to yell, especially within Leah's earshot. That was not Tom's way, and he had been more shocked than anyone when he heard the echo of his own rage. It was more than anger that had spilled out onto his wife, it was a pleading to keep the painting out of sight, because people would go crazy, they always did. It was the numbers. Didn't she see it was the numbers? Didn't she want to protect their child?

"I guess a part of me is," he said. "I'm sorry I yelled, Ellen."

"That's twice in the past few days, Tom. Me earlier, Reggie Goggins Saturday."

"I know." He tried to spot Leah and Allie and couldn't, though he saw a bit of Leah's shoes peeking out from beneath the pines. What were they talking about up there? He looked from the window to Ellen, who moved to the edge of their bed. "It wasn't so much that I felt angry, Ellen. I felt threatened. I just wanted to protect my family. I know it might not have looked like that to you, but I want you to believe me."

"We need to talk about this," she said. "That's what you always say, right? 'A good marriage is built on a solid foundation of communication.' The first commandment of the Gospel according to Dr. Thomas Alan Norcross. So let's communicate. I don't want to risk another fight, Tom. I'm so tired of it, and I know you are too. Sometimes it's just easier to swallow things or close your eyes and hope they go away. But sometimes I think the only place doing that will lead is back to where we were, and I won't let that happen."

"I'm better now," Tom said.

"No, you're not. And I'm not. And I'm sure Leah's not either. She was devastated when you didn't come with us this morning, especially after you weren't there yesterday."

"She set this town in an uproar over that first painting," he said. "She and Barney, anyway. You just threw gas on the fire, Ellen. Can't you see it did more harm than good?"

"Leah has a *gift*, Tom, and it's something I'm just trying to understand. God's touched her."

Tom smacked the windowpane. He turned to Ellen, trying but not succeeding in holding in check the rage locked inside himself. "What do you know about God, Ellen? If you only knew how much sanctimonious god-talk I have to hear, you'd know not to say anything like that. My job is to keep Leah *safe*, to keep her *well*, otherwise she'll end up"—*like Meagan Gladwell*, he wanted to say—"broken. She'll end up broken, Ellen. And you buying into the fantasy these people are building around her isn't helping."

Ellen did not back down this time. There was no forgive

and forget, no letting the next sunrise take care of things. She matched Tom's voice decibel for decibel. "How can you keep her safe if all you're worried about are your precious patients? Why'd we move here, Tom? Remember?"

Tom took a breath and tried to calm down. He didn't think Leah and Allie could hear them from so far a distance, but he didn't want to test that theory. And he was tired. In the end, that's what everything came down to, the reason for every problem that tangled his life—the simple weariness of trying to fix things that were forever broken.

"We moved here for a new start," he said.

"No, for a new *life*. Because our old one was broken. Because you spent so much time trying to keep your patients from losing themselves that you lost *your*self. I was losing you. And you made me a promise that it wouldn't happen again."

Tom left the window and sat on the bed. He took Ellen's hand and kissed it. Her skin was smooth and smelled of lavender. Blond hair swept down over her shoulders to the neckline of her T-shirt. And those eyes.

"You won't lose me," he said.

"Then talk to me. Tell me who she is."

He let go of Ellen's hand and asked, "Who *who* is?"

"Saturday with Reggie? Today with me? I thought the only thing they had in common was Leah. But there was something else, Tom. Both of those days were days after you worked. So tell me, who is she? Or is it a man this time?"

"Yesterday was a two-bag day," he said. A two-bag day and Meagan Gladwell, that woman with the faith of a child and the good sense of a rock. Who loved her God so much that she didn't care if she got the hell beaten out of her on a daily basis. Or if her unborn child did too. Tom took Ellen's hand again, squeezed it, looked at her *(those eyes)* and wanted to speak, wanted to tell her everything, because then she would know and she would understand. He said, "You know that's all I can say about that."

"No," she said. "Not this time, Tom. I want to know."

"Why? Why do you want to know, Ellen?" The words came out with heat behind them, shooting them forward too fast for Tom to think. "Do you really want me to tell you why we moved here? You need me to *remind* you?"

She laughed. It was a short sound, light on the ends but heavy in the middle—the chuckle you hear when laughter is expected for something not funny at all. "No, Tom, I don't need you to remind me. You remind me every . . . single . . . *day*. But go ahead. Tell me. Get it out already, because I'm so *tired* of this."

"I confided in you," he yelled, and at that moment Tom Norcross didn't care who heard. "Lilly was in trouble. She was *hurting*. She was on so many drugs that she wanted to *kill* herself, Ellen. I just needed someone to talk to, and I wanted to talk to *you*. And what did you do when I did, Ellen?"

Tom waited, would say nothing more until Ellen answered, because he wanted to hear her say it, needed for her to confess. That she already had didn't matter, not then and maybe not ever.

"I didn't know it was *Lilly*," she said.

It wasn't a confession, but it was near enough. And Ellen was right, she hadn't known the drug-addicted suicidal woman who'd sat on Tom's office sofa three days a week had been Lilly Wagoner, one of Stanley's most prominent citizens. He had only given Ellen generalities, nothing more, but when they'd attended one of the Wagoners' famous weekend soirees and Ellen had found herself with Lilly at her left hand and a bottle of wine at her right, those generalities became tinder.

Lilly Wagoner's insatiable desire for gossip and Ellen's insatiable need for acceptance? That was all it took.

Let me tell you about this woman Tom is seeing, she'd said. *Poor woman's so hopped up on drugs that she swears she's going to hang herself. She's driving Tom absolutely crazy. Could you imagine?*

It had been chance, nothing more. But it had been enough for Lilly to threaten Tom's license and enough for Tom to widen that wall between his family and his work—widen it so that no one could ever get in again.

"It doesn't matter that you didn't know," he said. His voice was still raised, but it had lost its edge. "That's what I need you to see, Ellen."

"You think I don't? I do, Tom. I *do.* And what I need you to see is that you spend most of your time telling people to give someone else another chance, but you won't give that chance to me."

Tom had no answer to that.

"Fine," she said, and the way she said it made him feel as if it truly might be fine this time. "Don't tell me who it is this time. Maybe that's what I deserve. But there's something else. Something about this . . . person . . . that's spilling out on me and Leah. I might not have a right to know about your patients, but I have a right to know about this because it's affecting our family."

She had a point. Tom looked out the window to the hill. Leah and Allie had crawled out to wall up their secret place with pine needles.

"It's Leah," he said. "The way she's been acting since the party. It concerns me. A lot."

"I get that. I'd be lying if I said it didn't concern me too. But, Tom, she has a *friend* now. She talks to people. Okay, maybe not a lot, but more than she ever has. The only other person she'd ever be around besides us was Mabel, for crying out loud."

"She talked to Mabel because Mabel wasn't a threat."

"Exactly. We've been beating our brains trying to come up with a way to get her out of her shell, and she's finally doing it on her own. That concerns you?"

"No, it's the suddenness that concerns me. This sort of thing takes time in a person, Ellen. It's small steps. With Leah, it's like someone flipped a switch."

"Maybe someone did, Tom. Or something."

Here we go, he thought. Tom didn't think they could talk for long without getting to the heart of the matter, which was part of the reason he'd kept his distance in the hours since Ellen and the girls had returned home. There was no getting around it now. But Ellen was right. Their options were either to talk or to let things slide back into the hell that had taken them two months and a new home to get out of.

"You mean this imaginary friend she has?"

"What if he's not imaginary?" Ellen didn't look at him. Tom thought she was thinking much the same as he—*Here we go*. "What if he's real?"

"Are you serious?"

"Her paintings, Tom. They're not what a little girl does. They're not even what most *adults* do. And then there's Barney and his numbers."

"Barney's good fortune had nothing to do with Leah," Tom said. "You said that yourself. I'll give you that something's happened to her, but you saw that painting. There weren't any numbers there."

"But there are in the new one."

"Yes, Ellen, there are. And that's why I didn't want you and the girls taking it down there. What do you think is going to happen when everyone gets a look at that painting? How many people in this town are going to go right out and buy themselves a ticket, thinking they're going to end up like good old Barney? And what's going to happen when those numbers don't pan out? How are people going to treat her then?"

Ellen looked down at her hand, and Tom thought she knew exactly how people would treat Leah. She hadn't thought of that. She'd been so caught up in possibilities—however far-fetched—that she'd been blinded to the reality in front of her.

"Our daughter sees imaginary people," he said. "You said that was a common thing. But even if it is, she's nine. Doesn't that seem a little too old for that sort of thing to happen all of a sudden? That's what's been bothering me. That this rainbow man, this *thing* in her head, is a crutch because Leah's given up trying to walk on her own. That's why I reacted the way I did this morning. And as for Reggie, I just think a notion of God is *another* crutch. Maybe a worse one." Tom took Ellen's hand and spoke low and slow to signify the fuzzy line he was about to cross. "It's one that I've seen for a long while now at work, including Friday and yesterday."

Ellen nodded. Tears gathered in the corners of her eyes. She smiled a thank-you.

"I don't want my daughter limping through this life, Ellen. I want her to stand tall and big and make her own way. You've always been able to see the bright side of things. You're so quick to believe and so slow to doubt. I'm just the opposite. And I think that's fine, because it helps both of us see another side of life that might stay hidden. But I just want us to be on the same page with this, for Leah's sake."

"Okay," Ellen said. When she nodded, tears spilled out of her eyes. "But, Tom, you go looking for monsters in every corner. That's your job. Maybe in this case there aren't any. I want you to at least consider that. Maybe there's just some strange beauty here. If there is, I want you to be a part of it. Barney wants us to bring the girls over tonight. He says he has something special for them. Please come. For me, and for Leah."

Tom smiled and said, "Okay."

He wiped the tears from her cheek and let his hand linger there against lavender skin. Ellen took his hand in her own and kissed it, kissed him.

As Leah and Allie spoke of Higher Things beneath the pines, Tom and Ellen Norcross offered themselves to one another. It was just like those Sunday mornings long ago.

4

Barney could barely summon the energy to turn the sign in the window from AHOY, OPEN! to BLIMEY, CLOSED. He hadn't put in a full day of work in twenty years, and not even during the glory days had there been a day so full that the door remained open past dark. *Blessing upon blessing*, Barney thought. His day had come, and it was about time.

But of course all blessings carried with them a bit of cleanup in the end. Barney had no idea just how many people had traveled in and out of the Treasure Chest over the past twelve hours. Scraps of paper littered the floor. Lincoln Logs were mixed in with the building blocks. Signs had been knocked down and trampled upon. An errant knee had cracked the side of one of the dollhouses. Several of the smaller items in stock—toy cars and trucks mostly—were missing despite Mary's assurance that she'd sold none. Barney wondered what else had been stolen in all the busyness, and he wondered how much of that pilfering had been done by people who weren't from Away.

Mary had volunteered to stay over and straighten up, but Barney had sent her home with a hug, a word of thanks, and a request to remind Allie to stop by later. He would clean up, he said, and it would be a pleasure. He swept the floor and righted what his energy would allow. The rest would have to wait until tomorrow, which promised to be just as busy. *Blessing upon blessing.* Mabel sat in her wheelchair by the cash register. The day had been even harder on her than it had him. Her head was bent down and to the right so that her chin touched near her armpit. She'd been like that since Mary left. One of the pins holding back her silky hair had loosened, spilling a strand over her ear and into her eyes. Barney resisted the urge to both fix it and make sure Mabel could wake. She needed the rest.

Doc March would come calling in a while to check on her cough and prescribe something for the fever. Those pills would be paid for this time. Barney patted the chest pocket of his overalls and heard the crinkle of his ticket. Yessir, he'd pay for them. He'd pay for them and maybe buy the whole dadgummed pharmacy while he was at it. But in the meantime, he'd carry Mabel up the stairs and boil some Ramen noodles for supper.

Barney was about to wheel her to the steps when he remembered the cash register. It wasn't that he needed the money (another pat and crinkle reminded him of that), but he thought it proper to empty the drawer of its cash and checks anyway, if only because it would be full again tomorrow.

He cranked the lever and winced as the bell rang and the drawer slid open. Thankfully, Mabel continued her rest. Barney looked twice to make sure what he was seeing was real. He made one quick count of the money and then a slower one, careful to make sure that in all the rush Mary hadn't accidentally slipped a few hundreds and fifties in with the ones.

No. She hadn't.

The drawer held thirty-five dollars in cash and a little over seven in change. In the slot where the hundreds and fifties should have been, there was only a thick stack of white slips of paper.

In his two days of being the most blessed man in Mattingly (a fact Barney reminded himself that Leah said would carry on, he and Mabel would be fine now, fine like Job, who got blessed even more in the latter of his days than he'd been in the former), that was the first moment when Barney Moore considered that something was wrong. That perhaps Reggie had been right. He pulled the slips from the drawer and laid them out onto the counter.

He counted one hundred and fourteen of them.

"No, I don't believe it. That can't be. There's gotta be something else."

He said that to himself, to the God of Blessing, to Mabel. None of them answered. Barney's words echoed through the empty store, only to return to a hollow place deep inside himself. The outline of the mockingbird on Leah's painting reached through the page, as if its eye had been turned inward to Barney rather than outward down Second Street.

"No matter." He nodded his head to convince himself and found it helped take the sting out of the lie. "Ain't no matter at all, Mabel. Reckon I can't blame 'em, it bein' so close to the news conference an' all. It'll be okay. 'Sides, it ain't like we need the business anymore. Maybe I'll just retire for real this time. Do it on my own accord instead of havin' it forced on me. We gonna live in style now, Mabel. We can find us a vacation place down Carolina way along the shore an' finally get you to the ocean. That sound good to you?"

Mabel didn't say.

Barney stacked the slips and left them on the counter,

leaving the money in the drawer. He walked to Mabel, dis-engaged the brake on her chair, and guided her to the steps. One of the wheels rolled over a missed Lincoln Log, lolling her head forward. Barney stopped and walked around to her.

"Sorry about that, Mabel," he said. He caught a whiff of rotten air and wondered how long she'd been that way. "Don't you worry about that either. I'll get you cleaned up proper once we're upstairs. Okay, then?"

Barney smiled. Mabel did not.

"Mabel? Ready to go upstairs?"

He touched her on the shoulder and shook.

"Mabel, you with me?"

Mabel did not flutter her eyes. She did not speak an *ahh* or *eck*, did not play the organ in her thoughts. She did not say I love you.

"Don't fright me, now," Barney said. He tried to chuckle, hoping that would chase away the fear that had crept upon him. "These old bones can't take much more excitement for one day. Come on now, Mabel."

He shook her again. Then he reached out two shaking fingers and felt her neck for a pulse. Felt harder. He had a sudden urge to both scream and loosen his bladder.

Barney Moore called out for the God of Blessing, and the God of Cruelty answered. He ran for the phone in his shop. The only sounds were his lament and the hollow crinkle of the ticket in his pocket.

5

For the second time in as many days, Reggie ignored the BLIMEY, CLOSED sign in the Treasure Chest's window.

He'd brought along the spare key Barney had given him after Mabel's stroke but knew it wouldn't be needed. Barney likely hadn't locked his doors in years. Why should he? To most, there was nothing inside worth taking.

The door swung open with a push of his hand. Reggie paid no notice to the painted mockingbird that questioned him. As troubling as the events earlier that day had been, they paled to what was happening now. The town, the "magic," shrank against the sudden reminder of life's brittleness. Let the little girl paint all she wants. Let her *say* anything she wants. Because in the end, Barney Moore hadn't called Leah Norcross or the Virginia Lottery or some imaginary friend, he had called his pastor. He had called his pastor even before dialing 911.

The lamps were on, illuminating a clear path through the cluttered store. Mabel's wheelchair sat askance by the staircase like an empty figure robbed of its soul. Reggie walked past it without looking. He took the stairs two at a time to the apartment above—the knee was better now, though it was ringed by a deep purple bruise—and gathered what clothes he could find into a suitcase. A part of him whispered that he need not bother. But this was what his old friend had asked, and this was what Reggie would do. It was an act of faith. Reggie was trying to live the Word.

He was halfway down the stairs when headlights flooded the windows. An engine stopped. Four doors closed. Reggie opened the wooden door of the Treasure Chest to order the wolves away and instead saw Tom Norcross standing in front of him. His knuckles were pulled back, ready to knock.

"Reverend?" he asked. He looked at the suitcase in Reggie's hand. "What's going on?"

Ellen stood behind him with Allie and Leah. Allie offered a "Hey there, Preacher Goggins" that Reggie couldn't bring himself to return. Leah's head cocked to the side. She reached for Allie's hand.

"Mabel's at the hospital," Reggie said. "I'm afraid she's not well."

"Oh no," Ellen said.

"Barney called to ask if I'd run over here and pick up a few changes of clothes before I head over there. He needs me."

Tom asked, "Is there anything we can do?"

"I don't think so, but I appreciate that, Tom. I really do. I should get over there."

Reggie stepped through the doorway as Tom stepped aside. He was almost to the car when Leah said, "Wuh-we're cuh-coming too."

Tom looked at her. "No, Leah. I think we should just go home and wait. Barney will call as soon as he knows something. Or the reverend. You'll call, won't you, Reggie?"

"I will," he said, thankful that Leah's father had said what he did. It meant Reggie did not have to say it himself. A hospital was no place for a little girl. Besides, Barney had called *him*. "I promise you, Leah. I'll call as soon as I talk to the doctor."

"Nuh-no," Leah said. "We huh-have to cuh-come, Ruh-Reverend." She tugged at Tom's arm and pulled him down to her eyes. "We h-have to guh-go, Puh-Pops."

"Tom," Ellen said. She offered a look that said more than the silence that followed.

"Okay. But we should take Allie home first."

Reggie moved from his car toward them. "Tom, I really don't think that's a good idea."

"I ain't goin' home," Allie said, though Reggie thought every bit of her face said going home was the only thing she really wanted. "I'm goin' with Leah. She's got a job, and so do I."

Reggie tried again. He gently put a hand to Tom's elbow

and guided him away from the rest. "Please, Tom. I don't think Leah and Allie should go. Barney was frantic when he called. Mabel was unresponsive and barely breathing. I don't know how this is going to turn out. If it goes wrong, I don't want children there. It could scar them. You're a therapist, you have to understand what I'm saying."

"I do understand, Reverend. And any other time, I would agree with you." He looked back to Ellen, who had one hand upon Leah's and the other upon Allie's. Her eyes were closed. Likely petitioning the Universe, Reggie thought. "But not this time. I can't be a therapist right now. I owe it to my family."

Reggie's mind did its best to sort out the dozens of ways he wanted to reply to such an asinine statement, but there was no time.

"Do what you think right, Tom. But understand that I have a job to do, even if you don't agree with it. I don't want any trouble."

"There won't be."

Reggie led the way in his SUV, followed closely by Tom's truck. He spent the ride praying and listening for (but still not hearing) the Still Small Voice that would tell him everything would be fine. The interstate was sparsely traveled that time of night, making travel faster and the world seem emptier. The hospital glowed beneath a rising full moon just off the first Stanley exit.

Reggie found two empty spaces in the back corner of the first parking lot. The group walked through the automatic doors in silence. Tom spoke with a woman behind a sign that read Information. Allie made her way from Leah to Reggie's side and took his hand. In those moments when trouble comes, you cling to those you've known the longest. The elevator took them to the fourth floor and opened into a maze of hallways and doors.

"This way," Tom said.

They turned right and followed the sounds of ringing telephones and quiet beeps until the hallway opened into a cavernous waiting room. Barney sat in a vinyl chair along the wall with his face in his hands. His glasses hung loosely between his ring and pinky fingers. He looked up as Reggie approached.

"Rever—" Barney rose but couldn't finish the word. His voice choked against fear and sadness. Reggie opened his arms to catch him. "I ain't heard nothin'," he cried. "I's just been out here all alone. I been prayin', but I ain't hearin' nothin' back, Reggie. I ain't hearin' a thing."

"It's okay, Barney," Reggie said. He remembered the silence that had followed his own prayers. There was wisdom even in the silence, he reminded himself, however hidden it may be. "Why don't you sit down and rest."

He guided Barney down into the chair as a tiny hand reached out and touched the old man's arm.

"Huh-llo, Mr. Buh-Barney," Leah whispered.

Barney raised his head—"Oh, thank the Lord"—and wrapped his arms around Leah's tiny waist. Her arms stretched around him barely past the shoulders and held there. Allie, Tom, and Ellen gathered around them. "Is he with you, Leah? The Rainbow Man? Mabel's in bad shape. I couldn't *wake* her."

"He's huh-here, Mr. Buh-Barney."

Tom said, "Leah, please," before Reggie could.

Leah's lip trembled. Her eyes blinked and would not stop, as if something had wedged itself in them. Allie watched her rather than Barney.

"You've no word on her yet?" Ellen asked.

Barney shook his head.

The door behind them opened. A young man wearing scrubs and a stethoscope walked through. He studied the room before his eyes settled upon the person who looked most upset.

"Mr. Moore?" he asked.

Barney stood up and said, "Yes."

"I'm Dr. Cox. May I have a word with you?"

Barney looked at Leah, who was now so upset that she could offer him no help. Reggie put a hand on his shoulder and nodded. He guided Barney to the doctor and announced himself as the Moores' pastor.

"I'm afraid your wife arrived too late. We suspect she recently contracted a mild form of pneumonia. Given her previous condition and her advanced age, I'm sorry to say there's little we can do but make her comfortable. She's resting and somewhat alert. You should go to her."

The words connected like a punch. Barney swayed to his left. Reggie tried to brace him. Ellen began to cry.

"That ain't true," Barney said. He sobbed and shook. Tom left his family's side and took Barney's opposite arm. "My Mabel's gonna be all right. It's my day."

"You can come with me," the doctor said. "I'm very sorry."

I'm very sorry. Reggie knew what those words meant. Barney's act of faith had been for nothing. Mabel didn't need a change of clothes to come home in because she wouldn't be coming home.

He said, "I'll go with you, Barney. Come on now. Mabel needs us."

Barney took two steps after the doctor and stopped. He looked to Ellen and the girls and said, "Please come, Leah? Please bring Him?"

Leah took Allie's hand and stepped away from Ellen.

"No, Leah," Reggie said. He turned to Tom. "Please, Tom."

"I huh-have to guh-go," Leah said. "I huh-have to, Puh-Pops. Puh-please."

Dr. Cox regarded Leah and said, "Mr. Moore, I'm afraid time is of the essence."

Leah's father nodded.

The doctor showed them to Mabel's room and closed the door. The bed was surrounded by machines that measured her pulse and offered her liquid comfort—more numbness for the numbness she already felt. Barney swiped at his eyes and sat beside her, took her hand in his own. He brushed the white hair out of her eyes.

"Mabel?" he whispered. "I's here now, Mabel. Leah's here with me. She's brought the Rainbow Man an' Allie. Reggie's here too."

Mabel offered a quiet *ahh*. Her eyes searched the room and found Barney beside her. She smiled.

Reggie moved to her other side and said, "Hello, Mabel. I'm going to pray for you now, okay?" He took the hand that Barney did not hold.

"Hello, Miss Mabel," Allie managed. She and Leah remained by the door. Both fought back tears. "I'm so sorry you're not feeling well."

Leah whispered into Allie's ear. They crossed the few feet between the closed door and the hospital bed together, Leah in front and Allie a step behind. Reggie's heart broke at the sight of Allie's fearful eyes, this little girl whom he'd welcomed into the world only hours after her birth, whom he'd baptized into Christ's loving arms and played catch with during Bible school, and who now was marooned in the presence of death because of the misguided faith of her friend and the foolishness of that friend's father.

He turned back to Mabel and the task at hand. "'The Lord is my shepherd, I shall not want.'"

Mabel's eyes widened. Her mouth gaped open and her head rose. Barney drew back his hand, unsure what was happening, and said, "What's wrong, Mabel?"

"Ahh," Mabel said. She reached her hand outward. Her fingers danced in the air. "Ahhhh."

"'He maketh me to lie down in green pastures.'"

"Mabel," Barney said, "I's right here, Mabel. Right here with you, girl."

"'He leadeth me beside the still waters. He restoreth my soul.'"

"Mabel?" Barney asked. "Reggie, what's she doin'?"

Reggie knew, but he would not say. He felt the Presence in the room, flowing all around, shredding the thin veil between one world and the next.

"You huh-hear him, duh-don't you?" Leah asked. "Duh-don't you, Muh-Miss Mabel? You huh-hear the R-rainbow M-man's song."

"Ahhh."

Mabel's shoulders were now above the bed. Barney tried to ease her down. She pushed against him, reaching out, smiling. Laughing.

Reggie closed his eyes to gather himself and then looked at Leah. His voice was calm, yet he could not hide the anger behind his words.

"Please let me pray, Leah. This is no time for folly."

Leah did not look at him. "You huh-hear it, duh-don't you, Muh-Miss Mabel? Isn't it b-beautiful? It's the muh-most beautiful muh-music ever. It duh-doesn't even sound like muh-music at all."

Allie tried to pull Leah away, to reason with her, but the

Norcross girl stood firm. Barney tried again to ease Mabel back into the bed, and again he couldn't. He looked from her to Leah and back, helpless.

Reggie said, "'He leadeth me in the path of righteousness for his name's sake.'"

"Do you nuh-know why it sounds so struh-strange, Muh-Miss Mabel? It's buh-cause his suh-song doesn't have a buh-beat. There's no buh-beat, Muh-Miss Mabel."

"I'm going to have to ask you to leave, Leah," Reggie said. "I'm trying to care for Mabel's soul."

"I am tuh-too."

"Stop it," Barney said.

Reggie nodded, then realized Barney was looking at him.

"Leave her alone, Reggie. Leah's takin' care of this. She's gonna help Mabel."

Mabel sat up, her arms trembling, reaching out, as if gathering in a cool rain on a hot day. Tears tumbled down her cheeks.

"There's no buh-beat, Muh-Miss Mabel. There can only be a buh-beat if there's tuh-time, and the R-rainbow M-man lives in a place where tuh-time isn't. There's no before or luh-later, there's juh-just now."

Mabel wept. Her arms went limp and she slumped backward. Barney caught her and gently lowered his wife into bed.

Mabel looked at him with her still-weeping eyes and touched his face—"I love you," she said—as the bedside monitor wailed an alarm. The light went out of her eyes.

"Mabel?" Barney asked.

He shook her shoulder, trying to wake her as he had all those times before. Allie cried at the foot of the bed. Reggie tried to finish his prayer and found he could not. The door burst open as nurses rushed in. Barney kept shaking, kept telling her to wake up, wake up now Mabel I love you it's time to go home. He turned to Leah as the world fell down upon him.

"Miss Mabel?" Allie asked. Her face was a mixture of fear and confusion. She took a step away from her friend toward Reggie. "Help her, Leah. Help Miss Mabel get better. *Tell him to make her all better, Leah.*"

But Leah did not move. Her eyes were forward to the bed. Her throat quivered. In a strange and embarrassing moment Reggie would never confess to anyone, he thought it more important that Leah Norcross was about to throw up than that Mabel had just passed into the next world.

"You said it was all gonna be okay," Allie cried. "Why'd you lie, Leah? That wasn't fair."

Leah's face fell ashen. Her lips parted to speak and then closed. She swallowed hard and then ran from the room, leaving Allie behind.

Reggie was glad she was gone.

6

Allie just wanted to go home to her momma. She'd never seen anyone die before—had never seen any*thing* die, really, other than bugs and the time her daddy hit a deer on their way to the Longview Mall—and it was just as awful as she'd imagined. Never mind that Miss Mabel was at peace now, like Preacher Goggins said to Mr. Barney after all the nurses left. And never mind that Allie was pretty sure Miss Mabel got a glimpse of the Rainbow Man just before she closed her eyes one last time. Neither of those things mattered. All that mattered was that Allie wanted to go somewhere safe, and she never wanted to look upon the face of Death again.

So when Mr. Doctor and Miss Ellen had said let's take you home, Allie, she had thought yes, that would be just fine and please hurry. But then in the darkness of the backseat Leah had taken hold of her hand, and Allie knew the stiffness in her friend's grip was but a mere crumb of the sorrow she owned.

No, she'd told them, I'd really rather not go home. And she'd told them that Miss Mabel was up in heaven right now getting fitted with her crown of jewels and playing that wonderful music and having a grand old time. Allie wasn't surprised that the two people in the front seat had nothing to say to that. She figured spiritual-but-not-religious folk didn't hold such things as genuine. But that was okay. She'd said it mostly for Leah anyway.

So they'd driven back to the yellow Victorian, where Miss Ellen had called Marshall and Mary to tell them the news and make sure it was still okay for Allie to stay over. Marshall had given an immediate no but was eventually overruled by Mary, who'd said yes but wanted to talk to Allie first. That had been a trying give-and-take, what with Mary wanting to know how Allie really was while Leah stood right there next to her. They'd exchanged cheery-byes with the promise that Mary would pick her up first thing in the morning. Mr. Doctor offered the girls what Allie knew to be a free head-shrinking session, which was politely declined. It's hard to talk about a wound right after one is received. Right after, all you can do is feel it.

Allie wasn't surprised that the decor of Leah's bedroom was excessively girly, but she was surprised at the size. The room looked bigger than almost Allie's entire house. Leah's pictures were taped all over the walls. One of those fancy beds with four wooden poles and a sheet draped over the top rested against the nearest wall. The comforter on the bed was a faded and melancholy yellow, as was the pillow. An armoire that looked like it could lead to Narnia stood against the far wall beside a bare dresser. Leah even had her own desk. Pencils and notebooks were stacked neatly on top, the notebooks in a range of colors that had been sorted into rainbow order. A bowl of thumbtacks sat near. Their bathing suits were still draped over the desk chair dry and unused (they'd never gotten around to their dip in the pool). And there was the easel, sitting in the corner all by itself like some grand mystery.

The two of them sat on the bed for what seemed like hours. Allie watched the shadows cast by the small lamp at Leah's bedside and listened to the sawing of a thumbnail. She didn't know what to do or say, so she figured she'd just start with, "How come you didn't know all that was gonna happen, Leah?"

"What do you muh-mean?"

"All the other stuff that's happened, you might not've known exactly how it'd come to be, but you knew it would. But I saw your face when Preacher Goggins said Mabel's at the hospital, and then again when we walked into her room. You were scared. And I'm just not sure how you can be scared with the Rainbow Man at your side, singin' those songs so pretty that they make dyin' women cry and whatnot. And you *lied*, Leah. You told Mr. Barney things would be okay now. I don't know how I'd describe things right now, but I know I wouldn't say they were okay. So I just want to know how come."

Leah wouldn't answer at first, she just kept right on with her thumb. The way she was bent down low with her hair covering her face made Allie think of a fearful child left alone in a dark place. The thing was, Allie didn't know exactly what her friend was fearing. Was it that the Rainbow Man was keeping some things to himself, or was it something worse? Her thoughts wouldn't settle long enough to decide. Half of her mind was upon Mabel laughing and reaching out into the air, and the other half kept hearing her momma telling her to be careful now and watch what she believed in that little girl.

"He didn't tuh-tell me," Leah whispered. "He didn't tuh-tell me that was going to huh-happen, and he wuh-won't say why. Duh-don't you go disbelieving me nuh-now, Allie. I nuh-know what you're thuh-thinking. You're thuh-thinking that maybe thuh-things aren't what I suh-say they are."

"Mr. Barney thought you were gonna save her." Allie's head bent low as well. Even though her pigtails weren't enough to cover her face, she thought the shadows would hide the tears she grew. "I loved her."

"The R-rainbow M-man was suh-singing for her to c-come home," Leah said. "I thuh-thought that meant she'd guh-go back to the Truh-Treasure Chest, but I w-was wrong. I guess her h-home was suh-somewhere else. Do you buh-lieve me, Allie?"

Allie evaded that question by asking one of her own: "Do you think he's God, Leah? The rainbow man?"

Leah looked up at her. "You suh-say his name duh-different now. You don't suh-say it like before."

And maybe that was true. Maybe before the rainbow man was a person, and now he was becoming just an idea.

"Puh-Pops says God isn't ruh-real. He doesn't buh-lieve in the Maybe. Muh-Mommy thinks she duh-does, but she duh-doesn't really. I think buh-lieving is like luh-love. If you buh-lieve in everything, thuh-then it's like buh-lieving in nuh-nothing at all. I'm not supposed to nuh-know those things, but I duh-do." Leah let go of her thumb long enough to wipe at her eyes. She pushed back her hair and looked at an empty place on the floor. "But if God's r-real, then I hope He's luh-like the Rainbow Man."

"Well, I say God is real, and I wouldn't give two nickels to anyone who says else. Even if it's your daddy, if you don't mind me sayin'. I just don't know if the God I believe in is the same one you're lookin' at." Allie looked at the same empty spot. "You look me in the eye, Leah Norcross, and you tell me he's standin' right there lookin' at us."

Leah did and said he was. "And he's not luh-looking, he's smiling."

"Is Miss Mabel there too?"

"No, she's huh-home now."

Allie shook her head. She was willing to accept on faith that God Himself could be standing there in front of her. Anything was possible, and she thought that might be the Maybe that Leah kept citing. Yes, anything was possible. Especially in Mattingly, where one and one sometimes equaled three and where other magic had gone on in the beforetime. Allie wasn't supposed to discern those things, but she thought that was much like Leah not being supposed to discern that her daddy didn't believe and her momma just pretended to and that faith was like love. Some things, kids just knew.

"Does he ever talk about me?" she asked.

"Yuh-yes. He loves you, Allie. He wants you to nuh-know that. He thinks you're a-a-awesomesauce."

Believer or not, that made Allie smile. She looked at the bathing suits draped over the chair. The idea that came was an odd one, but then, everything seems odd after you've been wounded.

"Do you trust me, Leah?"

"Yuh-yes."

"You think your folks are sleepin', or do you think they're bickerin' quiet?"

"Th-they're sleeping," Leah said. "They were kind tonight.

I think it's suh-sad that some people only act nuh-nice when muh-mean things happen."

"Then let's get our bathin' suits on."

Leah did so without question. They changed out of their pajamas and eased out into the hallway—Leah careful to point out where to walk so the floorboards wouldn't creak—then made their way into the backyard. The night was clear and lit by a full moon that looked like a giant Chinese lantern hung in the sky. Allie led her to the inflatable swimming pool by the shed.

"He here too?"

"Yuh-yes," Leah said. "Right beside us."

"Good. Because I don't know if this'll stick or not, or even if it'll mean anything, but I reckon it's worth a try. I don't know what's goin' on here or what's gonna happen, but I figure you'll need some protection. You know, just in case."

Allie stepped into the middle of the pool, which was little more than a puddle of cold water that barely touched the midpoint between her ankles and knees. "I'm gonna baptize you, Leah Norcross."

Leah looked at the pool and then to Allie. "What's that muh-mean?"

"It means I'm gonna call down the Spirit on you. It's kinda like bein' born twice. Like a do-over, I guess. It means you love God and you want everybody to know it."

"But I duh-don't know who God is."

"I think you maybe do. I think you maybe do more than anybody in this town. Now I ain't gonna force this on you, 'cause Preacher Goggins says forcin' God on unbelievin' folk is plain wrong. So I'll ask you this—do you love the Rainbow Man?"

"Yuh-yes."

"And do you believe him?"

"Yuh-yes."

"And will you do all the stuff he says to do, even if it's stuff that hurts?"

"I already h-have."

Allie didn't know why, but that answer made the backs of her eyes burn. She lowered her head and said, "Okay then, come on in here and let me dunk you."

Leah stepped into the pool. Allie tried to position her in the same way Preacher Goggins did the new believers in the dunking pool behind his pulpit. She managed that, but then found another problem.

"The water's too shallow. I reckon we'll have to get down on our knees." She placed Leah in front of her, Allie facing ahead toward the side of the yard and Leah facing the hill where they first met. The water splashed as they sank down and gave Allie the shivers despite the warm night. She took a deep breath and stared at the sky.

"Lord, this here's Allie. Leah's with me now. You know Leah, since I figure you mighta sent her a Rainbow Man. He's here too, I reckon, though I don't know where and I don't wanna break Leah's concentration by askin' her. I'm gonna be baptizin' her now. I don't know if it'll take, but I figure it'll do till we can find a proper preacher who ain't mad at her." She looked from the sky to Leah. "Don't be afraid now."

Moonlight shone on Leah's face. Her cheeks were twitching, and her hands shook. "I-I-I'm nuh-not," she said.

"Okay then. Leah Norcross, do you believe?"

Leah nodded.

"You gotta speak it, Leah."

"I buh-lieve."

Allie couldn't remember what came next, so she asked the question again. "Do . . . you . . . *believe?*"

"I BUH-BUH . . . LIEVE."

"Then, Leah Norcross, in the name of God and Jesus and the Rainbow Man and the Holy Ghost, which might all be the same thing but I don't know for sure and I'm sorry for that, I'm baptizin' you right now."

Allie took hold of the back of Leah's head with one hand and squeezed her nose with the other. Leah let out a muffled squeal, to which Allie whispered, "Don't worry, I got ya." She sank her friend's rigid body into the pool and stopped when Leah's head hit the bottom.

"Uh-oh."

"Wh-what uh-oh?" Leah asked.

"You ain't all the way under. I don't know if that means anything or not. Preacher Goggins always says you gotta get all wet."

"Wh-what do we do nuh-now?"

"I don't know. Roll around a few times and make sure you're all covered."

Leah rolled over in the pool, rolled over again, then rolled a third time to make sure water touched her everywhere. Allie took hold of her shoulder and said, "Down with the old girl, and get up with the new."

She raised Leah out of the water. Long strands of dark hair clung to her face and neck. Bits of grass and drowned bugs stuck to her skin. But Allie noticed her friend was smiling for the first time since their awful night began. Whether the baptism would stick or not, that was good enough for her.

"Feel better?" she asked.

Leah nodded. "I luh-love you, Allie."

"I love you too, Leah."

She brushed the hair from Leah's eyes. Shadows gathered over her face like flakes of black snow that fell diagonally rather than down. First one, then two, then more than Allie could count. She reached out to touch Leah's face just as Leah reached for her own.

"What's wruh-wrong with your fuh-face, Allie?" she asked.

The shadows weren't just on their faces. They were on the surface of the water and the sides of the swimming pool. They were in the grass and on the shed and arcing over the side of the house. Everywhere.

A cloud emerged from the edges of the lantern moon so thick that it nearly snuffed the light. Allie thought it was growing but then realized it was merely getting closer. Moving. Moving *fast*. It stretched out and thinned like a long finger and then swooped down upon them. Allie tried to scream and found her voice taken. Gray and white swirled around them like a rippling current, a dance that was at once violent and beautiful and hypnotic.

"What are they?" Allie asked.

"The-they're muh-mockingbirds."

The birds gathered in a single funnel that surrounded them. The air was silent but for the flapping of wings. A hot wind stirred Leah's hair. Hundreds—thousands—of tiny eyes sparkled in the moonlight. The mockingbirds rose upward over the trees, suspended in the night as if one body, and then they bloomed outward and spilled over town.

7

Leah sat at the end of the sofa in his office. A ball of thick tissues rested against her nose but could not stem the tears. They trickled down the ridges and valleys of the mottled bruises on her face. She wept, her body shuddering, and uttered,

I'm suh-so suh-sorry.

You don't have to apologize for anything here, Leah. Have you given any thought to what we discussed last week?

I'm a-a-afraid.

I know.

Do you th-think the R-rainbow M-man is puh-punishing me f-for the things I cuh-can't buh-lieve? Do you thuh-think that's what he's duh-doing, Puh-Pops?

No, Leah, I don't. I just think you're hurt. I'm going to help you.

You c-can't help me if you don't buh-lieve, Puh-Pops. That's j-just it. You c-can't under—"

The scream was in the back of Tom's throat when he woke. He heaved in air and jerked. Beside him, Ellen slept. He wanted to wake her but didn't. She would want to know what had frightened him so, and he would have to tell.

He stared at the ceiling instead, telling himself it was okay, everything was okay, everything was fine.

Outside the window, a mockingbird called.

Wednesday

Three Days Before the Carnival

1

The door struck the stop on the wall behind with a *thunk*, the force swinging it back as if to say move along, nothing to see in here, BLIMEY, CLOSED.

Barney pulled the wheelchair from the entranceway before the door bumped it. His mouth opened to say, *Sorry 'bout that, Mabel, reckon I gotta mind my own strength*, but only "Sorry 'bout" came across his lips. The chair was empty. Why was he out in the hallway with Mabel's chair?

From downstairs came what sounded like a voice but was most likely wind. Barney rubbed his head and entered the still-dark living room. Spots of colors appeared in front of his eyes—swimming first, then flashing, wobbling his knees. He was not conscious of moving to the sofa, did not feel the pinch of settling onto the broken spring. Feeling and motion had become as involuntary as breathing and heartbeat—there, but not so much as to be noticed.

He wondered how he'd managed to drive the old Dodge home, didn't remember doing it, then remembered Reggie had brought him. Reggie had brought them both.

Is that right?

Yes, he reckoned. That's what happened. Reggie had driven them home. Good old Reggie, who had prayed the Twenty-Third Psalm and smiled right along with Leah and Allie when the doctor announced Mabel was just fine after all.

Is that right?

The part of his mind that worked Barney's heart and breaths whispered, *Yes, that's right.* And then Reggie had said he would take them home, and Reggie was . . . where? Downstairs. Yes. Right. Because Barney had said he—no, *they*, he and Mabel—needed to get settled first. But where was Mabel? Had Barney already settled her? Had he been in the hallway to fetch Reggie?

Through the open windows, waning moonlight merged with waxing dawn. A mockingbird called from a nearby rooftop. Hoary shadows splayed upon the decaying walls, giving the room a dormant glow. To Barney it felt as if the very façade of the world was slipping away, leaving him to straddle the cleft between flesh and spirit. The wheelchair seemed more an It than a thing.

The lights remained off. Another voice in Barney's mind whispered they should be on (*Only a foolish old man traipses about in the dark*, that voice said), but this was one act Barney would not allow his body to perform without him. The lights might wake Mabel

(Is that right?)

and he did not want to do that just yet. She'd had a long night. Besides, the good voice, the one that had gotten him from the hospital to outside the door, cautioned that lights would bring brightness, brightness would bring clarity, and clarity would bring a truth he may not want to allow. Barney preferred the darkness just now, that state bereft of bold lines and right angles to tell him what was there and what wasn't. In the shadows nothing was ever really lost. Things were only hidden, and things never changed.

But things have changed, the bad voice said.

Barney called out, "Mabel?" in the way he always had. Both voices claimed victory when no one answered. One said it was because there was no one *to* answer. The other said that Mabel seldom answered at all so early in the morning. She had always been a deep sleeper, especially since her troubles. Not like Barney, who was always up with the birds.

"I love you, Mabel."

A flicker in the corner caught his eye. Barney turned to see a flashing *14* on the answering machine. He tried to remember the phone ringing that many times and couldn't, then decided the calls must have come while Leah had been healing Mabel. His finger moved to the Play button and froze when the good voice cautioned, *Don't you go doin' that, Barney, you might not like what you hear.* The wheelchair stared at him. It glowed in that alive way that Leah's easel had. That had been four days earlier, and one day before she'd said he and Mabel were going to be just fine. Sitting alone in the shadows, Barney decided that was right. Leah had been touched by God, and they had both made his wife well, just as Mabel hadn't answered because she'd always been a deep sleeper.

The voices devolved from arguing to shouting. Barney thought he could chase them both away if he'd just check the bedroom. He could show the bad voice Mabel, curled up beneath the sheets. Then he could lie down and drape his arm across her—for warmth, yes, but also to make sure those lungs were working—and he could wake her proper. He could shake her lightly and whisper, and he could once more behold the precious gift of seeing her eyes meet his and hearing "I love you" from her lips.

He heard shuffling downstairs. What could that be? Barney chuckled as the absurd thought of Reggie flashed in his mind. What would the preacher be doing downstairs at this hour? He rose from the sofa and walked down the small hallway. Both voices and the hoary shadows accompanied him. He paused at the bedroom doorway and wondered why he was afraid.

Mabel was curled into a ball beneath the sheets. Her knees were drawn upward to her chest as though nurturing the small ember of life her body still possessed. Gray and orange mixed through the open windows. Barney moved to the side of the bed and eased himself in.

"Mornin', Mabel," he whispered.

She did not move. The shadows around her shimmered as if she too straddled the cleft between flesh and spirit.

"Hey there. Time to get up now."

She'd always been a deep sleeper. Barney listened for the good voice to agree, but the only sounds were the sudden heavy thumping of his heart and a mockingbird outside. The lottery ticket crinkled in his pocket as he reached for Mabel's shoulder.

Barney's hand closed around shadow.

"Mabel?"

His hand searched the cold, unwrinkled sheets where she'd lain, feeling for her, willing her to come back. The mockingbird sang that Mabel could not. Would not. It sang that Mabel was in a place where there is no before or later but only now, and it was a fair land without shadow.

"But that ain't so," he cried.

Gray surrendered to orange as morning struck the window.

The only bit of Mabel left was a lone strand of silver hair on her pillow. Barney felt the chest pocket of his overalls and drew out what was inside. The mockingbird fell silent as the piece of paper was crushed and dropped to the floor. Barney took the strand of hair with two fingers and, minding his own strength, carefully placed it into his chest pocket.

The good voice spoke a final time in the tongue of more shuffling from the floor beneath him. In that small fragment of the human heart where lies are spun to ensnare truth, Barney believed that sound was Mabel waiting for him downstairs. He did not pause to hear if that was right. He ran, shouting Mabel's name, saying he was coming, that everything would be just fine.

2

The hard task of spreading the news of Mabel's death fell to Reggie, and his first call was to Brent Spicer. Five in the morning wasn't early for the deacon, as Brent started milking his cows two hours earlier. The conversation was going as well as could be expected. Brent was a good man, but his thoughts lived in a world of sunshine and fretted about the shadows.

Reggie told Brent he wasn't sure if Mabel's passing was judgment for Barney's foolish act or grace for her own condition or simply another part of the Mystery. No, there had been no discussion of a funeral date. There had been no discussion of anything, really. Poor Barney'd been in such a state that he hadn't accepted what had happened. It had taken Reggie nine full hours to convince his old friend it was time to go home.

"Lemme know," Brent said. "I'll pass word through the prayer line."

"Thanks, Brent. I'll give you a call when Barney's worked things out."

Reggie hadn't mentioned Leah and didn't say that Mabel's passing would have gone much smoother had the Norcross girl not been there. Five generations of Spicers were buried in a small corner of Brent's farm beneath stone crosses; he did not approve of people from Away, especially when those people went about speaking false prophecy and conjuring spirits.

From upstairs came "I love you, Mabel," and Reggie heard a sorrow and a fear in the voice.

He gripped the banister and took two steps before pausing. Let the man grieve, Reggie told himself. Outside, a mockingbird sang its night song as morning neared. Reggie couldn't remember wanting to say good-bye to a day more than the one finally slipping away around him. He spent the next moments helping as he could by straightening the mess left over from yesterday's business. Leah's painting hung in the window. Reggie tried to ignore it and found he couldn't.

A stack of papers sat by the register. Reggie recognized them as the ones Barney had handed out to Allison Summers and the man with the holey pockets. He put the broom down and went to the counter. There were at least a hundred of the slips, all in a pile almost as thick as Reggie's fist. He took one off the top and turned it over, turned over the next, then shuffled through the remainder.

They were all work orders. Not for marble rollers or dollhouses or wagons, but for easels.

"Oh, Barney," he whispered.

From the top of the stairs came shouts of "Mabel, I's comin'! Ever'thing's gonna be just fine."

Reggie placed the papers back onto the counter and ran.

He reached the mouth of the staircase and held his hands out, fully aware of the uselessness of that gesture. If Barney kept running, the only thing that would likely stop him would be the window. A brief thought passed through Reggie's mind that doing so might not be such a bad thing. That would at least take care of Leah's painting, even if the damage from that had likely already been done.

"Barney, it's me. It's Reggie."

Barney stopped. His body was turned to the side, his feet on successive steps. His face was red with tears, eyes wide and searching. It was as if he'd just awakened into a nightmare.

"Reggie?" he breathed. "I left Mabel down here, I think. After you . . ."

Reggie tried to settle himself. "After I what, Barney?"

"Mabel?" he called.

"After I what? Remember, Barney?"

"Mabel, where are you?"

Reggie took one step up and tried a quick prayer to summon the Still Small Voice. All he received was more mockingbird from somewhere outside. He placed his hand upon the banister and slid it upward until it rested on Barney's.

"Barney, she's passed. Do you remember that? She passed last evening."

"What? No, she—"

"Yes," Reggie said.

Barney shook his head. "She ain't dead, Reggie. I seen her upstairs."

"She's better now. Mabel's sitting at the Lord's Table."

"No, she's sittin' in *bed*, Reggie. But then I lost her an' I cain't find her no more." His eyes darted through the store and settled on Leah's painting. "Help me find her, Reggie."

"Barney, let's have a seat, okay?" Reggie squatted down

and kept his eyes on the old man. "That's it, come on down here a minute."

Barney's knees popped as he sat. Aside from the mockingbird, there was no sound. No movement. Reggie waited until Barney understood. They were alone—he and Reggie and no one else. No one.

"She gone," Barney whispered. "Ain't she, Reggie?"

Reggie nodded.

"Leah didn't help her."

"No."

"The Rainbow Man let her die."

"Barney, there's no—"

"Why didn't she help, Reggie? Leah always liked Mabel so."

"Leah couldn't help her, Barney. Her life's a dark one, so she had to go make a fantasy to make things brighter. That's what I've been trying to tell you. There's no magic to that little girl, just heavy sadness."

"But her pictures," Barney said. He pointed to the one in the window that he hadn't run through. "And my numbers, Reggie. She painted my numbers."

"No one else saw those numbers, Barney. I don't know what happened or how you won, but I still say it had nothing to do with faith. I saw those work orders over there on the counter. I know what they're for. It's all false hope, Barney. You succumbed to it, and because of Leah, everybody else is succumbing to it too."

Reggie knew those were hard words at a hard time. There was no easy way in this life, just hardness and the Mystery. It had always been like that. It always would.

"There's numbers on her new painting," Barney said, and that was true. The sunshine through the windows proved it—34720625, spilling out from the bird's beak.

"Yes," Reggie said. "But trust my words, Barney, those numbers will fall down on this town like a hard rain."

Barney's head fell into his hands. Soft sobs echoed through the aisles. He looked up and said, "She said my day's come. We'd be all right now. Leah's been lyin' all along, ain't she?"

"I think you two just fell into something, Barney. I don't know what that something is, but it's not what Leah says it is. She ain't Christian, Barney. She's a lonely girl. And she breaks my heart despite my anger."

"We gotta do somethin'," Barney said. "I don't want her hurtin' anyone else like she hurted me."

Reggie patted Barney's knee.

"Don't you worry about that. We'll quiet her down. I'll start on that today."

3

It wasn't the mockingbird that had kept Allie awake all night, though the incessant warbling hadn't made things easier. It was the noises from the bed above.

She and Leah had snuck back inside and dried themselves off just after the mockingbirds left. Even in the heat of the night, their skin was freckled with goose pimples and their teeth chattered. It was the magic, Allie remembered thinking. The Maybe had sucked all the warm out of the air and left them hunched over and prostrate as if in God's presence. Which, Allie figured, had maybe been the case.

Leah had offered Allie the bed. Sleeping there had seemed almost like a fairy tale, but such notions had given way to the manners Allie had been taught. Allie willingly took the floor. The four-poster's fluffy yellow comforter made a surprisingly soft mattress. When Leah added three pillows, the result had been more than on par with Allie's bed at home. They'd settled, then—as settled as two girls who'd watched someone die and a bunch of birds fly out of the moon could be, anyway. The house was quiet except for the one mockingbird still calling outside.

"Are you okay?" Allie had whispered.

"Yuh-yes," Leah had answered back. "Thuh-thank you for that, Allie. Even though I duh-don't feel much duh-different and I'm still scuh-scared."

Allie had replied that she was scared too, though she hadn't known why. "I'm glad Miss Mabel's up in heaven, but I'm sad Mr. Barney has to stay down here. He's got Pastor Reggie, though. And us, he's got us for sure. And I bet Pastor Reggie's already told him that Mabel's sittin' at the Lord's dinner table. He likes to say that to people, and I like to hear it. It makes me feel good that people are eatin' and havin' a good time up yonder. Don't you think so, Leah?"

"I guh-guess."

They'd said nothing more. Allie had tried to close her eyes and find sleep, but she found pictures on the other side of her eyelids; Mabel saying *I love you* and Mr. Barney fussing over his wife like he always had. That was the way Allie hoped Zach Barnett would treat her one day. She also hoped to still be walking and going to the bathroom on her own when that day came.

It was around one in the morning when Leah had started her talking. It was mumbling at first, sounds rather than words.

Allie heard "Are you shuh-sure?" and "Nuh-no" and "I duh-don't want to." "I'm tuh-tired." "Wuh-will you help?" Once Leah had leaned over the edge of the bed to make sure Allie was sleeping. Allie let out a snore that convinced Leah to resume her business. The speaking had gone on for about an hour until it finally died down. From then on, the only talk had been from the mockingbird outside.

Allie's momma often said this was a strange world, and trying to make sense of it would only drive a mind crazy. That hadn't been enough to stop Allie from trying to make sense of it anyway. Besides, if she couldn't make sense of things and her mind went all Humpty Dumpty, Mr. Doctor could put it all back together again before breakfast. Allie thought long and hard until the first rays of the sun poked up from behind the mountains and finally chased the mockingbird away. By then, the only conclusion she'd drawn was that her momma was right.

Allie pushed the doubled-over comforter back and went to Leah's desk, where she collected a sheet of paper and a red crayon. She pulled the comforter over her so that only a sliver of light passed through the bottom. A vertical line went down the center of the page. At the top left Allie wrote *Leah's lying*. At the top right, *Leah's telling the truth*.

"Okay, so there's Mr. Barney gettin' rich," she whispered. She wrote that on the right side of the page. "That's gotta be truth, since it happened. And then there's her second picture, the one with the birds, and she knew about Zach lovin' on me at her party." Two more for the home team. "Miss Mabel." Allie chewed the end of the crayon on that one, then reluctantly wrote it to the left of the vertical line and whispered, "Sorry, Leah, but you just kinda blew that one."

The score was three to one. Not bad, Allie thought, but not good either. Once she factored in the opinions of the people she trusted, things got worse. Allie knew her momma and daddy didn't really believe everything Leah was saying, even if they hadn't come right out and said it. Preacher Goggins *definitely* didn't. That put Leah a run behind. Mr. Doctor didn't believe (Allie didn't think he believed much of anything), and suddenly *Leah's lying* was up by two. Though Leah had said Miss Ellen thought she believed but didn't really, Allie scribbled her name in the *Leah's telling the truth* column anyway, just to make things closer. And there was Mr. Barney too. If anyone believed in Leah and the Rainbow Man, it was Mr. Barney. But that was after he'd won a bajillion dollars and before he lost Miss Mabel, and Allie didn't know what he thought now or if the hurt let him think anything at all. She wrote his name to the right anyway.

"We have a tie ball game, folks," Allie whispered. The air under the comforter was hot and stale. Allie began to sweat. "Bottom of the ninth, and that means . . ."

Allie didn't finish, didn't have to. Because it was a tie ball game, and the only person left to bat was herself.

One day ago Allie's would have been the first name written under *Leah's telling the truth*. Allie, who had stood on top of the fancy banquet table in the middle of the park on carnival week with fists raised, ready to pounce on any one of the townspeople or reporters who dared get near her frightened friend. Who had gone down to the Treasure Chest not once but twice to deliver Leah's holy paintings. (Or *holey*, Allie's mind said.) Who'd even taken Leah out into the backyard and washed her in the blood, and if that wasn't faith, Allie didn't know what was. But now, under the big blanket where only Allie and the first tendrils of sunshine dwelt, there came doubt. Not a lot, but certainly some. And even that little some was enough to frighten her, because that doubt came in the form of Mr. Barney sitting beside his fading wife believing Leah was going to make everything better.

In the end, all the pretty paintings and all the magical

numbers and all the birds from the moon didn't matter. No God was worth serving who was good at parlor tricks but bad when it came to what mattered. For Mr. Barney, all that had mattered was Miss Mabel.

Allie's hand went to the left beneath Mr. Doctor's name. Then to the right beneath Mr. Barney's.

Leah moved in the bed above. There was a sniff and then a yawn. Allie quickly folded her sheet of paper and tucked both it and the crayon into her pajamas.

"Huh-hey," Leah said. "Are you awake?"

"Yeppers," Allie said.

"Duh-did you sleep?"

"Like a log. I didn't hear you talkin' at all. You?"

"Kuh-kinda," Leah said. She rubbed her eyes and pushed her long hair behind her ears. "Thuh-thank you for last nuh-night. I feel buh-better now."

"I'm glad."

"Your mom will buh-be here suh-soon. I think I hear Muh-Mommy up. Puh-Pops will be up soon t-too. He should stuh-stay here, but I thuh-hink he's going to wuh-work."

"Sorry," Allie said. She wondered if her daddy would go to work too and decided he probably wouldn't. Mr. Barney would have to start getting his affairs in order. That's what people did when their loved one died. Allie didn't know what that meant, but she knew it often involved a lot of help. "Maybe you should ask him to stay."

"I've truh-tried that. The R-rainbow M-man says Puh-Pops is trying to fuh-find his way."

Allie tried to smile. "I reckon we're all tryin' to do that just now. C'mon, let's get up. I'll talk to your daddy if you want me to."

"Thuh-hanks."

Leah smiled, and with that Allie Granderson embraced once again her role of Guide to the Higher Things. She decided it wasn't because Leah had said the Rainbow Man wanted her to, but because it would be what God expected. And though she hadn't gotten the chance, Allie told herself that her name would go into the *Leah's telling the truth* column after all. She told herself that she was still young enough to believe in the magic. That she could see it even if others could not, woven into the slender threads that held the world together.

4

Tom stared at the ceiling and watched as light crept through the open window to his right. He didn't have a doubt in the world that he could lie there all day. He could watch the sun slowly arc from right to left as the yellow turned to orange and finally to red, signaling the end of the day. He could. He almost did. But in the end, he swung his feet out and over the bed.

It took courage to face this world. Tom knew that truth well—call it the second commandment of the Gospel according to Dr. Thomas Alan Norcross, surpassed only by *A good marriage is built upon a solid foundation of communication*. It was a statement drilled into the minds of every patient, followed by his or her first name to make it sound unique and personal: "It takes courage to face this world, _____." But Tom also knew there were days when the urge to wave the white flag was so deep and overwhelming that doing so seemed not only right, but good.

He rubbed his eyes and thought this would be one of those days. Knew it, just as he knew what was waiting for him on the other side of the closed bedroom door—more guilt, more misunderstanding. More pain. All things that would be easier to bear on the other side of a decent night's sleep. But sleep hadn't come to Tom last night, nor to Ellen. There had been too much Barney, too much Mabel. There had been no talk between them of what had happened that night or what would happen the following day, no mention of Leah and the look on her face when she came running from Mabel's room. There had just been the mockingbird and the nightmare.

Courage, he told himself.

He showered, shaved, and donned a pair of gray slacks and a white polo shirt that was much more comforting to his patients than to himself. The mirror showed the truth of all he tried to hide—the sunken face, the bloodshot eyes, the unnamable weight. From the hallway came the now-familiar *thunk, thunk, thunk* of Leah's plastic chair that meant it was time for breakfast.

Tom smiled the best he could as he came down the hallway. Ellen busied herself in the kitchen. Leah and Allie were already at the table with the plastic blue-and-yellow chair between them. Both girls were still in their pj's. Neither yawned, though Allie looked a bit droopy. Understandable, he thought. For not the first time in the last eight hours, Tom pondered the foolishness of allowing the girls into Mabel's room.

"Morning," he said.

"Hi, Puh-Pops," Leah answered. She eyed his clothes. "Say hi to the R-rainbow M-man."

"Hi to the rainbow man," he muttered.

"You look awful snappy, Mr. Doctor Norcross," Allie offered. She looked across the table to Leah and smiled. "Whatcha doin' today, mowin' the yard?"

Ellen spoke from the kitchen in a voice that was tired and flat: "It's Wednesday, Allie, which means Tom has to work."

She turned back to flip the pancakes on the stove. "Isn't that right, Tom?"

"I'm afraid so," he said.

There was nowhere he could look without facing some degree of either hurt or disgust—Ellen's back was still to him, Leah had donned her puppy-dog eyes, and Allie simply scowled as if she smelled something rotten.

Leah said, "Muh-Mommy, can you come help m-me pick out some clothes?"

"Can't it wait until after breakfast?" Ellen asked. "It's almost ready, and Allie's mom will be here soon."

"Puh-please?"

Ellen turned and met Leah's eyes. Tom was sure that what came next was evidence of the telepathic bond between mother and daughter, because then Ellen said, "Sure, let's go. Pops has plenty of time until he leaves. Isn't that right, Pops?"

Tom knew he didn't have a choice. And he did have time. Meagan's appointment wasn't for another hour and a half.

"Coming, Allie?" Ellen asked.

"No'm," Allie answered. "I reckon I'll just sit here and parlay with Mr. Doctor, if he don't mind."

Tom smelled a trap. The way Allie smiled, arms crossed in front of her, told him as much.

"That would be fine," he said. "I'd love to parlay with you, little Allie."

Ellen and Leah headed down the hall. Allie offered a wink as Tom took his seat at the table. That was fine. He had a few questions to ask Allie as well.

Allie leaned back and stretched. Slivers of sunshine fell onto the table from the slats between the blinds. The rainbow man's seat glowed. There was a brief but powerful moment when Tom realized the reasons behind his hatred of that chair.

Leah had placed it—and therefore the rainbow man—directly opposite him, as if challenging Tom's place as head of the family. The notion seemed ridiculous on the surface (not to mention more than a little childish), but Tom hung on to it nonetheless.

"So," she said. "Goin' to work today."

"Yep."

Allie nodded. "That's good. Miss Ellen's pancakes sure do smell fine, huh?"

"They do," Tom said. Whether it was the weariness that came from lack of sleep or the sort that came upon a person slowly, his patience began to wane. "Is this what you call a parlay, Allie? Because I've never had one."

Allie leaned back and looked down the hallway. "I'm supposed to be tellin' you how bad it is to go to work when Leah's hurtin' so. You know, 'cause we watched Miss Mabel pass and all. And I don't mind sayin' she's right."

"Okay," Tom said, "point taken. But it takes courage to face this world, Allie. Some people don't have that courage. It's my job to help them find it."

"I think you can live life just fine without courage." Her arms untangled themselves from in front of her and spread out onto the table. She touched the spots where the sunlight settled as if they were petals on a flower. "I ain't scared of nothin', mind you. But Leah is. I think Leah's scared of most things. But she has faith, Mr. Doctor. I don't think you need courage so much as you need faith. That makes the difference."

"Maybe so," Tom said. He thought he may have been right about Allie Granderson all along—she'd make a fine counselor.

"Anyway, I done chatted about that now. I know you're goin' to work no matter what I say. So I reckon we can move along to the real reason I wanna talk."

"Which is?"

Another look down the hallway. "If I show you something, we'll have that thing where you can't tell nobody, right?"

"You mean confidentiality?"

"Yeah. That. Right?"

"Sure," Tom said, and for a moment the questions he had for little Allie Granderson went away. His hand went to his chin.

Allie reached into the waistband of her pajamas—pink with the faces of several smiling Disney princesses; Tom would never have thought that was Allie Granderson's style— and pulled out a folded sheet of paper. She passed it to him beneath the table as if committing treason.

"What's this?"

"Just look at it."

Tom unfolded the piece of paper. Every crinkle made Allie's eyes blink toward the hallway. On the page was a line and a list of names and events, each placed under two catego- ries. It would have been cute had it not been so serious. And, considering the look on Allie's face, so damning.

"When did you do this?" Tom asked.

"This morning. I didn't sleep much."

"Me neither," he said. "Why are you showing me this, Allie?"

"Because you care for hurtin' people," Allie said, "and there's a hurtin' person in your house. Maybe two, 'cause I think Miss Ellen is sad about somethin'. And you don't seem so happy either, Mr. Doctor, if you don't mind me sayin'. But I think Leah's hurtin' most of all, and I'm worried for her." She looked at the plastic chair and back. "I don't know if God's in that chair, sir. He might be. But I reckon He might not. And after last night with Miss Mabel . . ."

There was Tom's opening. He pounced before Allie could say more.

"What happened at the hospital last night, Allie?"

She didn't answer. Tom moved a hand over hers and squeezed.

"I didn't want to let either of you go in there," he said. "I could explain why I did anyway, but I doubt it would make much sense. As soon as you two went back, I knew it was a mistake. And then when Leah came running out, she looked so scared. So . . ." Another squeeze. ". . . small."

"Mr. Barney thought the Rainbow Man was gonna make Mabel all better," Allie said. "Because of what Leah said before, about them bein' okay now. But Mabel weren't okay. I think she saw the Lord, Mr. Doctor. I know you don't believe in all that, and I reckon it's okay if that's who you are, but I ain't lyin'. Leah said that was the Rainbow Man's doin'. I don't know anything about that. I believed her before, like with Mr. Barney winnin' all that money, but what happened in that room didn't feel right in my bones. Leah hurt Mr. Barney." She looked at the chair and then to Tom. "She hurt me too."

"So you think Leah's not telling the truth now?" Tom looked across the table once more. "Is that chair empty, Allie?"

She looked and said, "I want to be Leah's friend. I think she needs one. I think she didn't have no friend, and that's why the Rainbow Man came. But I think she needs a real somebody to talk to, 'specially now. Momma says Leah might be stretched too tight on her insides, like a rubber band. You see that picture we took to Mr. Barney's yesterday?"

Tom nodded.

"It had numbers on it. I ain't no little girl. I saw how all them people acted down at the Treasure Chest when they saw them numbers tumblin' outta that bird's mouth. I know what them folks'll do. The lotto drawin's tonight. I wonder how many in Mattingly already got their tickets?"

Tom answered with a sigh. Allie nodded.

"Now, if they all win, I'll believe for real this time. I wanna believe. I figure everyone wants to, deep down, even you. But if Leah's wrong about those numbers like she was wrong about Miss Mabel . . ." Allie didn't finish. She didn't need to.

Tom looked at the sheet of paper in his hands. He saw his name on one side and Ellen's on the other. He also saw Allie hadn't written her own name on the page.

"You're a smart girl, Allie Granderson."

"Better wise than smart," she said, "that's what my momma says. I'll tell Leah I tried to talk you into stayin', but you said no. Which you did. But I won't say nothin' else, and I trust you ain't gonna either. I just wanna let you know what's goin' on. Leah says you love too much. I don't know what that means, but I think sometimes it makes you not see things you should."

From down the hallway, the bedroom door cracked open. Allie paused, and Tom turned to see two small eyes peering through the opening. Ellen followed Leah toward the dining room.

Leah smiled. To Tom, that smile looked like a rubber band stretched too tight.

5

The Old Firehouse Diner sat on the corner of Main and Second, just up the alleyway from the Treasure Chest. The two-story brick-and-stone square was built in 1872, which might as well have been yesterday in Mattingly terms. It served as a boarding-house for travelers stopping along the railroad until 1908, then for the next century it served as headquarters for the Mattingly Volunteer Fire Department, staging area for the yearly carnivals, and an emergency shelter for whatever hurricanes, floods, or blizzards the Lord saw fit to allow.

When Big Jim Wallis ascended to the mayorship in 2006, his first order of business was to convince voters that the fire department had to be upgraded. To Big Jim, it made more sense to build rather than renovate, and it made *much* more sense to build in a location away from downtown and more accessible to the surrounding hills and hollows where most of the townspeople lived. And as luck would have it, Big Jim himself owned ten acres of dead and rocky land out on Route 620 that would be perfect for a fire station—land that he was more than willing to sell to the town at a fair price. Why, he'd even use his own construction company—besides being mayor, Big Jim was owner of Wallis Construction, LLC—to make sure everything was built right. A special ballot was called the next year. The motion passed. And by May of 2008, Mattingly had a new fire department and Big Jim had unloaded a plot of worthless land and made a killing in the process.

Reggie considered all of this as Big Jim smiled at him from across the table through bloodshot eyes—in the end, the mayor's first priority was the mayor. Family came second, the town third, and sandwiched somewhere in between was the faith he professed every Sunday morning from the front pew of the First Church of the Risen Christ. Reggie would have to be careful here. This was happening. As much as he had thought in the past few days that it *would* happen, he didn't think it would be so soon. Yet here they were, the mayor, the preacher, and the head deacon—three of the most powerful men in town. Mattingly's version of the Bilderberg meetings.

Beside Reggie sat Brent Spicer, who had not bothered to

change out of his milking clothes—a subtle hint that he hoped their impromptu meeting wouldn't take long. He rubbed the white whiskers on his gaunt face and gazed out the window. Their talk quieted as other diners passed. The thick smell of sausage and gravy hung in the air like a fog. From the jukebox, Brad Paisley sang of how you'd never get out of Harlan alive. Allison Summers brought coffee and doughnuts and told Reggie to holler if there was anything else they needed.

"Heard about Mabel," Big Jim said. His blue suit jacket was open—the mayor had been unable to cinch his suit for years without the threat of a button popping off and putting out a constituent's eye—and his red tie was slung over his shoulder. He leaned in for a doughnut and took a bite. Without saying grace first, Reggie noticed. "How's Barney doing?"

"About as good as you'd expect," Reggie said. "Last night was a hard one."

Brent said, "Just gotta believe she's better off," and reached for a doughnut of his own. He rested it on the napkin in front of him but did not take a bite. "Barney's too good a man to have to suffer the evils that have befallen him."

"He's over at the Treasure Chest right now," Reggie said. "Left him awhile ago. I told him to sleep if he could. I expect the store'll be closed for a time. If you could spread word on that, Jim, I'd appreciate it."

"I'll tell Trevor to put something in the paper," the mayor said through the glazed crumbs that fell from his mouth. "And I'll see that the funeral arrangements are handled proper. Town takes care of their own. That's our way."

Reggie said nothing to that, only nodded. A week ago Barney and Mabel were afterthoughts to most in town. Aside from Reggie, the Barnetts, and the Grandersons (and, he supposed, the Norcross family), the Moores had no friends. But now Barney was one of their own. Big Jim reached for another doughnut.

"Why'd you get us here, Reggie?" Brent asked. "I got stuff to do."

Reggie sipped his coffee and listened for the Still Small Voice. The crowd around them chattered amongst themselves, sharing news of weather and crops and the carnival that was now only three days away. No doubt they had all heard about Mabel by now, though none seemed as affected by her passing as they were by the timing of it—poor old Barney couldn't even catch a break by winning more money than God.

"You seen that new painting of Leah Norcross's that Barney put up?" he asked.

"Nope," Big Jim said. He'd finished his second doughnut and reached for a third. "Heard it's pretty, though."

"It's an abomination is what it is," Brent said. "I's there when all them people were fawnin' over it. Don't know why you didn't kick Barney outta church after that sin he did, Reggie."

"Because church is *for* sinners, Brent," Reggie said. "And we're not here to talk about that, we're here to talk about Leah Norcross. She was at the hospital last night"—Brent opened his mouth to speak, Reggie silenced him with a finger— "Don't ask. But she was there, along with her parents and Allie Granderson. Barney convinced Tom Norcross to let Leah and Allie into Mabel's room. He thought Leah and her little imaginary friend could make Mabel well."

"You're kiddin' me," Jim said. His shock was so great that he momentarily forgot the doughnut in his hand. His tie slipped away from his ample shoulder. He tossed it back.

"You're surprised?" Reggie asked. "Come on, Jim. You know what's going on in this town more than anyone. That girl's convinced people she's got a direct line to the Almighty."

"Maybe she does. You ever think about that, Reggie?" The mayor smiled. "Or maybe you already have, and that's what's got you so riled."

Brent's face turned two shades of white. His lower jaw looked as though it had been disconnected from his mouth. "Y'all can't be serious," he said. "I mean, summa these other folks, okay, I can see them bein' tossed and turned by some notion of magic. But not you, Jim. And surely not you, Reg."

"Of course not," Reggie said, but at that moment the jukebox filled the air with music and he thought of Mabel, sitting up in heaven at the Lord's Table and listening to music that had no beat because there was no time. "She's just a confused little girl."

"Confused ain't the word, Reverend," Brent said.

"I ain't made up my mind yet," Big Jim answered. "So far there's just stories of that man she says follows her around. I know she's been good for the town. Plenty of Away folk been visiting us since that news conference, all looking for a sight of that young'un. Ain't no proof of nothing unless you buy Barney's story. And right or wrong, Reggie, you gotta admit that story has a ring of the magic to it."

"There ain't no magic," Brent told them. To Reggie, it sounded less like a statement and more like something he was trying to convince himself was true.

All Jim said was, "Like Reggie said, it's my job to know what goes on in this town."

"Well, right now," Reggie said, "two little girls have this town stretched to breaking, and last night Barney broke because of it. I'm telling the both of you, it wasn't Mabel's passing that hurt him so; it was that he trusted Leah and her imagination rather than give his wife a proper good-bye. And it's Wednesday. Lottery day. That painting Leah made, the one hanging in the

Treasure Chest's window right now, has more numbers on it. Now, how many people y'all think have snuck off to Camden or Stanley to drop some money on tickets? Money they don't have, mostly. Who are they gonna turn on when those numbers come up false? That family won't be safe in this town."

That last point wasn't a lie, but it was an exaggeration designed to provoke the very reaction that Big Jim Wallis offered. Suddenly his mind was less concerned with doughnuts and more worried about the potential political fallout of having a false prophet in town.

"What's in your mind, Reggie?" the mayor asked. "I appreciate the breakfast, but I got a lot on my plate today, and I'm tired. Dad-gummed mockingbird hollered outside me an' Gloria's window all night long. You want to run that family outta town?"

"Wouldn't be the first time town's resorted to such things," Brent offered. "It's plain they're trouble. I say run 'em out now while we can."

"I don't want to run them out of town," Reggie said. "I just want Leah to stop this nonsense before she hurts someone else. A warning, maybe. Like a petition."

"A petition telling her to stop . . . what?" Big Jim asked. "Believing in her imaginary friend? Painting her pictures? That ain't gonna work, Reggie."

"It'll work if the right names are on there. Might be enough to make Tom Norcross be a father for once and start getting hold of his child's imagination. And if not, well, we can say we gave them a warning. It's for the good of the town, Jim. It'll make things easier for you too. Better to nip this in the bud, especially with elections coming up next year."

And with that little tidbit, Jim placed the remaining two bites of his last doughnut on his napkin.

"See what you can do, gentlemen," he said. "But if you're right about everyone playing those numbers, might be wise to wait till morning before you commence. If we still got a town fulla poor, folks'll be lining up to sign a sheet of paper telling Leah to shut up." Big Jim paused and leaned in. His next words were a warning covered with sugar: "But if we have a town full of millionaires, it just might be you two they run outta Mattingly."

6

The smile on Leah's face quickly evaporated with news that Allie's parlay hadn't worked. Despite Tom's best efforts, there was no good way to tell his daughter that she would have to face the aftermath of Mabel's death the same way she'd faced the cameras and reporters—without her father. To make matters worse, Mary had arrived to pick up Allie just after. Ellen did her best to both comfort Leah and assuage Tom's guilt—"She'll be fine," she'd whispered as he left, "and so will we"—which was supposed to make Tom feel better but instead only made him feel worse. He arrived at work a full twenty minutes late.

A chill shuddered through him as he walked into his second-floor office and scanned the empty waiting area. Meagan was not there. Rita, however, was. She peered through the open section of her cubicle window, sighed, and shook her head.

"Won't ever leave early," she said, "but you'll show up late. What in the world happened, Tom?"

"I'll tell you later. Meagan's not here?"

Rita motioned to her left toward the closed bathroom door. Whatever fury usually seethed beneath her pale and

wrinkled face had disappeared—a bad sign. While most people centered their lives around the pursuit of some semblance
of peace and happiness (however fragile those things may be),
Rita was one of the few who thrived on anger. If she wasn't
mad, that meant something was wrong.

"Been in there about fifteen minutes," she said. "I was just
about to check on her. It isn't pretty, Tom. You put on your
doctor face when you see her. Anything else, and she's apt to
run right out of here and never come back."

"What happened?"

"That's your job, not mine, though I almost called the
police myself. Now get in there and get ready. I'll send her in
when she comes out."

"Between you and me," Tom said, "I don't know if I can
get ready this morning. Leah really needed me to stay home
today. Something happened last night."

Rita smiled and said, "You're a good man, Tom." She used
her grandmother voice, and now Tom *knew* she was angry,
because she only resorted to smiles and sugar when she was
ready to snap. "I don't know what's going down there in
Hooterville, and I honestly don't care. I'm telling you right
now, that girl in there is your first priority. Okay?"

"Yes, ma'am."

Tom walked into his office and set his briefcase on the
desk. The telephone stared at him, receiver tilted downward
to the right in the perfect angle to pick up the receiver and
give Leah a call, tell her he was coming home, that he was
sorry and wanted to—

The knock at the door crumbled those thoughts into dust.
Rita turned the knob and stepped aside so Meagan could enter.
The first thing Tom thought was how thankful he was that his
receptionist/bookkeeper/bouncer had given him a warning.

If she hadn't, he felt sure the calm, objective demeanor he'd cultivated since graduate school would have shattered into a gape of shock and rage.

The makeup on Meagan's face was meant to cover as much as it could, but all the lipstick and rouge had accomplished was to highlight what she wanted to hide. Both of Meagan's eyes were the color of deep holes. Red scratches covered her cheeks in a zigzag pattern that looked like some grotesque road map. The bruises that had covered her arms on her last visit were now joined by fresher ones, these yellow mixed with orange. Her hands shook as if she'd been left alone in the cold. She raised her right hand to cough—coughing was what most people did when embarrassed, though the why of that had never been explained in Tom's psychology books—and he noticed two fingernails were missing. In a fit of rage that he barely managed to keep hemmed beneath his doctor face, Tom hoped those two fingernails presently resided in Harold Gladwell's jugular.

He moved from behind the desk as Rita guided Meagan to the leather sofa and silently excused herself. Meagan made no move for the box of tissues on the coffee table. From the way she cradled her left arm, Tom didn't think she could. He moved the box to her right side.

"What happened?" he asked, and then he thought that was likely the most absurd question he'd ever asked a patient. It was obvious what had happened. Meagan had made another mess, and this one had been much worse than dropping a couple of dishes.

Meagan stared at a spot on the table. In a whisper Tom could barely hear, she said, "I told Harold about the baby. I prayed about it. God didn't tell me anything, so I took that as permission. I thought it might make things better. Harold said it wasn't his. He said I'd been sleeping around. 'Whorin' around,' is what he said. He said, 'You been whorin' around when I'm off working and providing for you. I been busting my back while you was layin' on yours.'" Her lips trembled, and her right arm curled around her left as if wrapping her in the sitting equivalent of a fetal position. "He said I'd lay down for anybody, and then he beat me. And then he . . ."

She didn't have to say more; Jack knew what had come after. Meagan reached for a tissue, but there was no explosion of tears and mucus. She simply balled it up in her hand and held it there as if that were her whole world, just a crumbly soft world destined for the garbage.

"Did you go to the doctor?"

Meagan nodded. "Harold took me. I think when it was over he thought I was dead, and he got scared. He told them I fell down the stairs. They believed it. They always do." She stared at the spot on the coffee table and slowly shook her head. "The baby's okay. They didn't say anything about the other things Harold did. What he did, he did in other places."

"I'm so sorry, Meagan," Tom said, amazed once more at the breadth of his counseling skills. Four years of college, another four of graduate school, published papers in more than a dozen psychological journals, countless seminars and awards, and at the end of it all was a feeble *I'm so sorry*. Bravo, Tom. Well done.

"I think God's forgotten me," Meagan said.

Tom didn't know how to respond. *I'm so sorry* didn't feel appropriate, nor did the more honest but less kind *Told you so* that had worked its way forward from the back of his mind. He sat across from Meagan Gladwell, the pretty brunette who was now little more than a pregnant piñata, and in his mind he saw Leah. He watched as Meagan stared at that spot on the coffee table like it was some gateway into another world that she could slip through and never return. It was as if she were tumbling into that spot even now, collapsing upon herself like a dying star, darkening like a candle snuffed out.

And Tom knew there was nothing he could do about it. Not now. Maybe not ever.

7

The yellow moon hung over Mattingly like a spotlight as the hands on the old clock tower in the middle of town met at eleven. The air was thick and still. Only the mockingbirds called out, uttering their raspy *chjjjs* and harsh *chawks*. They perched in trees and upon fence posts, atop mailboxes and telephone lines. They surrounded closed curtains and shut doors behind which anxious souls huddled around the blue glow of their televisions.

The only home without a glow was the faded and somewhat wobbly two-story structure at the end of Second Street. Barney Moore sat in the upstairs bedroom of the Treasure Chest, where the open window allowed the birdsong to reach him loud and unfiltered. He held the strand of Mabel's hair, stretching it out and then watching as it curled back downward. He no longer called out his dead wife's name (he had done so twice that evening only to discover it was not the following silence that frightened him as much as the hollowness in his own voice). Beside him on the bed, the covers were pulled down in anticipation of a rest that would not come. Mabel's pillow was turned long-ways so Barney would have something to hold. The crumpled lottery ticket remained forgotten on the floor.

Three miles away in the plain-but-suitable ranch house that served as the parsonage for the First Church of the Risen Christ, Reggie was telling himself he was still awake because of the baseball game on ESPN—a game he'd stopped watching in the early innings. A legal pad was on the coffee table in front of him. Handwritten on the top page were the charges to be levied against Leah Norcross (morally corrupting our fair town, inviting the wrath of God Almighty, and false prophesying among them). Following those were the amends both Leah and her parents would have to make in order to continue a peaceable existence in Mattingly (the gist of this was simple—stop with the painting and the rainbow man already). The mockingbird outside Reggie's window trilled such that it completely drowned a late-inning rally by the Red Sox. When the clock on the mantel read five minutes to twelve, Reggie turned the channel. He didn't know if the petition would ever be made public, but he had the satisfaction of knowing he'd already secured two signatures. Three, if he counted his own.

Across town, Allie had convinced Mary and Marshall to let her stay up late. She had no desire to sit with her parents in the living room—to Allie, the fear of which column on her *Leah's lying/Leah's telling the truth* list would grow in the next few minutes was more than she could bear—so she had gone outside to find the mockingbird that was cackling in the backyard. There was nothing but shadow in the mangled branches of the oak beside her small home. The bird grew silent as she stood watching and then called again the moment she turned away. To her it was a kind of magic, one not as wonderful as Rainbow Men or calling down the Spirit, but a magic just the same. When she went inside ten minutes later, Allie did not ask the question most on her mind, and her parents did not answer. They simply tucked her into bed and told her to sleep well.

Tom had decided he would kill his mockingbird if it came back the following night. It would be a gruesome death, the sort of ending he secretly desired for Harold Gladwell. The only thing that kept him from violence now was Ellen, who sat in the living room rubbing the crystal on her necklace.

He sat in bed and thumbed through a story he did not read in a magazine he did not remember picking up. The shuffling from the other side of the wall meant Leah wasn't asleep. Tom didn't think it was because of the mockingbird. He thought the reason Leah was still awake was the same reason he and Ellen and likely most of the town were still awake. Leah had said she was fine when Tom checked on her earlier, though her eyes had said otherwise. Those eyes had the look of someone who'd had to swallow something bitter and was just trying to keep it down. He was about to check on her again when the floorboards creaked in the hallway. Ellen opened their bedroom door.

"Her numbers were wrong," she said.

Thursday

Two Days Before the Carnival

1

Allie peeked out of her bedroom that morning long enough to say good-bye to her daddy, whose shift at the factory in Camden started at six. When Marshall Granderson bent down to eye level and rubbed her head, Allie knew what he was about to say. She knew it just as much as she knew that she'd called forth Leah's mockingbirds.

"I'm sorry, darlin'," he said. "Those numbers on Leah's painting were wrong. Not a one came through."

Allie hugged him—she would have hugged her daddy even if the numbers had been right—and went back to bed. When sleep wouldn't come, she rose from bed and added *Picked wrong numbers* to the *lying* half of her paper and then added her own name to the *telling the truth* side, though she knew it was for the wrong reasons. Then she dressed and went out to face what she knew would be coming.

The call came just after eleven, but not from Leah. Mary spoke with Miss Ellen for ten long minutes and divulged the details to Allie on the way to the Norcross home. Mr. Doctor and Miss Ellen knew about the numbers, but they hadn't told

Leah. She'd been in her room all morning and wouldn't come out, not even to eat and not even when Mr. Doctor tried to coax her.

"Ellen said Tom's always been able to coax Leah," Mary said.

Allie believed that to be likely. If spiritual-but-not-religious folk had anything akin to spiritual gifts, she thought that would be Mr. Doctor's.

They came up the long lane to find Mr. Doctor walking back and forth on the sidewalk and holding his hat. To Allie, it was as if he had an inkling he should pray but didn't know how. He led them inside and took Mary into the kitchen, where Miss Ellen waited with coffee. Allie excused herself and made her way down the hall.

She rapped three times on the door and said, "Hey there, Leah, open up."

There were tapping sounds from the other side, quick pops that wracked Allie's ears and then stilled, then started again. But no words.

"Leah Norcross, you open up this door and quit actin' like I ain't here, or I'm gonna just go right on home and I won't be here no more. You hearin' me?"

Allie figured Leah was too timid to not believe her. She had no intention of leaving, would camp right there until the Rapture if she had to. The popping stopped. The knob turned. Leah peeked out.

"Huh-hey," she said.

Her face was wet and her breathing heavy. The apron draped over her blue dress was stained with rainbow colors, along with a great deal of black and brown and gray.

"Hey back," Allie said. "You paintin' another picture for the rainbow man?"

"You're stuh-still saying his nuh-name different."

"Am not. Now let me in."

Leah shook her head and said, "I don't want yuh-you to c-come in."

"What's that s'posed to mean?" Allie cocked her head to the side and put her hands on her hips.

Leah offered no further explanation, though the door did ease partly open.

"We got stuff we need to talk about, Leah. Important stuff. So you gotta let me in, 'cause Momma didn't bring me all the way over here so I could talk to half your face."

"Okay," Leah said. "But duh-don't look at the easel, okay?"

"All right."

But of course Allie did, though the easel had been moved from the corner to the middle of the room and whatever Leah was drawing faced the wall. All Allie could see were the splotches of paint that had fallen on the piece of plastic under it. More brown and gray. A lot of black. The sight made Allie nervous. She didn't know why.

She sat on Leah's fancy bed and said, "So the lotto drawin' was last night. My folks stayed up. I did too, but not to watch it. I was looking for the mockingbirds."

Leah ignored her and walked to the open window that faced the road below. She rubbed at her thumb.

"Told you to stop that," Allie said.

Leah did. She looked at Allie and said, "Why'd your puh-parents watch the drawing?"

"Because of your numbers, doofus. The ones the mock-ingbird on your picture was singing. They were a bust, Leah. Momma said lotsa folks played those numbers, even if they won't say it outright. They all wanna be rich like you made Mr. Barney rich."

"But that was juh-just for Mr. Buh-Barney," Leah said. She looked out the window again. Allie thought she was waiting for something to happen. The way Leah was digging at her thumbnail again, it was something dark. "The R-rainbow M-man said it wasn't for anyone else."

"You mean they weren't lottery numbers to begin with?"

"I duh-don't know. If they duh-didn't work, I g-guess not."

"Well, you drew it. Don't you know what you're drawing?"

Leah looked from the window and said, "I just puh-paint what he sings. He's been singing all nuh-night from the c-corner. It's not like the other puh-paintings, Allie. I don't luh-like it. It scares me and it h-hurts to have to puh-paint it, but he says I have t-to."

Allie felt tired, like she was running in a maze and finding only thorny walls. She rose from the bed and met Leah at the window. The road below was bare of cars, and nothing was playing hide-and-seek behind the magnolias along the lane.

"Preacher Goggins says sometimes God wants us to do stuff that hurts because it'll make us better in the long run. I know you don't like the preacher much, but he's pretty smart."

"I like him just fuh-fine," Leah said. "I just don't think he l-likes me much." She looked to the empty corner and then out the window again, digging into her thumbnail as she did. "Things are guh-going to get h-hard, Allie. You'll stuh-stay with me, r-right? You have to pruh-promise you won't luh-leave, no matter how buh-bad it gets."

"I ain't goin' nowhere," Allie said, and then she promised it. She promised even though she still wasn't sure if God was really standing in the corner of Leah's bedroom, because whether He was or wasn't didn't matter much then. All that mattered was that her friend was hurt and scared and needed her help.

"Good. Luh-look."

Beyond the window, Pastor Goggins's truck came into view. It slowed at Mr. Broomfield's house across the road and then turned into the Norcrosses' lane, popping away and appearing again as it climbed toward the house. Allie couldn't see who was with him, but it looked like two people.

"Stay cluh-close to me," Leah said.

She let go of her thumb and took Allie's hand.

2

Barney thought of one long-ago town carnival when he'd tried to impress his daddy by getting on a ride the carnies called a Tilt-a-Whirl but the local kids dubbed the Juke-and-Puke. He'd only been seven then (or maybe eight, Barney was at that age when the beforetime lost its moorings and memories began to run together in a lump), but he remembered vividly how sure he'd been that he was man enough to do it. Harlan Moore, hard man that he was, told his son to go right on ahead. Barney's courage lasted right up until a bearded carnie with black teeth and moonshine breath cinched him in hard and fired up the motor. At that sound, little Barney Moore realized the foolishness of his decision. He cried out for the carnie to cut him loose, to please God stop, but by then the juking portion had begun and the carnie only smiled through those black teeth and said, "Ain't no turnin' back when the ride's done started," and Barney had been left to nearly drown in the geyser of tears and vomit that ensued.

He felt like that now.

He also felt as though he was becoming like Mabel, or at least the version of her that had sat beside him the last time he'd been up on the Norcrosses' lane. The hard lines of the world had gone soft and the bright summer colors had dulled. It was as if he were encased in shadow, like a gray shade had fallen over his life. His heart had been carved deep and hollow, and there was only silence to fill the empty spaces. Yet as Reggie's Ford weaved in and out of the magnolias, that shade inched up just enough to allow Barney a peek into what was about to happen. He stole a look at the papers on the console that fluttered in the humid morning breeze.

"Maybe we shouldn't do this, Reggie."

The preacher kept his eyes ahead, easing the wheel to the right and then the left, working his jaw.

"I don't think we have a choice anymore, Barney."

"Die's been cast," Brent Spicer said from the backseat. "We ain't the ones who threw it; that young'un did. You mind that, Barney."

Barney nodded as if he would. He knew better than to try and talk Brent out of something he'd already decided upon, especially when that something involved people from Away.

Still, "I can't help but ponder what Mabel'd think of this," he said. "We built our lives outta bringin' joy to the children. Now I'm fixin' to hurt one."

"Sometimes what hurts us makes us stronger," Reggie said. They were now ascending the last part of the hill. The magnolias gave up their guard. Tom, Ellen, and Mary walked out onto the porch. Leah and Allie were with them. "Just think of Job. He lost everything, but then he got more back. He was stronger for it."

That was true, Barney thought. But then he wondered if the more old Job got at the end had been enough to keep him from pining for what he'd lost at the beginning. Barney didn't think so, just like he thought the gain of two hundred fifty million dollars wouldn't make up for the loss of one sickly woman who was presently dining with Jesus. Because in the end God was cruel, and what He took was always greater than what He gave.

"Now, y'all just let me do the talking," Reggie said. "And I mean you, Brent. No sense in turning this into something more than it already is."

Brent said nothing. Barney thought that was so the deacon could say he never agreed to anything if things turned south. Reggie parked in front of the garage as Tom, Ellen, and Mary descended the steps to the sidewalk. Leah and Allie remained above them on the porch. They were holding hands.

"Morning, Tom, Ellen," Reggie said. His smile was wide and welcoming. "Hello, Mary."

Tom ignored the preacher. He moved to Barney and said, "Hello, Barney. How are you holding up?"

"Fair, I reckon," Barney mumbled, though he didn't *feel* fair. And he didn't see Tom's face as much as he saw that old carnie's, and his chest felt tight as if he was being cinched in. "Just tryin' to get along."

Allie had taken one step down from the porch. Leah's eyes studied her shoes. Barney suddenly wanted nothing more than for those eyes to look up at him, but they wouldn't.

"You know if you need something," Tom said, "anything, we're here."

Barney thought the next few minutes might change Tom's mind, but he said he appreciated it nonetheless.

Reggie kept his smile and said, "Tom, Ellen, this here's Brent Spicer. He's a farmer here in town and head of the deacons down at the church."

Ellen said, "Nice to meet you, Mr. Spicer."

Brent's face was like a rock.

"What brings y'all out here, Reggie?" Mary asked. She took a step and put herself between the preacher and the Norcrosses. "Seems like a church visit to me, and I think we all know where that road leads."

"More a town visit," Reggie said. He looked to the porch. "Leah, Allie, can y'all come down here for a second? We need to have a little talk."

"What's this about, Reggie?" Tom asked.

"About what's gotta happen," Brent told him. He took a step toward Tom and backed away when Reggie held up a hand.

Leah and Allie took the stairs and positioned themselves within easy reach of their parents. Leah let go of Allie's hand and stepped forward to Barney. She looked at him

(*Not* at *me*, Barney thought, into *me*)

with a pain that matched his own, a pain that said whatever magic had been in her life had now turned into something else. She reached out and wrapped her arms around his thick waist, pushing her face deep into the rough denim of his overalls.

"I'm so suh-sorry, Mr. Buh-Barney."

Barney put his hand on Leah's head. "Thank you, child."

"Tom," Reggie said, "Ellen, we're here today on official business of the town. I assure you this isn't something we take a great deal of pleasure in doing, but I'm afraid we don't have much choice."

He raised his arm. The papers were rolled up in his fist. Barney tried to tell Reggie to stop, please God stop, but he couldn't. The ride had started and maybe it had started long ago, and there weren't no turnin' back. He squeezed Leah and tried to cinch her in.

"I have here over a hundred signatures by upstanding members of the community, all demanding Leah put an end to both her paintings and this rainbow man nonsense."

"What?" Tom asked.

Leah pulled away and went to her parents' side. Mary gathered Allie into herself like a mama hen protecting its young from the wolves. Or, given that it was Allie, maybe she was just trying to head off the angry that was about to boil inside her daughter.

Ellen took the sheets from Reggie's hand and unrolled them. Her hands shook in the breeze. One of them went to a strand of blond hair that had blown into her eyes. There was a quick sniff as she tried to hold back the tears welling in her eyes. Mary bent over her for a look. Allie stood on her tiptoes for the same. Tom read the names as he laid a hand on Leah's shoulder. Barney wasn't sure if the doctor was trying to steady his daughter or himself.

"Half the church is on here," Mary said.

"More than half," Reggie answered. "Plenty more who belong to other congregations. And those are just from this morning. More's on the way. Once word got out, people couldn't line up fast enough for us."

"Us?" Tom asked. "Meaning you and this other guy—"

"Name's Spicer," Brent said.

"I don't care what your name is, mister."

"Sheriff Barnett and Katie aren't on here," Mary said. She continued to scan the sheets. "Neither is the mayor or Trevor. Or Andy Sommerville. You're missing some important names on this list, Reggie."

"Big Jim and Trevor have their own reasons," Reggie said. "As for the Barnetts and Andy . . ." He shrugged as if to say three names didn't really stack up to a hundred.

"No," Ellen whispered. The hand that was holding her hair back went to her mouth. She looked up. "You, Barney?"

Barney dropped his head and prayed the shade would close over him again.

"Barney was the third person to sign," Reggie said. "Right after me and Brent."

Leah asked, "You suh-signed the paper, Mr. Buh-Barney?"

Barney grappled with the gray curtain in his mind, tried to jerk it down and hold it there, but it only rose higher. Suddenly he could see and feel everything—the sharp green blades of grass beneath him, the way the sun angled down through the trees, the clanking motor of a distant tractor in the fields, the whiff of honeysuckle somewhere close. It was all a cruel reminder that he was still anchored to this world and as such would have to suffer right along with everyone else, that he was here and Mabel was dining with Jesus, and she could laugh and smile and talk again but he could not hear her.

"You said we'd be okay now, Leah. You said my day'd come." Barney's voice hitched. He reached for the shop rag in his pocket. "You *lied*. I know you didn't mean to an' I know you don't want me hurtin', but I is, little Leah. It *hurts*."

Leah wept. Allie went to her side. Ellen bent her knees to hold her daughter, and Barney wished someone would hold him too.

"We didn't want this, Tom," Reggie said. "I promise you that. But it was all that happened with Barney before, and then everything at the hospital with Mabel, and then the lotto numbers last night. People lost money they didn't have."

Leah moved her face from her mother's bosom. Her eyes were wet and red. A thin string of mucus connected the top of her mouth to the bottom of her nose.

She said, "I never suh-said those were lottery n-numbers. I nuh-never said that."

"But you never said they weren't, Leah," Reggie told her. "If they're not for the lottery, what are they for?"

"I don't nuh-know. He hasn't t-told me yet."

"Who?" Brent said. His arms were now folded in front of his spindly body and his head was cocked to the side. On his face was a mix of contempt and impatience. "Who ain't told you? That thing you think you see?"

"He's nuh-not a *thing*."

"Leah didn't lead them to the store to buy those tickets," Tom said.

"But didn't she?" Reggie asked him. "After what happened with Barney, what else would you expect?" He turned to Leah and said, "You can put an end to this once and for all, Leah. All you have to do is let us see him. Make him do something. If he's really there, then let's see a miracle."

Barney heard Allie whisper, "Do it," into her friend's ear, but Leah simply looked downward. The shake of her head was slow and almost imperceptible at first, then slowly grew.

"I cuh-can't," she said.

"That's right," Brent said, "you cain't."

Reggie said, "Tom, don't tell me you disagree. You're a reasonable man. I know deep down you see this rainbow man of hers as nonsense. That's right, isn't it?"

Tom and Leah looked at one another. Barney thought that maybe that's what fathers and daughters did—sometimes they spoke with words, and when words wouldn't work, sometimes they spoke with looks. Tom's look said all that was needed. He would defend his daughter. He would stand up to this town, tell Reggie Goggins that Leah could paint all she wanted and no piece of paper could tell them she couldn't, but in the end that was all Tom could do. He could support his daughter, but he could not believe her. Leah found her feet again. Her sobs were silent, shaking her body.

"Leah keeps her imagination to herself," Reggie said. "Her talents too. Town's spoken."

Tom tore the pages from Ellen's hand and threw them at Reggie. They smacked against the preacher's shirt and flowered as they fell. The breeze cartwheeled them away. One page became snagged in the white fence by the edge of the yard. The rest disappeared.

"You don't come on my property and threaten me," Tom said. His voice was gravelly, like there was a monster inside him about to be loosed. "You don't come here and disrupt my family and make my daughter cry. You leave. All of you. You leave before it's too late."

Barney pulled at the shade with all his might, but it would not block out the view of Tom looking at him.

"No," Brent said. He pushed past Reggie into Tom's face. "You leave. This here's your warnin'. You take your own and you get on, or else. This here ain't the city. Mattingly folk got their own way of dealin' with trouble like yours."

Reggie moved first. He grabbed Brent by the shoulders and pulled him away before Tom could cock his fist.

"Come on, Brent. Barney, you too." Brent moved to the driveway first. Reggie was close behind. He turned a last time and said, "I'm sorry. Truly." He looked at Leah but did not speak. Her chin seemed to weigh a ton, so close it was to the ground.

Barney followed last. Halfway to Reggie's vehicle, he turned and said, "Got fam'ly night for Mabel at the church tonight. I know y'all prolly won't wanna come, but I know she'd like you there. You can speak if you want, Miss Leah. If you can. I know you loved her in your own way. An' I know she couldn't show it much, but Mabel loved you too."

The Norcross family looked at him the way they would a stranger. If Barney was thankful for anything, it was that the gray shade closed down upon him once more.

3

Mary and Allie left soon after. Tom thought Allie would have put up much more of a fight than she did, but all it had taken was her mother's gentle hand upon her shoulder. There were promises from both—Mary that she would get with Sheriff Barnett and make sure nothing came of Reggie's paper, and Allie that she would call Leah soon. Ellen stood at Tom's side. Her face was contorted in an expression that was equal parts rage and hurt. Her hand whacked absentmindedly against her leg. Tom held her wrist before she bruised herself. Leah's expression was flat, almost serene. There was neither anger nor hurt in her eyes. This despite the fact that Tom had all but told Reggie Goggins what he did by bringing those papers to their house was wrong but the reasons behind it had been kind of right.

"We shuh-ud go to the m-mall, Puh-Pops," she whispered.

"What?"

"We shuh-ud go to the m-mall. The one buh-back in the suh-city that we used to always go t-to. We should g-go there."

Why? was the question he wanted to ask. On the surface it seemed the most ridiculous thing Leah could have said. But Dr. Tom Norcross seldom concerned himself with the surface of things, where eddies and tides spoke falsehoods and misdirection. He preferred the deep beneath the words where only truth dwelt. And the truth of what Leah just said was that she didn't want to go to the city, she simply wanted to go to a place where everyone was from Away.

"Let's go, Tom," Ellen whispered. She still gripped his hand, though the tension had gone out of it. Reggie, Barney, and the Spicer man were gone, and the shouting had been replaced by birdsong and the peacefulness of a lazy summer day. "Let's just go. It'll be good."

"Why not," he said. The alternative would be to sit around the house all day, Leah talking to herself in her room, he and Ellen in the den not talking at all, all of them peering out the nearest window to see if anyone else would be coming up the lane. Maybe leaving would be best. It could put some distance between what had just happened and what must happen next. Tom had decided there could be no more rainbow man. He would convince Leah of that. Not for Reggie Goggins or Brent Spicer or anyone else, but for the sake of his own family.

Of course, the very silence that sitting around the house promised accompanied them on the ride. Leah was cocooned in her own world, and Ellen was still too upset to offer much more than an occasional shudder. If either of them noticed the angry stares and mouthed curses from the people along Main Street (not to mention the CONGRADULATIONS BARNEY AND LEAH!!! that had been removed from the rescue squad marquee, leaving only TOWN CARNIVAL JUNE 25 and nothing beneath), they didn't speak of it. The only time Leah looked up was when they passed the park, where volunteers busied themselves with setting up the carnival's booths and rides. Ellen held his hand upon the console. At least there was that.

Tom allowed the hush to continue until they passed the town line. Then he asked, "You okay back there, Leah-boo?"

"Sure, Puh-Pops."

He saw the reflection of his daughter's smile through the mirror, wondered if it was genuine or not, then decided it was as real as it could be given the circumstances. Her left hand mimicked her mother's in the small space between the backseats. A tiny thought worked its way into Tom's mind—

Is someone sitting beside her? Maybe stroking Leah's fingers as I'm stroking Ellen's? Telling her everything will be okay, helping her find her strength, doing everything I should have been doing all along?

Ellen turned around in her seat and asked, "You sure you're okay, sweetie?"

"Sure, Muh-Mommy. Why?"

"Because if you want to talk about how you're feeling," Tom said, "that would be okay." He felt Ellen's hand tighten around his own. *Counselor mode*, that hand said. *Just be a daddy, Tom.* He knew she was right, but he also knew he couldn't help it. He was a counselor, and that was just as much a part of who he was as husband and father.

The interstate loomed ahead, a tangled mess of metal ants scurrying in two directions. Tom took the on-ramp. The sign at the edge of the asphalt read STANLEY 17.

Ellen said, "We're sorry about what happened, Leah."

"It's n-not your fault, Muh-Mommy."

"And I'm sorry too, Leah-boo," Tom said. "I know you might feel like I'm not all the way on your side, but I am. I want you to believe that."

Leah's fingers moved closer to the seat beside her.

"It's n-not my buh-lieving that's the pruh-problem, Puh-Pops. It's yours."

That statement hung in the air until they walked through the double doors of the Longview Mall in Stanley, Virginia. The Thursday afternoon crowd was large. To Tom, it was more people than lived in the whole of Mattingly, hills and hollows included. He briefly entertained the thought of sending Ellen and Leah off shopping while he stood by the entrance asking people to sign a petition saying Reggie Goggins should shut up and mind his own business.

They ambled through shops and stores, Leah between them, holding their hands. Ellen found a dress at J. Crew.

Tom treated Leah to a stuffed unicorn from the Build-A-Bear Workshop (because he loved her, yes, but also because a real unicorn could maybe come to take the place of an imagined rainbow man). For the first time in a very long while, they were a family. They laughed at corny jokes and talked about simple things and they loved. They loved most of all. There was no mention of paintings or fights or mean, nasty preachers. There were no mouthed curses or frightened looks from the people they passed. The world was right again.

The dinner line in front of the food court's Sbarro was long, but the pizza smell was enough to keep them from going elsewhere. Leah stood at Tom's right and offered her parents two maroon trays. She'd have the pepperoni, she said.

"Feeling better now?" Tom asked her.

"Yuh-yes, but we nuh-need to get b-back soon for Muh-Miss Mabel's service."

Ellen looked down and tilted her head. The line moved forward, creating a gap that was filled by an impatient customer. "You want to go to Mabel's service?"

"We huh-have to."

Tom wondered what would possess his daughter to say such a thing, but didn't ask. The odds were good it would come out wrong, and he didn't want to risk those words having the same effect as the look he'd given her in the front yard. Ellen was watching him, waiting. Tom nodded.

"Well, okay then," Ellen said. She leaned her head into Tom's shoulder and smiled. It was the first time she'd done that since she'd looked out from the living room window and told Tom and Mary someone was coming up the lane.

"How about you?" Tom asked her. "Better now?"

"I suppose," she said. She accepted the kiss on the cheek that Tom offered. Smells of pepperoni and pasta and shouts in

Italian filled the air. She leaned her head on Tom's shoulder. "We did good coming here, Tom. Guess we have the reverend to thank for that, huh?"

"I wouldn't go that far. If I did, then I guess I'd have to thank that idiot farmer who came with him."

"And Barney," Ellen said. "Can you believe he was in on all that? After everything Leah did for him?"

Tom started to remind his wife that Leah had done nothing for Barney but paint him a pretty picture, but then he felt the space beside him open up as the line moved forward again. He decided no, he wouldn't remind Ellen of that. Doing so would offer nothing but an opening for another argument. They had done good by coming to the city. He wasn't going to bring the country along with them.

He reached down to rub Leah's head, maybe squeeze her shoulder, tell her everything was going to be okay and he would help her find her strength, but his hand touched nothing but air. He turned his head away from Ellen and saw the empty spot where Leah had stood.

"Leah?" he called, but not too loud. Too loud would mean something was wrong, and there was nothing wrong. Everything was okay now. The world was right.

Ellen moved her chin from Tom's shoulder. The look on her face was much the same as she'd offered in the front yard that morning. It was a look of shock and mounting fear.

"Leah?"

Louder now. Tom scanned the food court for his daughter's long hair and blue dress. Families milled about him, mothers and fathers who knew better than to take their eyes off their children.

"Leah?"

"Has anyone seen our daughter?" Ellen asked. Her hands

shook and her eyes bugged. She reached for the closest person, an elderly man with glasses so thick that Tom doubted the man could see beyond his own nose. "Have you seen our daughter?"

Tom heard the faraway sound of his plastic tray clanking to the floor. The crowd stared. Fathers—good fathers—pulled their own children close in reflex.

Ellen took one end of the food court, Tom the other, but there were too many faces. When they met again in the middle of dirty tables and discarded food, the silence that had come to define their marriage had returned.

Leah was gone.

4

He knew many things, but at the moment the one thing that stood out was that forty dollars didn't travel nearly as far as it once had. Forty dollars used to feed you for two weeks. It could take care of your gas tank for pretty near a month. Forty dollars was darn near *rent* back in the day, though admittedly what that money had covered was little more than a hovel. And usually that money never made it to the bank at all. It often got poured down his daddy's gullet from a paper bag. He couldn't say anything about that, nor could his momma when she was around. "There'll be hell to pay" is what his daddy would say. Daddy'd whup you good if you opened your fat trap.

Yessir, forty dollars would once put the world at your feet. Now all it got you was a toilet assembly, some plumber's tape, and just enough gas to get you to the Sears and back home. Welcome to the new American Dream.

He carried his bag through the dense crowd that parted to

his right and left as they felt his approach. Many looked away. Some, he knew, looked back after he'd passed. They looked and they whispered, and he wanted to tell them he'd whup them good if they didn't close their fat traps.

Ahead at the doors, maybe seventy yards past the four steps he now descended, the rough outline of a child stood looking for something or someone. He checked his watch. Twenty minutes to get home. That woman better have supper ready. There'd be hell to pay if she didn't.

The child—it was a girl, he was now close enough to see that—had stopped her rubbernecking. The fact that she was now looking at him was bad enough. What was worse was that she would soon be invading his space. She had a look of horror that made him almost smile through his thick black beard. It was a look his woman gave him and a look most everyone copied in his presence—one that reminded him he wasn't a boy anymore and his days of being whupped were over.

He didn't have to be afraid anymore; everyone else did.

His boots made loud *thunks* on the floor that veered the old woman beside him to her right. He gave her no thought. It was the girl who had his attention now, the one watching as he approached with eyes as big as moons and a mouth that looked like it was about to scream.

Her space would be his space in five steps. Four steps. Three. She did not move. Two.

"Get outta my way," he told her.

She looked up at him and then down. The top of her head shook *No.*

"What'd you say?"

She shook her head again. The man smiled—that was what he did when he got riled in public, what Daddy did too, just before he whupped you—and said, "You're supposed to give way when an adult's coming. Didn't your daddy teach you manners?"

The girl looked up again. The dread was gone from her eyes. What had replaced it was a fire that burned white, one so bright hot that he winced despite himself.

She said, "You hated him . . . but now you're . . . him. You don't . . . have to be him."

She reached out her arm—*She's in my space*, he thought. *Daddy don't like nobody in his space*—and touched him on the chest. Her fingers shook as she did. People continued past as if they neither saw nor cared. It was as if the world had slowed and time had become stuck within the small bubble around him. His mind felt coated with molasses. His grip on the Sears bag loosened from all four fingers to the tip of only one. It dangled cockeyed by his leg.

The girl smiled, and there was a tired heaviness on her face. She lowered her head again and moved from the bubble. He stood there, staring ahead, letting her words wash over him like a cool rain, feeling that touch on his chest

(*She put something in me*, he thought, and then he thought, *No, she took something out*)

like a poker fresh from a waning fire. He turned, not knowing if he would call out for her or simply watch her leave, but there were too many people.

The girl was gone.

5

"Muh-Mommy found me," Leah whispered. "She w-was crying when she duh-did. It was the kuh-kind of crying that's huh-happy on one side and muh-mad on the other. Puh-Pops was just muh-mostly mad. He kept asking me why I d-did that, and I kuh-kept telling him, but he w-wanted to yell more than luh-listen. Sometimes when you luh-love too much, it c-comes out angry."

Allie blew a bubble with her gum, shook her head, sucked the bubble back in. On her other side, Mary reached out and tapped her on the leg. One more time, that tap said, and the gum would be hers.

"Why'd you run off like that anyhow?" Allie whispered.

"I juh-just needed to b-be by myself with the R-rainbow M-man."

"Is that what you told Mr. Doctor?"

"Yuh-yes."

Allie shook her head. "Sheesh, Leah, you don't know nothin'."

Miss Ellen shushed them and put a hand on Leah's leg. There was a squeeze along with the touch, like she wanted to make sure her daughter was really there and hadn't wandered away again. Mr. Doctor sat on Miss Ellen's other side. To Allie, it looked as though he'd aged ten years in the last ten hours. She figured he'd never been in a church before—probably not Miss Ellen or Leah either, for that matter—which was why he sat so stiff, like he was afraid the whole place was germy and he'd get sick.

Miss Lila sat up front at her organ. She gently pushed down on the keys so that what tolled out was soft and respect-ful rather than loud and full of praise. The chatter behind them ended at the door, where a steady stream of mourners flowed into the sanctuary.

"I had to guh-get by myself with the R-rainbow M-man," Leah said again, quieter. "Puh-Pops has to buh-lieve in the Muh-Maybe."

"Yeah," Allie whispered, "like Maybe he'll tan your hide if you ever do that again."

Her tongue worked up another bubble that her mouth swallowed before Mary could see. The gum had been Marshall's idea. He thought it might help take Allie's mind off the open casket that sat in front of the pulpit, where a dead person lay with her arms folded atop a white dress. Allie remembered Miss Mabel reaching up in her hospital bed with that teary smile. Preacher Goggins liked to say that bodies were like houses, and sometimes people get so big that their houses don't fit anymore and that was when they went to heaven.

That notion helped more than the gum. So did the fact that her parents and Leah were so near, and that practically the whole town had turned out for the occasion. Allie had never seen the church so full. They crowded the pews and stood in the back, spilling out into the outer aisles—men in suits and women in dresses and children awed to silence—all to say *Good-bye for now* to Miss Mabel and *I'm sorry* to Mr. Barney before doing it again for good the next day when she went underground.

Mr. Barney sat in the first pew in front of the casket. He wore the same blue suit he'd worn last Sunday when he stood up to say God loved him again. Mr. Barney had been happy then, Allie remembered. But now his shoulders were stooped and what little hair he had left was frazzled and uncombed. Preacher Goggins sat beside him and put a hand on Mr. Barney's shoulder as if to say, *That's just an empty house there, Barn, 'cause Mabel's up in heaven havin' some apple pie with Jesus.*

"Why ain't you got a dress on?" she whispered to Leah. "You wear a dress all the time."

"I juh-just couldn't," Leah said, and Miss Ellen tapped her

knee again. When Leah leaned over to hear her momma shush her, Allie heard a sharp crinkle from Leah's bulging back pocket.

"You got your picture? The one you were drawin' this morning?"

"Hush," Leah said. "N-nobody's suh-posed to know that."

"What are you plannin', Leah Norcross? You tell me now."

"I guh-gotta s-speak. When Ruh-Reverend Goggins suh-says anybody who w-wants c-can come up, I guh-gotta go up there."

"Why?"

"Because the R-rainbow M-man wuh-wants me to. I guh-gotta show everyone my puh-painting."

"You can't do that," Allie said. Her voice was loud—almost a shout. Heads turned in their direction. Marshall leaned past Mary and asked if Allie wanted to go outside. She said nosir and turned back to Leah. "This here's a remembrance, Leah. It ain't no art show."

"I huh-have to," Leah whispered. "I huh-have to do what he suh-says. And you huh-have to come with me, because I can't tuh-talk to all those puh-people on my own. I'll never guh-get it all out. Not even with huh-him standing there w-with me."

"My folks'll skin me," Allie said.

"Muh-mine too, but we s-still have to."

Allie thought that over. "What's on that picture in your pocket? If you want me to help, then you gotta say."

"It's important. T-to everyone. That's all I wuh-want to say, Allie. Saying more w-will just hurt."

The whispers from the crowd quieted as Preacher Goggins rose from his pew

("Puh-please?" Leah asked again)

and took to the pulpit above where Miss Mabel lay. He smiled as best he could, opened up his leather Bible, and cleared his throat. Leah began sawing on her thumbnail. Allie began to pray.

6

Reggie did not see Leah as much as he felt her, much like the day at the Treasure Chest when he'd turned to see her staring from the door. Looking at him. *Into* him. His eyes moved among the congregants to spot her, but the crowd was too big. Even in Mabel's feeble state and amidst the failure that had gripped her husband, she had been loved. Would that everyone in this dark world be so fortunate.

"The Book says the earth is the Lord's and everything in it." Reggie paused not so much for the amens—amens were rare on such occasions, though Deacon Spicer offered one from the front row—as for the sigh in his throat. He raised a closed fist to his mouth and added, "Though I suppose of late the Lord's rented out the night birds to the devil."

Chuckles rippled through the sanctuary. Half of those in attendance either lowered their heads or blew into their fists, victims of suggestion. The levity was brief but needed. This was a solemn time, yes, but not a hopeless one. Mabel was in

(a place where there's just now)

heaven, and that was cause for celebration even in the midst of mourning. Still, Barney sat unfazed and stared at the empty house that was his wife's body.

"We are not here to say good-bye, but to celebrate a life well lived. We are here to ponder the shortness of this world and the eternity of the next. We shall all meet Mabel Moore again on those fairer shores."

Still the eyes. Bearing down on Reggie, quickening his

heart such that sweat began to build beneath his suit and pool between his shoulders. He looked out and could not find her.

"Let us pray."

Heads bowed, eyes closed. As Reggie spoke he opened his eyes and scanned the crowd, searching for those whose heads would remain upright. In the back pew on the left, Tom Norcross sat stone-faced and chin high, refusing to admit God was larger than himself. Beside him was Ellen. Her head, at least, was lowered. In fact, the entire upper part of her body leaned forward so that her forehead nearly touched the pew in front of her. And to Ellen's right was Leah, who neither bowed her head nor closed her eyes but stared at Reggie as if he were an animal in a cage. The little girl smiled at him.

"Amen," Reggie said. His eyes remained on Leah. Her smile regressed. She looked away to a spot on Reggie's right, slowly cocking her head in contemplation.

"I've known Mabel Moore all my life," he said. "I remember her as a kind soul and a God-fearing woman. She loved her music. Sat right where Lila's sitting now for almost forty years and played that organ, praising God. I like to think she's playing that music right now."

Leah looked to him as if to say, *That's right, Reggie, I know she is, just like I know that music doesn't have a beat.* Her eyes returned again to Reggie's right in a stare so focused that Reggie had to fight the urge to look himself.

"If there is anyone here who'd like to come and say a few words, I'll invite you now."

Lila began the soft organ music, "When the Roll Is Called Up Yonder," one of Mabel's favorites. Reggie stepped aside. His eyes went first to Barney (who seemed not Barney at all but more an empty house himself) and then to where Leah looked. Nothing was there but the side door and a framed picture of Christ. Reggie realized Leah had likely never seen that face.

Mayor Wallis was first. He stood at the microphone and spoke long of Mabel and Barney's commitment to the town and the joy they'd brought to generations of children, as if Barney lay in a casket beside his wife. He said nothing of the lottery ticket. Reggie nodded in all the right places and looked at Leah. Leah looked at Jesus. Tom, either sensing his daughter's strangeness or seeing Reggie's stare, looked past Ellen to his daughter. He too followed the little girl's eyes to the painting. Reggie wondered what the man was thinking.

Sheriff Barnett was next; his wife, Kate, afterward. Lila McKinney cycled through all those old hymns. In an act Reggie could only describe as Spirit led, even Brent Spicer took the stage. Mary Granderson moved the crowd, as she often did. There was Boone Logan and Allison Summers and Andy Sommerville, on and on, one person after another, until more than an hour had passed and the people began to look as heavy and sullen as Barney himself.

"Is there anyone else?" Reggie asked, thinking there would not be and he could pray and get everyone home. But then came a rustling in the back of the sanctuary. Leah Norcross rose from her place, as did Allie. Both Tom and Ellen stretched out to try and stop their daughter but then pulled back, as though believing that scene would be worse than whatever Leah had in mind. A low buzz moved over the crowd as the two girls stepped into the aisle and made their way forward hand in hand. Lila continued her playing, though now the notes came clumsily and out of rhythm. Reggie thought that was because of the length of time she'd had to play, but then realized it was because she was looking at Leah rather than her own fingers.

Mayor Wallis straightened his back and leaned forward.

As did Brent Spicer, though Reggie thought that was so the deacon could kick Leah and her family out if the situation so evolved. Tom waited in the back. He still had that mocking air to him, like he was the only adult in a roomful of children. He watched Reggie and watched the painting by the door that had captured his daughter's fancy. Ellen's hands went to her head. Barney, as if sensing a change in the air, looked up for the first time as the girls reached the stage.

"What will you say, Leah Norcross?" Reggie asked. That he was nowhere near the microphone did not matter. He used his preaching voice. "Will you stand in front of this assembly and mock our ways?"

"Nuh-no," Leah said. Her voice was a whisper that somehow still carried. "I juh-just want to say m-my words."

The congregation waited. Some eyes asked Reggie yes, let her speak. Most told him no. But it was his church and his town and his decision, and in the end he knew that Leah had loved Mabel and Mabel had loved her back.

"Say your words, child," he said. "Just be mindful of them and do not mock God's truth."

Leah stepped to the microphone. Allie followed her as if conjoined. Their hands were so tight upon one another that they glowed white beneath the lights. Leah looked over the crowd and began to shake.

"I duh-don't know what God's t-truth is, I guh-guess," she said, "s-so I'm s-sorry if I s-say something you don't luh-like. Puh-Pops says the chuh-church is f-full of huh-hypocrites, and that m-means puh-people who s-say one thing and duh-do another. Like suh-some of you, I g-guess."

Tom's stare softened into a smile. Reggie bit his tongue.

"I nuh-know some of you are m-mad. Not b-because you think I'm a luh-liar, b-but because the lah-lotto n-numbers you pluh-layed off my painting didn't wuh-win you anything."

"Leah," Reggie said.

"Suh-sorry. I just wuh-wanted to say I l-loved Muh-Miss Mabel. She was kuh-kind to me." The microphone picked up a sniffle. Allie's arm went around Leah's back, holding her steady. When Leah rocked, Reggie saw her look at Mabel's body. "Wuh-we were alike, I guh-guess. Wuh-we were both truh-trapped inside ourselves. Now shuh-she's free. Shuh-she's in heaven nuh-now. I nuh-know that, and I expect you nuh-know how I nuh-know it." Her face was taut, the muscles in her neck bulged. Leah's words came harder now as she struggled against whatever she was about to say. Spittle flew from her lips. "It duh-doesn't matter if you suh-say the R-rainbow M-man duh-doesn't exist. Thuh-that w-won't muh-make him guh-go away. He's ruh-right here, wuh-watching all of you. He wuh-wants muh-me to shuh-show you thuh-this."

Leah reached over Allie's shoulder and pulled a piece of paper from her back pocket. Reggie's feet wanted to move but couldn't. Time slowed in the way it did just before a car wreck, when you knew what was coming and you knew it would be bad but you also knew there wasn't anything you could do about it. Leah unfolded her paper and held it over her head.

Audible gasps like air leaking from a tire spread through the gathering. From the front Brent Spicer called out, "What fresh hell is *this*?"

The page was covered with the burnt remnants of downtown buildings that a black sky had reached down and dismembered. Wailing faces called out into the darkness, perfectly painted hands grasping perfectly painted cheeks in looks of horror and anguish. Amber fires lit the corners of the page. Cars were overturned. Bodies lay in the streets. Blood flowed almost like a river. It was a horrible sight made strangely worse by the deep creases in the paper from being folded into Leah's back pocket. It looked like the town itself had been rent by a giant hand.

Reggie's stomach churned. He forced his eyes away. "Stop this," he said. "You put that away, Leah."

"I cuh-can't, Ruh-Reverend," Leah said. "He suh-says not t-to. There's a stuh-storm coming. There's no stuh-stopping it, because I've already truh-tried that. And everyone's going to duh-die unless you luh-listen to the R-rainbow M-man."

Someone screamed, and that fuse lit the powder keg that had walked into Reggie's church the moment Leah Norcross and her parents had arrived. Shouts rang out. Thunder rolled as people rose, their hips thumping the pews. Barney regarded the scene as though removed from it.

Allie's face grew as white as the hand that had held Leah's. She let go of her friend and whispered, "No, Leah, you can't be doin' this on Miss Mabel's day."

"Enough," Reggie called, and then louder, in his preaching voice, "Stop." He looked to Deacon Spicer and said, "Get them out of here," then he looked to the back and yelled, "Get out of here, Tom Norcross. Don't you come back. You leave us all alone."

Brent leaped from his pew, but there was no need for force. Tom and Ellen were already at the pulpit, pulling Leah toward them. Ellen bumped Mabel's casket and shrank back in terror. The family ran the gauntlet of shouts to the front of the church. Reggie watched as several in attendance rose to leave, either in protest of his order or in support of Leah's devil. Allie ran, not for Leah, but for her parents.

Reggie and Sheriff Barnett managed to restore enough calm twenty minutes later that the service could finally end in prayer.

There was no closing hymn. Lila McKinney had left as well, her side chosen.

<h1 style="text-align:center">7</h1>

The birds rang out that night, a cacophony of shrills and chirps, of justice sought or understanding craved or mourning released, depending upon the hearer. Yet each melody of every mockingbird carried the same truth, and it was a truth that crept upon them all and would not be chased away either by prayer or common sense. It was a truth that neither clenched teeth nor whispered doubts could deny.

A reckoning was near.

Friday

One Day Until the Carnival

1

For only the second morning in over fifty years, Barney Moore woke up alone. He had taken up residence at Mabel's bedside even in the days after her stroke, making sure her covers were tucked and the beeps from the monitors were steady and her chest rose and fell. Sitting in that worn vinyl hospital chair, helpless to do anything, his heart had been cradled by two unshakable truths—God was in control, and things could be worse. Now, as he rolled over and his arm found only the soft cold of Mabel's pillow, another unshakable truth took hold of his heart and squeezed—the best part of his life had ended.

He kept his hand on the pillow and rubbed it as he'd rubbed Mabel's shoulder so many times before. It was a hard truth that an end stalks us all, and no amount of wishing could make that end more bearable for those we leave behind.

The gray shade over him lifted enough that Barney saw himself gazing upon his wife's open casket the night before. He heard soft disembodied voices telling him that Mabel was in a better place. That she suffered no longer. That there was a blessing in everything, and Mabel's death was a kind of blessing to her.

He remembered the music Mabel so loved, the old hymns that spoke of love and hope and grace. He remembered the people who had stood up to speak of Mabel's kind heart and good soul. He remembered Leah. Leah holding that painting up, showing everyone that horror. He remembered hating her for it.

The mockingbird called from outside the window. It had done so all night. What little sleep it had allowed Barney had been filled with strange dreams that now dissolved like dew in the morning sun. He rose from bed and looked out to the vacant buildings beyond, but he could not find the source of the singing. There was only the song, as if it were a lost spirit calling out for a home it was destined to never find. Barney looked once more to the bed and plodded to the bathroom, where he brushed his teeth and emptied his bladder. The small linen closet beside the toilet sat ajar, revealing three unopened boxes of adult diapers.

Barney closed his eyes and waited for the shade to lower over him again and plunge him into deadness. Only when it had done so did he find the courage to leave the bathroom. He managed to make it into the living room before the shade snapped upward with a violence that nearly rocked him. It fluttered in his mind, and Barney winced at the sudden light that now blinded him, revealing in flashes of sudden knowing everything he did not want to know at all.

It was the answering machine. That dad-blasted, soul-stealing contraption from which no good had come. The one now blinking at him with its cold red eye, flashing a repeating 26, beckoning him closer.

26, 26, 26.

Barney stood at the living room's entrance and dared not

get closer. The shade in his mind still flapped, that light of knowledge still shone, and to him it was as if it illuminated not only what he had lost but also what he'd never had. His mind belched memory after memory like some broken old movie—Barney and Mabel waving to passersby on the street who turned the other way, Barney and Mabel stranded on the side of the road after Leah's party while vehicles rode past, the cobwebs and stale air of the Treasure Chest, standing in front of the church with ticket held high, the mound of white slips he'd found in the cash register.

He did not have to play those messages to know what they would say.

26

(*"Sorry for your loss, Barney."*)

26

(*"How's my easel comin' along, Barn?"*)

26

(*"Because times are tough, oh yes they are."*)

It could be nothing else. Because while most of Barney Moore was now as dead as the part of his wife that in a few short hours was going underground, another part had somehow come alive. He looked out the window, saw the town awaken, and Barney understood that everyone out there loved him not for him but because they believed whatever magic had reared itself up dwelt more in his craftsmanship than in Leah's rainbow man.

He retreated from the red light as if it were noxious and walked back to the bedroom. His blue suit hung from a hanger on the closet door. The pants and jacket were riddled with wrinkles from the night before. Barney decided that was okay. He turned to place the suit on the bed and heard a crinkle from under his foot.

When he looked and found his discarded lottery ticket, it was as if God Himself had spoken. Barney knew what he had to do. But first, he had to call Reggie.

2

Reggie did not know the Norcross family's routine, but he knew Tom worked on Fridays. He also knew that given the events of the night before, the good doctor would likely be staying close to home. That was both good and bad. Reggie had hoped Ellen would be the one he'd talk to, but he knew telling Tom would be best. Tom was the father and the husband, even if he didn't always act as such.

There was no one to meet him on the porch this time. That too was both good and bad. Reggie had spent the drive over pondering what Barney had asked of him and how he'd asked it, but now as he parked in front of the garage and slowly got out, he began pondering the likelihood of some sort of altercation. One could never tell with people from Away, but Reggie thought he could keep things civil. Besides, it didn't take long to deliver six words.

The steps to the front porch may as well have been a mountain ascent. The week had been hard, the last four nights sleepless. Reggie gripped the handrail and heard voices and a thumping from the backyard. He followed the noise and found Tom mounting a plastic owl decoy next to the maple by the house. The doctor's jeans and T-shirt seemed to settle the question of whether he would be working that day. He swung a mallet down onto the wooden stand the owl sat upon, driving it into the sun-baked dirt. The *thunk* was rhythmic and solid until he happened to pause in a down stroke and see Reggie by the side of the house. Ellen followed Tom's gaze and stepped in front of Leah. Her back was straight and her chin out, confident now that she was at her own home rather than in a strange church. Leah peeked around her mother and smiled.

"Huh-hello, Ruh-Reverend Goggins," she said.

Reggie nodded. What followed next was an awkward silence that was punctuated by the morning birds and a few wayward cicadas from the bushes. Somewhere in the distance, a dog barked and an unseen airplane droned.

"I apologize for the intrusion," he said. "I'm not here to argue or threaten. This won't take long."

Leah studied him as she had studied the painting of Christ the night before. Tom leaned on the plastic owl and considered the request. He turned to Leah and Ellen and said, "Why don't you two go inside for a minute?"

At first Ellen didn't budge. Reggie felt the spikes at the end of her stare. It was a sensation that was both hot and cold at the same time. She took Leah's hand and led her toward the back porch.

Leah turned and said, "Huh-hurry, Puh-Pops. Yuh-you'll be luh-late for work."

"Not going today," Tom said. "I'm going to cancel my appointments."

Leah stopped, extending Ellen's arm outward behind her until it wheeled her around.

"You huh-have to g-go, Puh-Pops."

"Why?"

"You huh-have to," Leah said.

Tom looked at Leah and then at Reggie. He said, "We'll talk about it in a little while, okay?"

"Okay," Leah said. And then, "Chuh-cheery-bye, Ruh-Reverend. See you suh-soon."

Reggie didn't answer. Answering seemed wrong in a way, as if it would somehow lend a measure of credence to Leah and what she professed. It would have also betrayed the anger that burned in him at the sight of the little girl's grin. The town had been torn asunder, lives had been tilted upside down, all because of her, this small one who thought it all some sort of game.

Tom waited until they were inside before he said, "You step on my property again, I'll have you arrested."

The words were as solid as the thunks Tom had given the owl, but Reggie smiled nonetheless. "Sheriff Barnett knows me a whole lot better than you, Tom."

"Maybe. But from what I hear, something happened a couple years ago that might lead him to back Leah rather than you."

Something inside Reggie buckled. His confidence wavered. How did Tom know about Jake? Who had told him, and how much?

"Speak your mind," Tom said, "and then get out of here. Nothing good ever seems to come out of our close proximity, Reggie. I think it's best if we just keep our distance from each other."

"Probably so." Reggie looked at the owl. Not the greatest decoy, but passable. Probably another of Henrietta Fox's left-behinds. "Mockingbirds giving you trouble too?"

Tom straightened the post beneath the owl and tamped down the dirt around it. "Haven't slept in a few days. What's on your mind, Reggie?"

"Barney called me this morning. I don't mind saying I'm worried about him, Tom. Loss is a hard thing for anyone, more so for him. He didn't have many friends left in town."

"Seems to have plenty now."

"Yes, but I think you know what kinds of friends those people are. Don't you?"

Tom's silence was all the answer Reggie needed.

"He wanted me to pass along something," Reggie said. "He said, 'Tell Leah not to come today.'" Reggie watched as those words sank in. Tom didn't seem to be surprised. "I'll ask—ask, mind you—that you abide by Barney's wishes, Tom. Give him a chance to say good-bye to his wife. This thing that's happened, it's gone too far. You know that. So do I."

Tom lowered his eyes and kicked the dirt. He nodded. "Since Leah's not here, I'll say I'm sorry about last night. Neither Ellen nor I knew any of that was going to happen. If we had, we wouldn't have been there. You tell Barney that for me, Reggie. And you tell him we'll stay away."

He went back to his fake owl. There was no good-bye, no have a nice day or see you soon. Reggie thought that was the best that could happen, given the circumstances. He turned, offered only, "Hope that decoy gets you some sleep," and walked back around the house.

As he was pulling away, Reggie turned toward the house. Leah stood in the living room window like a lonely ghost mislaid between two worlds, watching.

3

It wasn't the chirping that kept Allie awake as much as it was Leah's painting, and it wasn't Leah's painting as much as it was that Leah had chosen to keep the Rainbow Man's revelation to herself. A part of her still-dozy mind said that was wrong, that she should be more concerned with what the painting meant than the slight she felt, but the slight hurt more. It hurt like a deep bruise.

"Because we're in this together," she told the ceiling, and then nodded as if in agreement with herself. "That's what it means to be friends. There ain't no secrets, and you share even the bad stuff."

She pulled her knees up, transforming the bedsheets from plains to peaks, and rubbed her eyes. Outside, the morning sun was already above the trees on the edge of the yard. Allie had no clock in her room, but she knew it was late. She also knew the phone hadn't rung. She would have heard that, just like she'd heard her daddy say before leaving for work that he was going to kill that dang mockingbird.

What did it mean that Leah hadn't called? And did that matter now anyway? No, she thought. Because it was too late now. It was too late for a lot of things.

Maybe Mr. Doctor or Miss Ellen had grounded her from the phone because of what she'd done.

Allie didn't know why not, seeing as how she'd never witnessed such a conflagration of fury and disgust as she had the night before. The fact that it had all happened at a *church* during a *remembrance* had only made things worse. Why Leah had deemed that the best time to tell everyone a storm was coming and they'd all die if they didn't heed the Rainbow Man was beyond all logic.

"Maybe that's why Leah didn't tell me before. Maybe she wanted all those people to see my shock was like theirs"—*And my dander,* she thought, *because there was plenty of that on my face too*—"so the hate they carried for her wouldn't spill over to me. Maybe she just wanted to protect me like I done for her."

Maybe. Allie sighed and told the ceiling that she didn't understand why everything had to be so knotty.

She got out of bed and dressed. If Leah didn't call, then Allie would have to go over there. That wouldn't be a big deal. Miss Ellen had practically adopted Allie over the last week, and Mr. Doctor would be at work because he loved too much. Allie thought the only person who might object would be Leah, and that confused her even more.

Mary pigtailed Allie's hair and pronounced her fit to be seen in public. There was no talk between them of the night before, nor a reminder of what Allie must do. There was only a motherly hug, a peck on the cheek, and the promise of a prayer that things would go well.

"Thanks, Momma," Allie said. "They will."

The bike ride was short enough to keep Allie's legs from burning but long enough for her to consider everything that had happened in the last week—the party, the magic, Mr. Barney and Miss Mabel, Preacher Goggins's anger, the list Allie had shared with Mr. Doctor, the calling down of the Spirit, the mockingbirds. Her opinion of *Leah's lying/Leah's telling the truth* seemed to change depending upon the position of the pedals, but in the end Allie decided everything hinged not on Mr. Barney's ticket or Leah's paintings, but on the kiss she'd shared with Zach Barnett. Leah had known about that. Or the Rainbow Man had. Either way, it was impossible. It was impossible, and it also didn't matter anymore.

No one was waiting on the old Victorian's porch. Leah's bedroom window was empty. Miss Ellen opened the door just as she reached the porch.

"Hi, Allie."

Her voice was tired, and the words came out like they'd been spoken through a wind.

"Hey there, Miss Ellen. Is Leah here?"

"She's on the hill in the backyard. It's been a rough morning."

Ellen guided her inside and through the living room. The glass on the table looked like it was full of grape juice, but Allie thought it held something stiffer, given the fancy shape.

"Where's Mr. Doctor?"

"At work. He didn't want to go today, but Leah insisted."

"Really? Why?"

Ellen shrugged. "She said it'd be good for him. Especially after Reverend Goggins came by and said Barney wants us to stay away from Mabel's graveside service today. And though I can understand that, I know it hurt Leah."

"I didn't know the painting was of that, Miss Ellen. I swear it."

"I believe you."

The two of them stood at the back door and gazed out over the spacious but mostly empty backyard. Mr. Doctor had taken the swimming pool up, though the grass where it had stood was still flattened. The two pines on the hill sagged in the summer heat. Two feet poked out from beneath the maze of branches like two pale dots.

"I wish I knew what's happening," Ellen said. It was mostly to herself, but Allie nodded anyway.

"Me too."

"Do you really think God's touched her with magic?"

"I think something's touched her," Allie said, though whether it was magic or not she no longer knew. That was a question much harder for her to answer than it had been a few days ago. "But I don't know if it's God. My apologies if that ain't what you sought to hear."

Ellen nodded as if she'd had the same thought but not the courage to confess it.

"I'm gonna go talk to her," Allie said. "My folks were plenty mad last night at what Leah done, Miss Ellen. I gotta tell you that. And I gotta tell you they ain't so sure I should be friends with Leah anymore, even if she's got nobody else to tell her of the Higher Things. They like her, and they like y'all, but I reckon it's like Mr. Doctor in that they love me too much. So I'm just gonna go and set things right."

Allie didn't know if Ellen had heard her or not but got a pat on the head nonetheless. Ellen opened the back door and Allie stepped out. She stared out at the pines, trying to figure what felt right and what felt wrong, but everything felt knobby again. Allie supposed this must be what being a grown-up feels like, having to do things you're not sure you should be doing at all.

She took the space between the house and the hill with the steely resolve of a martyr, then paused where the shadow of the pines ended and said, "Well, this here looks familiar."

The toes peeking out from beneath the branches wiggled. A voice came back that answered, "I wuh-was afraid you'd c-come."

"That ain't no way to be, Leah Norcross." Allie stooped down and spread the branches with her hands. Leah was huddled inside. She drew her legs into herself and rested her lips on a knee. "You ain't ever gotta be afraid of me."

"I'm n-not afraid of you," Leah said. She looked at Allie with eyes that had accumulated a life's worth of pain in a week's worth of time. "C-come in here and suh-sit."

Allie wriggled herself between the trees, where Leah had spent so much time hiding from the world that the branches had bent and curved into a rough outline of her slumped body. "Everybody's muh-mad at m-me," she said. "Even Muh-Mommy and Puh-Pops. Mr. Buh-Barney. Ruh-Reverend Goggins. And you. You're muh-mad too."

"I don't wanna be," Allie said. "Maybe I wouldn't be if I

knew all that's goin' on. You shoulda told me about what you drew, Leah. And you *really* shoulda told me when you were gonna show it to everybody before you did it."

"I duh-don't want to t-talk about that," Leah said.

"Why?"

"I juh-just don't."

Allie looked around, careful of any wayward branches that could poke her eye. "Is the Rainbow Man here?"

"Yuh-yes, but I duh-don't want to t-talk about huh-him either."

"Well, I've had about enough of this."

Allie crawled out from the pines and took hold of Leah's feet. Leah let out a sharp cry as Allie began to pull. She grabbed for the nearest branch or root or rock, anything that would keep her in place. Nothing could. Allie was too quick and too strong. She dragged Leah out of the shadows and into the sunlight.

"I'm tired of you hidin' all the time, Leah Norcross, and I won't abide by you keepin' secrets. Know what my momma said to me last night? She said I can't be friends with you no more unless we fix this. Now, you tell me why you had to make a picture showin' something so awful."

"B-because the R-rainbow M-man told me to," Leah said. She propped herself up on her elbows and hiked down her dress.

"No," Allie said. "I don't believe that. The Rainbow Man's good"—*if he's real*, she did not add—"he's *good*, Leah, and no *good* Rainbow Man would tolerate you hurtin' Mr. Barney like that."

"B-but that's what he wuh-wanted," she whimpered. "Duh-don't you believe me?"

"Why wouldn't you let me see that painting?"

Leah stood up and shook her head.

"Why's there a storm coming?"

"I duh-don't know."

"When will it get here?" Leah shook her head again, and Allie screamed, "Why ain't you tellin' me stuff? Can't you see I'm tryin' to be your friend?"

Leah's lips trembled. Her throat went tight/loose/tight. She screamed in a voice so grieving that it sounded primal—"*Your muh-mommy's guh-going t-to duh-die.*"

The words struck Allie with such force that they robbed her of breath. She thought Leah had become confused, that she'd misspoken, that in the stress of the moment she'd listened to something the Rainbow Man sang and translated it the wrong way. But Leah said it again—"Your muh-mommy's guh-going to duh-die"—and this time it was softer and slower and Allie could hear it plain.

Leah's voice cracked beneath the weight she carried. Her face was contorted and her eyebrows bunched as if saying it hurt just as bad—worse, even—as hearing it. "I truh-tried to t-tell him to do suh-humething, to move the stuh-storm away. I buh-begged him, Allie, but he wuh-won't. He suh-said some things have to ha-happen and there's no chuh-changing them no muh-matter how we wuh-wish them so."

Allie slowly shook her head. The corners of her eyes began to burn.

"That ain't true," she whispered. "You stop that, Leah."

Leah bit her lip to fight back the tears. "I'm s-so sorry, Allie."

"You said if we do what the Rainbow Man says, we'll be okay."

"But nuh-not her, Allie." Leah reached out for her like a drowning person for a life preserver. "It duh-doesn't m-matter what happens, your muh-mommy's going to duh-die."

"You're lyin'!" Allie screamed. "You stop it."

"I cuh-can't." The tears were coming now. They flooded down Leah's cheeks like tiny rivers that glistened in the sun. "I cuh-can't stop it, Allie."

Leah closed the distance between them with a juddering stumble. She stretched out her arms, reaching for Allie, for the life preserver that had kept her from sinking.

Allie launched her fist forward and connected with the side of Leah's cheek, sending her sprawling backward into the grass.

"I hate you!" she screamed, and when those words drew tears, Allie screamed them again. "You're a liar, Leah Norcross. You're a liar and a fake and a rhymes-with-witch."

Allie stormed off, leaving Leah splayed in the grass. There were cries of please-don't-go and I'm-so-sorry and you-said-you'd-never-leave. Allie ignored them all, did not turn back. Nobody worth their bones wants anybody seein' them blubber, that's what Marshall Granderson said.

Miss Ellen came out onto the back porch and called out, "Leah?" She ran down the steps, not knowing why her daughter was crying and bruised, only that she was. "What happened, Allie?"

Allie did not answer. She only wiped her eyes and whipped her head in Leah's direction.

"I hate you!" she screamed. "You got a black heart, Leah Norcross. Black heart! And we ain't friends no more."

Allie Granderson pedaled home as fast as her legs could take her.

4

"What's gotten into you this morning?"

Tom had the vague notion that someone somewhere was

talking and thought that distant voice Rita's, but his mind was too preoccupied to answer. Despite his years of first plumbing and then unraveling the inner workings of the human essence, he was faced with the incontrovertible fact that he had no idea what he was doing sitting behind his desk. *Why* was another matter. Tom knew *why*. In the irony of ironies, he had decided to stay home from work to please Leah and was now *at* work because that was what she'd wanted instead. Even after Reggie had interrupted an otherwise decent morning to basically say the town no longer welcomed his family. As if they ever had.

He looked up. Rita stared at him through the thick glasses on the tip of her narrow nose.

"Sorry," he said. "Lots going on."

"Want to talk about it?"

Tom's eyes wandered to the windows that led to the streets below. The morning heat gave the illusion of ripples in the air. Sunlight glinted off passing cars. Horns blew. In the distance, a siren.

"I wanted to stay home today," he said. "All this stuff with Leah that you've no doubt read about in the paper but are just too nice to bring up? It's true. She really does think she has this invisible friend, and she's spent all week begging me to stay home from work. I didn't, of course. Because of . . ." Tom nodded toward the waiting area. Meagan was probably out there by now, and by now probably in a wheelchair like Mabel's. If she was lucky. "Know what I think, Rita? I think Leah's always had a father, but she's never had a dad. And I think she needed a dad so much that she had to go and invent one. This rainbow man isn't just a figment, he's the me I never was."

He waited for Rita to speak. She didn't.

"And now all these things have happened, one right after the other, like a snowball flying down a hill getting bigger and bigger, and it's smacked right into Leah. So I was going to stay home. Was going to call and tell you to cancel all my appointments, even Meagan's."

Rita raised her eyebrows at that last point, which was more emotion than he'd seen from her in months. As much as it pained him, Tom had to admit the little old lady in front of him was the one anchor he had in his life. She was the constant. He never knew when Ellen would be happy or sad, in the bottle or not. Never knew when Leah would hide inside herself or for how long. But he could always count on Rita to be Rita—aloof, cynical, and on the cusp of a fit. That seemed a sad way to live, but then, Tom realized, it was also a supremely stable existence. If Leah was right, and Tom's problem was that he loved too much, Rita's means of constancy lay in loving too little.

"So?" she finally asked. "Why are you here, then?"

Tom leaned back in his chair. "Because Leah told me to leave. She wasn't mean about it. There wasn't anything hurtful like, 'Get out, Pops.' She just said it was okay if I went to work. She said I needed it."

"Well, maybe you do."

"You don't understand. Leah gave up on me this morning."

"Maybe she just wanted you to come to work and help someone, because that's what you're good at. Speaking of which, Meagan will be here soon. I'll leave you alone. Listen for the buzz." Rita patted the back of the chair and walked toward the door. Halfway there, she turned and said, "If Meagan doesn't come, go home. Just go home, Tom. I'll cancel the rest of your appointments. Your family needs you, whether they say so or not."

Tom nodded. The door clicked shut, and the room was left in a silence that magnified the voices whispering in his mind—Reggie begging for Leah to just stop, Barney mourning Leah's lies, Allie weighing the either/or of the rainbow man, Ellen telling Tom to take the world off his shoulders. He heard himself say that some people loved too much and others not enough, but either way it took courage to face this world. He heard a mockingbird call and the office phone buzz. That one, at least, was real.

Tom picked up the phone. Rita's voice was clipped and pondering.

"She's here, Tom. Plus one."

"Plus one?"

"Yep. He's either the cabbie who brought her over here or someone she has on the side. Can't blame her for that, I guess."

"He'll have to wait outside."

"That's what I said. He seemed okay with it. She didn't."

Tom sighed and rubbed his eyes. "Fine, I'll tell him."

He hung up the phone and made sure the wastebasket was by the sofa and a new box of tissues was ready on the coffee table. Tom's hand hesitated on the knob and then opened the door. Meagan stood just outside. A faint but nervous smile was on her lips.

Beside her was the biggest man Tom had ever seen, easily six six or six seven, easily three hundred pounds. The man was not heavyset; all the weight centered itself in his midsection but was equally distributed through a chest that seemed almost inflated and arms that were thicker than Tom's legs. He wore faded jeans over a pair of black work boots. A red T-shirt was stretched to nearly bursting across his back.

Tom gathered himself so that his voice neither cracked nor gave any hint of intimidation. It took effort.

"Good morning, Meagan. Ready?"

"Yes," she said. The smile was still nervous but now more

there, like a secret about to be sprung. "Dr.— Tom, I'd like you to meet my husband, Harold."

Tom's training, all those years of school and real-world experience, had inoculated him from anything resembling surprise. When it came to dealing with secrets and regrets and pains so deep they seemed woven into one's DNA, shock was anathema. Shock could drive a hurting patient back on the street, never to return. But what Tom displayed was shock nonetheless.

"Harold?" he asked.

The man nodded. He offered a deep, gravelly, "Right."

The three of them stared at one another, and Rita stared at all of them. The pilot light in Tom's mind had been snuffed. He couldn't remember why they were all there or what they were supposed to do next.

"Why don't you two come on in," he finally managed. "Let's talk awhile."

Meagan and Harold entered the office—Harold had to practically duck and turn sideways through the doorway—as Tom and Rita exchanged looks of complete wonder. Meagan guided her husband around to the sofa, told him where to sit. She patted his gigantic knee. Tom saw all of this and realized that at least here in this space, she was in charge. He also saw that Harold was frightened out of his mind. Meagan's smile was full-blown by the time Tom sat in the chair in front of his desk.

"Well . . ." He looked at Meagan and then Harold and wondered at the weight discrepancy between them. A sudden and absurd picture flashed through his mind of the leather sofa seesawing and Meagan shooting through the ceiling. "I'm sorry," he said. "Honestly, I'm just a little . . ."

"Surprised?" Meagan offered.

"Yes."

Harold remained silent. His hands were in his lap. He looked around the office and met Tom's eyes. His jaws worked, rippling the muscles in his face.

"It happened," Meagan said. "It finally happened, Tom."

"What happened?"

"My miracle."

She looked at Harold and poked him in the ribs with an elbow that was still overlaid with black and green bruises. Those welts reminded Tom of the heavens in Leah's last painting. It looked like the sky that was swallowing the town.

"Go on," she whispered to him.

Tom crossed his legs. His left hand went to his chin, his right cupped an ink pen that rested upon a pad of paper.

"I know you're a little . . . overwhelmed, Harold," he said. "I understand that, I really do. And I think it's wonderful that you're here."

The words had the opposite effect than Tom had intended. Harold winced. Meagan's hand tightened on his knee, no doubt reminding him of some promise he'd made. Tom didn't think that would work (he was pretty sure Harold had broken his fair share of promises to his wife), but then he sighed and cleared his throat.

He said, "God spoke to me."

Oh no, not him too.

"God," Tom said.

"Spoke to me," Harold finished. "Meagan told me you wouldn't believe that. That don't matter. It's the truth."

"When did this happen?"

"Yesterday."

Tom wrote *Yesterday* on his pad of paper.

"Okay. Tell me about that, Harold. And this is all confidential. None of it leaves this room."

The big man winced again. Tom understood. Harold was the sort of man who was used to yelling instead of talking, and the only things he ever shared were his fists.

"I was at the mall," he said. "It happened at the mall."

At th—was all Tom managed to write down. The rest of the words somehow ended up in his stomach, where they swirled and gave him chills. He looked at Harold.

"The mall here in town? Longview?"

Harold nodded. "That's right. I was down at Sears, getting stuff to fix the crapper. Stupid thing's never worked right, and we don't have no money to fix it. That's why I was mad. I'm usually mad, I guess. I imagine Meagan's told you as much."

Meagan took her husband's hand in a gesture that said, *Don't worry about that, honey, everything's going to be fine now, our time's come.*

"So I'm coming up the mall toward the lot, and I see this girl."

"Girl?" Tom asked.

"Yeah. And she won't get out of my way, see? So we just stand there looking at each other. I tell her to move, but she won't." The words were coming easier now. It was as if what had been pent up in Harold was kinked like a hose, and that hose had suddenly been laid flat. "I was hot. Don't nobody do that to me. But then she steps up to me . . ."

He trailed off. The words wouldn't come. Tom could nearly see them lodged in the upper part of Harold's chest, stuck there by embarrassment or anger or whatever else. Meagan reached over and took a tissue. Harold slapped it away. Being in a counselor's office was pansy enough, Tom supposed. Having to bawl into a tissue would be even worse.

". . . and she *touches* me." Harold pointed to his chest, where the words had been stuck. "Right here. And she says,

'You hated him, but now you're him. You don't have to be him.'"

Tom wanted to write that down, but by then he'd forgotten the pen in his hand. He felt his cheeks flush and tasted the salt in the sweat that had gathered above his lip. He asked, "What's that mean?"

Harold shook his head and said, "I ain't saying. Maybe someday, but not today. But I swear on a stack, Doc, what that little girl said was something only God could know. It changed me. I went home so scared I was shaking, and that scared Meagan

("It sure did," Meagan said, and then she smiled in a way that made her beautiful)

but then I calmed down. That's when she told me she's been coming here getting counsel. I shoulda been mad at that but I weren't, and that scared me all over again. And now I'm here. I don't know why, but I am."

What Tom said next blurred the line between proper and not (at least professionally speaking), because it was asked not to provide insight into Harold's situation but to give light to a notion Tom could no longer dismiss.

"What time did this happen yesterday, Harold?"

"I dunno," he said. "'Round four. Maybe a little after."

Now the sweating was accompanied by a trembling that drew Meagan's eye. Tom's bowels tightened. He thought he might have to excuse himself.

"This girl, what'd she look like?"

"I don't remember."

"Was she short, tall, skinny, heavy? Black hair? Blond?"

"I don't know. Black, maybe."

"Did she stutter?"

"No, she didn't *stutter*," Harold boomed. Meagan's hand

left her husband's knee. She shrank back until her hip met the end of the sofa. Tom's pulse quickened. His bowels, once tighter than a drum, now became like warm Jell-O.

"I'm sorry," Harold said. "I get a fire in me sometimes. It's all hazy." He looked at Meagan, beckoning her to return. She didn't. He looked at Tom and said, "Ain't it enough that I'm here?"

"It is," Tom said. "I'm sorry, Harold. Let's keep talking, okay?"

And they did. For the next hour Tom asked vague questions he could not remember and received clumsy answers he did not hear. Home was all his mind could focus upon—home and Leah.

5

She did well as she traversed the shadow-speckled lane past the ranch houses and old Cape Cods, past the park where the carnival was about to begin, past the post office (where she even managed to wave and good-morning Sheriff Barnett without him seeing the tears leaking out of her eyes), up the big hill and down the other side, and then left at the old white clapboard church and up the second driveway on the right, but when Allie saw her momma tending the flowers in the front yard, the steel countenance proper for a Granderson shattered into a spasm of muted pleas and bottomless sobs. She let her bike topple into the browning grass and ran to Mary, who did not bother to ask what had happened or what was wrong but only closed her arms around her daughter and held on tight. Allie poured her fear and brokenness upon her mother's breast, all the pain and rage, and then collapsed into her until they both went to the grass.

No words passed between them. The only sound was the gentle *Shh* that followed what new tears Allie could summon. Mary slowly rocked her back and forth, just as she'd once done when Allie had stumbled into a yellow jacket nest the summer before. The result had been twelve stings that had not hurt nearly as much as what hurt now.

"Leah said you're gonna die."

Allie pulled away just enough to look into her mother's eyes, just as she'd wanted to look into Leah's when Leah had said the Rainbow Man was three biggers than her small and had eyes like clear pools. She watched to see if her momma's mouth gaped open in shock or her eyes widened in fear. But there was only a smile.

"She did now, did she?" Mary asked.

"She said there ain't nothin' anyone can do about it, that some things just are and can't be changed none."

She buried her head back into Mary's chest, who proceeded to rub the space between Allie's pigtails and offer only a simple, "I see."

"What are we gonna do, Momma? We need to tell Daddy. We gotta leave town."

Allie's head moved up and down with her mother's chuckle. Mary moved away and cupped her hands around Allie's chin, lifting it up into the sunshine. The gold cross around Mary's neck glimmered.

"Well, before we go and do all that, why don't you tell me what you said to Leah just before she told you that."

Allie sniffed and rubbed her nose. What came back was sticky and hot on her forefinger. She wiped it on the grass beside her momma's pink tennis shoe. "I told her she shoulda told me about that picture before she showed everybody, and then I said you didn't think we should be friends no more."

"So you told Leah that I didn't think you two should be friends, and that's when Leah said I'm going to die. You don't think that sounds a little fishy? Like maybe she said that because she was mad at me?"

Allie hadn't considered that. Then again, "Leah said the Rainbow Man told her."

"The rainbow man," Mary said. "And you're sure there's a rainbow man? Not just sure in your heart, because in your heart anything can be true. But I mean true in your head too? For a thing to be real, it has to feel that way in your heart and your head both. Everything that's happened with you two this past week, every bit of it, can be laid onto something besides a rainbow man."

"Not Mr. Barney's numbers."

"Which aren't there," Mary answered. "And who knows, maybe Mr. Barney saw something on that page. But if Leah had painted something, don't you think it would still be there?"

Maybe. Maybe that was true. Besides, if God wanted to give Mr. Barney a miracle, Allie thought He'd want everyone to see it. Because if something was real it had to be in the heart and the head at the same time, but it also had to be in the eyes.

"What about the mockingbirds, then? Leah painted that, and I was right with her when they came fallin' outta the sky, Momma. I don't know if you know that or not, but it's true. They were like clouds. That was right after I dunked Leah in the pool and drowned her in the Spirit."

"You did what?"

"I baptized her. At least I kinda did, I guess. That was after Miss Mabel passed. I thought it would help."

Mary said nothing to this, though it looked to Allie that she wanted to say a lot. Instead, she said, "What's so special about a bunch of mockingbirds? There's no charm in that, is there? Birds go crazy in the head sometimes. Remember awhile back when all those sparrows took a nosedive into the parking lot of the Super Mart in Camden? Besides, I don't think it was the mockingbirds Leah's painting was talking about, it was the numbers. And we all know how that turned out. Just like you said she tried to save Miss Mabel and couldn't. Because Leah's just a little girl, Allie. Just like you. Nothing more than that."

She looked at Allie and smiled again. It was the same smile she'd offered after cleaning up all those yellow jacket stings and covering Allie's arms and legs with Band-Aids (they were SpongeBob, Allie remembered, and that made her cry again because for reasons she could not recall, SpongeBob gave her the willies), the same smile that had always nursed Allie back to health whenever she got the flu or the croup, the smile that proved Mary Granderson was the most beautiful and good woman in the whole wide world.

"Whatever magic might have brushed up against Leah is gone now, if it was ever there at all. I don't abide by what Reggie's done to Leah and her folks, but I do agree that she's just a confused little girl who got in over her head. And if you think with your mind as much as you're feelin' with your heart, I think you'd believe the same."

Allie closed her eyes to the sun and contemplated her next words. They would be serious words, ones that would likely get her into not a little bit of trouble, but ones that needed telling. Because while her momma may have been right about everything she'd just said, there was still one thing that stood in the way. Something no one else could possibly know.

"I let Zach Barnett kiss me." Allie spewed those words as fast as she could—*IletZachBarnettkissme*—thinking the speed would dull the pain, like when you yanked off a SpongeBob Band-Aid in one clean pull.

"You did what?" Mary asked.

"Ilethimkissme. Or maybe Iaskedhimto, I don't know. But that's not the point, Momma, and I hope you ain't mad. The point is that Leah *knew* it. I asked her to prove the Rainbow Man was real, and that's what he *told* her."

Mary sat silently in the grass—Allie noticed her momma's hand was no longer atop her own but fingering her pink Nikes—and thought a moment. She smiled and said, "Leah was up on that little hill for the whole party until you brought her down, right?"

"Yes'm."

"I would imagine a body could see most everything there is from up there. All the house and yard, clear on down to Mr. Broomfield's house."

Something sparked in Allie's mind at that notion. She did her best to roll back through the memories of what she and Leah saw during their many stays in their secret place under the pines and found it was true. Leah could have seen them plain and in fact had. Allie wondered at her own stupidity.

"We don't have anything to worry about, do we?" Mary said.

"No'm," Allie said.

The smile that came through her drying tears was one not as beautiful as her mother's, not as supremely *good*. Not yet. But it would be one day. Everyone in town would say so.

"Good," Mary said. "And we'll not mention your dalliance with Zach Barnett, especially to your father."

Allie thought that settled things, though a small part of her (head or heart, she couldn't tell) believed there was still plenty to worry about—that a big scary something was sneaking up on them all to say *boo*. But by then her momma's hand was back atop her head. In the end, that was all that mattered.

6

Tom didn't realize he'd just crossed the town line, nor did he understand that he'd done so at forty miles over the posted speed limit. The world had tunneled along with his mind. Trees and houses blurred past while he himself felt unmoving, as if the yellow Victorian were coming to him rather than he to it. But of course such a thing was impossible. Contrary to the immutable rules of the universe. And to upend those rules would be tantamount to, what? A miracle?

"There's no such thing as a miracle."

He uttered those words as if trying to speak their truth into existence and dispel the doubt that had now taken root inside him. Leah was just a little girl. Little girls aren't supposed to guess winning lottery numbers and convince strangers to confront their deepest agonies.

But Leah had been at the mall that day and had gone missing at that very time. The girl who spoke to Harold had black hair—maybe. Leah had black hair.

But the girl hadn't stuttered. Which meant it couldn't have been Leah

(Could it?)

because she would have most certainly stuttered to a man like Harold Gladwell. Leah would have been spluttering like Porky Pig.

Tom thought yes and then he thought no, and all the while the doubt inside him grew like a vine around his heart.

Ellen walked out onto the porch as he parked by the

garage. A dish towel hung limply from her hand. Her face was drawn, her eyes like two dim holes. She regarded Tom with a look he had seen each time a new patient sat upon his sofa and reached for the box of thick tissues on the coffee table. It was a look of surrender. A look of *What now?*

"Why are you home so early?" she asked.

Tom climbed the steps and took hold of Ellen's arms. The dish towel smacked absently against her leg.

"Where's Leah?" he asked. "We have to talk to her. It's important."

"Locked in her room," Ellen said. Her words were thick, but Tom smelled nothing but coffee on her breath. "She won't come out, Tom. She just . . . won't. She and Allie had a falling out this morning." The towel smacked harder against her leg. Ellen was shaking like an engine about to sputter and die. "Allie *hit* her, Tom. With her *fist*. I saw it myself. I don't know what's *happening*, and I can't *stop it*."

Tom looked inside the house. He wanted nothing more than to walk inside to Leah's room and ask her—even if it had to be through the door—what had happened at the mall. Ellen sank into the hollow of Tom's chest, her heaves muffled by his shirt. He held her as they stumbled to the swing in the corner like two beaten fighters. Ellen's weeping was soft, childlike. Her hand curled around the collar of Tom's shirt and held him there. Leah's window was directly behind them; even closed, Tom thought she could hear whatever they said.

A thought struck Tom then, one that seemed equal parts absurd and impossible and felt like an itch deep in his ear that he couldn't scratch. He wondered for the first time if everything had perhaps been engineered according to some kind of design—if Lilly Wagoner was supposed to sit beside Ellen at that party so Ellen was supposed to get tipsy enough to divulge secrets she normally would not, because Tom was supposed to partition his life and lose himself in his work so they would move to Mattingly, because Leah was supposed to have her party so she could get her easel, because Barney was supposed to buy his ticket so Reverend Goggins would deliver his petition, because Tom was supposed to run away with his family to the Longview Mall so Leah could confront Harold Gladwell so Tom could be so torn, so utterly confused between doubt and belief, that he would be sitting there at that moment holding his wife and about to do the one thing he swore he would never do again.

Because maybe Barney had been right—it was all connected. Everything and always.

"I have a patient," he said. "A woman. Not much younger than us, really. I've been seeing her for a while now. She isn't getting better."

Ellen's tears lessened. Tom thought she understood the magnitude of what she heard. The grip on his shirt grew tighter.

"Her husband abuses her. She's pregnant with his child, but he accused her of infidelity and then raped her. He's a monster, Ellen. I never really believed in monsters until I met her. I've told her to leave him over and over. I don't normally do that, but when a life's in danger—and in her case it's two lives—safety comes first. But she wouldn't go. She kept saying God was going to save her."

Tom paused there. He had to breathe before he said more.

"She actually thought God would save her. I guess you can believe that, maybe. Not me. I've never believed such things. I guess I still don't. I felt so helpless, sitting there listening to her. I was watching this woman die right in front of my eyes, and there was nothing I could do about it. That's why I reacted to Reggie the way I did at Leah's party. It's a reason, but not an excuse."

Ellen began to cry again. Tom thought these tears were different—shed not out of pain, but of being included in his secret life once again, however sorrowful the story he told.

"I saw Leah in her. They look alike, but it's more. Deeper. They're both small, not just on the outside, but on the inside too. Her husband came in with her today. Just like that. I know a lot about people, Ellen. Stuff like that just doesn't happen. So I asked him what brought him there, and he said . . . he said God spoke to him through a little girl he met at the mall yesterday afternoon."

Ellen's head shot up with such force and speed that it nearly clocked Tom square in the jaw.

"Yesterday afternoon?" she asked.

Tom nodded. "Around the same time that Leah ran off. I asked him to describe the girl, but he couldn't. He said everything was hazy."

"Leah, Tom? You think that was Leah? Because if it was . . ."

Ellen didn't have to finish that sentence. Tom knew full well what it meant. It meant having to change everything he believed in and didn't.

"That's why I came home," he said. "To ask her."

They rocked. Tom gave Ellen enough time to gather herself and process what she'd just been told. When he thought she was ready, he said, "You can come out now, Leah."

The screen door squeaked open just enough to be heard.

"Hey, Puh-Pops," Leah said. "Didn't think you h-heard me."

"Why don't you come out here for a second."

The door opened wider. Leah stepped through. Her steps were cautious at first, but grew bolder as she closed the distance between them.

"Did you hear what your mother and I were discussing?"

"Yuh-yes, sir."

"Is that why you wanted me to go to work today?"

Leah shrugged and asked, "Is it important?"

"It's very important," Ellen said. "You won't get into trouble either way. I promise. We just need to know the truth. Where'd you go at the mall yesterday, Leah?"

"D-do you want the real t-truth or the t-truth you wuh-want to hear?"

"The truth, Leah," Tom said. "No more playing. Just tell us where you went."

Leah's eyes fell to the wooden planks beneath her. She kicked at a wayward acorn, sending it skittering off the porch. A hot breeze gathered and played with the ends of her

(black, it's black like the little girl's)

hair. Her eyes tried to find something else to kick, something else to look at, anything that would keep her from having to answer. But the porch was bare, and all she could do was lift her head and say, "Nuh-no."

"What?"

"Nuh-no," she said again. "I'm nuh-not saying. Maybe I just wuh-wanted to run away b-because I was t-tired of everyone luh-looking at me like a fruh-freak. Or m-maybe the R-rainbow M-man suh-sang to me because s-someone else needed muh-magic. Muh-maybe giving that muh-magic was the only wuh-way you would ever buh-lieve."

"Believe in what?" Tom asked.

"In the Maybe, Puh-Pops. In what's ha-happened and what's guh-going to happen. I can't tell you where I wuh-went because then you'll nuh-know, and that's nuh-not faith. Faith is buh-lieving in a thing you've n-never seen but's only been pruh-promised."

"Leah, what are you talking about?"

"About the R-rainbow M-man. He wah-wants you to buh-lieve in him, Puh-Pops."

"Tell me what he looks like, Leah," Ellen said. "Describe him. Give me a picture to see."

Leah shook her head. "It's too huh-hard."

Tom said, "When we were at church, Leah, you kept look-ing at that picture by the door. Is that what he looks like? Is that the Rainbow Man?"

She only said, "That's not his fuh-face."

"Then what's his face look like?" Ellen asked. "Tell us that."

"It luh-looks like you, Muh-Mommy. And you, Puh-Pops. Allie and Mr. Buh-Barney. Miss Mabel. It looks like Ruh-Reverend Goggins. His fuh-face is everyone's. Everyone who's ever buh-been and even everyone who'll ever buh-be."

For reasons Tom did not understand, Ellen began to cry. She rose from the swing and went to her daughter.

"Tell me," she said. "Please. I've helped you. I've done things for you. I want to believe, Leah."

"Could I have duh-done that, Muh-Mommy? Puh-Pops? Could I have guh-gone up to that muh-man and suh-said what was tuh-told to him? It duh-doesn't m-matter if it's certain or even likely. Is it *puh-hossible*? Don't answer with your huh-heads. Answer with your huh-hearts."

"Yes," Ellen said, and the tears came one last time. "My heart says yes."

Leah smiled at her mother and turned to Tom—"Puh-Pops?"—who felt the vine that had choked his heart now bursting it open. The squeak from the swing was louder, the sky clearer, the air fresher. In a way he could not fathom, everything around him seemed bigger and more alive. Was it certain? Likely? No.

Was it possible?

Was it maybe?

"Yes," he said. "Maybe."

"Will you huh-help me, then? Buh-both of you? I don't think we huh-have m-much time."

"Help you do what?" Ellen asked.

"C-come to my room. I'll shuh-show you. I've been wuh-working on it all duh-day, since Allie went away. I was guh-going to g-get her to huh-help me, but now it has to b-be you. It's going to be huh-hard, and the R-rainbow M-man says he's suh-sorry for that. But he says we huh-have to."

Ellen took Leah's hand as they walked to the door. The two of them waited there for Tom, who joined them despite the voices in his head.

7

Oak Lawn Cemetery was a gated span of stately trees and manicured lawn that encompassed nearly ten acres on the southern end of town. Among the hundreds of earthly remains interred there were those of Zedekiah Almarode, Mattingly's founder, and Nathaniel Cohron, who in 1864 had pulled together a ragtag collection of farmers and shopkeepers and chased a contingent of Yanks back over the mountains where they belonged. Now the town gathered to sink another of their dearly departed into that dark soil, rendering to the earth what belonged to it now that God had taken what belonged to Him.

Barney pondered these things as he sat in the first of what seemed a hundred rows of metal folding chairs and stared at Mabel's coffin. He wondered, if his wife's body belonged to the ground and her soul belonged to heaven, what exactly was there left for him? Nothing but memories, he reckoned. And one empty wheelchair, three boxes of diapers, and a single strand of snowy hair in his pocket. Even surrounded by so many people, even with Reggie's voice near and Allie Granderson's tiny hand squeezing his knee, Barney had never felt so utterly alone.

"Amen," Reggie said, which was followed by a smattering of echoes from the crowd. Barney hadn't realized everyone was praying. He hoped God wouldn't hold that against him and thought He probably would anyway.

There followed an a cappella rendition of "To God Be the Glory" that Barney endured as best as he could. The gray shade over his mind still flapped (he had tried pulling it down several times since seeing the *26, 26, 26* on the answering machine but had finally given up). Just when the need for numbness was greatest, Barney saw and felt everything. He didn't know if that was by chance or design, and chose to believe the latter. It would help him to say what needed to be said.

Reggie looked at Barney and nodded for him to stand. He squeezed Allie's hand, offered a ghost smile to Mary and Marshall, and walked to the front.

The afternoon sun shone bright against a sky so clear that Barney thought he'd see Mabel and Jesus if he looked straight on into it. The plot he had chosen was near the entrance— better when it came to visiting, though he didn't know how often that would be now—and was situated such that her stone would be visible regardless of which direction one faced from the intersection beyond. The streets would normally be busy that time of day; even in a slow place like Mattingly, there was always a going and coming. But as Barney looked out beyond the iron gates that would now forever hem in his wife, he found them empty but for three specks that approached from the distance. Barney adjusted his blue suit and tugged at the knot in his tie.

"I reckon I been thinkin' on things. That's all I have now. Ever'thing else's gone, an' when you ain't got nothin' left all you got time for's to think. I didn't like what came to me. I got to thinkin' that a body ain't got to die for a person to go to hell. Sometimes hell comes when you're livin'." He turned and looked at Mabel's casket, now closed and ready to be lowered. Dust to dust, the Book said, and that was true.

"Y'all just sang 'To God Be the Glory.' I wonder if this is the glory of God an' a great thing He hath done. I don't think so. Mabel didn't deserve the end she got. She used to run the Bible school in the summertime an' the Christmas program in the winter. An' she helped me out plenty, back when folks would come to the shop for toys to give to others. That ain't how it is now. Now y'all come for toys you think I will give to you."

Nervousness moved like a wave that lowered heads and hunched shoulders in the crowd. The three specks coming down the street were closer now. Barney saw each speck was holding something aloft.

"Life or God or whatever turned on her, just like y'all turned on us. Or maybe it just turned on me, and poor Mabel got caught up in it. Left her like a child who needed help to eat an' move an' clean herself. She couldn't even speak no more. All she said was 'I love you.' I reckon y'all know that, though."

Signs. The three specks were carrying signs. And they were no longer specks, they were people. Two big ones and a small one in the middle.

"Now, y'all tell me, could you live with your loved one in such a state and still give reverence to the Lord? What God worthy of reverence could allow such a thing to one of His own? How can He pardon the darkness of this world and allow it to strip my Mabel down?"

"Barney," Reggie said. The preacher stepped closer and placed a hand on Barney's elbow, trying to guide him away.

Barney jerked away and said, "Nosir, Reggie, I need to say this. I lost my business, I lost my wife, an' then I lost my faith. And then I lost y'all too. All my friends. My Mabel's life got shrunk down to the bare bones, where 'I love you' meant hello an' good-bye an' thank you an' praise the Lord, an' maybe that's what it should mean for all of us. But it don't. Lemme ask y'all this, and you can answer in your own heart—how many of y'all would be here today if I hadn't won that money?"

The people beyond the cemetery gates had stopped on the opposite corner. Barney watched as they huddled together and then spread out, hands high.

"What's that?" he whispered.

A few heads turned in the direction of Barney's gaze, Allie's included. One of the people—the little one, Barney thought, and he also thought it was a girl—shouted something. More heads turned. Allie mumbled something that Barney couldn't decipher. He didn't know what was happening, but something inside whispered that he'd better get on with it.

"I'm leavin'," he said. It was as loud as he could make it, and it must have done the trick, because all but Allie turned back to face him. "I'm leavin' Mattingly. Cashin' in my ticket an' goin' away. Mabel always wanted us to retire down Carolina way, right along the shore. That's what I'm gonna do. I don't wanna be round people who only like me for what I got and not who I am, an' that's all I got to say about that."

Reggie stepped up to him and said, "Barney, you can't mean that."

"Done made up my mind, Reggie. You's always nice to us. None of that was about you. The Barnetts too." Barney looked at Allie and said, "That goes for you and your folks too, Allie."

Allie didn't hear him. Her head was turned in the opposite direction, past the fence to the street corner where the sign people were. The little one was shouting while the big ones were quiet. Nervous too.

"That's Leah out there screamin'," Allie said.

Leah called out again. Barney thought it was *Let Mabel go to bed*, but Allie said it was *Listen to what the Rainbow Man said*. The crowd pulled away from the service. Someone called out for Leah to shut her city mouth. Reggie stood near Barney. He did not beckon the townspeople to return. Mary and Marshall stepped closer to the fence. Allie reached out for Barney's hand and led him as far away from Mabel as he would allow.

Leah stuttered another shout. The sign she raised was the painting she'd shown everyone at church. Flanking her were Ellen and Tom, each of them visibly embarrassed yet refusing to do anything but keep their own signs aloft. LISTEN TO THE RAINBOW MAN, Ellen's read. The letters were drawn in purple with the squiggly lines of a hand either too old or too young. Barney thought he knew which. DON'T BE FOOLS said Tom's, his in the same style but with a yellow color.

Leah yelled, "Luh-let the R-rainbow M-man save you buh-fore it's too luh-late."

Several of the townspeople now moved outside of the open gate. They gathered on the opposite corner from the Norcross family, the empty road between them like a no-man's-land.

"Git on," Brent Spicer yelled, waving his hands as if trying to scare vermin from his barn. "Don't nobody want you here."

Leah called louder, "Tuh-ime's running out. Puh-please listen to me."

"Don't nobody want to *hear* you," came another voice, and that drew more away from the graveside and through the gate.

Allie held on to Barney's hand. "What's happening, Mr. Barney?"

Barney thought, tried to reason things, but found nothing. He merely shook his head and said, "It don't matter, child. It's all been written with a pen that don't erase. We got no power in this life; you just gotta let the world roll over you. You best learn that now."

What happened next played out in front of Barney like a movie. Leah continued to call, and the crowd continued to call back. Tom and Ellen gathered around their daughter, their signs slowly lowering until they settled at Leah's chest as if making a shield to keep her safe. Sheriff Barnett burst through the crowd and stood in the middle of the street, yelling for a calm that Barney thought even Jake knew was not meant to be. The townspeople crept closer. Leah held her ground even when Tom and Ellen tried to back her away. Her yelling only grew louder, more defiant, her face red and her eyes wide and scared.

No one saw the rock until it struck Leah in the head. Barney watched as she fell to the concrete curb like a discarded doll. She lay there motionless, just as Mabel had right before the light went out in her eyes. Ellen and Tom howled. Reggie yelled, *"No!"* and ran. Allie began to cry.

Barney turned from the spectacle and passed his hand down the top of Mabel's casket, the hell rising up around him no match for the hell within him. He thought the screaming and crying a natural consequence of the rottenness that lurked just beneath the goodness of his town. In the distance, a mockingbird called.

8

This was not how it was supposed to end. Not at a doctor's office with an injured little girl, however guilty that little girl may be. The town—his town—was better than that.

Dr. Henry March's tiny office was situated only a block away from the cemetery. The close proximity of the two had long been a running joke, but on that afternoon no one was laughing.

Fortunately for all involved, it just so happened that Doc was one of the few to remain behind after Leah was attacked. She was conscious but dazed. Though a patch of her black hair was stained crimson, she had been much calmer than either of her parents. Jake ushered Doc and the Norcross family into his Blazer and sped off, the situation so dire that he went to the extreme length of fastening his blue light atop the roof. Mary and Marshall remained behind to tend to Allie and Barney. Reggie supposed the care for the latter lay within his purview, yet he felt a greater responsibility elsewhere. He left shortly thereafter, and that was how Mabel Moore's funeral began with nearly two hundred souls in attendance and ended with only four.

Jake's truck was parked directly in front of Mattingly Family Practice. Reggie parked and walked through the still-open doors. The bare waiting room held that peculiar mix of sterile and sick. Tom and Jake sat in two wooden chairs by the window thumbing through magazines that told last summer's news. Tom looked up as Reggie approached.

"What are you doing here?" He rose with such force that the chair banged against the wall. "Come to pray, or come to tell us to leave town? Either way, Reggie, I'm going to make sure the next bloody person the doctor sees is you."

Jake dropped his magazine, stood up, and guided Tom back down with a strong hand and a gentle warning. "I don't want no trouble, Tom," he said. Then, to Reggie, "You either, Preacher."

"No trouble," Reggie said. He held up his palms as if to say there was nothing under his sleeve. "I just wanted to make sure Leah's okay."

"Doc's back with her now," Jake said. "He said it was a glancing blow, not head-on. Looks like she'll be fine."

Reggie closed his eyes. He thought Tom would scoff when he offered a *Praise the Lord*, but none came. "Tom, I know we have our differences, but I never wanted this. You have to know that."

But Reggie didn't think Tom knew that at all. He thought the only thing Tom knew was that someone had smacked his daughter in the head with a rock. Nothing else mattered, and where to set the blame was pretty far down the list. As far as Dr. Norcross was concerned, the whole town was guilty. And maybe that was true.

"Let me sit with you," Reggie said. "Just to make sure she's fine. I won't pray and I won't preach. I promise."

Tom crossed his arms in front of him and said nothing. Jake nodded at the empty chair across from them. Reggie sat.

"Where were you when all that happened?" Jake asked.

"With Barney at the graveside."

Jake raised his eyebrows. His black cowboy hat was turned upside down on the small table beside him. He worked the toothpick in his mouth and pondered.

"You see who threw that rock?"

"No."

"Sure about that?"

"I'm sure, Jake."

The sheriff nodded an okay, though his smile said otherwise. Reggie was glad the questions ended there. Tom gave up leafing through his magazine. He tossed it onto the table, looked at Reggie, looked at Jake.

"What kind of hole did you find, Sheriff?" he asked.

Jake's toothpick stopped moving. "What's that?"

"Barney told me that winning the lottery was a miracle and Leah's rainbow man was real. That was Sunday. I doubt he thinks that now, but he believed it then. He said it wasn't the first magic this town had seen, that you'd found a hole someplace called Happy Hollow. He said it was all connected. I didn't know what that meant, and honestly at the time I didn't really care. But something happened to me this morning, and I'm thinking about it now. So what kind of hole did you find, and what's that have to do with my daughter?"

Had Reggie been standing, the tumble he would have taken upon hearing that question could have certainly bloodied him enough to require Doc March's care. As it was, the only muscles of any consequence that gave way were those surrounding his mouth. Jake at least managed to keep a proper façade of ignorance.

"I don't know nothing about that," he said.

Tom smiled. "You're lying, Sheriff."

Jake took the pick out of his mouth, snapped it, and tossed it into the small plastic trash can beneath the table.

"Tell you what," he said, "once this is all over and if you decide to stay, you come find me. I'll tell you what I found. I'll tell you everything."

"*Jake*," Reggie said.

"Tom's got as much right as anyone else," Jake said. "Maybe more, considering his young'un. And besides, maybe Barney was right. Maybe it is connected."

The door beside the nurses' station opened before Reggie could protest more. Ellen was out first, Dr. March last. Leah was sandwiched between them. She wore a tired smile and a bandage around her head that Doc swore looked worse than it was. Tom rose and gathered Leah into his arms, picking her up and turning her as if performing a dance. Leah opened her eyes and stared at Reggie. Her cheeks were streaked with the muddy brown of dried tears and dirt.

In a calling in which woeful sights were abundant, Leah's sunken eyes and beaten body were the most woeful Reggie had ever seen. He had always considered himself a good man—not perfect, but good—a man who'd given his life to God and longed only to see His face. Yet that had all been tested the moment he watched Brent Spicer pick up that rock, and it had been shattered when he knew the deacon's intent and did nothing to prevent it. The Book said there was no great or small sin but sin alone, but that was one scripture Reggie now doubted. What he had done—what he had allowed—lay beyond forgiveness for a man who longed to look upon the face of his God. And as Leah looked upon him from the safety of her father's arms, Reggie felt sure she knew all of this. She knew all of this and more—that in the eyes of God Reggie might as well have heaved that stone himself, and with no feeling but hate and no other purpose than to maim.

Saturday

Carnival Day

1

The worst day in Mattingly's long and relatively quiet history began as if it would be among its finest. For Barney Moore, it began as good-bye.

He sat on the edge of his empty bed and watched the coming morning unfold like petals on a flower. In a scraggly maple beyond the open window, his mockingbird repeated the mournful lullaby like a skipping record. Twice in the middle of the night Barney had gone downstairs to throw what rocks he could find. Twice that bird had been silenced. And twice it had sung again once Barney was back upstairs.

No matter, he told himself. Let the bird sing. He'd never hear it again, anyway.

The first rays of the sun lit the sides of the abandoned buildings along the alleyway a brilliant orange. There were plenty in Mattingly who would say they were afforded better vistas—mountains and hollers and pastureland and river—but Barney always thought his and Mabel's view was just as good. Seeing that orange glow upon the old Foster's Seed building and the boarded-up Billington's Small Engine Repair meant that Barney was home, that no matter how bad things seemed or how much worse Mabel became, there was still the chance that a new day could bring change.

He rubbed his hands over the suitcase balanced upon his knees, the contents of which represented the sum total of all that seemed necessary to take—three changes of underwear, two pairs of overalls, eight white socks, a Ziploc bag containing Mabel's strand of hair, and his glasses. The lotto ticket was in his front pocket—a quick pat of the chest made sure of that—and his keys were waiting on the coffee table.

"All right, then," he announced.

Barney nodded twice at the window and rose from the bed. It took all the willpower he could summon not to look at Mabel's side of the bed, just as he'd avoided the pictures of them together that dotted the house's shelves and tabletops. The part of Barney that could peek out from behind his mind's gray curtain was afraid the bright eyes and pearly smile that defined Mabel's better days would be gone, replaced by the furrowed brow and pursed lips of disappointment. It had only been hours ago that Barney was convinced that leaving town was the right thing to do. But then sleep wouldn't come and that bleeping bird had started chirping again. Doubts slowly entered, disguised as one reason among many why so few Mattingly folk had ever strayed from the town of their birth and ventured into the corners of the world.

You don't roam far from the bones of your loved ones.

That didn't matter in Mabel's case, at least that's what Barney had decided. There was more of her in the strand of hair in his suitcase than there was in the empty house that was buried on the wrong side of the ground over at Oak Lawn. She wouldn't mind. Mabel had always loved the ocean. Besides, when you're in heaven you're no longer distressed about the world's goings-on. You know that even if people are standing still, they're still roaming about, looking for home.

He'd have to leave soon. It was carnival day, and Barney wanted to stay as far away from that tangle of people as possible. They might try to talk him out of leaving or tell him how sorry they were. Or ask how their easels were coming along. It would take him a couple hours to make it to Harrisonburg and cash in his ticket. He'd tell them to wire it to his account—everything in this dad-gummed modern age was wires—and then he'd get on the road. Assuming the old Dodge could make it, Barney figured he'd be looking at the Atlantic from the Carolina coast by sundown. Whatever came after didn't matter. There was only now. Leah had taught him that.

The light on the answering machine blinked *ERR*. Barney didn't know what that meant other than the messages had grown too big for the machine's insides to handle. He took the keys from the coffee table and left. The mockingbird trilled. Barney imagined it was because he'd left the door open, but he didn't retreat to close it.

Downstairs, he took what cash had been left in the register since

(since Mabel died)

Tuesday and shoved it into his pocket. Gettin' round money is what he called it, though forty-two dollars in cash and change wouldn't even cover the gas. The thick stack of easel orders remained on the counter.

He didn't know why he stopped at Leah's painting in the window. Perhaps it was the way the morning sun glinted off the glass, framing it with a kind of alpenglow. Barney's eyes settled over the mockingbird and the town, the way the clouds gathered just over the horizon. And the numbers. Numbers that hadn't amounted to much of anything except to rile the town. They didn't even look like lottery numbers at all, and he should know.

34720625.

Barney said those numbers aloud—"three-four-seven-two-oh-six-two-five"—then said them again slower. Then he grouped them—"three-forty-seven, two, six-twenty-five."

His hands went to his cheeks, where they slipped downward over the corners of his mouth and paused at his chin. The end result was an expression of slack-jawed awe that comes when wisdom enters where ignorance once dwelt.

Only later, when the horrible mess was over and the time for reflection had come, would Barney remember that the mockingbird outside stilled at that moment. And he would ponder the Maybe that it had done so because its purpose had been fulfilled. But at the time he neither reflected nor pondered at the window of the Treasure Chest. He only whispered, "Oh my sweet Lord."

2

"Would you look at that? Just *sitting* there, like it knows what it's doing. Have you ever seen anything like that?"

Tom turned from the window for an answer that didn't come. Ellen was still in bed, turned away from the window (as if that would help) with the pillow over her face.

He looked out the window again and shook his head. It was bad enough that the plastic owl he'd found in the garage hadn't worked, but to see the mockingbird perched on *top* of it, screeching from it, was too much. Tom balled his hand into a fist and banged three times on the window—*bam, bam, bam.* The bird went silent.

"That's right, shut your yammer."

"My hero," Ellen mumbled.

The alarm clock on the dresser read 6:04. Tom thought if he hurried, he could actually get about three hours of sleep before Leah came looking for him. He'd just crawled back into bed and pulled the sheet over his head when the bird called again. This time the song was neither melodic nor mournful, but three angry staccato *birps* that matched the banging from moments ago—*birp, birp, birp.*

"I give up," Ellen said. "I know you abhor violence, Tom, but if you don't kill that thing, I will."

"Maybe Marshall knows what to do," Tom said. "He's half hillbilly."

"Last time I talked to Mary, Marshall hadn't slept either. No one has. It's like a bad Hitchcock film—death by sleepless-ness." Ellen got out of bed and pulled on her robe. "I'll go make coffee."

She opened the door to let in sounds echoing from the living room beyond the hallway. Ellen leaned out into the hall-way and looked back to him.

"The TV," she said. "Leah must be up."

Ellen continued down the hallway as Tom got out of bed and dressed. "Leah, honey, what are you doing?" he heard Ellen ask. He followed his wife's voice into the living room and stopped as his mind tried to interpret what his eyes saw.

Leah sat on the edge of the sofa, back straight and hair combed. Her knees were close together and her hands care-fully folded into her lap so as not to wrinkle her yellow birthday dress. The living room curtains were still drawn. What little morning light peered through the edges was drowned in the blue glow of the television screen. The shine made the black eye she'd sprouted overnight burn a sickly green. Tom realized he might be pacifistic enough to spare an aggravating mock-ingbird, but if he ever caught the person who threw that rock, he'd kill him. He'd kill him and not think twice about it.

Leah looked up and said, "M-morning, Muh-Mommy. Hey, Puh-Pops."

"Why are you up so early, Leah-boo?" Tom asked.

"Had to wuh-watch the w-weather."

"Since when do you get up before the sun and check the weather?" Ellen asked.

"It's c-carnival day," Leah said. "We have to go, Puh-Pops. It's important."

"I don't think we're going to the carnival today, Leah-boo," Tom told her.

Leah didn't respond at first. She picked up the remote and flipped through the channels, passing over cartoons she never missed and clicking through the nature channels she loved. Her thumb stopped on the weather channel.

"We have to go, Puh-Pops. Muh-Mommy, we huh-have to."

"Why?" Ellen asked.

Leah's lips moved, but she said nothing. Her eyes were centered on the screen. Tom took a step to the side and looked at the television. What crawled along the bottom was what Leah's lips were reading—sunny, upper 80s, slight chance of thunderstorms.

"Because it's the cuh-carnival," Leah said. "What's a sluh-light chance mean, Puh-Pops? Like a number."

"I don't know. Maybe one or two in ten?"

"But you duh-don't know for sure?"

"No. What's wrong?"

A noise that was thankfully nothing like a mockingbird came from outside. Ellen walked between Leah and the tele-vision and peered through the curtains.

"Barney," she said, opening the curtains.

Tom felt the muscles in his stomach tighten. So much for a quiet morning. "What's he doing here?"

"I don't know," Ellen said, "but at least he's alone."

Leah found another report, this from across the mountains in Charlottesville. The bright yellow sun the weatherman pointed to was hidden behind wavy letters that spelled out HAZY. Beside that were a question mark and a bolt of lightning.

"What do you think that muh-means, Puh-Pops?"

Ellen went to the door and opened it. The smile on her face was one that wasn't entirely sure if it should be there or not.

"Puh-Pops?" Leah asked. She pointed to the screen. "Does that muh-mean maybe it could r-rain today duh-down at the carnival, or duh-does it muh-mean like muh-maybe we could get attacked by aliens?"

"Sun's shining, Leah," he said. "I'd go with the aliens."

Barney's head slowly appeared from the bottom of the window as he took the steps onto the porch. Tom noticed he was not smiling, even if Ellen almost was. A rolled piece of paper was in his left hand. Ellen offered a curse word upon seeing it that Leah did not hear. She was too busy trying to find a third opinion on the day's forecast.

Ellen held the door. Barney stopped just short and said, "Hello, Ellen. Sorry to visit at such an early hour. Mind if I bother y'all for a second?"

"Please come in, Barney."

"Much obliged." He stepped through and nodded at Tom— "Mornin', Tom"—and then turned to Leah. "Hello there, Miss Leah."

Leah's head and neck twitched at the sound of his voice. "Huh-hello, Mr. Buh-Barney," she said. "Do you nuh-know if a slight ch-chance of suh-something and a question muh-mark means suh-something will be, or are you muh-more inclined to think it wuh-won't be?"

"I don't rightly know," Barney said. "Reckon we don't have much say in whether a thing is or ain't, only what we'll do either way."

Tom didn't know what any of that meant and so passed over it in favor of more important things.

"Barney," he said, "I know I speak for the whole family when I say—"

"Don't have to, Tom," Barney said, waving him off. "Appreciated, but not necessary. Just wanted to come by an' tell y'all what I said at the funeral. Y'all didn't hear it, you bein' occupied with disruptin' things. I'm leavin' town. This mornin', actually."

Neither Tom nor Ellen spoke. Tom could not help but feel a sense of responsibility over everything that had happened. It had been only a week since Barney had pulled up the lane with Mabel to deliver Leah's easel. Things had been good then. Not perfect, but certainly better. For them all. And now Mabel lay in the ground, Barney in pieces, and the town that had turned out for the party now shunned them. It was amazing how quickly life could turn. One minute you're stroking it until it purrs, and the next it's baring its teeth and tearing at your flesh.

The sharp thump of the remote hitting the living room's floor snapped Tom back to the moment. Leah had dropped it. Evidently something had happened that was more pressing than mostly sunny and HAZY with a slight chance of question mark.

"You can't luh-leave, Mr. Buh-Barney." She rose from the sofa. Her left foot bumped the remote and sent it scattering across the floor. "Puh-please don't. You d-don't understand."

Barney nodded. The edges of his mouth wanted to curl upward but managed only halfway. The smile that could have been came out as a frown instead.

"I reckon I don't. Haven't for a long while, Miss Leah. I thought I understood, Tom. Ellen. For two whole days, I thought I finally understood. But y'all know what? It's when we think we got it all figured out that God says not so fast and reminds us just how small-minded we are. First I won that money an' I thought the Lord wanted me to be rich, but then He took my Mabel so I could see how rich I already was before. Then when Mabel left I thought that meant I should leave too, but then I looked at this one last time."

He unfurled the paper in his hand—Leah's second painting. The town. The gathering clouds. The mockingbird and the numbers tumbling from its mouth. Tom looked at it and realized that at some point since Barney had arrived, the mockingbird in the backyard had finally stilled.

"You say you put those numbers in my first painting, Miss Leah. You know what they was for. You know what these here numbers this bird's singing are for too, don't you?"

Leah did not answer. Her left hand reached for her right thumbnail with the deftness of a professional. Ellen watched her, mouth open and lips pursed in a way that made Tom think of an overbearing parent willing her child to perform. He could not think ill of his wife because Tom realized that he too was willing Leah. Willing her to say, *Yes, I know what those numbers mean, just like I spoke to Harold Gladwell at the Longview Mall.* That's what Tom's own lips were mouthing, because in the end Tom Norcross was the kind of man who would rather be proven crazy than wrong.

Barney looked at Tom. He pointed to the numbers and then turned so Ellen could see as well.

"Three-forty-seven, two, oh-six-twenty-five. Those ain't lotto numbers, Tom, Ellen. People played them an' lost because they weren't lotto numbers a'tall. Ain't that right, Leah?"

There was only the crinkle of the painting against Barney's trembling fingers and the *sst sst* against Leah's thumbnail. Tom's lips kept moving, his eyes kept watching Leah, seeing how scared she was, how nervous. The secret voice in his head wavered. Instead of saying YES, it whispered that his daughter was just as sure about those numbers as she was about the weather.

"Three-forty-seven is the building number of the Treasure Chest," Barney said. "On Second Street. Oh-six-twenty-five, that's—"

"Today," Ellen finished. Her eyes fluttered to Tom.

Leah returned to the sofa and sat. Tom thought she had been just as shocked. Her hand found the cushion next to her. She rested it there and squeezed her fingers together in a kind of half fist, just as she'd done on their ride to the mall.

"Leah," Tom asked. "What's going on?"

"I duh-don't know," she said.

Barney took a step toward her and eyed the empty cushion beside Leah more than Leah herself.

"What's those numbers mean, Miss Leah? Somethin' gonna happen today?"

"You cuh-can't leave, Mr. Buh-Barney. That's what those n-numbers mean. It means it's your tuh-time."

"But you said that before, child."

"I nuh-know." She squeezed her hand again. Whether it was the effects of the sleepless night or some sort of willed mirage, Tom swore he could see the pads of her fingers flatten against an unseen hand she held. "But *I* suh-said it before. He's suh-saying it now. Do you buh-lieve me, Mr. Buh-Barney?"

Barney rolled the painting up slowly, an inch at a time, careful that the ends were even and did not telescope out. Tom knew what that act meant. He'd employed similar methods whenever faced with a patient's thorny question. Barney was buying time.

Leah rose from the sofa again. Her steps were not as bold as her first advance nor as shaky as her last retreat. She took Barney's hand in her own and eased him down to her eye level.

"I'm so suh-sorry, Mr. Buh-Barney. About everything. I luh-loved Muh-Miss Mabel, and all I suh-said about her at the s-service was true. All I was duh-doing was what the R-rainbow M-man asked. I didn't understand why, but I duh-do now. He wanted as many puh-people to hear as could. Do you understand? Puh-lease try. And puh-lease don't go yet. C-come to the carnival with us."

"I weren't plannin' on goin' to the carnival," Barney said. "I's s'posed to be down Carolina way by sundown."

"We weren't planning on going either," Ellen said. "But plans can change. Can't they, Tom?"

The three of them looked at Tom, who nodded a silent yes.

"All right, then," Barney said. "Reckon there ain't no harm in stoppin' by." He nodded like he'd just convinced himself and looked out the window. "Besides, s'posed to be a pretty day after all."

3

Reggie thumbed the switch to Off and found himself whistling a tune he could not place. Probably it was a fragment of a hymn, though there were times when he would begin a few random notes and let the Spirit take over. Sometimes the result was pleasing, other times not so much. This melody sounded well enough that the source did not matter.

Sweat gathered above his brow though the sun was still weak on the horizon. His T-shirt was wet and cold at the neck and under the arms. It had been a long job, and tougher than he'd realized. But it was done. Reggie stepped back to take stock of his handiwork and saw that it was good.

He laid the chainsaw in the grass beside the ladder and settled into the backyard's only chair, one of those plastic jobs the Super Mart in Camden gathered en masse in front of the store and sold for five bucks apiece when the weather turned from cold to hot. Aside from that, the only other object that occupied the concrete slab outside his back door was a small charcoal grill covered by a tattered canvas and a thin layer of spiderwebs. Reggie took a sip of milk—not his first choice but his only, as that was all that was in his refrigerator. Across the way, Jeff and Pauline Hartzog peeked out from behind their curtains, no doubt wondering why their preacher was making such a racket so early on carnival day. Reggie toasted his glass of milk to his only neighbors and carried on his tune, pausing only to chuckle at Pauline's confused and somewhat petulant look.

She and Jeff could slumber in peace now that the once mighty maple outside Reggie's bedroom window had been reduced to a pile of kindling. Cutting down the tree had only expanded the emptiness of the backyard, but it had been worth it. Oh yes it had, because Reggie's backyard may now be devoid of all but the tumbledown woodshed that marked the boundary between his property and the Hartzogs', but it had also chased off his mockingbird.

"Let's see you sing now," Reggie said to no one in particular, and then he whistled again.

He looked at his watch, surprised at the hour. There was

no time to shower, which was fine because there really was no need. Strange how the minutes could slip away when you had so much to do. Sort of like how God could hang a CLOSED sign on the door and go fishing when you needed Him the most. Reggie thought of Leah, tiny Leah, powerful Leah, thought of her saying, *See you soon, Reverend*, and of Brent Spicer's rock hitting her in the head, but most of all Reggie thought of God and how he'd spent his life in search of Him and how now He seemed so very far away.

The ride into town took longer than it would have on a normal Saturday. The downtown area was already filling with trucks and cars. Horns bellowed and hands were lifted. Anticipation filled the air like electricity. People passed from one side of the street to the other, most of them not bothering to make sure the way was clear. They carried blankets to lounge upon and chairs to sit in. They pushed baby carriages and pulled coolers, laughing, shouting, celebrating the day. Many waved to Reggie as he passed. A part of him wanted to wave back—it would be the Christian thing to do—but his hands were too tight on the steering wheel and he could not seem to pry them away.

He realized the tune he'd been whistling was not the Spirit's but that of a man named John Newton, who long ago had cried out for God's mercy during a storm at sea and had become a good man because of it. Reggie whistled the melody as he passed the town square and saw Barney's truck gone. Left for Carolina already, Reggie supposed, and may God go with Barney Moore. He repeated it as he drove by the rides and games and fun that awaited in the park. Then he parked in the lot of the First Church of the Risen Christ, where every Saturday for the past twelve years—rain, shine, or carnival— Reggie Goggins had gone to put the finishing touches on the next day's sermon.

He was whistling still when he dropped five quarters into the vending machine just down the hall from his office and selected C2. Having a candy bar for breakfast may not have been synonymous with treating one's body as a temple of the Holy Spirit, but when you were gripped by the three-headed monster of anger, hunger, and exhaustion, only chocolate and peanuts would do. The metal loop that held his breakfast gave way with a whir, pushing the candy bar free. Just as it was about to fall into the bin below, the whir stopped. Reggie's eye twitched at the sight. The tune he whistled caught in his throat. He walked back to the office for something that could help. Lines of townspeople marched by the window. He turned and saw Mary and Allie Granderson walking hand in hand toward the park.

Whistles echoed through the hallway as he returned to the vending machine and the reward still dangling beyond his grasp. Reggie brought the softball bat down upon the thin sheet of Plexiglas. It shattered into long, thin shards that bounced off the junk food inside and plinked onto the floor. Reggie reached in and gently pried his breakfast from the metal ring. He turned toward his office, candy bar in one hand and the bat swinging in lazy circles in the other, whistling again words John Newton had penned after his storm was over—of the dangers and foils and snares through which he'd already come, and how it was Grace that had brought him safe thus far and Grace that would lead him home.

4

Allie had been fine all morning, but now a sudden fear swept through her and sent her hurtling headlong into the crowd, thoughtless of whom she swatted out of the way as she cleared a path with elbows and excuse-me's. She could not get past how it had happened so suddenly. One minute she was admiring the bags of pink and blue cotton candy next to the dunking booth, the next she was all alone. Weren't the orders to be mindful and stay close? Yes. In fact, Allie recalled those very words. And yet there she was, surrounded by everyone but the one who mattered most.

The park was already close to capacity. The clatter of people mixed with the constant hum of the rides and the whirs and beeps from games made even Allie's voice just another small element to be swallowed by the din. She spotted Jane Markham holding court near the dunking booth with half a dozen fellow fourth-grade survivors, all of them laughing (Allie briefly wondered if Jane had just said anyone who'd ever get in a dunking booth would need srain burgery), their worlds careless and innocent. She wondered how things would have turned out if she'd simply told Leah last Saturday to go on to the Treasure Chest and drop off Mr. Barney's painting on her own, that Allie Granderson couldn't be friends with someone from Away, she'd rather sit there on the sidewalk and share a Popsicle with her good friend Jane.

Allie decided it best to find higher ground and climbed atop one of the waxed and gleaming fire trucks. What she saw from that vantage point only made things worse. Rising up over the distant blue mountains was a string of cotton-balled clouds that looked like angels at the tops and demons on the bottoms. Just as the sort of panic that was all claws and teeth began to build, Allie spotted Jake Barnett making his way out of the park.

"Hey, Sheriff." She waved, but as she did two of the Clatterbuck sisters (that would be Margie and Mattie, "So big

they near block out the sun," as Allie's daddy sometimes said)
passed in front of her. When they made their way on, Allie
saw that the sheriff had paused in his going but was looking in
the wrong direction. She waved again and said, "Sheriff, over
here."

Jake waved back and tipped his hat. Allie dismounted the
fire truck and ran up, so thankful that she almost gave him a
hug.

"Mornin', Allie," he said. "Zach's over by the Ferris wheel.
If you're interested."

He added a wink on the end that told Allie he knew interested was exactly what she was, which would have been true
enough under normal circumstances. But something inside
her—barely there, but there nonetheless—said things were
about as far from normal as they could get.

"I was lookin' for my momma. She was right beside me a
little bit ago, but then she weren't."

Jake nodded. "She with your daddy, maybe?"

"Nosir, Daddy's at the factory today. I gotta find her,
Sheriff."

"Well, I'm sure she's around here somewhere," Jake said.
"Why you lookin' so worried, Allie? Everything okay?"

Allie wanted to say no, but she knew if she did Jake would
want the particulars, and all the particulars she had at the
moment was the Barely There inside her that was still going
on about how things had turned wobbly.

"Everything's roses," she said. "Where you off to, Sheriff?"

"Gotta head back to the office. Kate thinks she left the
coffeepot on. Want me to help you look first?"

"No thanks."

Allie started a smile, but she turned to see the clouds
closer now, pushed along by a gathering draft that ran like a

fingernail down her back. She shivered and jumped as if the wind that had just touched her was a living thing.

"Sure you're okay, Allie?"

"Yessir. But if you might, Sheriff, could you do me a favor?"

Jake said, "That's why I'm here."

"Could you just take a look around at things when you get to your office? After you turn the coffeepot off, I mean."

"Anything in particular I should be looking for?"

"Can't say."

Jake took a step toward her. He pushed back the brim of his hat. "Can't, or won't?"

Allie measured her next words and hoped their sum spoke more than their parts. "I reckon both, Sheriff. Just like I reckon sometimes we gotta turn over the secrets we come across ourselves before we go sayin' what's right and what ain't for other folks."

Jake's look was one of decision, a weighing of whether wanting more of an answer would be proper or inviting trouble. It was as if a different sort of Barely There was in him as well, whispering that Allie knew of the magic that had touched him in the dark woods of the Hollow. That maybe she didn't know all of it, but some.

"I'll make sure all's well," he said. "Now, you get on and tell your momma I said hey."

"I will, Sheriff."

Allie felt Jake's eyes linger as she threaded her way back through the crowd, pausing at the pie contest and the quilting exhibit and the bake sale—the sort of places Mary Granderson would be drawn. No one had seen her. Worse, no one seemed particularly alarmed. And though the clouds were still a ways off and were just as likely to head toward Camden as not, they now looked a bit more demon than angel. Allie felt a knot work its way north from her stomach to her throat. Her eyes squinted in reflex. That's when she knew she was going to cry, she was going to cry and there was nothing—

"Hey, sweetie."

Allie knew the hand that squeezed her shoulder. She wheeled and reached for her mother's waist with a speed and strength that forced Mary to let out a faint *whump*.

"I told you to stay close," Allie said. She gripped her mother tighter. "I said those exact words, Momma. Didn't you hear me?"

"Well, I'm sorry." The words came out in a heave that Allie would have normally

(*But things aren't normal*, said Barely There)

found humorous.

"Please don't leave me again. Please. If you have to, you gotta tell me where you're gonna be."

"Well, yes, ma'am," Mary said. Or tried to say. By then the heaves had morphed into a low whine. "Can you let go of me, Allie? I can't breathe."

"Sorry." Allie released her and smiled. It was a real one, not like the one she'd given to the sheriff, who hopefully had turned the coffeepot off back at the office and was now busy taking a look around at things. "I just want you to be safe."

Mary bent down and said, "I'm safe, Allie. I was safe before too. And I'm going to be safe later on. Here. Won you something at the dime toss."

She reached into her pocket and pulled out a red plastic band. In the center, wobbling in a pool of clear liquid, floated a tiny compass. Mary cinched it around Allie's tiny wrist as far as it would go.

"Got it on my first try," she said. "You like it?"

"I love it," Allie said.

"Good. I'm going to go help the Women's Auxiliary set up for lunch. I'll be right up on the hill by the pavilions. Now, it's carnival day, and you're gonna go have fun. Stop fretting and enjoy yourself." She pointed to the compass and said, "If you get lost, I'll be north."

"That's not funny," Allie said.

"It's kind of funny. Now go have fun."

Allie said she would try, and she meant to well enough. But it was hard not to fret with her momma walking farther away and those gray clouds coming on faster. And then it became darn near impossible.

Because just as Mary melted into the crowd, Allie saw Mr. Barney approaching with a candy apple in his hand, followed close by Mr. Doctor and Miss Ellen.

Leah was with them.

Mr. Doctor saw her before she could move. He raised his hand and said, "There's Allie."

5

Tom wriggled his hand from side to side when he thought Allie hadn't noticed them.

Leah stopped in front—Tom couldn't recall how she'd managed to maneuver herself into conductor of their four-person train, but she had—and he halted behind her. Ellen bumped into his shoulder and gave a startled cry that left her face red. Given what had happened just the day before, Tom didn't blame her for being tense. Truth be known, he wasn't feeling so comfortable himself.

At the end of the train, Barney let out an *oomph* as he bumped into Ellen, which caused another cry.

"Hello, Allie," Barney said.

Allie remained still long enough to answer, "Hey there, Mr. Barney," and then disappeared behind a row of games.

"What was that all about?" Tom asked.

Leah rose to her tiptoes and looked into the crowd, only to give up and slump her shoulders. "It duh-doesn't matter," she said.

They continued through the crowd as if through the valley of the shadow of death, guarded not by a spirit but by a brokenhearted old man who had yet to realize that what burdened him in the Virginia mountains would be waiting for him at the Carolina shore. Tom knew as much. That had been the third commandment of his gospel, right behind marriage being built upon a solid foundation of communication and the fact that it took courage to face this world—run from your sorrows, and all you'll find is futility.

But he also knew better than to offer his counsel when it had not been invited, especially in the midst of such commotion. There was little doubt that beneath the bright colors and festive music of the carnival lay a dark rage aimed directly at the Norcross family, one that would surely bubble over were it not for the presence of the one man whose rage seemed most warranted. But it looked as though the fight had gone out of Barney Moore, if ever there had been much fight in him at all. He sidled up to Tom, more interested in his candy apple than in his beleaguered mind.

"Ain't a crowd like usual," Barney said. He glanced ahead to Leah and said, "Reckon you scared a lotta folk away with your talk, little Leah. Won't get you many points with the fire department. They need this money to run on."

Leah said nothing. Tom wanted to apologize for her but didn't. There was no way of telling whether Barney spoke the truth, and from the looks of things the fire department would make out just fine.

"Lunch'll be up at the pavilions in a bit," Barney said. "Ever'body down here now will be up there then. After that's when the concerts and dancin' start. I plan to be on the road by then, little Leah. Wanna beat those clouds yonder."

Leah stopped the train again and looked back over her shoulder toward the mountains. Tom followed her eyes to the approaching clouds. Their bottoms were dark and pregnant with rain, their tops white and afire with sunlight. Though the speed at which they'd gathered seemed odd—Tom could swear those clouds hadn't been there when they'd left the house—they looked no different from any other clouds on any other summer day. That made the fear on Leah's face more puzzling. It was as if another sort of storm, one smaller but just as violent, passed through her eyes as she regarded the marshaling sky. She reached back and took hold of Tom's hand, used the other to take hold of Barney's. The old man winced at her touch and then surrendered like someone receiving unpleasant medicine for a wound. Tom didn't ask why she did that. A part of him knew he would be afraid of her answer.

The people around them offered nothing beyond their usual sneers. Tom thought whatever insults they might have had a mind to speak were silenced out of respect for Barney, who met every stare with a quiet, "It's okay now, they's with me." Those words did little to assuage either the townspeople's disgust or Ellen's fears. She allowed not even a sliver of daylight between herself and Tom. Her hand was clamped into his and spasmed with every bell from the games or whistle from the rides. Her other hand was upon Leah's shoulder, who was the conductor once more despite Tom's guess that she had no idea where they were going.

The sad thing (and this bothered Tom even more than the sneers) was knowing that the carnival could have been fun if things had been different. If he had asked Barney to make Leah a dollhouse instead of an easel, those looks would likely be of acceptance at most or indifference at least. Anything besides the hate they displayed. Tom whiffed the hot peanuts and fresh funnel cakes and could almost picture Ellen helping in the concession stands. He heard the clanging bell of the miniature train and saw Leah sitting alone in one of the back cars, gripping the flaking red paint on its side with her scarred thumbnail, trying to smile all the way through three looping circles around the baseball field. In Tom's mind he saw himself huddled with his wife and daughter over plates of barbecued chicken with slaw and corn bread on the side, maybe a slice of apple pie after, and a cold Coke ("Co'Cola," he'd say, just to fit in) to wash it all down. He saw all of this and wondered how he could feel loss over something he'd never had. A gust of wind tickled the back of his neck and sent gooseflesh down his spine. It was a heavy breeze, and cold.

"What are we doing here, Leah?" he asked.

"I d-don't know, Puh-Pops."

Ellen said, "Well, if you don't know, sweetie, then maybe we should just go. I don't want more trouble."

"Won't be no trouble, Miss Ellen," Barney said. He offered a hello to a younger woman in a waitress uniform and said he was sorry, but his easel-making days were over. He smiled and patted the dejected woman's arm, then turned back to Ellen. "Folks'll mind their manners so long as I'm with y'all, an' I won't wander off. An' don't you worry about Reggie, Tom. He'll be over at the church readying tomorrow's sermon."

Leah stopped and turned. "The ruh-reverend isn't here?"

"No, ma'am," Barney said. "You'll be fine, Miss Leah."

They turned and made their way through the center of the park, where Tom and his family were heckled not for who they were but what they were—paying customers. Everything from American flags to fire department T-shirts to Mason jars filled with clear liquid marked "medicine" was being hawked. People haggled for profit and pleasure. Leah kept moving, pausing only to turn around and make sure her company was still present. Barney was the only one who seemed to be enjoying things. His candy apple was little more than a stub now. Every person who came up to him was given a hello again and a good-bye forever in the same sentence. When he smiled, his lips were lined with a thin sheen of caramel.

There were four pavilions scattered through the park, two near the baseball field (where Tom assumed the town had gathered Monday for Barney's press conference) and two on the hill above. It was in these upper wooden rotundas that lunch was about to be served, as evidenced by the slow migration of people away from the fairgrounds. Tom caught a passing glimpse of Allie above as they made their way up the winding steps. He thought he heard her call out for her mother.

They reached the pavilion just as the first thunderhead passed under the sun, encasing the entire park in shadow.

"That looks like it's going to put a damper on the day," Ellen said.

"It does," Tom answered, and when the wind blew again he heard an echo saying, *There's a storm coming, there's no stopping it, because I've already tried that.* He turned to Leah, sure that she had said those words. But her eyes were on the park, where those who chose to forgo lunch for further entertainment played and laughed.

What people were not gathered beneath the open shelters of the pavilions had spread out blankets and beach towels around it. Tom guided Ellen and Leah to the far end, where he thought they would go unnoticed. Barney joined them. It was a kind gesture, Ellen whispered, and Tom agreed.

Mayor Wallis took the microphone and asked Brent Spicer to come and bless the food. Tom bristled at the sight of the old farmer, who was about to use the same tongue to say Dear Lord or Praise God or whatever those people said that he'd used just days before to threaten Leah and Ellen. But just before he spoke, the first peal of thunder rocked the hill.

Ellen jumped as the shock wave rattled the corrugated roof of the pavilion. Several children huddled close to their mothers and fathers, their faces a mix of terror and embarrassment. Barney mumbled something about not being able to outrun those clouds after all and then shuddered as a cold wind swept across the baseball field and up the path, scurrying paper plates and napkins and toppling half-empty drink coolers with a hollow, mournful thud. Tom felt the pressure in the air drop. Ellen reached out and found Leah's hand.

The fervor that had permeated the carnival's lunchtime gave way to a confused silence, as if the townspeople were trying to match the blue skies of just moments ago with the laurel-green dusk that had quickly engulfed them. Thick raindrops fell upon the roof like nickels onto metal, sending those who had been scattered around the pavilion scrambling beneath it. Tom saw Mary Granderson run back down the hill toward the fairground and wondered where she could be going without Allie.

"No worries, folks," Mayor Wallis said. He held out his hands and pushed them down like a teacher calming a group of unruly students. "Just a little shower's all. Be over before you know it."

Far in the distance came the low whine of the siren atop

the Mattingly Volunteer Fire Department. A corresponding noise that was not quite panic but close enough to fear rippled through the crowd as the wind picked up again, this time stiff enough to send the rain sideways through the pavilions. Another siren, this one sharper and closer, pierced the air. Sheriff Barnett's truck skidded to a stop on the slick pavement just beyond the pavilions. He bolted for the crowd, leaving the driver's side door swinging in the wind. His mouth was open, arms waving, but the wind and rain swallowed Jake's words until he reached the gathering.

"Tornado!" he yelled. "Tornado's coming. *Everybody get out.*"

Screams filled the air. The world came down.

6

It wasn't that Reggie didn't sense the storm approaching, he was simply too preoccupied to understand the growing awfulness of it. His ears registered the rain and wind (and the hail now, that plinking on the stained glass had to be hail), but his mind had been divided neatly into thirds—the weariness he felt, the sermon he was supposed to be preparing, and the lingering image of the shattered snack machine in the hallway. The weather was far down on his list of concerns.

That was about to change.

His worn leather Bible lay open in front of him to the next day's scripture (1 Thessalonians 5:18, which went well with the topic of "Giving Thanks for What's Difficult to Be Thankful For," which was already printed in the church bulletins). He cleared his throat and gripped the sides of the pulpit, tried again, and got no further into his sermon than the three preceding efforts.

He thought again of the mess in the hallway and wondered what a church member would think if he or she stumbled upon it. Wondered, too, how exactly that had all happened.

The sun was gone now, casting the sanctuary in a strange gray that seemed more twilight than noon. Thunder from outside. *That'll put a damper on the carnival.*

Reggie tried again, working his way down the notes paperclipped onto the opposite page of his Bible, trying to find his groove, trying to summon the Spirit. But even as he tried, the hallway came back to him, that feeling of being out of control and his mind snapping in half, caving inward and shooting out as the Plexiglas had. The Spirit could not dwell where sin dwelt. The dark sanctuary pressed in around him. Shadows formed like tiny circles in the empty pews as if they were reservations for the souls who would sit there the next day. People who trusted the words of their preacher, who put their faith in him to be a pillar of the community and a man who lived the Word.

He cleared his throat again, all the while knowing that what was keeping him from speaking wasn't the last bit of chocolate caught in his throat but the means by which he had obtained it. Had that been living the Word? Would a man of God resort to such actions?

"No," he said. The sound reverberated through the sanctuary and mixed with the wind and hail to produce a sound unlike applause. It was one word, but it was the most honest and heartfelt word Reggie had uttered since taking the pulpit that morning. And to his amazement, that one word felt so freeing, so *right*, that he said it again—

"No."

He thought once more of Elijah's maelstrom, the wind and fire and shaking, and that small part of him not focused upon his God reminded Reggie of another maelstrom brewing just beyond the walls of his church. Still he hung on, eyes clenched, searching for that Still Small Voice that had eluded him for days.

Longing for it, begging it to answer.

7

Chairs screeched and tumbled backward from the panicked force of people who now understood they were in the midst of no passing shower. The green-black sky unleashed its rage in violent retches of wind and water. Barney felt the table beneath his hands vibrate. He turned to see Tom's chair toppling end over end down the hillside to the fairgrounds, where people now ran in all directions. The doctor grabbed Ellen by the wrist and Leah by the shoulder to pull them away. He was yelling. Barney didn't know what Tom was saying. It was as if everything around him was happening too fast for words to stay beside. The gusts scattered the people's screams as hail the size of quarters kept them hemmed. They scuttled in all directions, only to be driven back by the thunder's deep knells. There were shoves and curses and the cries of those pushed to the ground. In that moment the townspeople's brittle façade of community and kinship was peeled back to expose the beasts that lurked beneath.

They were all going to die. Barney accepted this conclusion as a fitting end, one that held a great deal of pain at the beginning but promised Mabel's sweet face at the end.

He would remain. Yes, he would stay there in his chair and let the thunder roll and the lightning strike and the winds lift him heavenward. *Close the shade,* he asked. *Close the shade and let me drift.*

And then there was Leah.

He sensed her in front of him, waiting despite her father's pull with a calmness so inappropriate that it drew Barney's gaze. He looked up and saw a pair of soft unblinking eyes that held a light despite the silence in them, a light that conveyed not thoughts but pictures. Barney did not know how long Leah's eyes tethered him nor how much rain had happened in the meantime. He did not know that the Ferris wheel had rocked and then toppled onto the fairgrounds below, did not hear the screams that rang out from the people around him. There were only the pictures of him on the Juke-and-Puke as a boy, holding on because once the ride started there was no getting off, of Mabel's smile and the pursed lips of his fellow townspeople, her love and the town's fear that his failure was a virus that would spread if they did not keep their distance. He saw the numbers in Leah's first painting and the not-numbers in the second and he knew oh God he knew he knew everything.

"Ever'body come with me!" Barney shouted. He stood, and when the throng did not respond he shouted it again.

Tom was still trying to pull Leah away. He stopped upon the discovery that not only was his daughter not moving, Ellen had paused as well.

"Ever'body follow me. We'll get in the basement at the Treasure Chest. It's the only place." The rain now fell sideways, so hard that it stung needle-like upon Barney's skin. He turned to Tom and Ellen. "Come on now, let's get goin'."

8

Allie no longer cared who saw her cry. There were plenty of other people doing just the same. She saw grown-up women teary and shaky. Strong men buckled beneath the enormity of the storm around them. Boys and girls older than herself cried out for their parents, and Allie cried too. She cried because she understood that people don't weep because they're weak, but because they've been strong for too long.

She could not find her momma. She could not find her momma and there was a storm and Leah said her momma was gonna die and there was nothing anyone could do about it. Some things have to happen. There's no changing them. No matter how much we wish them so.

The pandemonium around her had reached its zenith when the Ferris wheel fell. Allie cried out again as hard and as loud as she could. Tears and snot clogged her throat, crying out, *Momma, Momma, please come get me.* Mr. Barney said something. Allie didn't know where he was but she heard him again, telling everyone to follow him. Fear stuck her feet to the pavilion's concrete floor like flypaper. Someone shoved her aside, and she briefly wondered who could do such a thing to a little girl.

There came a call of "Allie" from the back. Allie turned, her heart exploding with joy, only to see not her mother but Miss Ellen barreling through the crowd. She swept Allie from the floor and cradled her like a newborn.

"I can't find my momma." Tears flooded her eyes again. The wind swirled, sending a sideways sheet of rain through the pavilion that washed her face. Lightning flashed overhead like a million tiny flashbulbs. "Do you know where my momma is, Miss Ellen?"

Mr. Doctor worked his way beside them, carrying Leah in his arms. When Allie asked him if he'd seen her mother, a black pall came over his face.

"I saw her going down to the fairgrounds," he said. "Just before the siren sounded."

And Allie knew then, at least some part of her knew, that Mary Granderson had gone out into the teeth of the storm to find her daughter. And the greater part of her understood that if her momma died, it would be Allie's fault.

Miss Ellen pulled Allie close to her breast, but even the wind and hail and the suction of her wet skin could not keep the "She won't find Allie" away from Allie's ears.

"Where's your daddy?" Mr. Doctor asked.

"He ain't here. I want my momma. You gotta get my momma." Allie wiped her eyes, scratching her face with the compass bracelet on her wrist. And then, realizing there was no other choice, she added, "Leah, please tell the Rainbow Man *to get my momma.*"

Leah looked at her. Her face was wet. Allie knew it was not from the rain.

"Listen to me," Mr. Doctor said. "Your mother's going to be fine. She's going to find a safe place to stay. But you have to come with us, okay? Your momma will be fine."

But Allie knew he was wrong. Leah's tears told her so.

9

Brent Spicer spoke for many when he shouted, "The Treasure Chest'll be the first to fall. That heap will be the end of all us."

"You run you die, Brent," Barney said. "This is the only way."

"There's no time," Sheriff Barnett said. Kate and Zach were huddled close to him. "Everybody follow Barney. He's got the only basement close. It's our best chance."

Barney stepped forward. Tom, Ellen, Leah, and a bawling Allie Granderson came after. He wanted to ask where Mary was, but Tom shook his head. The crowd split between those who saw the wisdom in following the most cursed man in town to the ricketiest building in town and those who understood the foolishness of it. Many ran for their cars, Brent Spicer among them.

Those who remained—Barney supposed there were fifty at most, though by then the storm was such that he could barely see—huddled close to the sheriff at the far end of the second pavilion. Barney led them out into the gale. Trees bent and snapped. The air churned with both refuse and an electric charge that made the hairs on his arms stand on end. They formed a long single line, each person holding the hand of the one in front and behind, Barney first, the sheriff last.

"Head down, one step at a time," Barney yelled. "Slow and easy. Don't look up."

The Treasure Chest lay two blocks away. It was an impossible distance, but they would make it. Barney was sure of it. That and that alone was what was in Barney Moore's mind as he stepped out into hell itself.

Because Leah's eyes had given him more than pictures. They had also told him his time had come. His time had come, and God loved him. Barney thought God maybe even loved him most of all.

10

They walked and stumbled under the black sky, pushing their feeble might against the wall of wind, their hands tight against one another. She waited until it was time and then slowly drew the hand behind her forward and the hand in front of her back, and when they met, both relaxed just enough to uncouple before clamping down again. That those hands now gripped a different person didn't seem to matter, especially since at that moment the transformer just outside the park blew, sending a shower of sparks and a muffled cracking sound into the air.

There was no time.

She ducked into the wind—not an easy task given her size—and kept her head down. The long line of people slowly passed in front of her, their backs hunched and heads tucked into their shoulders to protect themselves from the flying debris. The walk back seemed like hours. Water rushed into every orifice and through every opening—into her shirt, down her jeans, soaking her shoes. Roof shingles and flowerpots flew past, forcing her to duck and weave as if she were stuck in some twisted game of dodgeball.

Twice she lost her footing as the wind swept over her. Blood mixed with water as the hailstones cut into her scalp and face. Streets were turning to rivers, alleyways to creeks. The water was now to her ankles. Her clothes added a weight she could barely carry.

She looked up to find both pavilions gone, collapsed into two heaps of fluttering metal. The path to the fairgrounds was blocked.

There was no time.

It would be the long way around, then, which was a kind of blessing in that she could steady herself by gripping the iron bars that fenced the park. Cars and trucks sat dented by the hail, their windshields shattered. Many of the large oaks within the park had been felled. One of them had fallen onto the banquet table where only days before they'd sat and faced the wolves. The park had been full then, the sun shining. Though the park looked empty now, she knew it wasn't. There were others there, hiding, praying, calling out for help.

She paused at the front gate—she knew she was supposed to keep walking but she had to rest, her legs were so tired—and looked out over the wide expanse of carnival rides and booths that were now unrecognizable, mangled by the storm. Above her the green-black sky vomited lightning and thunder. Angry clouds released tails of small funnels that swirled downward only to be gathered back up.

It's coming. Hurry.

She took two steps away from the gate before looking back. A woman ran toward a small wooden equipment shed beside the baseball field. She tripped on a tree limb and fell. When she rose again, the front of her shirt and jeans were covered with mud. She flung the door of the shed open and closed herself inside.

Leah stood by the gate and screamed, screamed with all her might, but the woman didn't hear. Couldn't. And there was no time. She cried out when the wind took the equipment shed with a deafening *WHOOSH* and dared not look back for fear of what she would see.

Battered and soaked, she walked on as best she could, her head down as the water rose past her ankles.

11

The garbage can and broom that Reggie needed were housed in the church kitchen, which sat midway between the sanctuary and the pastor's office. The room also afforded two windows that looked over the parking lot and the park beyond. What greeted him through those panes was a sight so horrible that his heart nearly lurched from his chest.

Only one of the big elms in front of the church was standing.

The rest lay toppled and splintered, stacked like some giant's kindling. Not blown down—sheared away. Torrents of rushing water descended from downtown like waterfalls that pooled in the low places, rendering the church little more than a sinking island. The wind beat against the windows, expanding and contracting the glass as if the building itself was gasping under the pressure. Lightning streaked across a dark, churning sky. Thunder boomed. Reggie stood in shock. The world was ending, and he'd been too busy wallowing in his own self-pity to notice.

He ran for his office phone and tried Jake Barnett. The line was dead, as was the power. The windows outside Reggie's office were larger and offered even more destruction. He wanted to leave, to help, but both seemed impossible. No one could survive being caught in such weather. His only hope was that everyone at the carnival had found safety indoors.

The rafters above him shuddered against a violent gust. The walls moaned. From far down the hallway, Reggie heard the sound of a door slamming and squeaks against the linoleum floor. Quick at first, then slowing. Reggie went to the door and peered down the hallway. Shadows engulfed everything past the shattered vending machine. The steps grew closer.

"Hello," he called.

The footsteps stopped.

"Who's there? Is everything okay?"

The squeaks came again, slower than before. Almost timid. The darkness coalesced just beyond Reggie's sight. What came from the black was a frightened and waterlogged little girl. Her long black hair clung to her face in thick strands. Blood seeped from her head to her face. Her fingers were mangled. Small tennis shoes left puddles in their wake.

"Leah."

Reggie rushed to her just before she collapsed. He sat her down against the wall, careful to place her between the kitchen's windows and the vending machine's shards.

"What are you doing here? Where are your parents?"

"With Mr. Buh-Barney. People are going to the Truh-Treasure Chest. It's the suh-safest place. We have to luh-leave. Tuh-t-tornado's coming. It muh-might already be too luh-late."

Her lips were white and trembling. Rivulets of blood ran down her bare arms. Leah was in shock.

"Now, you just sit here a minute," Reggie said. Leah tried to say no, but he was already at the kitchen. He returned with three dish towels and did his best to wipe her face and arms. "You should be with your folks."

"I cuh-came for you," she said. "We have to go, Ruh-Reverend. We have to guh-get to Buh-Barney's."

Reggie said, "We're not going anywhere," and as if to define the wisdom in that statement, a sheet of wind-driven rain slammed into the side of the church so hard that the foundation itself seemed to shift beneath them.

Leah staggered to her feet and took Reggie by the hand. "We have to guh-go. You d-don't understand."

"No." Reggie jerked his hand back. "We're staying here, Leah. The storm will pass. If we go out there now, we might die."

Her hand found his again and was joined by her other. The squeeze she gave was frail and unsteady. "If we stuh-hay in here, we w-will die. The R-rainbow M-man told me. You have to *buh-lieve.*"

Reggie's hands began to shake. His lips twitched. The anger bubbled up again, just as it had when he reached for the chainsaw and ladder in his shed and as it had when he grabbed the softball bat after putting his five quarters into the vending machine. It bubbled out of frustration and fear, and then it spewed regardless of the one in its path.

"No one believes more than *me*, Leah. Especially *you*. Why can't you just leave me *alone*?"

He didn't know if it was the cold rain outside or the hot fury in his voice that made Leah's bloody body quiver, but in that moment Reggie saw how small the object of his scorn appeared.

Leah let go of Reggie's hand. Before he could apologize and beg the forgiveness of both her and his God, that hand reached back and flew forward, slamming into the side of his neck.

"You . . . *nuh-n-ninnyhammer*," she screamed. "Do you think I wuh-want to be huh-here? I wuh-want to be with my muh-mommy and my puh-pops, not *huh-here*." Her tears came like the pummeling rain outside. "I'm supposed to huh-*help* you."

Reggie felt his neck but could not massage away the sting of Leah's hand. Nor could his mind massage away the sting of her words. His knees weakened. He slumped against the wall.

"Pluh-lease," Leah said, quieter now. She took his arm. "We huh-have to g-go."

Reggie could not move even if the church around them mostly did. From up the hallway came the shattering of windows. Leah yelped and gripped him tighter. Reggie paid no mind.

"I'm so tired," he said. "It's that mockingbird. Just wouldn't stop singing. Did you make that happen too?"

He laughed despite himself. Leah said nothing and followed his gaze.

"All I wanted was breakfast," he said, nodding toward the vending machine. "A candy bar isn't the healthiest thing in the world to eat, but I usually eat one every Saturday morning before I practice my sermon. Practice makes perfect, Leah. You remember that. The Spirit can speak through you, but you have to do your part."

"Ruh-Reverend, we duh-don't have t-time."

"I put my money in. Pushed the buttons. But I didn't get my reward. Do you understand, Leah? I followed all the directions and still didn't get what I was hungry for."

"I duh-don't understand," Leah said.

Reggie smiled. "No, I guess you don't. And you still wouldn't even if I explained it."

"You c-can explain it on the way."

He wanted to say no, they weren't going anywhere. That despite their differences she was still a child and he was still an adult and he would not put either of them in danger. But then the last of the giant elms gave way and was thrown through the kitchen windows. Glass sprayed through the open door into the hallway, sending Leah into Reggie's arms. The howl beyond consumed them. Reggie couldn't understand how a storm could last so long and still continue to grow, but he knew Leah was right. If they stayed, their lives were at risk. If they went, their lives were at risk. But the Treasure Chest had a basement, and it was only a few blocks away.

He did not release her but struggled to his feet with Leah in his arms. They made their way down the dark hallway, sidestepping glass and wood. The side door was the closest exit. Reggie pushed against it, but the wind held it closed. He pushed again and managed to open the door just enough for them to squeeze through.

The wind took his breath. Reggie struggled against both it and the current of the rising water. They made it as far as the edge of the parking lot before he lost his footing, sending them both into the water. He tried to pick Leah up again.

"N-no." Leah screamed the words, but they registered as barely a whisper. "I c-can walk. It'll be fuh-faster. Just huh-hold my hand."

Reggie did. The two struggled across the road to the far side, where the park's iron fence provided them with at least a handhold. They pulled themselves along with Leah between Reggie and the fence, head down, rain stinging their bodies. What adrenaline had been coursing through him gave way to a wave of exhaustion that made continuing on impossible. Reggie looked up to see a van parked along the street that would perhaps offer enough cover for them to rest, if only for a moment. He took two steps toward it before seeing the crumpled mass.

"Close your eyes," he yelled.

He didn't know if Leah did, didn't even know if she'd heard him. Reggie tried to keep himself between Leah and the corpse. The body lay crosswise in the street beside a yield sign bent nearly in half. Reggie uttered a silent prayer as the battered, lifeless face of Brent Spicer watched them pass.

The howl increased to a thunder all its own as the wind suddenly shifted. Reggie's ears popped. He looked to his left just as the funnel reached down, swirling and angry and massive. Debris like circling birds hovered around its gaping maw. The sound was of Mattingly itself screaming in agony as the world around it was rent. Windows shattered, entire buildings seemed to explode. There was a bong and then a giant crushing sound as the clock tower in the middle of town fell. The updraft lurched the First Church of the Risen Christ upward from its foundations and spun it in the air like a child's toy before dropping it into shards and splinters.

"We're almost there," he yelled. "We have to hurry."

They fought on, one iron bar at a time, inching their way

forward as the horrid sounds of collapsing buildings and snapping lines exploded overhead. The air swirled with what could not be battened to the ground. Mailboxes, bicycles, street signs, garbage cans, whole sections of siding, all pirouetted around them. Lightning struck a telephone pole nearby with a boom that left Reggie's ears bleeding. Trees folded like blades of grass. The air stank of sulfur—brimstone, Reggie thought, and then he was sure they were all in judgment.

They reached the gate to the park when Reggie turned to see the newspaper box hurtling end over end toward them. He called out and pushed Leah out of the way, toppling her into the water just as the metal box slammed into his chest and sent him sprawling into the street. The rolling water was not enough to keep his head from smacking the pavement. Pain swept over him in one swelling wave after another. His bladder loosened. Far away, Leah screamed.

12

Barney saw the tornado first, just as they reached the wooden front door of the Treasure Chest. The sight of that black funnel diving out of the sky struck him with a terror so consuming that his body's every involuntary function ceased. His very blood froze.

And it was an even worse terror when Tom asked, "Where's Leah?"

The crowd stumbled inside like refugees behind them, filling the storefront. Dollhouses and marble rollers tumbled soundlessly to the floor. Blood streaked the barrels of Lincoln Logs and building blocks as people barreled past. Tom turned to Ellen. His face was contorted into an expression of vague confusion. He looked like he'd just misplaced his keys rather than his daughter. The hand he held was not Leah's but Allie's.

"Ellen, where's Leah?"

Ellen shook her head as if Tom's question had been asked in a foreign language. The people pushed in like sheep without a shepherd. Mayor Wallis and Jake Barnett tried to point them in the direction of the basement. Many were frantic, practically baying. Many more, like Tom and Ellen, had simply chosen numbness over madness and had found their own gray curtains.

"Allie," Barney said, "where's Leah? She was holdin' your hand, and Tom was holdin' hers. We was all together."

Now it was Allie's turn to shake her head. Tom looked around as the understanding of what was happening broke through his haze and hit him with a force even greater than the storm. Sheriff Barnett and Kate guided the people down the stairs as quickly as they could, one eye on the next in line and the other on the half of the funnel cloud that was visible through the front window.

"Allie," Tom said, "do you know where Leah is? She was holding our hands." He held up his own as an example. "I felt her slip out, but then I grabbed on again. Did you feel that too? Did I grab on to you instead?"

"I don't know," Allie said, dreamlike. "Where's my mommy? Do you know where she is, Mr. Doctor?"

Barney felt cold even as the air outside somehow grew hotter. Thicker. And the noise. He'd always heard a tornado sounded like a freight train, but the one outside was more like a jet. Like the biggest jet the world had ever known.

Jake yelled, "Barney, Tom, Ellen, y'all get downstairs. Hurry up now."

Tom turned to Ellen and said, "Go."

"No," she cried. "No, Tom, please God—"

"*Go*," he said again. And then to Barney, "Make sure you get her downstairs. Allie too."

"Where you goin', Tom?"

"To find Leah."

Tom ran for the door and didn't pull it open as much as it burst inward. The wind found that small opening and created more, sweeping through tiny cracks in the walls and floors and between the window, sending papers and toys sprawling. What townspeople remained in the storefront cried out, some in fear and some to God. Shards of glass bit into Barney's face. He fell backward into the cash register, knocking it to the ground. White slips of easel orders fluttered in the air like tiny helicopters before being sucked outside and disappearing forever.

Jake went to the door and yelled, "What are you doing?"

"Leah's out there," Tom answered. "We can't find her."

"You can't go out there, Tom. You'll never make it."

"I have to."

Tom shoved Jake aside and tried the door again, though by then all he had to do was climb through the broken window. Barney grabbed him by the shoulders and spun him around just as the Old Firehouse Diner disappeared.

"You gotta leave her," Barney roared. "You gotta trust, Tom. Ain't nothin' else for you now."

"No," Tom yelled. "She's out there alone."

Barney shook his head. "She ain't alone, Tom."

The walls of the Treasure Chest began to crack and snap. Ellen was crying, faced with the impossible choice between child and spouse. In the end, it was Allie who saved them all. She pushed through the wind and took Tom by the hand.

"You gotta trust," she screamed. "Leah went to find my

mommy. I know she did. You'll see, Mr. Doctor. What's gonna happen when she's okay an' you're dead?"

Tom was as still as he could be within the yawing building. His hand stayed upon the doorknob, ready to pull. The rest stood in a half circle around him, holding on to what they could, waiting. Barney supposed that each of them had been forced to choose sometime that week whether to believe or doubt. This was Tom's time to decide. And whether he made that choice or the crushing approach of the twister made it for him, he stepped away from the door and ushered Ellen and Allie toward the stairs.

Barney was last. He closed the basement door just as the Foster's Seed building erupted in a volcano of bricks and mortar, and he knew what was disappearing would never be had again. There would not be a rebuilding. The town was too poor and the government money, even if it came, would not be enough. He turned and followed the sound of Jake Barnett's voice. The basement was cramped and rank with the smell of wet and mold. There were no lights; the darkness was thicker than even the darkness outside. The only sounds were the sobs for the dead and dying and the jet engine overhead. For the first time since Mabel's death, Barney began to pray.

13

The funnel's bottom began to lose its cohesion as it rumbled over town. What came next was an unraveling not unlike a top that slowly lost its spin and wobbled until falling limply upon a table. The twister left as suddenly as it had come. The sky had had its fill of the earth.

Reggie looked up. The thick blanket of green clouds had

given way to black; gray was not far behind. They did not creep but rather moved with a speed he believed impossible. Reggie watched those clouds roll by and decided he had not moved in forever and would not move forever still. He would just lie there and rest. Yes. That would be like heaven.

The water was still around him, over him, though its current and depth had lessened. Reggie knew this, though he could not feel it. Everything was numb but for the sharp pain that accompanied every sporadic breath. He tried to lift his arm but couldn't. His head lolled to the side—Reggie thought it was the water and not himself that had done that—and saw his left arm bent in a grotesque L. The once regal buildings around him were now piles of stone and wood and steel. Jagged stumps remained where ancient trees once stood. Cars were overturned, trucks flipped onto their sides. The air was still and silent.

His chin moved closer to his chest. What looked like a dark sun appeared at the top of his vision and slowly eclipsed downward. It paused and then spoke, "Are you okay, Ruh-Reverend?"

Reggie's eyes adjusted—that function, at least, was still working—to reveal not a star, but Leah's face. She bent over him. Her hair was wet and bloody, her white T-shirt clung to her bony neck. Reggie realized she had placed his head in her lap.

"You're bluh-bleeding all over," she said. "I was g-going to be okay, but thuh-thank you for suh-saving me." She sniffed. One hand moved from what Reggie guessed was his cheek and wiped at her nose. "I t-told you to please be c-careful of the nuh-newspaper box. I tried yuh-yelling, but no one's c-coming. No one's c-coming, Ruh-Reverend. I don't nuh-know what to do."

Reggie's hand appeared from the corner of his eyes and took Leah's, though he was not conscious of moving it. He forced his lips open. His tongue felt thick and heavy.

"It was supposed to. Be. Me," he said.

"But it wuh-wouldn't have h-hit me, Ruh-Reverend."

Reggie shook his head

(so tired)

and tried again.

"God. Supposed to speak through me." He wanted to offer more, but what came out was a bloody cough that splattered onto Leah's shirt. Red droplets expanded into tiny circles. "I always believed . . . Leah. Did the. Right thing. Used correct . . . *change*. But it got stuck. You got my blessing." Leah began to cry. Reggie thought he squeezed her hand but couldn't be sure. "Why. Did he come for. You?"

"He d-didn't come for me, Ruh-Reverend. He c-came for you."

Reggie coughed again. He felt nothing now. He was bleeding everywhere, but numb. God's graces continued even if His blessings did not. They continued on until the end.

"Did you huh-hear, Ruh-Reverend? He c-came for you. I nuh-know that nuh-now. Puh-please don't d-die yet. Everything huh-happened so we c-could be right here n-now. Can you hear me? Puh-please say yes."

Reggie tried but couldn't. His tongue had gone the way of his legs and arms—dead, even if his mind hung on. He sighed instead and hoped Leah would understand.

"He c-comes to us all, Ruh-Reverend. He's always w-with us. You and me aren't duh-different. No one's duh-different. It's just that I nuh-know I'm small and everyone else thinks they're buh-big. That's why no one else c-can see Him. They pruh-pray and sing and say they luh-love Him, but d-deep

down they think they know beh-better than He does. They
d-do their own things because they thuh-think they're b-big
enough. But they're not. No one's big enough."

Tendrils of smoke rose above them and gathered into the
parting clouds. Leah began to fade. Everything began to fade.

"I nuh-know why the m-mockingbird sings," Leah said.
"It sings at nuh-night because it's l-lonely and wants another
m-mockingbird to love. Can you huh-hear me, Ruh-Reverend?
Puh-lease say yes. The m-mockingbird sings b-because it's
looking for a b-better life. Please don't c-close your eyes
yuh-yet."

Leah bent closer. Water dripped from the ends of her hair
and fell upon Reggie's face, bringing him back.

"You c-can see Him nuh-now, Ruh-Reverend. Yuh-you're
not b-big anymore."

Reggie sighed again. Tried to nod. He did not know what
she meant. Did not care. All Reggie knew was that Mattingly
was gone. It was gone and it would never return, and he felt
helpless to do anything about it. The townspeople would need
him now. They would look to their reverend for succor and
peace, they would bay for their shepherd, but Reggie knew
he would not be there for them. He would be gone soon, not
because he had lived a full life and stood ready to exchange
one world for the next, but because he—Reggie Goggins—
had sacrificed himself for this unbelieving child. Because he
had forgotten how important he was, how big, and for one
moment had chosen to make himself so . . .

Small.

Leah tilted his head to the side. The air began to stir and
shimmer in reds and oranges, yellows and purples, only to
gather into a form that was both there and a place faraway, a
form that reached out for him. Its face shone with a light from

deep within that pulsed and heaved with aliveness, a face that both moved and didn't as it changed in both shape and complexion. Flame rippled outward from its skin, turning Reggie's cold and dying body into a sea of warmth—of peace—and he knew then that it was not flame at all, it was the light of the world and all other worlds. Only its eyes remained steady and unchanged—deep pools of blue that penetrated Reggie's heart into even his darkest places and yet loved him still.

The Rainbow Man.

And yet Reggie knew it was also not, that what he gazed upon was not all the Rainbow Man was, but merely all Reggie was able to understand.

Reggie began to cry.

The Rainbow Man began to sing.

Like waves over shells, like a baby's laugh, His words falling down like sweet syrup over the broken places in Reggie's heart, strengthening it, healing it, making it strong. It was a song like rain upon parched earth that coaxed life from places long rendered dead and lost. It was life eternal. It was Grace that led home.

Reggie began to laugh. His body felt light, like a feather pulled up by the gentle breeze of his last words—a quiet whisper of "Fly over me."

And then Reverend Reggie Goggins reached out into the still air, and he found his rest.

14

They emerged from the darkness to a world of fire and water, and of the range of terribleness that greeted them, nothing was so terrible as the realization that all they had once taken for granted now existed only in memory. Gone were the town square, the Old Firehouse Diner, the sheriff's office. The two-story building that housed the headquarters of the *Mattingly Gazette*. So, too, the movie theater and Wenger's Pharmacy and every other business within one square mile, all arranged in piles of rubble and waste that held neither order nor meaning. Cars sat upon the splintered remains of rooftops. Stalks of straw were embedded within tree trunks that were otherwise untouched, while mere feet away stood foundations of entire buildings that had been picked up and tossed away like refuse. The air was filled with the smell of fresh-cut wood. Fires raged untended.

Only the Treasure Chest remained, rising up from the ruins like a beacon.

The survivors fanned out in all directions. They could not know where they were going—all sense of direction had been lost along with every landmark they'd ever used to navigate by. Tom and Ellen ran for where they thought the park once stood. Barney and Allie were close behind. Echoes of names called out. Many wandered the streets with the stuttered steps and bent necks of the undead. They shook their heads and muttered no, as if their denial would make it all go away.

They found the remnants of the pavilions, and the path blocked. What lay below was little more than a sea of flotsam. Tom led them around the park. He held Ellen's hand and found himself praying for the first time in his life, asking neither for forgiveness or mercy, but only that his daughter was alive.

Let me find her alive, and then I will believe. I will believe and I will never doubt You again.

They found her near the gate in the middle of the street beside an overturned newspaper box. Reverend Goggins lay with his head in Leah's lap. Ellen screamed when she saw his caved chest. Blood caked in foam around his mouth. Tom ran. Inside the park beyond the iron gate, he heard Allie call Mary's name over and over. Barney searched the remains of what was once a wooden shed.

The first rays of the sun reached down as they neared, washing the reverend's body in a glow. Ellen took hold of Leah just as Barney took hold of Allie. One of Mary's pink tennis shoes dangled from her right hand.

Leah's eyes went to the sky. Tom heard the single word she spoke. It came clear and with no stutter, and there was softness in her voice.

"Good-bye," she said.

Saturday

Carnival Day

One Year Later

They came that night, those who had borne the storm and those who had on that morning one year prior seen the coming clouds and heeded Leah's warning, remaining close to basements and root cellars. They came from hills and hollers that were still littered with Mattingly's detritus, from neighborhoods not yet rebuilt and farmsteads that had yet to fully recover to a downtown that was slowly rising again. They came, if for no other reason than to remind themselves that they had stood up when they wanted to lie down and believed when all that was scattered before them called for doubt. They came to sing and dance and break bread not in spite of their bent hearts but because of them.

The rows of booths and games were back, as was a new Ferris wheel. The fire trucks, which had seen so much mud and dirt and soot on that day, now gleamed under the soft glow of the setting sun. Lila McKinney won the baking contest with her grandmother's recipe for coconut cake. She had witnessed Leah Norcross's magic during Mabel Moore's remembrance and left that very night to stay with family in

Highland County. She returned the day after the storm to do what she could, even if it was only to play a secondhand keyboard at the funerals. She dedicated her blue ribbon to the fifty-seven dead and the one still missing, and especially to Reverend Reggie Goggins, a good man who could finally look upon the face of the God he loved.

The Ladies Auxiliary fixed supper that evening in new pavilions on the hill, these made of reinforced concrete and steel. The consensus was that, at least in this case, new was not bad. Up-to-date rides and games and pavilions meant things were moving forward. It meant the healing had begun.

As sun gave way to moon, the celebration turned from the park to the town square, where Mayor Wallis sat upon a makeshift stage beside the covered bronze statue where Allie Granderson now stood. She had donned her best dress for the occasion, white with yellow flowers. It had been her momma's favorite, and so now it was Allie's.

She peeked beneath the curtain before being shooed away by the mayor, then weaved among the waiting townspeople. The hem of her dress swished against her knees. Allie heard her father's call above the buzzing voices. She turned and waved back between a passing family.

"I'm right here, Daddy."

"Don't wander far."

"I won't," she said, and waved again.

Marshall Granderson nodded and did his best to smile, though all that made it through the stubble on the face and the red in his eyes was a sad grin. Allie could see the worry on his face. Her daddy never liked her to go far nowadays. He made sure no one was watching—no one was, Big Jim had just got to the microphone—and took a sip from the flask in his back pocket. Allie turned away as he did so. Marshall didn't like Allie to see that even more than he didn't like her to wander far.

She walked on as the mayor began his speech, reminding the townspeople of what had been so hard to put away—that the tornado cut a path a mile wide and twelve miles long and had been on the ground for twenty minutes, how it destroyed not only the whole of downtown but much of the surrounding area as well. Mayor Wallis paused after each sentence and looked out over the people. He tried to swallow. His voice cracked. He dabbed his forehead with the handkerchief from his pocket and tried again. The only thing that allowed him to continue were the glances he offered to the covered statue beside him.

Allie's legs continued to move as if on their own, guiding her through the crowd. She said hello to those who said hello first and tried to ignore the poor-little-girl stares she was offered. Still going, still within the reach of the mayor's shaky voice, past where the Old Firehouse Diner had stood and would soon stand again and where the Treasure Chest sat empty, her feet upon sidewalks freshly laid and gleaming, her head down, trying to siphon from the crowd a part of the joy that was in them.

And then, "Allie?"

She looked up to see Mr. Doctor and Miss Ellen holding hands.

"Hello, Mr. Doctor," she said.

Miss Ellen bent to hug her. Mr. Doctor drew her close. He looked in her eyes (*Studying them,* Allie thought, *because that's what head doctors do*) and smiled. His smile was brighter than her daddy's.

"How are you?"

"I'm okay," Allie said.

"We've missed you," Miss Ellen said.

"I know. I got busy with school an' all. I was one of the

kids who got sent to Camden for the year. An' I have to care for Daddy now."

Mr. Doctor's cell rang. He excused himself and answered.

"How are y'all doin'?" Allie asked, though mostly out of courtesy.

"We're good," Miss Ellen said. "Lost the house, of course. But we bought a little farm out on Route 40. Things are good."

"That's real nice, Miss Ellen."

Mr. Doctor returned and snapped his phone shut. He was smiling when Allie heard him tell Ellen, "That was Rita. Meagan called to say she and Harold found a sitter for Monday, so they can keep their appointment."

"Good," Ellen said.

"You still doctorin', Mr. Doctor?" Allie asked.

"I am. I decided to go back full-time. With Ellen's blessing, of course."

He kissed Miss Ellen on the cheek, and Allie thought of the way her daddy used to kiss her momma like that. She thought of that and of how her daddy would never be able to do that again.

"Allie," Miss Ellen said, "Leah and I have started going down to the new First Church. We haven't seen you there. We'd be happy to pick you up—"

"No, ma'am. Daddy loves too much, I reckon. I do appreciate that, though."

Ellen smiled and said that's fine, but anytime, anytime at all, just let her know.

"Leah's across the street," Mr. Doctor said. "She said she could get a better view from there. You should go say hello, Allie."

"Daddy don't want me wanderin' far," Allie said. "I best be gettin' back. Good to see you both."

The crowd applauded as the mayor moved on from the story of that day to stories of the days after, when Mattingly began to rise again. Of how the town had pulled together as one just as they'd done in wars and in want, and how the past year had been like a war of its own, only one fought with faith and hard work rather than guns and bombs. People cheered and whistled, and the mayor pointed to the covered monument beside him as proof. They chuckled when reminded that as horrible as the storm was, it had at least chased away the mockingbirds.

Daddy would be wondering where she was. Allie made her way back, mindful of her wandering and mindful also that her legs were not cooperating. She was being pulled along again. Guided across the street by some invisible tether to an empty spot beneath a shining streetlamp.

Right where Leah stood watching her.

Neither of them spoke. In Allie's heart she knew Leah had done nothing wrong, that Leah had in fact warned her of what would happen. But it had hurt and it hurt still, not simply because Allie still loved her, but because in the end Leah had chosen to try and save Preacher Goggins rather than her best friend's own mother.

"Hello, Allie," Leah said.

"Hey there, Leah."

The mayor had moved on to the names of those who had gone above and beyond in the rebuilding of the town. He mentioned Sheriff Barnett and Marshall Granderson. He mentioned Mr. Doctor. And last had come Mr. Barney, who Big Jim said showed everyone how good a Christian man he was, considering his heart had been so full of sorrow. The crowd cheered again.

"How are you?" Leah asked.

Allie shrugged. "You?"

"Fine."

Allie saw that was true. It was not so much that Leah had grown as it was that she stood taller. And the stutter was gone. Allie's daddy had told her that had happened, that Mr. Doctor had said she'd finally outgrown it but Miss Ellen said it had been something else, a bit of the Rainbow Man's shine that had been left behind.

"I miss you," Leah said.

Allie said, "I miss you too," and cradled in those words was an apology for going away and a request to come home.

Mayor Wallis continued on about how Mr. Barney had walked into what was left of the town's offices two weeks after the storm and laid a torn and nearly indistinguishable lottery ticket on top of the desk. His gift to the town, Barney said. And by the hand of God Himself, the total after taxes had been just enough to cover the rebuilding.

"Leah, do you . . . ?"

Leah looked at her. The smile she offered was both bitter and sweet, like a memory that hurt so long as it wasn't pondered.

"No," she said. "I can't see him anymore. But just because you can't see something doesn't mean it isn't there."

"Thank you for coming to the funeral." Allie's eyes stung. She eased her way out from under the lamppost, happy that the darkness caught her. "There was just her shoe in the casket. I guess you know that. That's all we found. The rest of her was taken by the wind. I don't know if it's better to believe she's up there with all the other folk, or if she just got lost somewhere and she's making her way back home. Which do you think is right?"

"I don't know, Allie. Maybe it's both."

Mayor Wallis was still telling the story. Everyone had been so happy to know that the future was bright again, he said, but Mr. Barney was still sad. And then he told how Jake Barnett had found Barney at the Treasure Chest a week later, slumped over his desk. Doc March had pronounced it a heart attack, and no one was surprised. When two people love each other as much as Mr. Barney and Miss Mabel, they share a heart. And when one of those people moves on, the other finds that half a heart won't get you through for long. Allie thought of her daddy. Her eyes stung more.

"Would this have happened if he hadn't come, Leah?"

Leah's yes came quick, as if that question had tumbled through her mind as well in those long days between the town's death and its rebirth.

"Some things must be," she said. "But if he hadn't come, a lot more people would have died. The town wouldn't have been saved and Mr. Barney wouldn't have saved it, and Reverend Goggins wouldn't have gotten his reward. The town's healing now. People will move on. They'll be better."

Allie's voice was as soft as Leah's once was—"I won't."

"You will. Sometimes you think a story's ended, but really it hasn't, and all you have to do is turn the page. The magic's still here, Allie." Leah's lips thinned into a smile. "Most everybody round here believes in the magic. My best friend told me that once."

Those words clicked in Allie's mind like tumblers opening a lock. At first she had thought (and she had also prayed) that the memory of that day would fade, that it would recede and then crumble like a bad dream at first light. But then Allie had come to realize that it would be with her always. She touched the plastic bracelet her momma had given her that day. It was worn now, a dull pink instead of the bright red it used to be, and the compass had stopped working sometime during the storm. Allie knew her mind would gloss over a million other memories, but the memory of Mr. Barney holding her tight where her mother had been taken up would always be fresh.

Some things must be.

And a thought came to her then, one that she would only understand later—that God would allow her to remember not out of some punishment but some mysterious good. Because the story hadn't ended that day, and a page would soon turn.

Mayor Wallis finished his speech. He took a step to his left and pulled at the curtain covering the statue. It dropped to the ground as the crowd roared.

The town had chosen bronze because they'd wanted something that would last forever. And though Allie had no idea who had been the carver (or even if the statue had been carved at all), she thought it was a right fine job. Everything was the same—the hat, the glasses, the overalls, the smile. Especially the smile. She wished Mr. Barney could be there to see how important he was now, how much he was loved. Then she figured he was kind of there after all.

"I'm never gonna let my momma go," Allie said. "If she's out there somewhere, I'm gonna find her."

"I know you will," Leah said, and Allie thought she really did know somehow—as if the Rainbow Man's leftover shine had done more than fix her tongue, it had also given her a glimpse into what was yet to be. Maybe that was so.

Maybe.

The cheers carried through the summer air and were drowned in a series of deep thumps. Leah took Allie's hand and brought her back into the light of the lamp overhead.

"I love you, Leah."

"I love you too."

As their fingers linked, Allie's felt Leah's thumbnail and found it smooth. That made her smile more than anything else. Even more than the fireworks that burst overhead, striking the dark sky with a thousand tiny rainbows.

Reading Group Guide

1. Faith is an important element within *When Mockingbirds Sing*, in this case faith in someone most of the town of Mattingly can neither see nor hear. For much of the book, the only people who truly believe are two children and a man who has lost his worldly worth. Why do you think that is? Does faith come easier to such people?

2. Did you ever have an imaginary friend? How old were you? How long did you have him (or even it)? And most importantly, when and why did that imaginary friend go away?

3. Do you think God would ever choose to speak through someone like Leah, who confesses that she doesn't even know who God is? Why do you think He chose an agnostic little girl rather than Reggie Goggins, who had devoted his entire life to his faith?

4. The final chapter infers that Tom Norcross's promise to believe in the Rainbow Man if Leah survives the storm has gone unfulfilled. Why is it that some people shy away from belief even in the midst of a miracle?

5. There is a fair amount of suffering in the story. Barney loses his wife, Allie her mother, and Meagan Gladwell is marooned in a violent and loveless marriage. Yet it is Leah who seems to grieve the most, even as she comes face-to-face with the Divine. Do you think this is fair? Would encountering a holy God be a blissful experience, or do you imagine it would be a painful one?

6. Sacrifice and loss are major themes in *When Mockingbirds Sing*. In the end, which character do you think lost the most? What was gained by that loss?

7. When Allie begs Leah to ask the Rainbow Man to stop the storm from coming, Leah replies by saying some things have to happen and there's no changing them. Do you agree with that notion? Why?

8. During Mabel's funeral, Barney relates to the gathered how he had lost his business, his wife, his faith, and his friends. Yet with the tornado bearing down, he comes to believe that perhaps God loved him most of all. What accounts for this change of mind? What was the insight Barney received in that moment?

9. Barney seems to sum up his outlook on life when he tells Leah, "Reckon we don't have much say in whether a thing is or ain't, only what we'll do either way." Do you agree with this sentiment?

10. Much of the conflict in the story can be traced to the Rainbow Man not fully explaining everything to Leah, but rather guiding her step by step and telling her only what she needs to know at the moment. Is this how a life of faith is often lived? What pitfalls and benefits does such a life offer?

Acknowledgments

Despite the joy it delivers in the end, writing a novel can be a painful and lonely experience. I'm blessed to have a special group of people who provide the necessary antidote to both.

My wife and children loved me through the many long nights and empty stares that are an integral part of a writer's life. They let me work. They brought me coffee. And most of all, they never failed to remind me of the need to stop writing about life and go live it.

Kathy Richards patiently endures my ambivalence toward a great many things in general and technology in particular. Her hard work has made my life immensely easier, and I am continually grateful.

Daisy Hutton welcomed me to Thomas Nelson with all the grace and warmth of a true Southern lady. Her vision and optimism inspire me. I'm blessed to know her.

I am especially indebted to my editor, Amanda Bostic. She is the sounding board for so many ideas, and she possesses the wisdom to know what works and what doesn't. My thanks as well to LB Norton, who kept reading this story when I no longer could. Whatever is right in these pages is because of them. Whatever is wrong is because of me.

Ruthie Dean, Becky Monds, Katie Bond, and Jodi Hughes worked tirelessly to get this book into your hands. I could not trust my words to better people.

And to you, dear Reader. I save the most thanks for you.

Buried secrets will bring one family
to their breaking point when . . .

The
Devil Walks
in Mattingly

NEW FROM BILLY COFFEY
IN MARCH 2014